Ben-Hur: The Odyssey

Barry Clifton

Writers Club Press
San Jose New York Lincoln Shanghai

Ben-Hur: The Odyssey

Published by Writers Club Press
an imprint of iUniverse.com, Inc.

For information address:
iUniverse.com, Inc.
620 North 48th Street
Suite 201
Lincoln, NE 68504-3467
www.iuniverse.com

ISBN: 0-595-08857-0

Printed in the United States of America

For Grandma Graper,
who taught me how to dream

Epigraph

In the end, there are only three types of people. There are those who do not ponder the existence of God. These become fools and discover depravity. There are those who ponder the existence of God and find the evidence unconvincing. These become philosophers and discover despair. Then there are those who ponder the existence of God and find the evidence compelling. These become believers and discover delight.

Author's Note

Some may question the presumption of writing a sequel to General Lew Wallace's classic novel *Ben-Hur*, particularly since Wallace attempted to fill out the life of his fictional hero in the closing chapter of his book. However, many who have enjoyed this great book over the years have regretted the brief and incomplete end to the story. The final 35 years of Ben-Hur's life are summed up in what is essentially a mere three page appendix. But an Odyssean character like Judah Ben-Hur comes along rarely in literature, and it seemed a shame to leave half of his story untold. And so, borrowing inspiration from the hints Wallace provides in his appendix (of Judah's marriage to Esther and his connection to the Roman church) and rearranging a detail or two, *Ben-Hur: The Odyssey* is an attempt to complete this moving saga. With great indebtedness to General Wallace for giving this inspirational story to the world, the author humbly submits the remaining chapters in the life of Judah Ben-Hur.

Part 1: A.D.59

Chapter 1

Rome

The slave's mottled hands shook uncontrollably as he took the razor out of the leather case. Gingerly, he placed it on a tray alongside a dozen other razors, each one set in a carved ivory handle. Though his face was that of a young man, his hands were worn with the strain of a life of servitude, and seemed to be aging further even at the moment.

In his trembling, he disturbed the symmetry of the razors on the tray, and when he tried to straighten them, he only made the arrangement worse. A frantic moan escaped his lips. Standing next to him was an older slave who held in his hands a silver vase, inlaid with ribbons of gold. He looked on with a paternalistic grin, clearly amused by his friend's anxiety.

"Wonderful time for the palsy," he smirked.

"I'm fine!" said the other sharply. As he tried to center his thoughts, the older slave placed a consoling hand on his shoulder.

"Look—you're just going to shave the Emperor's beard," he said. "He sleeps, he sweats, he farts, he grows whiskers like any other man. His face is no different than the hundreds of others you've shaved. So relax."

With this encouragement, the shaking subsided some. A third slave entered the room holding a bowl and brush coated with foam. Sweat rimmed his forehead and he looked physically ill. His face was as white as the foam. He put the bowl and brush down, and dropped into a chair, exhaling deeply in relief. "Your turn," he said to the servant with the tray of razors. "I wouldn't want your job."

The timid slave's trembling resumed in earnest. He cleared his throat and looked pitifully at the one with the vase, who nodded affirmingly and pointed to the door. "Remember—just like any other man," he said.

At this, the servant in the chair wheezed. "Right!" he said, doubling over. "Cut his face, he'll cut off your head!" He snorted in laughter as the nervous slave glared back at him. At last, he gripped the tray tightly, straightened his shoulders and walked through the door with the older slave behind him.

They stepped into a small chapel which was jammed to capacity with a hundred or so members of the nobility of Rome, and seated squarely at the center of the chancel was Emperor Nero. He was wrapped with white, clerical vestments which seemed to strap him to his chair, and his stocky face was hidden beneath a thick layer of foam. He stared straight ahead above the audience, looking proud—or at least as proud as a youthful adult with a lathered face could.

Since his ascension to Caesar's throne five years earlier at the age of seventeen, Nero had hosted numerous coming-of-age celebrations, and this was his latest gift to his people. In commemoration of the shaving of his first full beard, he had declared the observance of the inaugural *Neronia*—a week-long festival of games and performances fashioned in the spirit of the Greek Olympics. There would be competitions in singing, gymnastics and chariot-racing. Nero's baths would be thrown open to the public with complimentary body oil given to the bathers. And it all began now, with the offering of his facial hair to the Roman gods.

Seated along the walls behind Nero were his closest associates and family members. His mother Agrippina looked on, and if examined closely, it could be discerned in her face where Nero's pride came from. Her eyes were like two suns, burning brightly with arrogance. This moment was as much hers as her son's. He had risen to power on her wings. She had taken him from earliest infancy and raised him for this hour. Every act of discipline, every academic lesson, every companion of his childhood was chosen with delicate precision, as a sculptor measuring each stroke of the chisel. And now as she beheld her masterpiece, she could not suppress the smug vanity that showed on her face.

Seated beside her was Octavia, Nero's wife. If light had once beamed from her young, restless eyes, it had long since been extinguished. She was not ten feet away from Nero, but ten miles away, and longed to be much further than that. She wanted to throw the tiara off of her head and vanish. And yet there was no person in that room more beautiful than she. Like a wilted rose, she exuded a grace and dignity that was obvious to everyone.

The two slaves approached Caesar, who extended his chin out further. The slave with the razors awkwardly set his tray down on a stand erected next to the emperor, nearly knocking over a gold box already resting on the stand. Inside the box were the dry, black hairs of Nero's beard which had been clipped earlier. The slave selected a razor and leaned over the emperor.

He managed to suppress the quaking of his hand long enough to make a smooth swipe across his face, and was relieved to find only foam and stubble clinging to the blade. Heartened by his success, he scraped the razor clean on the edge of the box, then disposed of it by dropping it into the vase held by the older servant. He picked up a second blade and continued shaving. Pockets of conversation echoed throughout the room. Toward the back of the chapel, two elderly women leaned over to each other, each one mindlessly toying with her jewelry as they watched the ceremony.

"Octavia looks care-worn," whispered one, sounding bored.

"Yes," the other agreed. "They say the emperor has lost his affection for her and is dallying with another—the wife of his friend, of all things."

"The poor child. She's lost everything. Her father is dead. Her brother was murdered by *you know who*." She cast a disdainful glance at Nero as she said this.

"Shhh!" the other reacted with alarm and looked around, picking nervously at her diamond necklace. "Britannicus died naturally."

"Of course he did. How convenient for *you know who* that his chief rival dies of a fit of epilepsy at his own birthday party."

"Keep your voice down!" The other was quite agitated by now, and quickly tried to change the subject. "Agrippina looks in her glory this afternoon."

This brought a scowl from her friend, who whispered, "The emperor should never have let her back into the court. She'll kill him before she gives up her power again."

Her voice began to carry, and the diamond-lady was now fidgeting recklessly. "Unless he kills her first. Or maybe they'll kill each other." The diamond-lady was about to have her own seizure. "Why is the royal family so demented?" The diamond-lady coughed loudly and turned completely away.

Suddenly, there was a collective gasp from the audience. Nero had pulled back sharply from a nick of the slave's razor. The slave froze in anguish for what seemed an eternal moment as he waited to see if the skin had been broken, and then to his utter horror, he saw a small red line appear on Nero's face. It was scarcely visible, hardly more than a drop, but to the slave it was like a river of blood. He may as well have driven the blade into Nero's chest. Nero's hand slowly went to his face and touched the blood, and when he saw it smeared on his finger, his eyes became instantly livid.

The storm that clouded Nero's face seemed to darken the room. The Ahenobarbi family from which Nero came was notorious for the fury of its congenital temper. In the room at that moment were those who remembered Nero's father running down an innocent boy on the Appian Way rather than swerve his chariot the width of a wheel. The same demon was in his son, but until this moment it had been well suppressed. Now a birthing of something wicked seemed right then to be taking place.

Nero turned his head and looked full into the eyes of two men sitting next to his wife—Annaeus Seneca and Afranius Burrus. Seneca was the soul of Rome— a famed philosopher, senator and writer. For the past twelve years he had served first as Nero's tutor, and now as one of his most trusted advisers, along with Burrus, who as the prefect of Nero's Praetorian Guard, was Italy's highest ranking military officer. With a shielded, downward motion of his hand, Seneca urged Nero to control his rage, while Burrus remained somber and still. Nero swallowed, and then directed a punishing glare at the slave.

"If you intend to disfigure me, a smooth swipe behind either ear should be sufficient," he said, and nervous laughter broke out from the audience.

The slave felt paralyzed, unable to decide what to do, like a deer caught in the path of the hunter, but in that moment of puzzled inactivity, Nero's patience was exhausted and he snatched a towel from the slave's arm.

"Will you let me bleed?" he exploded. "What are you, a Carthaginian assassin? Dismiss yourself at once!"

The slave mumbled a cry and fled from the room, while a tense silence fell over the assembly. Nero wiped his face, and then looked up from the towel, scanning the room of observers. When his gaze met Octavia's, he saw her look quickly down to the floor in a blushed mixture of embarrassment and fear.

Nero looked at the other slave who had remained firmly rooted in place as this unfolded. "Can I trust you to complete this messy business, or are you his accomplice?" he asked, attempting to gain some composure. The servant merely nodded, and immediately placed his vase on the table beside the box. Without delay, he took a fresh razor and continued the shave.

Nero tipped his face in the direction of his advisers, and cracked a weak smile. "Now I know why you never shave, Burrus," he said, and the bearded prefect nodded in return, while the audience again fell into pathetic laughing.

In a few moments, the slave finished. He toweled the emperor's face clean, snatched up his materials and left, while a priestly figure approached. The cleric placed a lid upon the gold box, then took the box and walked with it up a short set of stairs into a small foyer where a towering gold statue of an eagle stood. As he did this, everyone in the room stood reverently to his feet.

The priest bowed, lifted the box above his head, and in a deep, penetrating voice which rang out through the chapel, intoned, "To the glory of the gods of Rome, we offer the first-fruits of manhood of your divine son, Nero—emperor, lord and Caesar. May your blessing rest upon him as he leads our empire into further greatness."

In unison, the voices of the assembly rang out, "Hail to our lord Caesar, rich in mercy! May his glory continue forever!"

Toward the back of the room, one elderly woman muttered under her breath, "May the gods save anyone who looks to *you know who* for mercy."

*   *   *

Caesarea, Judea

The jailor shuffled down the corridor, barely disturbing the open flame of a lantern hanging from the wall. The steps of the two guards that walked behind him were tentative compared with his own comfortable gait. Clearly, the jailor felt at home here. Looking at his wrinkled, pale-white skin, the guards wondered if he ever left the dungeon at all.

They walked past a row of cells and through the barred doors, could see the prisoners. Most were sleeping, one was pacing and another was engaged in vigorous debate with himself. Eventually, the light was all but consumed by the shadows, and the guards instinctively drew together side by side, but then the glow of another lantern burning up ahead picked up their path and so they continued.

Finally, at the very end of the corridor, they came to a cell in which they could see a man kneeling down beside his cot with his head buried in his hands. The jailor reached into a pocket of his faded yellow tunic and withdrew a ring of iron keys. At this sound, the prisoner raised his head and looked over. A rich, gray beard hung from his face—a face not nearly as listless as the others had been. It was difficult to tell, but he even appeared to be smiling.

The jailor selected a key and inserted it into the door. "My friend," he said with familiarity, "there's no time for a visit today. You have an audience with King Agrippa this afternoon. Isn't this your lucky day?"

The prisoner rose to his feet. He was short, with thin arms and stout legs which were obviously accustomed to walking great distances. Across the lean of his bulging calf muscles were numerous scars showing the checkered pattern of the Roman whip. As he stepped toward the door into the light, the guards were surprised by his gentle dignity. They had expected defiance or despair—the fraternal twin emotions bred by incarceration. But not serenity. Not in this place. But there it was, written on his face. And then he laughed, saying to the jailor as he stepped out into the corridor, "Who knows, but perhaps it is the king's lucky day."

The jailor returned the smile, showing an uneven row of yellow teeth. He reached behind him and took a set of manacles from one of the guards. "You and I know how needless these are, but we must keep Governor Festus happy," he said. The prisoner extended his wrists, as though familiar with the routine, and the jailor chained them together. A second set was then stretched around his ankles. "Well friend, you know the way," the jailor said as he straightened up. "I'm going to stay and clean up your room, though I hope the king will not send you back."

"So you wish for the king to cut off my head?" the prisoner asked.

"Don't jest about such things!" gasped the jailor. "Dear God, no. May he see what I see—an innocent man. And I should say after seeing thousands pass through these walls, that I know the difference."

"If Agrippa calls for a witness, I shall summon you, good Cornelius," said the prisoner, and he laughed as the jailor's eyes opened wide with fright. "But fear not, I have a strong defender." He looked at the guards, and then began walking as they nudged him forward.

The journey out of the dungeon was not quick enough for the guards, but they had seen enough to know that they ought not rush this man in chains. A nobility shined through his smelly prison rags, and dimmed the glory of their own regalia. Soon, torches were no longer needed to light their way as sunlight began to flood the corridors. Noises filtered in—the clanging of iron, then someone belching. They passed through the intersection of hallways and chambers that signaled the end of the prison and the beginning of the palace. The prisoner seemed more and more out of place as they walked past clusters of people in formal dress, who stopped their conversations to look at him and dropped their voices in whispers after he walked by.

Finally they came to a large marble doorway where the bottleneck of traffic was most obvious. The guards drew the attention of one of the posted soldiers there, who disappeared, then returned and signaled for them to enter. They passed through the doorway into the main hall of the palace.

Herod the Great had spared no expense when he constructed the palace in Caesarea 75 years earlier, and its magnificence still was evident. In the center of the room was a parade of marble statues, each honoring one of Rome's historic figures. The more spectacular sculptures were of Rome's Caesars: Julius, Augustus, Tiberius, Gaius, Claudius, and finally Nero, whose was the most ostentatious of all. The image carved in stone gave him the appearance of seasoned manhood, and some would argue even divinity. Its eyes seemed to follow them as they walked past, but the prisoner appeared not to notice.

Beyond the gallery, the hall opened up into a spacious rotunda crowded with more people who moved quickly aside to avoid any contact with the prisoner, as though he were an animal carcass the guards were dragging into the room. A wide path was cleared which allowed them to march to the front of the room, where across the width of the floor was a raised platform, divided by marble colonnades and heavy, velvet curtains.

In the center section of the platform, all eyes were drawn to two men and a woman who sat upon thrones. They were draped in robes which spread around them like tents and appeared far more unwieldy to wear than the curtains themselves would have been. The woman and her apparent partner had small crowns on their heads and fully looked the part of royalty. He was robust with a thick beard and a calm, confident gaze, but all eyes were drawn to the woman who was younger by perhaps ten years, and strikingly beautiful, with long hair and a soft face.

By contrast, the second man was pathetic. He was short and stumpy, and sat in his seat with a crooked posture, and crooked eyes, and looked quite out of place sharing the stage with the other two. Nevertheless, when the prisoner and his escorts emerged out of the crowd and came forward, this man spoke first.

"King Agrippa, this is the man I was telling you about." He pointed a crooked finger at the prisoner. "This is the one whom the Jewish leaders want dead. The Jews have certain points of dispute with him about their own superstition and about some Nazarene who was dead. But he asserts that the Nazarene has come back from the dead. I care nothing for their troublesome religious convictions, but he shows his face in Jerusalem, and the place explodes in rioting. They want him executed, and now he has appealed to Caesar. But I don't know what to write Lord Nero about him. Perhaps after you, King Agrippa, and your sister have examined him, I will have something to write."

Agrippa leaned forward and looked at the prisoner with a penetrating stare. Their eyes met and it was as though for a few seconds the two of them were wrestling together in invisible space. Not a wrinkle blemished the prisoner's serenity. He seemed unimpressed to be standing before one of the most powerful men in the Judean province. If the men were engaged in an unseen contest, it was the king who backed down first. He tipped his head to the side, scratched his beard and with a touch of condescension said, "So, you are Paul, prophet of the Galilean messiah, thorn of the Jews, and troubler of my kingdom?"

The prisoner nodded his head. "It is an honor to speak with you, your majesty."

"No, the honor is mine!" the king bellowed. "Yours is a household name. You are famous!"

"Infamous, you mean," the woman said, her beautiful face contorting into a sneer. "As though our nation, already troubled with rebels and thieves, could easily afford the distemper of a heretic." This brought murmurs of agreement from among the crowd which had now pressed in around them to hear the proceedings.

The king laughed. "Peace dear Bernice! Already you condemn the man. Let us be fair and not judge so swiftly. Let us hear the testimony of this great man." He again leaned toward Paul. "As I understand it, you once persecuted the faith that you now adopt."

For the first time, Paul looked down, then winced. "With unbridled zeal, so great was my ignorance."

The crooked man pounced at this. "And so it is guilt that propels you all over the empire, spreading the seeds of your so-called *gospel*."

Paul immediately regained his poise. "On the contrary, Governor Festus. It is the grace of the God of my fathers which compels me to this work. King Agrippa, you yourself have heard my story—how I was journeying to Damascus with authority to imprison every Christian I could find. And at midday, I saw on the road a light from heaven, brighter than the sun, shining around me."

Paul's hands went up and his eyes blinked rapidly as he told the story, as though he were seeing the vision all over again.

"And when I had fallen to the ground, I heard a voice saying to me, 'Paul, why do you persecute me?' 'Who are you?' I asked in amazement. And the voice answered, 'It is I, Jesus, whom you are persecuting.'"

Paul looked at Agrippa. "And do you know what Jesus said to me?" Agrippa shook his head, unable to hide the fact that he was eagerly waiting to find out. "He said, 'Now rise and stand on your feet, for I am sending you to bear witness to me, and you will turn many from darkness to light, that they may receive forgiveness of their sins, and a place among those who are redeemed.' And so, King Agrippa, I have not been disobedient to this heavenly vision, but wherever I go, I declare that men should repent and turn to God."

The crowd could scarcely restrain itself at this, nor Governor Festus who shouted, projecting a mixture of words and spit, "Absurd! Paul, you are insane. Your great learning has turned you mad!"

"I am not mad, most excellent Festus, but I am speaking the sober truth." Paul's voice was deep, steady, and obviously well trained. "The king knows about these things, I am certain. I cannot believe these events have escaped his notice, for this was not done in a corner. And besides, our scriptures have foretold these events for centuries. King Agrippa, do you believe the prophets? I know that you believe!"

The rhetorical mastery Paul had used in switching the light of judgment onto the king caught Agrippa off his guard. The king took a nervous sip from a cup on a nearby table. He laughed, but unconvincingly. "In a short time you think to make me a Christian!"

Paul pressed his case further. "Whether short or long, I would hope that not only you but everyone who hears me this day might become such as I am—except for these chains."

Agrippa sat back now in his chair and pondered this exchange. He was a deeply religious man, and indeed was well versed in the Jewish scriptures. He had seen the length and breadth of religious practices throughout the empire and was disgusted with most of what he saw. The gods of the Greeks and Romans were susceptible to all the lusts and scandals of human nature. The philosophers had long observed that a worshipper becomes like the object of his worship, and so it was not surprising to Agrippa that Roman culture—for all its splendor—was largely debased. Above this dark and confusing spiritual landscape, the star of Jewish monotheism shined brightly, and Agrippa was drawn to it, but only from a distance.

What Herod Agrippa knew in his head could not win over his heart, which was at that time inflamed with incestuous passion for his sister. He was a pagan in practice, yet he despised the pagan gods, which presumably approved of his behavior. And so as he looked at Paul, he felt a certain admiration, and even envy.

"Except for these chains." Paul wore chains of forged iron, and yet was otherwise free. Agrippa's wrists were unbound, but his life was shackled. Who was the real prisoner? The king broke from his reverie. He now regretted the burden of Roman law, which had to be respected.

"This man has done nothing to deserve death or imprisonment," he said with such force that no one in the hall dared to disagree. He looked at Paul. "You could be set free if you had not appealed to Caesar. But we are a lawful people bound by law. Because you have appealed to Nero, to Nero you shall go. Yet Paul, because of *my* grace, I will grant you assistance along the way. A legal advocate shall be provided for you to accompany you and defend you on your journey."

This news was unexpected. "An advocate?" Paul said, and then he swept his hand through the air as though to reject the offer. "I have requested no advocate, nor do I—"

The king waved him quiet. "The mercy of Rome is great. Before the request is even on your lips, she has acted on your behalf, and why shouldn't she? You are one of her own citizens, whether my sister likes it or not." He cast a glance at Bernice who scowled afresh. "Rome is an intimidating city to the newcomer. And so we offer you the companionship and counsel of one of her finest representatives, to help make your reception there a bit more pleasant."

At this, the king looked to the back of the hall and gestured to the soldiers stationed there. Paul looked back as well, and through the crowd, could see the soldiers coming forward, creating a wedge of space for an obvious dignitary. The man was dressed in a dazzling purple and yellow vest. And he was older too. He wore no hat, and Paul could just make out the top of his resplendent silver head. As the soldiers squeezed through the wall of people, the man stepped forward into the open and Paul immediately gasped. His expression melted into one of stunned astonishment, and tears began to glitter in his eyes. He walked over and caught the arms of his advocate.

"Judah!"

The older man returned the smile. "My friend and brother," he said.

They paused for a moment, frozen in place, both pleasantly numbed by the rekindling of an apparently old and meaningful friendship. Slowly, Paul's friend turned to face the king and his companions.

"King Agrippa, Governor Festus, Lady Bernice—I am Quintus Arrius the Younger, known in Judea as Judah Ben-Hur. In accordance with the correspondence which you have already received, and the arrangements which have been made, the people of Rome and her Senate request the transference of your prisoner into our safe-keeping, for presentation before Caesar's tribunal."

The king nodded, then looked to Governor Festus. Festus smiled, crookedly, and said, "With pleasure…and relief."

The king was fascinated by the apparent familiarity the two men shared with each other. "So you two have met before? How is that possible?"

Judah and Paul looked at each other and a grin simultaneously appeared on their faces. Finally, Judah turned to Agrippa. "When Paul was going to Damascus to imprison Christians, my name was at the top of his list of those to arrest."

The king's eyes widened. "Now this is utterly intriguing," he said, refreshing himself with another drink. "You must tell me how this strange thing came to be. I know your story somewhat, Arrius. You were a Jew by birth and through some peculiar circumstances became a Roman by adoption."

"And then through even stranger circumstances, became a Christian—by choice," Judah added, causing Bernice to blanch. "In time, I became a leader among the early followers of Jesus. When Paul began his rampage, I fled with my family to Antioch, but he tried to cut off our escape to the north. He got as far as Damascus."

"So his story is true?" the king asked.

"What else could explain what happened?" Judah replied, and Paul nodded his head in silent affirmation. "Several nights after Paul had his vision, the Lord directed me and another man to seek out the one known as *Paul the Persecutor*. When we found him he was alone in a room. His eyes were seared shut as if they had been burned. He hadn't eaten or slept for three days. He looked more dead than alive."

"I haven't improved much since then," muttered Paul as he looked down at his filthy hands and soiled rags, and not a few members of the audience snickered as he said this.

"From that moment on, Paul and I worked together," Judah continued, "helping small congregations of Christians in Damascus and Antioch, until the time when I returned to Rome to inherit my father's estate. So yes, King Agrippa, we know each other well. We have a rare friendship built on twenty-five years of shared history."

The king shook his head in disbelief. "And I suppose you also would like to turn me into one of these Christians?"

Judah's eyes beamed. "For what it's worth, your majesty, I too have seen the Jesus Paul preaches."

"Before or after this purported resurrection?" asked the king.

"Both," was Judah's simple answer, and a chill swept down Agrippa's spine.

He washed down one final drink to ease the drying of his throat, then said, "These are most curious tales you both are spinning, but as much as I would care to hear more, you have a ship to catch which sets sail shortly. We have assigned you an armed guard. You may go." The soldiers began to clear a path for them to leave, and as Judah and Paul followed, King Agrippa called out, "By the way, Arrius! How is our young emperor?"

Judah turned and said, "It has been years since I have walked in the Senate chambers, your majesty. To be truthful, I have not met the Emperor yet."

"When you do, will you greet the illustrious Nero for me?" the king asked. Judah nodded with an agreeable smile, and they then paraded from the hall.

*   *   *

Rome

Several hours after his beard had been shaved, Nero called together Seneca and Burrus to a private consulting chamber in his palace—the Domus Transitoria. With them, was Ofonius Tigellinus, a boyhood friend of the emperor's who was usually found somewhere within his shadow.

The chamber was designed like a scene from any hunter's favorite dream. It was filled with statues and carvings of a myriad animals and birds. Wild game trophies hung from the plastered walls—the head of a bear, a lion, a ram, and an eagle with its magnificent wings fully extended. The three advisers were seated around an oval oak table which was itself a work of art. A woodland scene of a herd of elk was delicately chiseled into the tabletop, and was supported by four wooden deer legs. Two doors, as elaborately carved as the table, led out of the room from opposite sides. One led to the interior of the palace and the other to a courtyard which could be viewed from a small circular window cut into the door. Nero stood before the window, gazing reflectively into the courtyard.

Seneca was the first to speak. He was thin, due in part to a lifetime of asceticism. Though he was sixty, his smooth, bald head helped to conceal his years. All of his wrinkles seemed to cluster around his eyes, leaving the rest of him looking remarkably ageless. "Congratulations, Emperor. You look..." and here he paused to consider his choice of words.

"Careful, Seneca," warned Nero, turning to him with a playful frown.

"Shall we say," Seneca continued, "that Rome has again entered a glorious age of youthful vigor?"

Burrus laughed, which was unusual for so stoic a soldier as he. "Delicately spoken, my philosopher friend."

Valor and dedication on the field of battle had crippled one of his hands and wore out his body, but his spirit was as valiant as the day he first drew his sword. He was dressed in full uniform, and he reached beneath his bronzed breastplate with his good hand and withdrew a coin from a pocket in his vest. He tossed the coin, on which was molded an image of Caesar with his beard, onto the table.

"We'll certainly need to mint some fresh currency."

Nero picked up the coin and studied it for a moment. There were times when the thought of the power he possessed swept over him like a wave, and he could scarcely stand beneath the wonder of it. But as he stood admiring his silhouette on the coin, another image intruded into his thoughts. He grimaced slightly, handing the coin back to Burrus.

"I suppose you two wish to tell me that I was—how to put it?—*barbaric* with the barber?"

"Poetry drips from your lips, Lord Caesar," Seneca said. "Your response was measured and restrained. I think at an earlier time you would have had him beheaded on the spot." The others smiled in agreement. "But I think it is worth repeating, if I may be so bold, that when the strong rule with gentleness, the people will follow with eagerness."

Nero stood behind Tigellinus and placed his hands cordially on his muscular shoulders. By appearance alone, Tigellinus looked more like a ruler. Nero was of average height, with a stocky build and plain face. Tigellinus was handsome, dark and Roman.

"Seneca and Burrus, without your instruction I would be as hopeless a case as Tigellinus here," he said, slapping his friend on the back.

Tigellinus remained unaffected by this friendly jab. He was not given to emotional swings of any degree but was steadily somber, and his leaden countenance continually made those near him wonder if he enjoyed their company or perhaps was plotting their deaths. But Nero knew him well and did not expect a reaction. He eyed his counselors once again.

"Do you have more you wish to discuss gentlemen? I find myself in need of some rest."

Seneca looked at Burrus and then spoke. "Lord Nero, it's Agrippina."

Nero grimaced. "What has my mother done now? I have restored her to the court in compliance with your suggestion."

"Yes, but it appears that she has not quite learned her lesson," Seneca continued. "And I'm afraid some remedial refining ought to take place."

Nero frowned in exasperation. "By the gods, Seneca, would you speak to me plainly."

Burrus intervened. "What he means is that she continues overstepping her bounds. It's plain that she is still thirsty for power. She orders my guards around as though they were little children."

"She mingles with the Senate," added Seneca. "She conducts diplomatic business with no authorization. Fraternizes with every tribune in sight."

"This is your doing!" Nero chastised with a short, stubby finger extended at the philosopher. "You suggested that—"

"But it will be your undoing," said Seneca with firmness. "She's far more ambitious than anyone realized."

"Oh please Seneca," Nero fumed. "I've known it since I was a boy. So what would you have me to do?"

"Temper her enthusiasm. Several public rebukes ought to work nicely," said Seneca without hesitation.

He looked over to Burrus for reinforcement and the prefect continued. "Tomorrow you receive the Armenian ambassador. The health of the East depends largely on his reception, and the negotiations which follow. Agrippina has established a certain intimacy with the ambassador."

Nero laughed. "What? She's slept with him already? They've just reached Rome."

Burrus shook his head. "No they've never met. But in her curiosity for the affairs of government, she has written numerous letters to him, and we suspect that she will attempt some sort of demonstration of her influence tomorrow."

"What type of demonstration?" asked the emperor.

Burrus now looked to Seneca. It was clear that the two advisers had developed a comfortable rhythm with each other over the years. When one faltered, the other was there to offer support. "With her imagination, it could be anything," said Seneca. "But it will surely stand out, and when she displays her feathers, you must decisively ruffle them."

Nero scowled. "I will watch her more carefully."

Seneca proceeded with caution now. "There is another matter, Lord Nero."

Besides Agrippina, only Seneca could push Nero beyond his normal limits of toleration. With every one else, Nero had learned to use his power to squelch criticism. Even so, Seneca was sensing that Nero had begun to develop an immunity to his counsel. At the emperor's insistence, Tigellinus was now included in all official consultations. He represented a group of companions who had an increasing influence on Nero. Never in the history of Rome had the transition between generations been as abrupt, or—in Seneca's eyes—as ominous. Nonetheless, he spoke the truth as he saw it, hoping for the emergence of some yet unseen streak of statesmanship in his emperor. Nero gestured impatiently for Seneca to continue.

"Your affair with Poppaea Sabina is stirring up the people."

Nero exploded. "Seneca!" he yelled, slapping the palm of his hand against the wall. "The city of Rome does not belong in my bedroom. Stop meddling in my private life!"

Seneca had braced himself for the storm and chose to confront it directly. "You must listen to me, Emperor!" Nero leaned over the table shaking. "First of all, she is the wife of one of your...friends, Salvius Otho."

He paused, hoping something would slip past the armed guard of Nero's anger. "But secondly, and more importantly, Octavia is the daughter of your predecessor Claudius. You are his adopted son. To tamper with the cords that tie you to Octavia is to tamper with the cords that tie you to the throne."

"I am *Caesar!*" Nero roared, now slamming a fist onto the table. "And have been for five years. Britannicus is dead. And still you dare to insinuate that my claim to the throne is illegitimate!"

"What I think is irrelevant, my lord," said Seneca. "What the people think is everything." Nero walked over to the window, and sullenly looked out with his hands clasped behind his back. "The only security for a ruler lies in the love of his subjects. Your subjects are emotionally attached to Octavia. I would not yet toy with those affections." Seneca wished for Burrus to step in, but the prefect had leaned away and clearly wanted nothing to do with this exchange. Nonetheless, Seneca pulled him in. "I believe the prefect shares my convictions."

Burrus shot an icy stare at his friend, and then after a brief silence, spoke. "We would just remind Caesar to exercise caution."

Nero leaned closer to the window and his breath caused an island of mist to appear on the glass. Without turning to them, he said, "I think our lessons are through for the day. We will meet again tomorrow in preparation for the ambassador's visit. That is all."

Seneca and Burrus exchanged a look of disappointment, then stood and slowly left the room, while Tigellinus remained frozen in his chair. Once they were gone, Nero turned to him and sternly asked, "And where are your affections?"

Like a statue coming to life, Tigellinus spoke at last with a deep voice to match his dark and sinister disposition. "Never question my devotion to Caesar."

Nero smiled. "No, Tigellinus, I don't. From childhood, you have been by my side. Seneca, Burrus, they are not of us. The values and ideas of their generation are growing increasingly musty. Seneca disapproves of my love of music. Burrus frowns upon my athletic ambitions. Agrippina hovers around me like a vulture. One day we shall sever our connections to their world, and reshape Rome into our own image."

He paused to let his anger die down, but then his eyes lit up with a spark. Snapping his fingers, he said, "And let it begin now. Tigellinus, you are to prepare and deliver a note to my *good friend*, Otho. The distant and dangerous province of Lusitania is in need of a governor. Of course, the man I appoint will have to go alone. Lusitania is not a place for a family. Or a woman. My mind draws a blank. Perhaps you can help me draw up a name. When you do, see that Otho is told. Even tonight."

Tigellinus bowed his head and left the room. Nero returned to the window, and in its glass he could see his reflection, and the small cut on his face. At once, a scowl returned to his face and it widened as he touched the scab.

Chapter 2

Caesarea

Nearly a century earlier, the coastal city of Caesarea was built from the ground up by King Herod to serve as the center of the Roman provincial government in Judea. He named his city after Caesar Augustus, and it made for an ideal harbor once the king had constructed massive stone breakwaters to the north and south. Its central location between Lebanon and Egypt insured that it would be a major trade station as long as the *Pax Romana* was in force.

Herod was a shrewd ruler, and by placing his principal residence here he could both satisfy the Romans and pacify the Jews. The Romans conquered first with her armies and secondly with her culture, and Caesar expected monuments to Rome's greatness to be visible throughout the conquered territories. In Caesarea, Herod could erect an amphitheater, dedicate numerous temples, and liberally scatter statues of the emperor, thus giving Judea the appearance of a serene Roman province. The Jews could not protest for this was not their city. The emperor could not complain with a city that was entirely his.

But Herod knew that behind this marble curtain was a nation simmering with patriotic fervor. The tinder of Jewish passion was very dry, and the ruler of such a race must not be prone to setting off sparks. He understood these people, and could govern with great magnanimity such as when he opened up the royal treasury to rebuild their sacred temple. He could also govern with great cruelty, not hesitating to execute his own wife, or sons, or a village of innocent infants if it suited his purposes. And so history labeled him "The Great", for good or ill, and none who lived during his 36–year reign could question the indelible mark he left on Judea.

As Judah Ben-Hur and Paul the apostle walked out of Herod's great palace, they were accompanied by a small army of Roman soldiers who hemmed them in on each side. They slowly marched to the harbor, along with a column of other prisoners. The late autumn sun was gently riding overhead, and Paul had to momentarily shield his eyes as the light skipped wildly off of shields, swords and water.

He had been imprisoned for two years and had seldom been outdoors during that time, so suddenly he felt an exhilarating sense of freedom which he relished even if it was illusory. The scent of the sea breeze was intoxicating, and he imagined the wind on his face to be the brush strokes of angels' wings. And then beside him was an old and dear friend. This moment was surreal.

He turned to his friend. "Judah, I cannot believe I am walking beside you. If you tell me you are a phantom, I would readily believe you."

Judah laughed. "I know you have had visions, but this is not one of them."

"So you are really here, and after all these years we are together again!" Paul marveled. "When did we last see each other? Was it the Council in Jerusalem?"

"More than ten years ago."

"And then you, Silas, Timothy and I had adventures in Galatia, and afterwards we said farewell in Troas. You returned to Rome; we went on to Macedonia."

"And making trouble as you went," Judah said with a smile.

A centurion in command of the procession rode up beside them. His golden crest stood atop his helmet like a lion's mane. Judah signaled to him and asked, "Are all of these soldiers necessary to escort us to the harbor? An old man in chains cannot escape very far."

The centurion steadied his horse. "It's not his escape we're worried about," he said. "It's his murder." He galloped away toward the harbor, and Judah looked at his companion with an inquisitive smirk.

"As I said, making trouble as you go. As I recall, you never were very good at making friends."

Paul was amused. "Friendships can be complicated. Enemies are much easier to manage. But Judah—*old man?* I'd say the years have not been kind to you either!" At this he issued a raucous belly-laugh that surprised the nearby soldiers who were not accustomed to hearing hilarity during a prisoner transport. "Judah, I am so pleased to see you. I am puzzled, but I couldn't be more pleased.

You would come all this way from Rome, to turn right around and travel with me back to Rome?"

"As you say, friendship can be complicated," said Judah, poking Paul playfully on the shoulder. "To be honest, once we knew you had appealed to Caesar, it was a very easy decision to make. The church in Rome unanimously decided to send us."

"Us? Then Esther is with you?"

Judah nodded. "I wouldn't go anywhere without her. And you'll be happy to hear that Luke and Aristarchus have agreed to join us on the voyage. They've all gone ahead to the ship to prepare our chambers."

"Judah, that's wonderful! And here I feared that my voyage would be monotonous, and the Lord has sent me the most splendid company. I can't tell you how uplifted I feel. It stirs up memories of our first fellowship together." He looked over at Judah and a misty tear formed in his eye even as he spoke. "You and Barnabas were the first two to bring me in and embrace me as a brother. I never will forget the lesson of trust you taught me. And I still quote you today in my preaching—*Love always protects, always believes, always hopes, always endures*—great words. Marvelous words!"

Judah looked down at the sand. "Words that can easily lose meaning when you live in Rome," he said listlessly.

Paul could not miss this change in tone. "What's this? A breeze of disillusionment blowing in the air? You need a good prison cell to lift your sagging spirits." And he laughed again, causing Judah to brighten. "I hear you have been very good to Rome. You've planted a church of hundreds. You have trained and able leadership. Converts among the house of Caesar. Judah, I applaud you! When I first encouraged you to take the gospel back to Rome, I never could have imagined the things that God has done through you. In fact, while praying for your success in public, I secretly feared that you'd return to Judea having fallen short. You are a triumph. A trophy of grace!"

Paul was known by the churches in Asia as the *apostle of joy*, and that he was, though it seemed incomprehensible if one saw the marks of torture on his body or knew even partially of the sufferings he endured for the sake of the Jesus he had met on the Damascus Road. Judah felt mildly admonished by the resiliency of his friend. But then Paul always was a man of vision and passion. Judah would never forget the one conversation with Paul years earlier that had changed the course of his own life.

It came at the end of a special year of shared ministry in Antioch, as they worked side by side along with their good friend Barnabas. The fellowship between the three pastors that year was rich, and it was a time they would each look back on later as something rare and immeasurably sweet. But the happy triumvirate knew that the work of the kingdom of God must advance, and each one sensed that the fellowship had to be broken that a higher good would result. Toward the end of their time together, Paul took Judah aside to share with him a burden that had been weighing upon his heart.

"Judah, why do you think God first took you to Rome?" he asked soberly.

Judah responded, "It was clearly part of God's plan for my deliverance. Nothing else could explain the favor that was shown me. To be a doomed galley slave one day, and the adopted son of a Roman consul the next was nothing short of a miracle of God."

"That's very true, Judah. No one could deny it. But did God have even a higher plan beyond your own redemption? Could he have been thinking of the redemption of Rome when he sent you there?"

Until that moment, Judah had never considered the possibility. After he was betrayed by his Roman friend Messala and sent to die on a slave ship for a crime he did not commit, Judah assumed that the purpose for his years spent in Rome was merely to prepare him for the work of redeeming his family once he returned to Judea. Now Paul had challenged him with an entirely new interpretation of this tragic history.

"Think of Joseph, sent to Egypt first as a slave, only to be exalted by God to the right hand of Pharoah," Paul continued. "And why? For the redemption of his family, of course, but more so, for the redemption of all Israel. And Joseph's power and Joseph's influence were all elements which God used as part of his plan. Think of it, Judah! You have connections to one of the highest families in Rome. Your adoption as a son of Arrius gives you access to the Roman Senate and to the house of Caesar itself."

Judah shook his head. "But my father died two years ago."

"But your citizenship is still intact?"

"Only because of my father's noble and generous spirit. During the days of my zealotry, I returned my ring of adoption to him, but he dismissed my action for what it was—foolishness—and sent the ring back with further tokens of his love for me. His hope was that I would one day return and fulfill my destiny as his son, but that was always out of the question. What God is doing here is far more important. In another year, his property becomes forfeit to the Senate, and my flirtation with Rome will end."

"No Judah! Your thinking is too narrow," said Paul, with mounting fervor in his voice. "What God is doing here is important, but think of what God could do in Rome. Think of a church planted in the heart of the capital city. Think of the possibilities! Messengers could be sent to all parts of the empire, from Britain to Persia, to Carthage and Spain, and within a few years we can fulfill our Lord's commission. We can reach the ends of the earth with the gospel! But we must win Rome first. And Judah, you're the one who can do it. Don't you see? You are Joseph!"

Paul's rhetoric was stirring, but Judah was yet unconvinced, so Paul pressed him further. "Judah, you have the gift of bringing churches to life. And you have the opportunity of doing so in the empire's greatest city. You must do so! We must do whatever we can to save some. If it means becoming a slave to win a slave, then we do so. If it means becoming a Roman to win a Roman, then so be it. Judah, do you understand? I know a man of vision such as yourself can see the truth in what I'm saying!"

After much time spent in prayer, Judah and Esther did come to see that Paul was right. And while the opportunity yet remained, they said farewell to the land and people they loved, and sailed west. And except for one occasion three years later when Judah returned to Jerusalem to help settle a point of controversy concerning the relevancy of Jewish laws to Gentile converts, the two friends took two very different roads which now, to the delight of both, had converged again.

There was no question that what God had done during the years of their friendship was astounding. Paul had gone on to win renown as a great pioneer and missionary, planting not one church, but many, scattered like diamonds throughout the empire. And in Rome, Christianity was now firmly rooted and there to stay. Both men were now more than sixty years old. But where Paul was still energetic and tireless, Judah was worn out and exhausted. And it showed in his face and in the slight way his shoulders sagged as they approached the harbor.

The cry of a gull flying overhead brought Judah out of his daydreaming. He turned to Paul.

"You won't still consider it a shortcoming if Esther and I return to Jerusalem before long? We may have been good to Rome, but it has surely taken its toll on us."

"You do look tired, Judah," said Paul with a nod.

"We've been away for thirteen years. Years I wouldn't trade for any. But both Esther and I find ourselves yearning to be home. Suddenly this irresistible longing to fill out our days in Judea has welled up within us. And now seeing our country again, hearing Galilean dialects, smelling the aroma of Jewish ovens, it has awakened in us so much emotion. It's very strong and compelling."

Paul smiled with understanding, but his eyes beamed with another light. "And Judah, my friend, I desire nothing more than to climb aboard that boat and sail west. And never look back. I want to scale those Seven Hills of yours, preach on the Forum, baptize in the Tiber, and if Nero allows me, I'll sail on to Spain and bring the gospel to every creature I find. Isn't life funny? Isn't God funny? The paths that he takes us on—they are so different. And yet each one brings him glory. Isn't it overwhelming?"

"What overwhelms me is seeing that you've lost none of your flame," said Judah. "I am glad for that. And glad that our paths have crossed one more time."

After a brief silence, Paul spoke out. "Judah, why don't you stay? You're here. You have family and property in Jerusalem. Your companionship is welcome, but as you can see...", and here he pointed around them to the surrounding soldiers, "...Caesar will take good care of me."

Judah shook his head. "No. Not yet. My official duties call me to prepare you for the emperor."

"Ha!" said Paul. "Or prepare the emperor for me!"

As they approached the harbor, a trio of sailing vessels came into view, the larger of these being a service ship used to transport an assortment of goods from around the empire back to Rome for the indulgence of the conquering race. The cargo varied with each shipment. Sometimes it included sand for the circus usually accompanied by a menagerie of wild beasts, or exotic fruits and rare delicacies for the dinner tables of the elite, and always prisoners. Since the days the Julian dynasty began, the dregs of the Roman empire were scraped up for the entertainment of Caesar and his courtiers. They were converted into gladiators or broken into slaves, and the stream of captives never ran dry. Ship after ship hauled them to Rome for "justice".

Paul was just one of a larger group of prisoners boarding the ship. Yet as a Roman citizen, he was to be handled with greater delicacy under the watchful eye of the centurion. As an appellant to Caesar he would be given even more privileges such as private quarters not far removed in comfort from ordinary chambers, and with a senatorial advocate by his side, he would virtually be a free man, but for a personal guard who would shadow him.

As the parade of soldiers and prisoners drew near to the ship, a woman's voice danced out across the pier. "Judah! Paul!" They looked up and saw a woman standing on the ship, with two men beside her.

Paul smiled. "That can only be dear Esther."

Judah nodded, with a certain pleasure washing over his face. "And her voice still makes my heart melt."

"It's a miracle you lovebirds ever had time to accomplish anything for the Lord!" mused Paul with a playful twinkle in his eyes, and Judah laughed.

The trail of prisoners was ushered onto the ship like cattle, but as soon as they were on board, the centurion separated Paul from the others and brought him to the main deck, where he assigned a guard to watch him. Esther ran forward to them. Disregarding the soldiers, she threw her arms around Paul and kissed his neck. "Paul! God's peace to you." A purple veil hung loosely over her head and short white locks of hair fell out beneath it onto her forehead. Her face was soft, and her warm eyes radiated with gentleness.

"And you, dear sister," he said with great affection. "You look as beautiful and youthful as ever." He leaned closer to her ear. "Your husband on the other hand…"

"That's quite enough," Judah interjected with mock solemnity.

Paul straightened and greeted the two men who had come near. "And Master Luke, the good doctor. How I've longed to see you again. And you've brought along faithful Aristarchus, the pillar of our Thessalonican flock." The three men embraced.

"You're smiling, as always," said Luke. "Some things do not change."

The centurion was giving final instructions to the guard when Judah drew his attention. "Centurion. Your name is Julius, I believe." The centurion nodded. "I have a favor to ask. As a legate of the Roman Senate, I would ask that Paul's chains be removed during the voyage."

The centurion paused momentarily and then motioned to the guard to unlock the chains. "But only while we are at sea," he said, walking on.

Judah smiled and looked at Paul. "Now, what were you saying about me earlier?"

Paul again leaned toward Esther as the guard freed him. "Salt of the earth. Esther, have I told you? Your husband is a wonderful man."

*   *   *

Rome

The emperor walked into the receiving hall, tapping the front end of his shoes against the mosaic tiles that spread out across the floor in a rich coral patchwork. Dozens of people milled about the room. The women clustered together like birds in a flowerbed, happily chirping away in their multi-colored stolas, each one showing off her jewelry or creative hair style. The men huddled in groups of three or four, draped in togas, arms folded, each one comporting himself with elitist laughter and noddings of the head.

Nero ignored all of them. He himself wore a white toga with a brilliant purple sash draped over his shoulder. The laurel wreath atop his head symbolized for the Roman mind military prowess—of which Nero had none—but custom forbade Rome's emperors from wearing gold crowns. Rome was not ruled by a king but by the *Princeps*, the '*First Citizen*'.

Nero looked nervously about from one end of the room to the other and then approached Seneca and Burrus who were standing within reach of the heat cast off by the room's oversized fireplace. "Where is my mother?" he asked, backing off from the fire, which was large enough to roast a boar.

"All members of the royal court are in place but for her," said Seneca matter-of-factly, adjusting his own white toga, worn only by members of the Senate.

Nero bit at the end of a fingernail. "What are her intentions?"

Seneca shrugged. "To make some noise, I imagine."

"We will not wait for her," Nero said. "Let's get on with it." He leaned toward a soldier standing nearby. "Usher in the Armenian ambassador."

The audience came to a sense of order as Nero walked to the center of the room and joined a receiving line composed of numerous senators and patricians. He scanned the room, then sharply asked, "Where's Octavia?"

She emerged from the crowd and reluctantly walked across the room to take her place beside him. She wore a stunning white silk gown, spangled with amethyst, which flowed down to her feet. Her long, dark hair stood atop her head in a cascade of elegant curls, and the bronzed skin of her face seemed to glow. She left more than a few open mouths in her wake, except for Nero who frowned impatiently.

"Really Lady Octavia, your place is at your lord's side, not cavorting with the gentry," he lectured, not minding that his voice carried. "Did your father not teach you any sense of protocol in these matters? Sometimes you really embarrass me."

She looked down, not attempting any response, and he lifted her chin with a rough flick of his finger. "And please stop looking at the floor," he continued. "You're my queen, not my housemaid."

At that moment, the doors opened and the Armenian delegation entered, led by the ambassador who approached Nero with a broad smile pasted above his neatly clipped goatee. He wore a bright red tunic, held at the waist by a gold belt. He bowed before the emperor, who savored the adulation for a moment before bringing him to his feet. "Ambassador, welcome to Rome, and to the Domus Transitoria, my home."

The ambassador was older—perhaps three times the age of Caesar, and noticeably taller. As a veteran of diplomacy, he was a capable actor. So his face showed only deep regard for Nero though his immediate urge was to laugh at this boyish, stumpy person in front of him. He straightened and said, "My Emperor. Our highest congratulations to our lord on the shaving of his first beard. It is a deep honor to share in this noteworthy occasion."

Nero leaned closer to him. "And in your entourage, you have brought athletes and musicians to compete in my games?"

"Most certainly, Emperor," said the ambassador. "Though in deference to the greatness of Rome, we are hardly worthy of sharing the same stage with Rome, let alone aspiring to compete with her." The ten or so people in his party rapidly bobbed their heads in mock agreement, looking not unlike a group of barnyard chickens.

"Ah, but I've heard that the Armenian chariots are the envy of the gods," Nero said, "and I am most anxious to observe your drivers."

"Only observe?" asked the ambassador, twisting his face to show disappointment. "We had hoped that my lord would himself race. We had heard of your interest in the sport and hoped we might witness your great talent."

Nero feigned modesty. "I have built a private circus for my own pleasure wherein I tinker, shall we say. My advisers feel that it is not quite suitable for the First Citizen to stoop to such amusements."

"Such a tragedy," the ambassador said, fabricating a frown. "I believe your people would worship you all the more if you participated with them in their recreation."

"That day will come, Ambassador," Nero whispered in his ears with a certain emphasis. He led the ambassador down his receiving line. "And this is the daughter of Claudius, my wife Octavia."

Now the ambassador smiled with genuine enthusiasm. "Ah, Empress. Your face adorns the halls of many of our temples. You are truly worshipped by our people."

Octavia smiled and with a soft voice said, "I am flattered, Ambassador."

A member of the Armenian coterie reached forward and handed the ambassador a luxuriously ornamented box. He turned and offered it to Octavia. "And for you, my lady, I have a gift. A collection of rare and fragrant Persian perfumes. Though how does one complement perfect beauty? If there was a way, it would be found in these vials."

Octavia received them with humility. "I will wear them with honor," she said.

"The Emperor surely appreciates the treasure he has in you?" asked the ambassador looking at Nero, whose lips curled in an awkward, forced smile.

Nero quickly directed the ambassador to Seneca and Burrus and initiated swift introductions. The ambassador then searched the remainder of the attending audience, and asked with distraction, "But where, might I ask, is Agrippina, your mother?"

"She was expected, but is apparently indisposed," said Nero bluntly.

"What a shame," mused the ambassador. "From the nature of her correspondence, I presumed she would be a part of our negotiations this afternoon."

"That she would give that impression is of no great surprise," Nero said. "But, sometimes my mother is prone—"

Here he was cut off mid-sentence by a sudden disturbance at the doorway as Agrippina burst into the room with a provincial clamor, startling the guards and attendants alike. Nero winced as Agrippina obtrusively strutted forward and presented herself to the ambassador. She wore a gaudy purple robe and her face was caked with enough makeup to paint every woman in the palace.

"Why, this must be the distinguished lady herself," the ambassador said with perfect composure, though his histrionic talents were now fully stretched.

Agrippina raised her hand to the ambassador, who kissed it, not failing to notice her long purple nails and fingers bedecked with jewelry. "Ambassador, I am Lady Agrippina. I apologize for charging in so. It is rude of me."

"Quite," Nero muttered under his breath.

"My lady, to see your face at last fills my heart with joy," the ambassador remarked. "I'm so glad you have joined us."

Nero suppressed the fire burning in his bosom. "Mother, we were preparing to be seated to begin our discussion."

"Why in that case, I won't delay the proceedings any longer," Agrippina blurted out. "By all means, let's be seated and I'll take my place beside you, if I may, Ambassador." She took the ambassador's arm and began to move toward a raised dais on which were arranged an assortment of chairs. Seneca suddenly stepped forward toward Nero and took him aside.

"Caesar, Agrippina's presumption of sitting on the dais with you is an encroachment on your authority," he whispered intently. "Allowing her to participate officially in these negotiations will give her an appearance of power I'm not sure you wish for her to have. You must stop this now, or it may be impossible to dislodge her later."

Nero scowled and swiftly moved forward. He reached out and firmly grasped Agrippina's arm, then spun her slightly to the side and redirected her to a chair on the main floor. "Agrippina, we have an assigned seat for you right here, near where your daughter-in-law will sit," he said, trying to sound cordial. But as he nudged her into the chair, he leaned forward and spat quietly into her ear, "How dare you assume to join me on the dais. You'll answer for this!"

She smiled as though he had merely blown on her ear, but if anyone had looked closely at her face, he would have seen minute cracks appearing on her makeup. Only her eyes showed the boiling of her blood.

Nero's polite formality returned as he pivoted around and ushered the ambassador and his party onto the dais, where for the remainder of the afternoon, the stage of performers went through the motions of diplomatic civility, playing their parts with precision and flair.

That evening, Nero entertained his guests with a lavish feast, which was intended less to feed his visitors, than to remind them why Rome was master of the world. The banquet hall stretched out for 150 feet. Stone pillars encompassed the room at ten-foot intervals, supporting a vaulted ceiling that left those who looked up at it breathless. Behind the columns was a walkway leading to other parts of the palace, and from it emerged a steady stream of slaves who brought one course after another, only pausing long enough to wash the guests' hands when requested.

The food was heaped up on low tables, each one surrounded on three sides by long velvet couches. Up to twelve people could recline comfortably around one table and leisurely pick at the food with their fingers. The emperor lay at the center table, with Octavia to his left, the ambassador to his right, and his mother and advisers occupying the remaining positions. Three other tandems of tables and couches for the remaining guests were spread out around the emperor, but space was left in the middle of the room for the entertainment which was a traditional part of every feast. Dancers, clowns and poets appeared throughout the long stretches of the evening.

The *gustatio*, or appetizers, included honeyed dormice sauteed with poppyseed and oil, as well as stuffed thrushes served with quail eggs in an asparagus sauce. Eggs, olives and grapes accompanied the salads. The Romans delighted in forming their dishes into exotic shapes, and Nero was especially pleased to see his favorite gelatin made of peacock brains appear on his table molded into sea urchins. Later the stuffed pork was brought, pressed to look like a wild goose. The Romans loved to cook with sauces, the most popular being *garum*, a potent blend of salted, fermented fish remains. All of it was washed down with the finest wine the emperor could supply.

Nero and his guests lounged on their couches for five hours, and as the wine took hold, a disheveled restlessness took over the party. Nero grew increasingly loud and vulgar the more drunk he became, and tried to fondle every slavegirl that came within arm's length of him. Octavia drifted into a troubled sleep.

Seneca became more philosophical, and annoying. Agrippina spent the night in pursuit of the ambassador, and her persistance finally broke him.

While turning a pomegranate over in his hand, he suddenly winked at Agrippina, then licked the fruit with a seductive lap of his tongue. She blushed and batted her eyes in return. At this, the ambassador issued an ear-splitting belch, which rattled off the ceiling and caused Octavia to nearly fall off her cushion. Nero applauded him, and echoed back with a belch of his own, and soon, a chorus of bodily noises shook the room.

"Thank you, everyone," Nero exclaimed with a boorish lifting of his hands. "I'm glad you are all pleased. We have made new friends today." Every head nodded in ready agreement, and then with the ambassador's lead, everyone raised a glass to Caesar and hailed his greatness and divinity.

As the glasses were lowered, the ambassador turned to Nero. "So my Emperor, I am from a different culture and am unfamiliar with the fine points of Roman custom. Why is it that the Supreme Ruler of the earth is denied the pleasures of formal competition in the circus? Of what consequence is a trivial horse race to your imperial authority?"

"Because Ambassador, sport is beneath the dignity of the Roman ruling class," Nero answered pertly. He looked at Seneca who lounged across from him. "Or so I have been told. Isn't that right, Seneca?"

Seneca nodded unapologetically. "It has long been the Roman perspective that athletic and artistic pursuits are of minimal use in preparing a person for public life," he said.

The ambassador's earlier condescension of Nero now evolved into a distaste for the entire Roman race. "But certainly gentlemen, to guide the chariot to victory in the circus is a worthwhile preamble to guiding the chariot to victory on the field of battle," he said with aplomb. "To conquer the wrestler in the ring must surely prepare for success in actual hand-to-hand combat!"

Seneca was always invigorated by debate. "Then how does one explain the debasement and enthrallment of Greece, for whom the games occupy the center of existence?" he asked. "The Greeks lack for no training, as you suggest. But how many of them would you want with you in battle, Prefect?"

He turned to Burrus sitting next to him, who sternly answered, "Give me a hundred Roman slaves to fight with over a thousand Grecian athletes."

"Then music would be of even less value yet?" Agrippina asked, jumping in with an offhanded innocence to her voice.

Seneca scoffed. "For us, all these pursuits weaken the moral strength of a leader."

Nero had scarcely heard Seneca, because he found in Agrippina's comment the adder's bite of a mother's sarcasm. He glared at Agrippina. "Now it is curious that you broach the subject of music, my mother, since you know my great love for it. And I can only imagine that you are attempting to embarrass me...," and at this, Agrippina protested with a look of shocked feminine denial, "...since you are aware of the fact that this week I intend to give my first public performance as the centerpiece of my *Neronia*."

This announcement was greeted by stunned silence. Seneca was clearly disturbed, but he gathered himself together. "A public performance of music, of song?"

"No Seneca, I will stand on a stage and crow like a rooster," Nero fumed.

"I was not aware of my lord's intentions," said Seneca. "No emperor has ever performed for his people before. It's quite unprecedented, and dare I say, unusual."

"My beard is off now, Seneca," Nero responded coldly. "I am capable of solitary decisions." He wiped his mouth with a napkin. "And you will all be present, as Roman custom evolves before your eyes."

As each person stewed in the uncomfortable silence that followed, the ambassador finally rose to his feet. "Caesar, it will be our highest privilege to witness this event. A true cultural milestone. Our people commend you. For now, accept my gratitude for this marvelous repast. Would you please excuse me and my company? We have official duties to attend to before retiring."

Nero signaled his approval with a nod of his head and the Armenian delegation quickly picked themselves up and left the room. Those that remained sat around their tables in awkward isolation, until Seneca again ventured to break the silence.

"Emperor?"

"Seneca," grunted Nero unenthusiastically.

"Are you certain that this is a step to take at this time?"

"At what time would you prefer?" Nero snapped. "When, if not now? Would you suggest I cannot sing?"

"Having not heard my lord, I cannot offer an opinion."

Nero then turned to his wife. "Octavia, you have heard me sing. What do you say? Am I pleasing to listen to?"

She grimaced to be drawn into the conversation. "Yes, my lord," she said quietly without raising her head.

"I'm sorry. I did not hear you," Nero said.

Octavia looked up and met the gaze of her husband with eyes that were both frightened and weary of being frightened. "I said, yes. I enjoy hearing you sing."

"And the public could stomach an entire performance of mine?" he pressed.

"Yes, they would enjoy hearing you sing as well."

Nero ignored the lifelessness of her words.

"There it is. A ringing endorsement from the house of Claudius. Then it is settled. Burrus, I will expect a visible presence of the Guard on that evening. And Seneca, you will assist me in seeing that the Senate is given full encouragement to attend. Remember in whose honor these games are held, and allow me the discretion to dispense with tradition if I see fit. I am Caesar. This discussion was to have been held later, but Agrippina, as she is prone to do, has forced the issue as it suits her. For now, I would like to dismiss the rest of you as I discuss this matter further with my mother."

Agrippina shook her head. "Really Nero, I am tired and—"

"You will stay until I am through," Nero said with blunt severity. He nodded and everyone else rose and left the room, while Agrippina and Nero sat up straight on their cushions.

Nero spoke. "Agrippina."

"I am your mother," she replied. "Don't address me by my name."

"Oh, you are my mother?" he asked with disdain. "For a short moment this afternoon, I had the distinct impression that you were the Emperor. Excuse me if I appear confused."

"Don't condescend to me!" she hissed.

But he roared back. "And don't patronize me! How dare you trivialize my authority by attempting to give the impression that Caesar's power is shared!"

"It was a simple oversight," she said. "In my hurry…"

Nero's eyes widened. "An oversight? You intentionally delay your entrance so as to command our attention. You pander to the Ambassador as though he were a long-lost suitor, and then I discover that you have engaged in lengthy correspondence with him. Of what business are the affairs of Armenia to you?"

Agrippina eyes filled with fraudulent tears. "It was all quite innocent, I assure you."

"Innocent!" Nero shouted. "You lost your innocence before I was born."

She quickly forgot her tears. "Why you ungrateful wretch!" she spat. "Everything you have is because of me. Everything you are is because of me. Without me you would be eating crumbs from the table of Britannicus!"

Nero crashed his hand down upon the table. "Do not mention his name!"

Agrippina fired one final volley. "He would not disgrace the throne of Caesar with his voice."

"*Silence!*" Nero bellowed, rising to his feet like a cobra. "You have gone too far! You have crossed the final dividing line of my favor. I welcomed you back, and immediately you betray me. The breach now is irreparable. Tomorrow morning, an escort of soldiers will lead you out of Rome, and if you manage to make it as far as your villa, you will never set foot off of the property again. For the day you set your sights on Rome again, is the day you join your husband!"

"O Nero, Nero, don't do this to me!" wailed Agrippina with real tears now, because they flowed from an inner pool of self-pity. Nero stopped her.

"Go! Be gone now. I am so weary of you," he said, and she picked herself up and fled from the room, with her long, hard sobs echoing behind her. Nero sat back down into the cushion and closed his eyes, attempting to still the angry trembling of his body. He remained motionless for more than five minutes, after which time a guard tentatively looked into the room and then entered.

"Emperor," the guard said timidly. He waited until Nero looked up. "You have not yet assigned the password for the evening watch this week."

Nero wiped his mouth and then spoke with exhausted dullness. "This week's password is the 'best of mothers'." The guard saluted and marched from the room.

*　　　　*　　　　*

Paul sat quietly upon his bed, his head bowed in a posture of prayer, while across the tiny room his guard hunched over on a cramped wooden bench looking annoyed. The cabin was little more than cubicle with two short bunks built into the wall, and enough room for a man to stand and dress. Night had fallen, and the guard occupied himself by studying the shadow cast on the walls by a flickering candle. The shadow seemed to breathe in time with the gentle rocking of the ship—inhaling, exhaling, shrinking, expanding. His analysis was interrupted by a knock at the door.

Paul looked up as the door opened, and Judah's face protruded into the room, with Esther's silhouette visible behind him. "Are you comfortable?" Judah asked.

"Very much so," said Paul. "I've traded in a prison cell for a king's suite. I couldn't be happier. Please come in, both of you."

They entered, and the guard eagerly obeyed when Judah signaled that he could be dismissed. Esther took his bench while Judah sat down at the end of the bed.

"The centurion tells me that we will be trading vessels once we arrive in Lycia," said Judah. "There'll be a hold-over for several days and he has given his permission for us to go ashore. Our Julius is a good man."

"Yes, I would agree," said Paul. "I have a soft spot in my heart for him. I imagine we should be able to meet with some of our Asian brothers if we are given a few days to rest on shore. Think of it, Judah. You and I performing an encore, together again as at the first!"

"I have a hard time thinking of ministry as rest," said Esther, slightly chagrined.

"Ah, but you forget, dear sister. I have had ample rest, of late," Paul noted. "I have had two years to catch my breath in Agrippa's dungeon's. More than enough laziness for one lifetime. I am more than ready to be exhausted for the Lord's work. I want to serve him like a good piece of firewood, that gives off heat till it's completely consumed. There's nothing worse than green wood that sputters and goes out."

Judah was contemplative. "Your words are harsh, my friend. You are speaking to two very tired people. We are indeed exhausted for the Lord's work."

"But weariness is nothing to be ashamed of," Paul remarked. "It is clear that we are like two vessels floating past each other—one heading to sea with a full arsenal and a ready crew, and one limping to harbor after a great conquest, victorious but depleted. I understand fully."

"To be honest, Paul, there have been times when we have envied you," Esther mused after a momentary silence.

"O! And why is that?" asked Paul with playful curiosity.

Judah answered for her. "The life of an apostle is never dull. Always moving, always planting, every year a new congregation. The work is always fresh and exciting and unpredictable. Not so for the pastor. What is planted he must tend. He must outsmart the insects and outlast the weeds."

"And goodness, the weeds!" Esther sighed. "Paul, the time you wrote to our people in Rome, civil war had nearly broken out in the church. And over what? Meat of all things! Grown men, brothers in Christ, quarreling over butchered cattle. What petty controversy will it be next—the songs we use to worship with?"

"But dear ones, believe me, how often I have envied you!" exclaimed Paul. "To be able to settle in one place and watch your work mature. To see seeds you've planted come to bear fruit. We apostles lack a sense of accomplishment for our work is never finished. And yet the shepherd's heart within us is always pricked with suspense at how our flocks are progressing. Some nights I cannot sleep at all for tossing in restless prayer for them."

Judah was struck with a pang of conviction. "*Thou shalt not envy*. And look at us now—wanting what the other person has. Sometimes I even imagine that Moses or David are jealously watching us from heaven, itching to return to earth again and jump into the fray. Meanwhile, we envy what they have."

"Now there's a provocative thought!" laughed Paul. "Which is better? Fitful rest united with our King, or faithful service separated from our King? Which is better—to live or die? Judah, no man can jar my thinking as you can!"

Paul reached out and slapped Judah's knee as he said this. "But this is why I say that contentment is the greatest gift a man can have. And why shouldn't it be so? Think of how short a time we are here. I remember skipping stones on a lake near Tarsus as a young boy, and I remember it as though it were yesterday. And now look at the three of us. That lake is still there with young boys still beside it, but we are old and gray. So soon it all passes. Contentment is best. So I stand repentant with you. Let's hear no more talk of envy."

"Agreed," said Judah, and Esther nodded approvingly.

And so their conversation continued amiably for several hours as they exchanged stories of their respective adventures and shared their dreams for the future. Judah and Esther's years in Rome had been as fruitful as Paul had originally envisioned. Most of those who were acquainted with Quintus Arrius were pleasantly surprised when his adopted son unexpectedly arrived in Rome to lay claim to his inheritance, with the exception of Emperor Claudius whose eyes had eagerly fallen on the Arrius estate as the time for its forfeiture drew near. The imperial coffers were still languishing from the opulent excesses of his predecessor, Caligula.

When Judah appealed to the Senate for official reinstatement of his property and name, Claudius hovered in a temporary state of indecision. But the Arrius family was deeply loved, and any refusal on Caesar's part would have incurred deep senatorial resentment which Claudius could then ill afford. Begrudgingly, he released the property, and three years later, when Claudius banished the Jewish community from Rome, some traced the expulsion to the anger he felt over the younger Arrius' return. Caesar could not touch Arrius, but he could wound his people.

But Claudius did not comprehend that the younger Arrius now belonged to a new community of people that transcended race; it was neither Jewish nor Roman. It was never perceived that a new and potent spiritual force had been unleashed on the city, which was even then quietly filling the empire. From the time Claudius expelled the Jews, it would take fifteen more years before the Christians would be recognized as a unique religious entity—a discovery that would be made by Nero, with devastating results.

After his return to Rome, Judah—in honor of his father's name—began a short career as an advocate in the Senate, arguing cases for those who could not afford private counsel. His ready wit and steady logic won him many cases, not to mention the admiration of several men of influence, including the senator Seneca. Yet Judah's heart was elsewhere.

By this time, there were already many believers scattered in pockets throughout the city who had traveled in Judea and had been convinced and converted by the Christians they met. But they lacked the galvanizing leadership needed to pull them together as one congregation. When word spread that an intimate associate of the apostles had come to Rome, Judah quickly found himself with a substantial following, and by the time of the Jewish expulsion, he found it necessary to abandon his career in the Senate to attend to his flock. He quietly retreated into the backdrop of Roman politics.

Paul was intrigued by the intricacies of the Roman court. "So tell me about Nero," he interjected as Judah was continuing with his story. "I know he is young, and I have heard that he is the benefactor of an ambitious mother."

Esther scowled. "Agrippina is a wicked, scheming woman."

"And I fear that Nero is cut of the same cloth," Judah said. "After his wife died, Emperor Claudius married Agrippina, even though he was her uncle. Incest is of no account to these people." The distaste in Judah's voice was obvious. "Claudius' natural son Britannicus was the rightful heir. Yet somehow Agrippina bewitched Claudius into adopting Nero and designating him as his legal successor. Shortly after this, Claudius became violently ill and died. It was obvious to everyone that he had been poisoned. But before anyone in the Senate could act, Nero was in power. He was seventeen years old when he ascended."

"A harmless little pup," Paul said.

"The pup grew fangs rather quickly," added Esther.

Judah continued. "Britannicus came of age the very next year and died at his birthday party, in plain view of his friends. Poisoned, of course."

"It's a saying in Rome that mushrooms are the food of the gods," Esther added. "In eating one, you may very well die and become a god."

Paul scoffed. "Well, that goes to show you how little the Romans know about theology, or cooking for that matter. So who is actually running the empire at present?"

"No doubt Agrippina thinks that she is," Judah replied. "But then others feel the real strings are pulled by Nero's closest advisers. His prefect and the philosopher Seneca appear to have their hands in everything."

Paul's eyebrows raised. "I once met Seneca's brother Gallio in Corinth. He was a spineless man."

"And likewise Seneca," said Judah. "He's much too in love with his philosophy to be an effective ruler. No, I think the one we will ultimately reckon with is Nero himself."

Paul ran his fingers through his beard. "So has any of this violence touched the church?"

"So far we have been left undisturbed," Judah said. He looked at Paul with dark, sober eyes which seemed to glow in the candlelight. "But as anyone who has fished the Sea of Galilee knows, the storms can suddenly come on you unannounced."

Chapter 3

The emperor's first public performance was the talk of all Rome. It was the sole topic of conversation from every barber's chair to the back alley vegetable stands. Those that were older saw it as a sure sign of imperial humiliation and cultural decay. Those that were younger favored it, seeing in it an act of courage and innovation by a contemporary leader who would not let Rome stagnate in a cesspool of foolish traditions.

The performance itself was the capstone of a glorious day of final competition as the *Neronia* wound to its climax. Augustus was the first Caesar to learn the full power of offering games to enhance his popularity. The average citizen cared little for the substance of government, as long as he was fed and entertained. *Bread and circuses!* was the mantra of the populace. Each successive Caesar tried to outdo the one before in providing them, and so by Nero's time, the people were thoroughly addicted to the games. To watch the emperor sing was something bold and different, and the people's approval of Nero soared to new heights.

When the night came, the theater was overflowing with spectators several hours before the program began. It was an open-air amphitheater which comfortably sat 8,000 people, but on this night more than 10,000 were crammed into the half-circle of stone benches that cascaded up the theater floor. Behind the massive stage towered a 75–foot stone wall, divided into sections by decorative marble columns which rose up in the shape of giant flower stems, enshrining the entrances to the stage. Soldiers stood posted all along the sides of the theater, while ushers rushed up and down the stairs like ice-breaking barges, futilely attempting to keep the aisles clear.

At last the program began. It was an exhausting four-hour parade of musicians and dancers who swept across the stage, while a panel of judges sat

frowning or yawning in a row off to the side. Nero watched the competition
from the shadows of one of the stage entrances. Seneca and Burrus stood beside
him, while Tigellinus lurked behind them in the darkness.

The performer who preceded Nero was a beautiful young woman who sang a
lengthy, haunting ode to *Heliades*, the joint name for the daughters of Apollo.
When their reckless brother Phaeton was killed by Zeus with a thunderbolt, the
inconsolable grief of Heliades so unnerved their father that he changed them into
poplar trees, and still the sisters weep with tears of amber sap to this day. The
woman's voice rang through the theater with disarming beauty, and everywhere
people were dabbing away tears from their eyes. Even some of the judges turned
aside their heads for a moment. Nero looked on, attempting to suppress the
effect the singer was having on him.

"By all the gods, that woman has the voice of Circe," he said to his two advisers. "Who is she?"

Seneca nodded his head approvingly. "Yes, she's quite gifted. She is a senator's
niece, from Pompeii I believe."

Burrus too was enamored with her singing. "By far, she is the best entrant in
the voice competition." Seeing Nero scowl, Burrus quickly added, "Among those
we've heard so far."

Earlier in the evening, Seneca and Burrus had informed the master of ceremonies that they would make one final attempt to dissuade the emperor from
performing. Seneca saw this as the decisive moment.

"My lord, your presence at these games ennobles them. Your desire to participate in them insures that they will never be forgotten. For you to actually compete can scarcely add more luster to the glory of this event. I would suggest that
if you wanted to honor this woman, you forego your performance, and award
this woman the victory wreath which would surely be yours otherwise. The
judges would certainly agree."

"What a magnificent idea," Burrus said. "Emperor, I would heed him."

Something unpleasant flashed in Nero's eyes. He looked at his advisers with
exasperation. "Your counsel smacks of impropriety, gentlemen. Accept a prize I
have not earned, then under false pretenses, present it to another? You can honor
a fool that way, but certainly not a woman. And you continue to miss my point!"

His voice grew louder and carried out onto the stage to the woman who looked nervously behind her while she continued to sing.

"Ribbons and wreaths are not the issue here. It is my singing. It is art! Every Caesar has led in battle and expanded the boundaries of Rome. But what Caesar has expanded the culture of Rome? Our conquests are worthless if we do not at some point seek to elevate the human spirit. An empire is not ultimately advanced by the sword, but by the soul. And tonight I will make that point very clear. Award your wreaths to whomever you choose. Tonight your emperor will sing!"

Nero folded his arms and looked back out at the woman, signaling an end to the discussion. A short time later the woman finished, and the theater shook with the sound of the audience's robust cheering. A rainbow of flowers showered onto the stage, which the woman quickly scooped up before running off. The master of ceremonies came to the center of the stage, and when the crowd had quieted, spoke.

"A most engaging performance. If the contest were to conclude right now, we would have to call it a rewarding evening." He glanced back in the emperor's direction and sought out Seneca, who waved him on with a discreet flick of his hand which Nero could not see.

After clearing his throat, the emcee looked back to the audience and continued. "And now, we are all soon to be witnesses to a most noteworthy event. Never before in the history of the empire has the emperor performed before his people. Tonight that changes, to our delight. With humility and honor, I now relinquish the stage to our divine lord, Caesar."

Nero had made public appearances since he was a boy. Shortly after his tenth birthday he gave his first speech to a large audience gathered on the Forum. As a young teenager, he was allowed to plead two cases before the Senate; one he made in Latin and the other in Greek. There was no setting where he felt uncomfortable being the center of attention, until now.

His knees shook as he walked onto the stage. Attendants brought him a stool and a lyre and as he took his seat, he saw staring down on him not an audience of subjects, but an assembly of critics and judges before whom he could fail. The irony of the moment was that the spectators were equally tense. Every throat was dry. Every hand quivered. As much as Nero longed to be seen as solely an artist at his craft, the audience could not play at that charade, and yet no one was quite sure what the rules of this game were, and so for one long and terrible minute everyone sat in strained silence.

All at once, one soldier along the back wall began to applaud, and his clapping was quickly echoed by the other soldiers near him, and then as a matter of duty, every military man in the theater sounded their acclamation. The ovation was then picked up by those men who felt they had the most to lose if they were not observed supporting the emperor. The men of rank and power—the senators and patricians—stood to their feet and shouted their approval. Next to follow suit were the members of the equestrian order who did not have as much at stake, yet they knew it was never wise to waste an opportunity to flatter the emperor. Finally the plebeians joined in, with nothing to gain or lose except the pleasure of acting riotous. The collective effect was sheer pandemonium and Nero was so overwhelmed by their praise that his fear completely vanished.

He lifted the lyre into position and when all was hushed, he began to play. As an instrumentalist, he was competent and could even be enjoyed. Most recognized the opening notes as part of a familiar ballad, *The Fall Of Troy*. What most also knew was that this particular ballad began with a demanding vocal arrangement, and as Nero approached this part of the song, the audience held it breath. Some looked down. Seneca bit his lips. And then Nero sang.

His voice was husky but not rich. It was adequate but not praiseworthy. The best that could be said of it was that it did not cause pain. But neither did it inspire pleasure. It was a voice to be endured, like a bland casserole. Sadly, for those who heard it, this endurance contest lasted more than ten minutes. Yet the length of the performance did have one positive effect: it compelled the audience to be highly interactive.

When his voice rose to hit the high notes, they winced. When he held his fermatas, they prayed. When he arrived at the end of a verse, they exhaled in relief. By the end of the ballad, everyone in the theater was completely wrung out in exhaustion, as though each one had accepted personal responsibility for carrying Nero through to the final bar. And so when the applause began again, the excitement Nero heard was less for himself, and more for the spectators, who found the silence delicious.

So they clapped and stood and cheered for Nero with obnoxious enthusiasm. He sat there basking in it as he wiped the sweat off his forehead and palms. If the people had known at the time that their hypocrisy would condemn Rome to nine more years of Nero's singing, they all would have ripped out their tongues and cut off their hands at once, but no one could see any further than the next hour, and all the people wanted was to leave the theater and breathe in mouthfuls of cold, fresh air. So they showered their disingenuous acclaim on their emperor in the hopes that he would soon dismiss them.

The master of ceremonies was particularly demonstrative in giving praise as he walked onto the stage toward Nero. In his hands was a bright, green wreath and when he reached the emperor, he motioned for the audience to be still. Kneeling before Nero, he proclaimed, "We are a most blessed and happy race that the gods have given you as leader over us. Even before your performance was completed, the judges rendered their unanimous verdict that you, O Nero, are the fairest recipient of the wreath of champions. We present it to the glory of your divine voice!"

The clapping resumed as Nero dipped his head to receive the wreath. Off to the side of the stage, Burrus leaned over to Seneca while both men applauded with lifeless smiles pinned to their faces.

"Praise as you grieve, noble Seneca," he said. "Praise as you grieve."

*   *   *

The ship sailed north along the coast of the Roman province of Syria. After a short stop in the town of Sidon (during which time the centurion Julius allowed Paul to visit briefly with friends he had there), they continued north around the island of Cyprus. Winter was coming, and already the winds had begun to turn against them, but the ship managed to labor along. The vessel then turned west and crept along the small coastal provinces of Asia Minor, until finally it landed at Myra in Lycia, which was an important hub for the fleet of grain ships which regularly sailed from Alexandria to Rome.

With the onset of winter, the captain of the ship would sail it no further, so its cargo—prisoners and all—was unloaded and transferred to larger vessels. During the two or three days needed for the centurion to book another passage, Paul and his companions were given permission to go ashore. They found lodging with the local group of believers and arrangements were quickly made to call together as many Christians from the surrounding region as possible to meet with Paul and Judah.

News of their arrival spread quickly and reached as far north as Colossae, and on the appointed evening, several hundred believers had converged on Myra to hear the words of these legendary heroes of the faith. They met at the marketplace which by nightfall had been abandoned by the merchants and shopkeepers, and in no time at all the Christians had converted it into a modest sanctuary suitable for worship.

The congregation stood and sang numerous hymns of praise to God and to his Messiah, and as the beautiful music of this choir drifted through the deserted streets, dozens of listeners were drawn to its source. The worship of the Greeks and Romans was usually frenzied, orgiastic, and left the spirit barren. But this was entirely different. This worship strengthened the believer's resolve for moral purity and summoned reason to its highest calling in contemplating the holiness and majesty of God. This worship gathered together in beautiful harmony the heart, soul, mind and body of the worshipper. There were some people that night who were stirred to faith simply by observing the worship of the church.

When the singing was through, the believers greeted each other with warm and sincere affection. Here were Jews, Asians, Cretans and Greeks completely ignoring their racial and cultural differences. There were some that night who were moved to devotion by observing the unity of the church.

When this time of sharing peace with one another had concluded, everyone sat down in anticipation, except for a younger man who remained standing and addressed the crowd when all was quiet. "Brothers and sisters, we are the happiest of God's children tonight," he said with his face beaming. "The Lord has sent to us two of his greatest pillars—Judah Ben-Hur, the shepherd and founder of the church in our capital city, and Paul of Tarsus, who has tirelessly spread the good news throughout our region and beyond. Both have seen the Lord with their own eyes, and both are here tonight by God's appointment to encourage us."

When he turned to the two friends who were sitting by each other, Judah gestured to Paul who stood and spoke first. To hear Paul preach was to sit on a hillside and watch a thunderstorm move in from a distance. He began quietly, with only an occasional rumble of passion breaking through the soft timbre of his voice. He spoke with pain of his past, and as he came to the moment of his decisive encounter with Christ, the wind of his words began to whip with increasing intensity. He told of his calling to ministry and of his burden to reach the Gentile nations, and it was then that the storm broke in all its fury.

Hail and lightning poured from his mouth as he testified to the mighty power of the risen Christ working through him. The people sat in mute awe before him as he told of the opposition: the imprisonments, the beatings, the mob violence, and the endless harassment from his own people. The chains around his wrists only deepened their admiration for him. They marveled as he told of the triumphs: the conversions, the miracles, the stilling of demons, and the shaming of critics. This Paul, who claimed in private that he was a stumbling, stammering speaker, was in public a flawless mouthpiece of the living God.

And then slowly the storm passed over, the sun broke through the clouds and the warm breeze of his encouragement blew on his listeners. Paul gently exhorted his hearers to be soldiers for Christ, to gladly endure any suffering and loss in light of the joy that awaited them, and to consider as rubbish the greatest possessions of this life which when placed in the scales of eternity beside the full weight of heaven were no more than dust. And there were not a few that night who became disciples when they heard Paul the apostle speak.

Paul then asked for Judah to lead the church in a time of prayer. Judah was as emotionally spent as everyone else, but he stood nonetheless, and in that holy moment, shared these words with the congregation.

"The course which God lays out for us can at times seem wildly unpredictable. But he gives us many moments of grace along the way to refresh us—moments such as this one."

As Judah looked out at the unknown faces before him, his heart was filled with compassion. "Now we are on our way to Rome. I know it is difficult at times during these days of Roman rule to believe that God is still in control—to believe that we have not been abandoned. There was a time in my life when I was consumed with hatred toward Rome, and I could not understand why God had allowed his people to fall into bondage once again."

The two guards sent to watch over Paul fidgeted slightly as they stood at the back of the assembly. "But then I met the One who showed me that my bondage was not to Caesar, but to my broken, rebellious heart. And that One took the dagger of anger out of my hand. Twice in my life, I received water from the hands of Jesus. Once as a galley slave of Rome, he quenched the thirst of my flesh, but I continued in thirst thereafter. And once as a slave of sin, he quenched the thirst of my soul. And I have never needed another drink since."

At this, many nodded in familiar agreement. "I still do not understand everything. And life is so often hard and perplexing. As we return to Rome, we have no guarantees concerning what the outcome will be. But we do know that no matter how the story develops, God will write the final chapter. And so we press on—enduring, overcoming, rejoicing. Rome is great. But God is greater. Caesar is powerful. But God is almighty. Life is uncertain. But eternity is sure."

At this point, Judah led the church into a time of heartfelt, earnest prayer. And as the people poured out their souls to God in that hour, praying for one another, asking for the protection and expansion of the Church, even interceding for Caesar and all in authority, there were again some who were brought to faith on the wings of those prayers.

When it was all through and the believers had returned to their homes, Judah took Esther by the hand and walked with her away from the town to the beach near the harbor. It was a beautiful, crisp autumn evening, and the sky was heavy with stars. The lapping of the water at the shoreline where they walked added to the tranquility they already felt. They walked along in a lover's silence for nearly a mile. Finally, Judah disturbed the quiet.

"What are you thinking about, my love?"

"Many things," she answered. "How beautiful tonight was. How welcoming the family of God can be. How good it is to see Paul. And how sad I feel to be returning to Rome. All these emotions are churning inside of me."

"And which is weighing most heavily on you?"

She stopped and faced him. Her eyes were moist. "Oh, Judah. I feel so teased by our time in Judea. It was too short. I wish we could stay longer. It really is our home."

"But you know as well as I, Esther, where our real home is," said Judah, in a feeble attempt to comfort her. "Our true citizenship is in heaven."

"Why then are these feelings so strong, Judah?" she protested. "Don't you feel them as well? I know you do! I've found you weeping in prayer to be able to return home."

"Of course those longings are there," he admitted, regretting his sanctimoniousness. "I'm sorry for acting like your pastor and not your husband. You know me too well, Esther, and you read my heart, as always." They continued walking down the beach. "I can't shake these desires either. They are very strong. And I cannot help but believe that the Lord will bring us back and we will fill out our days where we belong—in Judea."

"What about Paul?" Esther asked. "How long do you think this will all take?"

He shrugged. "Roman law is cumbersome. It may take a year, maybe two. Which is why we need to be there, to make sure that Paul doesn't end up rotting in a prison cell as he has been. The man has suffered so much and yet look at him—he shines! Have we lost some of that?"

"Maybe we have," she said. "But maybe that's why we need to come home." They walked on a little further and Judah again stopped, but this time he faced Esther and held both her arms with firmness. "Esther, I promise you, as soon as Paul's case is settled, we will come home. I want to spend my last years with you, in our home, with our people, in our land." She looked fully into his eyes, which burned with conviction. "My love, I promise you this!" And there beneath the stars, with the water at their feet, they embraced and Judah sealed his promise with a long and tender kiss.

*   *   *

Later that evening, Caesar retired to his private chambers to drink with Tigellinus. The apartment was divided into two levels. Nero paced excitedly back and forth along the upper level, which was simply a bare alcove that led to other rooms and offices. Two sets of marble steps on either side of the room led down to the main level where Tigellinus was sprawled out on cushions, studying a silver chalice in his hands.

"Tigellinus, I feel so invigorated. Tonight it has begun!" Nero exclaimed. He thrust his victory wreath into the air with one hand which seemed to set him off balance, but the flask of wine he held in his other hand was the ballast that righted him. "Tonight we throw off Augustus' shadow," he said, but with his drunken lisp, the shadow actually belonged to *Auguthtasha's*.

In between the two sets of stairs was nothing but a large ceramic amphora, and Nero bumped it as he staggered about, coming precariously close to sending it over the edge. "Tonight we remake Rome!" he continued. "Do you see this wreath?" He tossed it down to Tigellinus who caught it, examined it and placed it squarely on his own head. "Do you know what that wreath symbolizes?"

"That judges can be bought," Tigellinus said impudently, but Nero ignored him.

"That wreath is an awakening. A renaissance!" he declared. "You understand, don't you? Tonight Athens and Rome become one. All of Rome's greatness up till now has been nothing. It has been a mirage."

He managed to walk to a staircase and began a tentative descent, but he suddenly stopped and pointed emphatically in no certain direction. "Outside these walls is the city created by our forbears. So austere and primitive. Its architecture, its buildings are not worthy of us. We should call in ten legions of soldiers right now, command them to lay siege to the city and level it. Then we could begin again. Such a waste of marble. Babylon was a finer city 600 years ago."

He took a long draught of wine then resumed his speech. "But tonight it changes. Did you hear their applause, Tigellinus? The citizens wanted it. They're tired of generals wearing Caesar's mantle. They want an artist. They want me. They need me! And I will lead them." He inched closer to the edge of the steps. "Ah, Tigellinus, I am so full of energy!"

With this he leaped out from the staircase and fell clumsily onto the cushions, narrowly missing Tigellinus, but causing him to spill his wine down his front. Tigellinus was unimpressed, and with a tinge of irritation, said, "When you pretend to be a musician, no one gets hurt; but when you pretend to be an athlete, you put all of us at risk." As he said this, he launched the remaining bit of wine in his chalice directly into Nero's face.

Nero laughed and rolled to his knees, pointing a finger at Tigellinus. "Because you are my friend, I will overlook your insult." He then bounced several times on the cushions like a little boy, before falling over in an exhausted heap. After a few seconds of rest, he leaned toward Tigellinus who was still scowling. "So, how do we celebrate this great new day that is dawning for our empire?"

Tigellinus took the edge of his sleeve and wiped the wine off his face. When he lowered his arm, any trace of intoxication was gone from his expression, as though he had wiped his drunkenness away by a simple act of his will. He looked at Nero.

"A few years ago, you had a very innovative way of expressing your pent-up passion," he said. "You mentioned leveling the city earlier. We could begin the work of demolition this very night."

Nero's eyes lit up with mischievous pleasure. "Why Tigellinus, you mean the evenings we used to dedicate to my precious mother in the early days of our adulthood? What a magnificent idea!" He stood up and offered a hand to Tigellinus, then helped him to his feet. "Yes, I agree. It would be a perfect end to this night. Go, my friend, and gather some comrades of ours. Let's revisit the past even as we recreate the future."

Tigellinus bowed his head slightly and left the room, after which Nero fell back once again on the cushions and closed his eyes, his inebriated smirk frozen in place.

Shortly after his ascension to the throne, Nero began to feel overwhelmed by his new office. The regal balderdash of the court and the sudden responsibilities that were thrust upon him all worked to compress his adolescent spirit, and so it was inevitable that he would seek for a way to vent this building pressure. He found it by occasionally slipping away undetected from the palace at night in the company of some friends. After covering up with masks and makeup, they would roam as a pack through the deserted streets, vandalizing property and harassing passersby.

But their adventures came to a sudden end one night when one of their victims caught Nero with a vicious cuff to the head, sending him to the ground and jarring loose his mask. The man gasped to discover that his assailant was his emperor, and Nero was similarly startled to see standing over him an influential senator. The two men observed an uncomfortable silence afterwards, and Nero's desire for these escapades quickly waned, though more from shame than a transformation of character. But now two years later, the mixture of excitement and alcohol softened Nero's heart for an encore.

And so later that evening, a mob of seven hoodlums covered with sheets and masks ran through the streets of Rome breaking into shops, knocking over flower boxes, smashing statues, assaulting anyone who had the misfortune of crossing their paths and leaving a swath of ruin behind them. Soldiers tried in vain to corner them and victims called down curses on them, but no one could stop their lawlessness until they themselves were weary of it.

After several hours, the seven congregated beneath the stone archway of one of the city's bridges. They were quite out of breath, and each one fell to the wet grass doubled up in exhaustion and laughter, with the current of the Tiber River running lazily at their feet. "Now what would your mother say?" asked Tigellinus as he and Nero stripped off their masks.

Another of the vandals piped in with a high-pitched impersonation of Agrippina. "*Now Nero, this is not how I raised you. Wherever did you learn such behavior!*" The others erupted into more cackling.

Nero leaned upon his elbow. "I ruin buildings. My mother ruins lives. At least I can repair the buildings in the morning. And Tigellinus, see that the district we visited receives royal compensation. As emperor, my heart is grieved that such violence can still occur in our great city."

Tigellinus could not suppress a dark smile, then said, "These vandals must be stopped, my lord."

"Yes, it's a dreadful blight," Nero uttered gravely, but he couldn't hold back his laughter which soon broke through again. "Ah, just like old times. I feel quite young again."

"You look quite young again," said one, reaching out and slapping Nero's smooth face. "The boy emperor returns!"

Just as a frown was about to rise on Nero's face, the same person suddenly pulled a brass jug of wine out from under his cloak and held it up to Nero, and with that, his impish grin was back in place. "I accept your peace offering!" Nero declared, taking a healthy swig before passing the jug around the circle.

As things began to settle down, Tigellinus looked at Nero. "Caesar, I do believe that we are in the vicinity of a grieving young woman named Poppaea who is recently bereft of her husband."

"I have heard of her," Nero said. "'Tis a sad story."

Tigellinus added, "Official responsibilities have taken him to a distant province for a long, long time."

Nero stood up, brushing off his tunic. "My faithful companion, I do believe you are right. I think I shall visit this lady in distress and extend to her my comfort. It's the least I can do as emperor. Please excuse me, gentlemen. And by the way, if you find these hoodlums who are out foraging through our streets, see that they are properly chastised." The men saluted him irreverently, and Nero ran off into the dark streets.

He ran for three or four blocks, and then turned up an alleyway, where there was a long row of larger houses. He spotted the particular house he wanted, and jumped over a small gate, and ambled up the narrow walkway. He straightened back his hair, and sampled his breath by blowing into his hands. He frowned a bit at the odor that stung his nose, but shrugging his shoulders, he straightened up and knocked loudly at the door. He knocked again after a few seconds, and a small peephole in the door slid open, and then slid shut.

At last the door opened and a young woman with long, unkempt hair appeared in the doorway. She was wrapped in a blanket, barefoot, and her face was pale and dull with sleepiness, but to Nero, she was the most ravishing sight on earth. As soon as she saw him, her face contorted with grief, and she began to tremble. Large, opaque tears bubbled up in her eyes.

"Emperor Nero!" she cried. "Why did you send my husband Otho so far away? How could you separate us like this? What kind of demon are you? It will be months before I see him again." She started to sob openly.

Nero smiled sadistically, growing increasingly aroused. "Correction, my Lady Poppaea. It will be more like years."

She looked up at him as he said this and in an instant, her sorrow transposed into an intimate, seductive smile of her own. She reach up and wrapped her arms around him, while he slid his hands beneath her blanket, and they kissed each other with a sudden, thunderous passion. Locked in this embrace, she pulled Nero into the house and closed the door behind them.

Just after sunrise the next morning, Tigellinus and two guards came up Poppaea's walkway and knocked bristly on her door. None who saw Tigellinus would have recognized him the night before. He was dressed in a soldier's uniform, and his granite expression showed no hint of frivolity, nor any indication that he was capable of it. After a moment, the peephole slid open, and Poppaea opened the door. She had draped her blanket carelessly around her naked frame, and her immodesty prompted the guards to blush and look away. Tigellinus simply glared at her and said, "The emperor? We must see him right away."

Poppaea was scarcely awake. She rubbed her eyes. "Nero left several hours ago."

Tigellinus' eyes widened in anger. He turned to the two guards and barked, "You both told me that he never left! I thought you were watching him!" The guards were about to offer a sheepish protest, but Poppaea interjected.

"Oh, he was too drunk to use the door. I think he climbed out the window. He's probably walking by the river."

At this, Tigellinus turned and whisked away in a huff of irritation with the guards timidly following after him. They walked down to the river and began to march along the bank. A heavy mist hung over the water. After walking nearly a half-mile, Tigellinus saw a crumbled heap laying on the ground up ahead of him. Tigellinus increased his pace until he came up to the motionless form. It was Nero. He was in such a deep sleep that he was face-first on the ground and not seeming to mind.

"Lord Nero!" Tigellinus said firmly. "You must get up!" Nero uttered a faint sigh, but then resumed drawing in sleep-filled breaths. "Emperor!" Tigellinus shouted.

Nero fidgeted and turned his head. His face was marked with creases from the grass. In a croaking, weak voice, he muttered, "Tigellinus, let me sleep."

Tigellinus felt in no mood to pamper Caesar. To the shocked disbelief of the guards, he bent over and pushed Nero straight into the river. The effect was comical and instantaneous. Nero at once came to his senses and struggled to regain his footing in the shallow mud of the river bank. He kicked and howled like a caged hyena, and when he finally did gain a foothold, he screamed as loudly as his croaking voice would allow.

"Curse you, Tigellinus! You forsaken fool! I'll have your head for this!" As he dragged himself onto the grass, a river of profanities poured from his mouth, but the angrier he became, the more foolish he looked, and even the guards had to suppress their laughter. Nero choked and spat out water from his mouth, and then came to his knees and glared with fire in his eyes at Tigellinus, who did not bother holding back his enjoyment of this moment. "How dare you laugh at me!" Nero hissed.

But Tigellinus remained calm. "An emperor who chooses to walk away from his bodyguards deserves to be laughed at. Just be thankful it's me who threw you into the river." Nero quieted down, and then started shivering. "You need to return to the palace at once. Last night, we intercepted a letter. A very compromising letter. A very treasonous letter. Written by the hand of—"

Nero nodded his head in understanding. "My mother." He stood, but very slowly. "And so it's come to this at last. Let's return to my palace, where we will deal with Agrippina. And afterwards, I will deal with you, my friend." He stuck a thick, trembling finger at the nose of Tigellinus, but Tigellinus waved it off and turn to walk to the city.

Chapter 4

After several days in Myra, Julius the centurion found a privately owned grain ship from Alexandria sailing to Rome. With some delicate negotiating—and the promise of imperial compensation—he purchased passage for the soldiers and prisoners in his charge, and notified Judah to be prepared to embark the next morning.

Judah and his company arrived at the ship the next day, leading across the harbor beach a small, motley army of friends from the Lycian church. Women, peasants, slaves and children hovered warmly around Paul and Judah, which humored the shipmates and soldiers who watched them approach. As they reached the pier, Paul reached down and picked up a little child that had been dancing around his feet, and swung him around playfully.

After setting him down on the sand, he turned to the Christians and said, "Family of God, I commend you all into the care of our Heavenly Father. Keep watch over yourselves." Patriarchal tenderness rang in his voice. "You are God's precious flock, and nothing can ever separate you from his love. Difficult days are yet ahead but you can do all things in Christ who gives you strength!"

They all nodded and some had a few tears in their eyes. At Paul's invitation, they dropped to their knees in the sand and prayed, committing each other into the care of God. As they prayed, one of the soldiers with Julius leaned over to his commander and said, "They're all deluded fools, believing there's a paradise."

But the centurion was sympathetic to the Christians. "When life is hell, why judge a man for dreaming of something better?" he scolded.

The soldier grunted at the centurion's reproach and walked away. When the Christians were finished saying their farewells, they turned and came aboard the ship. As they passed Julius, Paul turned to him and said, "Good Centurion. If it is permissible, I need to speak with the owner of this vessel."

Julius seemed confused by this request, as did Judah. "I'm sure he is not accustomed to speaking with prisoners," the centurion remarked.

"He may choose to see either my chains, or the advocate of the Roman Senate who stands beside me," said Paul, nudging Judah.

The centurion looked at Judah and then with a slight frown said, "I'll see if he is available."

As he walked off, Paul winked at Judah and Esther. "King Agrippa was right. It looks as though you are useful after all."

Judah did not look amused. "Why thank you," he said dryly. "As your counsel, I don't suppose you could let me in on your secret? I don't think we should stretch the good graces of the centurion. He's worked hard to book our passage."

"I had a dream last night, Judah," said Paul, more soberly. "I'm sure it was the Lord."

He waited, and Judah prodded him to go further. "You know I trust your intuition. What did you dream?"

"This vessel did not make it to Rome," said Paul, and Esther gasped as he said this.

They boarded the ship, and as they walked to find their quarters, the centurion called out to them from across the stern. Beside him stood the owner of the ship and his captain. The owner was the older—and uglier—of the two men. Years facing down a sea breeze had etched permanent creases into his brown, leathery skin. "Counsel, you know this is a busy moment for me," he said gruffly to Judah as they came near. "Can't this wait?"

His expression and posture made it clear that he completely disregarded Paul, but Judah was simply not ready to speak for his friend at this moment. "This man, Paul, is greatly burdened with a message for you," he said. "I think he should share it himself."

Paul did not wait for the owner's consent, but spoke at once. "Sir, I ask you to pardon me for my frankness, but I must strongly urge you to consider delaying your arrival in Rome and finding a port to winter in."

"*What!*" bellowed the owner. "I don't have time for this." He glared at the centurion and turned to walk away.

"I think you should listen to him," said Judah quickly.

The owner spun around and said with pronounced venom, "Who is he that I should listen to him? Rome is recovering from a famine and I am standing atop a barge loaded with wheat. We *will* be in Rome before winter."

Paul was perturbed, and pressed his case. "What is your final port before Rome?"

"This is our final port!"

Paul did not relent. "But the ship will pass the island of Crete."

Taut, angry veins, thick as mast rope, appeared on the owner's reddening neck. "*This* is our final port!" he screamed, turning to walk away again, while the young captain looked on solemnly.

"If you do not seek harbor on Crete, this barge will be on the sea's floor before winter." Paul spoke with such vigor and authority that the owner could go no further. Once more he turned around, barely suppressing his urge to strangle this Jewish prisoner.

"What makes you so certain of the fate of my ship?"

With firm insistence, Paul stated, "The God whom I worship has told me this."

The owner looked down and then laughed, but only to cover the rage he felt at being dragged into this conversation. "Well, I worship the gods of gold and silver," he said. "And if this ship does not reach Rome by winter, then I'll be an atheist." He then looked at Judah. "With respect to your authority, sir, I'd prefer to not see either one of you the remainder of this voyage." He stomped off with the captain, and the centurion followed after them, looking back at Judah with an unmistakeable scowl.

"The fool," muttered Paul.

Judah sighed, not sure what to think. "To the bottom of the sea we go," he said and they went to seek their quarters.

*   *   *

Nero had just emerged from his bath when Seneca and Burrus answered his summons to come to the palace. As he toweled off, he shared the intercepted letter with them. Burrus read it first, then Seneca, and as Nero was pulling on his robe and sandals, Seneca handed it back to Tigellinus.

"So my mother is unhappy flirting with senators and courting ambassadors," said Nero. "Now she is soliciting the favor of our most powerful provincial governor."

"She is certainly persistent," said Burrus.

"Treacherous," corrected Tigellinus with a snarl.

"I don't know if the contents of this letter imply treason," said Seneca, disturbed by the implications of Tigellinus' accusation. "She sounds more like a desolate and lonely widow."

Nero sat down in front of a floor length bronzed mirror and dried his hair with the towel. "By the gods, Seneca, there's only one reason she has written this letter. It's time to accept the fact that Agrippina is our adversary, made all the more deadly by her connections to the throne. Treason knows of only one penalty."

"You wish your mother dead?" asked Burrus carefully.

"Don't you think this breaks my spirit?" asked Nero with unconvincing grief, his voice temporarily muffled by the towel he jostled over his scalp. "Don't you think I have a tender cord inside me? But it is plain that my mother died a long time ago. This demon masquerading in Agrippina's body opposes me. Opposes us! Have we not shared all this together? Seneca!" He turned and pointed a finger at the philosopher. "All along you have warned me of her. At last I acquiesce. At last I listen."

"But I have never counseled her death," said Seneca grimly. "And even now, I would yet caution restraint."

He looked at Burrus for support. "Agrippina is greatly loved by the people," said the prefect in response.

"The people, the people, the people!" said Nero in exasperation. "Did you hear the people last night? It was not Agrippina they were worshipping. Seneca, Burrus! Has your age so dimmed your vision that you cannot see what is plain to the rest of us? Last night, a page was turned. Caesar is no longer a boy. The people understand that. When the kernel is ripe, the husk is no longer of use."

Thinking his argument was unimpeachable, Nero proudly reached for an ivory comb and drew it across his hair, but Seneca quickly stole the metaphor for his own use. "Therefore the husk need only be thrown aside, and not destroyed. If Caesar has come of age, then his spirit will radiate with mercy. Send your mother into exile, and you will both save yourself and secure the people."

In that moment, Nero came to a crossroads in his soul. He knew Seneca was right, but the pride percolating within him prevented him from listening to reason. After a moment of wavering, Nero turned to them. "My teachers, thank you again for coming so early in the day," he said. "Go and enjoy breakfast with your families."

After they left, Nero looked Tigellinus straight in the face. "What Seneca calls mercy is nothing but hesitation and half-heartedness. This moment calls for action that is decided and permanent. Tigellinus, once again, I appeal to your creativity. Devise a way to satisfy my wrath and satisfy *the people*—," and these words he spat with great disdain, "and I will satisfy you." But before the words were on Nero's lips, Tigellinus' mind was already actively applied to the task.

As Seneca and Burrus strode side by side from the palace, both men were silent but visibly unsettled. When they reached the perimeter of the palace grounds, Seneca suddenly stopped and turned to his friend, looking around to make sure they were alone.

"The emperor was correct. A page has been turned. And I fear that Agrippina is not the only husk to be thrown aside."

"We can no more keep Caesar from asserting his independence that we can prevent winter from coming," said Burrus gravely.

"No, nor would I want that," said the philosopher. "The purpose of our tutelage all along has been to give to Rome, at the right time, a wise and judicious leader."

Burrus nodded. "Like you, I believe that our tutelage is not yet complete."

"No, you misunderstand me. I fear that our tutelage has been in vain!" said Seneca with a tinge of pain. "A lion cub can be taught to play with sheep, but the day comes when the growing lion smells blood. And so either one is good by nature or one acts a role which cannot be maintained. Do you follow me?" The prefect looked away, knowing full well what Seneca meant. "How will you respond, Burrus, if in the end it turns out that all our time has been wasted?"

Burrus met his gaze with eyes of steel, and then said slowly and deliberately, "My loyalty is first to the glory of Rome's future, then to the glory of Rome's past, and only then to the glory of Rome's Caesar's."

"Then we understand each other."

"We will keep closer watch," said Burrus.

Seneca nodded and the two friends parted and returned to their homes.

*   *   *

In the early days of the voyage, the ship pressed forward slowly against a fierce coastal wind. At last, they reached the southern shores of the island of Crete. The open sea awaited them beyond Crete. Once they sailed past, they would be committed to facing whatever adventures awaited them, so the decisions made in the next few days were critical. The winds died down as they reached the inlet at Fair Havens, and the spirits of the officers brightened some. But Paul remained adamant that great misfortune awaited them if they set out from the island, and so the crew was agitated, not knowing whether to trust the owner's ambition or the visions of a person rumored to be a great holy man. Despite its name, Fair Havens offered unsuitable shelter for the large ship, and so with the break in the weather, the owner greedily decided to press on.

The next day, Judah and Paul stood on the deck looking out at the rim of the rocky shore disappearing to their north. The further from land they drew, the more choppy the seas became. "Esther is ill," said Judah. "Your waves are unkind to her."

"My waves?" Paul protested. "No. These are God's waves. And no one can resist God's waves. Not you, nor I, nor Caesar himself. Fear not though, Judah, we will not go down with the ship. We have an appointment with Rome to keep."

Judah looked dismal. "I hate shipwrecks, you know," he muttered, looking over the edge at the green, churning water which seemed to be hissing at them.

Even as they spoke, in another part of the ship two of the pilot's officers approached the pilot and owner. "The storm is reviving," said one. "We should return to Fair Havens while we still can."

The owner cut them off. "Did I hire either of you as captain of my ship?"

The second sailor spoke. "The men are restless, sir. We just assumed you might care to hear more than one opinion. The vessel is in danger and with winter fast approaching, it is difficult to predict the severity of these storms."

"Do you confuse me for a cadet, that you lecture me?" the owner shouted, the creases in his face widening. "I was sailing these waters before you were born. Return to your posts, both of you! We will maintain our present course. And tell these restless men to concern themselves only with the duties I hired them for."

The sailors retreated, but not before giving a pleading glance to the pilot to intercede for them.

"What a damnable voyage!" the owner muttered to himself. "Slaves and simpletons telling me how to run my ship."

Trepidly, the captain spoke. "Yet the men have a point, sir. If we venture too far from Crete, we lose all hope of saving ourselves should this turn into a real northeaster. If we stay close to land, the western port of Phoenix would still be in reach if things got too rough." Quickly, he added, "But it's your ship, your wheat."

"My wheat," spat the owner. "As though anyone were concerned about my wheat." He waved his hands in disdain. "Fine. Do as you will. Set sail for Phoenix. Winter there for all I care. But you and your men are bound to this ship by contract until we arrive in Rome, and do not expect extra wages for extra months at sea."

He stormed from the cabin, and as he passed by on the deck, he saw the two Christians on the other side of the ship, and the anger burned all the more in his belly.

*   *   *

Behind his palace, Nero had dug out a circular, artificial lake, five hundred feet across and hidden behind a protective grove of cypress and fruit trees. The lake was what he liked best about the Domus Transitoria, but was still not enough to compensate for what he felt were serious deficiencies in his home. Even then, work was proceeding on a new palace more suitable for his eclectic tastes. In his eyes, Roman culture paled in comparison with the great civilizations that preceded it, especially Greece, and he felt embarrassed that Roman roads and armies should ultimately be found more useful for empire-building than Greek art and philosophy.

So he loved to spend long hours near his lake escaping the compression of the city, composing poetry, or swimming, or sometimes hosting novel forms of entertainment which only he could provide. One of his favorite diversions was recreating naval battles on the lake using miniaturized replicas of the Roman fleet. Each ship was no bigger than a chariot and could be guided on the water by one man standing beside it, pulling on a long wooden dowel which jutted out from the ship's side. A small but workable catapult was rigged inside each of the ships, and with it, the operator could launch wooden, melon-sized balls at enemy vessels. One ball to a mast, or a head, could effectively scuttle both ship and crew.

Several days after Agrippina's letter had been intercepted, an unseasonably warm afternoon inspired Nero to call together a group of friends for a bout of war games. The rules were simple enough. The twelve ships in Nero's toy armada were divided into two opposing fleets, battle lines were agreed to, and the bombardment began. Once a ball ripped down a sail, splintered the hull, or forced an operator to release his hold on his ship, then the ship was considered destroyed and had to withdraw. The final battle of the afternoon found Caesar and one companion, whose ships flew black sails, bearing down on a lone white sail. Nero lobbed a ball and it arched high, narrowly missing the white sail's captain.

"Look astern, Galen!" Nero shouted gleefully. "You nearly went down with your ship."

Nero's partner then demanded, "Surrender your vessel and prepare to be boarded."

"And become your slave? Never!" Galen yelled back defiantly.

Nero and his comrade reloaded and fired, and this time the volley was deadly. Both balls sliced through the sail, and Galen was forced to dive into the water to avoid being struck. "Then sink to the River Styx!" screamed Nero triumphantly, and those waiting on shore who had already been eliminated howled and jeered at Galen for his ignominious defeat.

As the combatants pushed their ships to shore, Tigellinus appeared from a courtyard behind the trees. Two servants were with him, and they carried a simple, unornamented ship of their own, though not a warship but a roughly shaped dinghy, and in place of a catapult was a solitary lever protruding off its deck.

"Why Tigellinus, you've come late to the ball," Nero called out. "And naked as well. Where is your sail? Where are your armaments?"

Tigellinus stepped directly into the water, and motioned for the servants to follow him. "This is no battle cruiser," he said. "It is an escort ship."

Galen pushed his crippled ship out of the water. "We can see that you fool. Of what use is it for our war games?"

"It's of great use for destroying one's enemies," Tigellinus responded, as he nudged the ship further out into the water. Nero watched him with great interest. "First, you make overtures of peace, lulling your enemy into a dull contentment. Then you honor your enemy by granting him—*or her*...," he said slowly, looking at Nero, "...safe passage to the peace table aboard this fine vessel. While en route, disaster strikes."

At this, he pulled back on the lever and at once, the ship pulled apart into two halves, which promptly began to sink. Nero's friends looked on with bemusement. One of them called out from the water's edge, "May the gods be merciful, Caesar. Your safety is entrusted into the hands of a madman."

"You need a woman, Tigellinus," yelled another. "You spend too much time playing with yourself." With that, everyone but Nero began to laugh. Nero stayed frozen in the water, captivated by Tigellinus' demonstration.

"Do you approve of my solution?" Tigellinus asked him, though softly so the others could not hear.

Nero marveled. "My mind is racing, Tigellinus. Frankly, your brilliance has caught me off guard. Are you proposing that we build a vessel such as this, which mid-voyage will just split apart and sink?"

"To be honest, Caesar, the idea originated in Anicetus' calculating mind."

"Ah! Our fine commander of the fleet in Misenum," said Nero. "So you've brought him in on our little game?"

"I know how fond Anicetus is of your mother," Tigellinus said with a twisted smile. "He and Volusius Proculus are most eager to assist us on this project. It would be a shocking tragedy, that your dear mother should be lost in a sailing accident. And at the very time when you were being reconciled with her. The gods are very cruel."

"Is the engineering of this possible?"

"Proculus already has men working on it. It will be ready in less than two weeks."

Nero nodded his head approvingly. "What I love about you, my friend, is that you appeal to my love of the theater. So let us set the stage at once." He leaned over and touched Tigellinus' arm, whispering, "Agrippina must know as soon as possible how repentant her son is. And he desires for her to join him at his island villa in two weeks. There he will make his peace with her. Yes?"

Tigellinus tipped his head. "You have commanded it."

*   *   *

No sooner did the captain and his crew attempt to bring the ship parallel to the coast, than a violent northeast wind drove it out to sea, as a predator drags its victim into isolation before slaughtering it. The storm which broke out upon the travellers in the grain ship traumatized all but the Christians, whose faith was an unbreakable anchor in the face of the twenty and thirty–foot swells the sea hurled at them.

The gale raged on for more than a week. Every measure was taken to secure the ship and preserve its passengers. Food and water were rationed. Rope was pulled under the ship to reinforce its hull. All cargo but the wheat was tossed into the water, the tackle was thrown overboard and what was left of the shredded sails had been pulled down. Yet they were tossed like paper before the wind. Even the seasoned sailors soon abandoned all hope as the elements pounded on them from above and the seas tossed relentlessly beneath them.

Somehow the ship managed to stay afloat, and at nightfall on the fourteenth day, the owner summoned the pilot and his officers, as well as Judah and Julius, to his cabin for a consulation. But Judah did not come alone, and the owner erupted when he saw Paul standing in the doorway also.

"Not him!" he cried, with a condescending shout. "I'll have no slaves setting foot in my cabin!"

But Judah rebuked him at once. "This man is no slave! And had you listened to him to begin with, we would not be facing this crisis." The owner's face stayed red, but he looked down to the floor, having nothing to say in response. Judah spoke again. "Maybe you will listen to him now."

He turned to Paul who touched his beard thoughtfully before speaking. "The God whom I serve spoke to me again last night as I prayed—which shows you something of his mercy, seeing how we did not listen to him the first time." His eyes burned brightly with conviction, which caught the attention of the centurion who could not look away from his prisoner. "Last night, my God gave me this message for you. He said we are not to fear. My trial with Caesar must take place, and therefore each of your lives will be spared. The ship will be destroyed, but no one will lose his life. Not a hair of anyone on this ship will be hurt."

"There are more than 250 people on this ship," said the pilot. "If this ship sinks, the loss of life will be frightful."

"Not this time," Paul replied. "Such is God's love for you. Now I know that we are near to land." At this, the owner looked up sharply and stared at Paul, and the officers looked at each other in bewilderment. "Isn't that true?" Paul asked the pilot.

"Why yes," he answered in amazement. "The crew took soundings not an hour ago. We are entering shallow water."

At this, the owner blurted out icily, "And what does your God say about that? We can't see a half furlong in front of us. We'll be smashed on whatever rocks are out there! We're going to lose everything, you know."

"No, not everything," Paul said. "Only the ship."

"And my fortune. And my career," the owner muttered, and there was desperation in his voice.

"Without your life, you can restore neither," said Judah.

Paul spoke again. "It's been more than a week since anyone has eaten a substantial meal. I think it's time to feed everyone. It will give us the strength to swim ashore."

The owner scanned the exhausted, pale faces of the men cramped into his tiny quarters. "This time I will listen to you," he said quietly. "Centurion, see that the food stores are opened up and the passengers fed. We'll then make preparations to abandon the ship if we run aground." He dismissed all but his captain, and when they left, he pulled the door shut and spoke to the young man with a hushed and secretive tone. "If things remain as they are, ready the dinghy and alert the rest of the officers. We'll leave the ship at midnight."

"But the other passengers?" the pilot asked.

"Let them drown," blurted the owner. "I for one will not stand around and die waiting for a Jewish god to save me. Tell your men if they know what's best they'll join me at midnight." The pilot swallowed hard, but nodded his head and left the cabin.

Once the food had been parceled out to the passengers, Judah took a bowl to Esther who was lying sick in their tiny chamber. "My love, eat this," he said gently. "You'll need strength for what awaits us."

Esther struggled to sit up. Her face was white and dry from countless bouts of nausea. She let her head fall against Judah's side as he sat beside her on the bed. "I'm frightened, Judah," she said weakly. "I don't think we can last much longer."

"We are in the hands of God," he said to assure her. "Is there a safer place to be?"

"I'm still afraid, Judah," she whimpered. Judah shifted his weight slightly, and Esther clutched at him. "Don't leave!"

"I'm right here, love," he said softly.

"O Judah, I don't know how I could survive without you with me."

He embraced her. "Esther, we will live together. And we will die together. I will never leave you alone. I promise." He pulled her tightly to him, drew a blanket up over her shoulders, and rocked her tenderly as the ship rocked them mercilessly.

Several hours later, Julius reported back to the owner that the passengers were fed and resting. As he turned to leave, the owner called out to him. "Centurion, I don't need to remind you of your duties as a Roman officer." He placed his arm on Julius' shoulder. "If this ship runs aground, Caesar expects you to execute every prisoner. I want you to make sure you begin with the Jewish prisoner," he said.

Julius showed no expression except for the slightest tipping of his head, and as he walked away, the owner spoke once more. "And you can count on me, Centurion, to put in a good word for you when I give Caesar my report." Julius hesitated at the doorway, then continued walking.

Chapter 5

The Festival of Minerva was an annual celebration which Caesar traditionally observed at his island villa in the waters of Baiae, off the coast from Cape Misenum, which lay just north of the fertile vineyards of Pompeii. As the festival approached, Nero began to offer public intimations that he desired reconciliation with Agrippina.

"We children must put up with the mood swings of our aging parents!" he joked before the Senate, and the hearts of the public were gladdened that peace seemed to have finally come to Caesar's household. Agrippina herself was initially suspicious of her son's sudden change of heart, but she knew full well of his shifting tempers, and so convinced herself that the tumult was passed. She accepted Nero's invitation to join him at Misenum.

On the day of the festival, she chartered a small ferry and crossed the bay, accompanied by a female servant and two bodyguards. The short two-mile cruise was made miserable and long by wintry winds and unsettled seas. Agrippina looked ashen white as the rowers finished bringing the small boat alongside the dock. Her bodyguards looked at her with concern but said nothing, for Agrippina bristled furiously at any insinuation of weakness.

Nero was waiting for her as she arrived, and in his hand was a heavy bouquet of flowers. Behind him, a dozen members of the imperial guard stood at attention in a receiving line, as they would to grant honors to the highest of dignitaries. Agrippina's pride was thoroughly stroked by this reception, which was exactly the effect Nero intended. Yet Agrippina suppressed her pleasure and showed only the expression of an aggrieved mother. Nero rushed to her side like a compliant child, which was exactly the effect Agrippina intended.

"Mother, you look pale," said Nero as he took her hand and escorted her to a marble walkway which led away from the beach.

"The seas are very choppy today," she said quietly.

"My captains tell me that there are fearful storms out to sea right now. No doubt we are feeling their effects." He walked with her up the path, and the body-guards and soldiers followed after. "Mother, I am so very pleased that you accepted my invitation. These past few weeks have been bitter as I think of the pitiful way in which we parted."

Agrippina said nothing, though her face betrayed a thin smile. They walked arm in arm up the hill, through a stretch of woods and came to Nero's villa which was nestled into the bare rocks which crowned the island, and overlooked the entire bay. Nero led her inside to an glass-enclosed atrium, elegantly furnished, and filled with a cataract of sunlight which poured through a sun-roof three stories above the floor. In the center of the room bubbled a fountain of turquoise water, and around the fountain in an octagonal pattern was a symmetrical collection of sofas and tables. On one of the tables was a rich spread of food. Already seated around the fountain were several of Nero's friends, including Tigellinus and Anicetus. The scent of danger hung in the air and Agrippina stopped.

"Seneca, Burrus, they are not here?" she asked.

"Seneca is vacationing with his family in Neapolis this week," Nero replied, "and Burrus is in Rome, polishing his medals I suppose."

Tigellinus stood and took Agrippina's hand. "Agrippina," he said respectfully, as he stooped to kiss her fingers. She trembled. Anicetus also stood and greeted her. He was nearly forty, plain-faced with shifting eyes and long, straight hair that hung recklessly off his head. Anicetus had been Nero's first tutor, but Agrippina grew to despise him for he seemed too independent and resisted her influence. His appointment as the naval commander at Misenum, which came at her encouragement, was more to remove him from Rome than to promote him. She stiffened as he reached for her hand.

Nero then clapped his hands to break the mounting tension. "Gentlemen, I see that you have laid food out for us. My thanks to you. I would like to ask if my mother and I might have some time alone. We have much we need to talk about."

They all nodded and withdrew from the atrium except for the necessary guards and attendants. Agrippina slowly sat down, and Nero held out for her a plate of fruit, which she picked from. Then after he had poured for both of them a glass of wine, he fell back on his own couch. "So mother, could I ask what you have been thinking about since I last saw you?"

She summoned up a look of pain and said, "I was very hurt, and very frightened, by what you did."

"Understandably so," said Nero, looking tender and repentant. "I said things I greatly regret. Why is it that we are prone to abuse those whom we are closest to? I take similar liberties with Octavia, and I love her so much."

Agrippina resisted the urge to spit out the wine she was swallowing. She set the glass down. "And where is your wife?" she asked.

"She is home, sick. Sick of me, no doubt."

Agrippina said nothing for a brief moment. She was anxious to pry into her son's motives and thoughts. "You accused me of terrible things which are not true in the least."

Nero leaned forward and picked a piece of bread from off a serving tray. "Well Mother, as you know, our perceptions do not always mesh with reality. Too often, we are bothered by things we do not fully understand. Today it is my full intention to clear away anything that is bothering me." He smiled as he took a bite. "One of the things that bothers me is that my attempts to govern are suffocated by the opinions and advice of those who yet see me as a child. And Mother, that includes you."

"I will stay out of Rome," she said.

"Yes, but will Rome stay out of you?" he asked, pointing a finger at her. "What I must ask you is that you completely relinquish any ambition you have. Give it up." She began to fidget and protest but he held up his hand to stop her. "Ah, you know it's there. Shall I recite for you the list of victims who have fallen prey to your ambition? Marcus Silanus, Narcissus…"

"Nero stop this. Don't torment me," she said, looking down. "And don't forget my son, that you are the beneficiary of my ambition."

"But that was then, and this is now. And your son is no longer a boy." He waited until she glanced up so he could look into her eyes. "Mother, what I want for you is to marry again. And I want you to marry not for wealth, not for power, but for love. I just want you to be happy."

She was more light-hearted now. "You just want me out of the way."

Nero laughed. "Yes, there's a point," he said and he poured more wine into Agrippina's glass.

*   *   *

Several hours after nightfall, Paul emerged sleeplessly from his cabin. It was well past midnight, and as he had stretched upon his bed in troubled prayer, he felt a prompting within him to walk upon the deck. Sheets of rain stung his face, driven by the wind which blew on unabated. As he struggled to reach the deck, he heard voices coming from the other side of the ship.

He stumbled, slid across the wet wood and grabbed hold of the railing, then looked in the direction of the noise. Halfway down the outside of the boat, he saw four sailors standing in the ship's dinghy, laboring to lower it into the sea. Leaning over, looking on from the deck, was the owner, the pilot, and the remaining corps of officers. Paul's weariness immediately disappeared and a certain fury swept over him.

"You there!" he shouted at the top of his lungs. His voice cut through the wind and drew the surprised attention of the owner, whose hands clutched a coiled up rope-ladder. Paul stepped closer to him and pointed his fingers at the dinghy. "Unless these men stay in the ship, you will not be saved, not one of you!"

For the first time, the owner felt fear as he stood before Paul, much like men of old felt fear in the presence of Moses or Elijah. There was nothing he could say and he began to shake. The rope dropped from his hands. The four men stopped their frantic activity.

"Tell your men to cut away the boat!" Paul ordered. The sailors in the dinghy looked up first at the owner, then the pilot, for a confirming sign.

"Now!" Paul commanded.

Without a word, the owner gestured for them to do as Paul had said. The sailors wasted no time scrambling back up into the ship, and then they each withdrew knives from their belts and cut at the ropes holding the boat. In a matter of a few swipes of their blades, the dinghy was loosened from its hold and it plummeted into the water with a dull splat. Within seconds, it was swept away out of sight by the current. Paul glared at the owner and walked away, with angry mist rising up from his silhouette as he disappeared into the darkness.

*   *   *

By the end of the day, Nero had won the heart of his mother. She seemed to be so eagerly eating from his hand that he even felt a slight spasm of guilt thinking about what must transpire. But when night had come, Nero begged tiredness and brought their time to a close. With the soldiers and servants following after, they walked back to the pier, and as they emerged from the woods upon the marble path, Nero said, "Mother, this day has been special."

"Yes, very," she agreed. The night sky was filled with stars, and by their light, she could see that the water was now idly stroking the shore. "It looks like the storminess has subsided," she said with relief.

"Yes, it has," said Nero. "Oh, but you mean of the water? Yes—and for us as well."

Nero now sprang the trap. He looked over at Agrippina's boat, and his head tilted to the side with curiosity. "Mother, your boat appears to be coming apart. Look here." He grabbed a torch from a guard and walked right into the water, pointing to the side of her boat where three slats of wood had pulled loose from the frame. "Tigellinus, come and tell me what you think."

Tigellinus stepped into the water and examined the boat, and then shook his head. "It's hardly seaworthy, emperor."

Caesar looked at Agrippina. "Mother, it's a miracle you even made it here."

Agrippina looked distraught. "I didn't notice us taking on any water. What will I do now?"

Nero came out of the water, shaking his hands of the wetness. "Why don't your men stay and repair this boat with materials we have on hand. My soldiers will escort you home now in my private ferry. They can follow later." He pointed to another boat bobbing innocently in the water. "Consider it a seal of my affection for you mother."

"Oh, this is most inconvenient," she said, looking over at Nero's boat. Like other small royal charters, this had one main level and built into the center hull was a private cabin, comfortable for six people at the most, and then above it, was a small pleasure deck which rose up above the main floor. Its gold and silver molding glistened in the torchlight. Agrippina paid no attention to the two large levers which were built into the hull on either side of the deck, next to each oar.

"No, not inconvenient at all," said Nero. "I won't be leaving for a couple days. But please, just promise me that you won't let riding in the emperor's ferry go to your head. I Nero, your son, am emperor."

Agrippina frowned playfully at her son. "Then let's be gone before it's too late and I miss my bath. I would like one of my men to come with me though."

Tigellinus looked at Nero, but Nero showed no hesitation. "Very well. Take your pick." He then pointed to two of his own guards. "Men, if you would be so kind. Take my mother home, and make sure she gets her bath." Saluting, they climbed aboard the ferry and stationed themselves at either oar, while Agrippina, her attendant and lone bodyguard situated themselves within the cabin.

Nero waved after her. "Thank you mother. A pleasant journey." Once the boat had pulled far enough away, Nero looked to see if Agrippina's other body-guard was distracted, and then leaned toward Tigellinus. "She never apologized to me once. Not a single, simple, 'I'm sorry'."

"She still is a very dangerous woman," muttered Tigellinus.

"For yet a little while," said Nero. "After all, it is amazing how a little bath can change one's perspective." He laughed, trying to ignore the lump of anxious guilt that welled up in his throat. The boat vanished beyond a bend in the bay.

*   *   *

The additional soundings that the sailors took in the next few hours confirmed that they were fast coming near to land. Just before daybreak, they rammed the first rock, violently jerking those who were on the deck to one side, and arousing everyone who was beneath the deck to rush to the top. On the ship were 276 souls, each one with a name known by God and a unique story to tell, and each one fearing that his or her story was coming to an end too soon. Merchant and seaman, prisoner and officer, slave and free, all stood upon that deck bound together as one community, united in suspense, with one common destiny that awaited them.

With the inevitability of running aground, the owner was forced to undertake one last measure in an attempt to keep the ship from exploding apart on the rocks. He had waited as long as possible, desperately hoping that something could be salvaged from this disaster, but now that hope was gone. Navigating the ship to shore required that it be as light as possible. He ordered his pilot to dump all of the wheat into the sea.

Never had dawn come so slowly, but at last the horizon began to show through the dark mist. The sight of any land at all would have lifted the spirits of the ordinary travellers, but the sailors knew that land alone could not save them. Without a beach or bay, the loss of life would be great.

The horizon brightened and suddenly, a great cheer swelled up from the ship, for visible a half-mile off was the dark phantom form of an island. Fifteen minutes passed and another softer shout was heard, this time from the sailors. A small inlet appeared between the rocks, framed by a long, clear stretch of welcoming beach. Immediately, the crew sprang into action. Each anchor was cut loose, the rudders were untied, and a makeshift foresail was hoisted up to catch the wind, as every effort was expended to head for the beach. The tide providentially prodded them closer.

Suddenly, the ship was jolted again, and once more, the helpless passengers were tossed about like loose grapes on the floor. A loud, mournful creaking sound lifted up from the sea, and the sailors began shouting, "We've run aground! We've struck a shoal! We're breaking apart!" Only the seasoned hands of the crew brought a semblance of order to that moment of chaos. The owner ran from bow to stern shouting to his men, "Get everyone in the water now! Everyone in the water! Grab a hold of loose planks and get ashore!"

Two soldiers ran up to the centurion with swords withdrawn from their hilts. "Centurion—the prisoners!" they said with duty-bound firmness.

Julius grabbed both of them by their cheeks to make sure he had their attention. "Save yourselves and leave the prisoners alone! Do you understand?" They nodded vigorously. "You tell the others. Two soldiers will die tonight for every prisoner that dies this morning!" Again they nodded and ran off.

Judah, Esther, Paul, and their companions assembled together in one corner of the ship as the turmoil and terror unfolded around them. Each one of them was interceding before God with determined passion, but none could say that his faith at that moment was untainted by fear. Each of them was very much caught up in the stark human drama of the impending shipwreck, and no one knew what the next moment would bring. When the decisive moment came for them

to leap into the cold, turbid water, each one felt the breathless, unpleasant sensation of being in dark isolation—a lone plunging into the hands of God.

Judah had tied a rope around his and Esther's wrists, and when he surfaced, he
reached for her. She was vomiting. The bitter sting of being immersed in the cold
salt water induced a new bout of nausea, so he clung to her and held her up until
her shaking had subsided. He kicked as vigorously as he could to stay afloat, and
just when his strength was nearly gone, they floated into a field of debris. The
moment was not without its perils, for the waves tossed splintered wood around
them like spears. Cautiously, Judah grabbed hold of a sturdy plank that drifted
by and then kicked away from the ship, which the sea tore into pieces before
their eyes. The strange cacophony of screams, buckling wood and boiling water
added to the horror.

As they drew nearer to shore, they scarcely had to swim at all. The surf drove
them to land with precision and power, and soon deposited them rudely but
safely on the sand. With what strength they had left, they crawled higher up onto
the beach and then they collapsed weary and beaten in each other's arms, the
rope still joining them at the wrists.

*   *   *

Agrippina sat in silence within her cabin contemplating the events of the day,
mulling over every word of conversation, calculating her gains and losses. And
one thing was for certain—all was not lost. There was still some ground beneath
her feet. Her world had not yet collapsed around her. Until that moment.

Neither Agrippina or her attendants had noticed that the boat had stopped
moving and that the noise of the oars splashing on the water had stilled. Not the
least suspicion was aroused until the two soldiers knocked loose the footings
holding up the ceiling of the cabin—a ceiling that had been purposefully loaded
with a quarter ton of lead. When the ceiling collapsed, the layer of lead fell
directly onto her bodyguard, breaking his neck and killing him instantly.
Agrippina and her servant slumped down on the sofa, and were saved when its
raised sides caught the ceiling and held fast.

In the darkness, the two soldiers leaned over the wrecked cabin and surveyed
their work. Their orders were to sink the ship only after everyone had been killed.
They could see that the ceiling seemed to be propped up on one end, and then to

their dismay, they heard shuffling movements and muffled voices. They paused indecisively for a moment, then with one nodding at the other, rushed to the two levers and simultaneously pushed them forward. The wooden clips that had efficiently held the two sections of the ferry together in one watertight piece disengaged, and within seconds, water began to pour into the boat, separating the pieces. The two soldiers found themselves each on a different half, drifting apart from the other, and the two ends of each half slowly begun to tip up vertically in the water.

The two women were effectively pinned to the sofa until the boat began to come apart. As that happened, a pocket of space was created that allowed them to slip free of the cabin and drop into the water. Both women gasped at the initial shock of the frigid water chilling their skin. Agrippina's maid swam out away from the boat ahead of her mistress, and then turned around to grab hold of the sides of one of the sinking halves. She coughed up water and screamed out, "Help! Save me! Agrippina!"

The soldier nearest her, thinking the maid to be Agrippina, drew his sword and immediately plunged it into the unsuspecting woman's chest. She floated lifelessly past Agrippina who still remained out of sight, clinging to the other half of the boat.

Up until that moment, Agrippina was still confused as to what exactly was happening, and it was yet her thought that a terrible accident had occurred. She was on the verge of crying out herself until the soldier drew his sword upon her servant. In one flash of light, she now understood everything, and immediately, the ruthless instinct for survival which had preserved her for so many years reared up within her. The body of her guard was bobbing facedown beside her in the water, and Agrippina coolly reached underneath him and groped for a weapon that might yet be attached to his uniform. As she felt his chest, her fingers traced the edges of a poniard, and with a calm determination, she reached inside the lining of his jacket and removed it.

The soldiers now had reason to grow concerned for their own safety as the boat halves began to plunge beneath the water, nearly fifty feet from each other. "Was that Agrippina?" shouted out one to the other.

"I'm not sure. Do you see the other bodies?"

"No. They must be dead," he answered.

Agrippina slipped off her outer cloak and shoes, and while treading steadily, made sure that she kept behind the bottom of the boat which was now like a wall in the water, hiding her from the one soldier she knew was with her. As the boat rose vertically, she also knew it was only a matter of time before he had to jump into the water, and then a moment later, she heard the splash. Only five feet of the boat now remained above the water, and as it sank, she braced her left hand upon the wood and adjusted her grip on the knife with her right hand. The boat disappeared like a curtain on a stage, and then suddenly, the curtain was gone, and there she was face to face with the soldier. She caught him completely by surprise, and all he could say was, "Here—!" before she drilled the dagger into his throat.

As this was happening, the second soldier had slipped into the bay, but he was too far away to see anything, and what he heard was garbled by the water that lapped around him. He called out once, then twice, and only then began to suspect trouble. Agrippina's thoughts raced within her. Did she have the strength to swim to the mainland? If she had to outswim a pursuer, she knew she would fail. The advantage of surprise was still hers, so she decided to wait for the other soldier to act by floating as though dead on the water. She quietly nudged the the dead soldier away from her, then drifted toward the other bodies. As she imagined he would, the soldier slowly swam in her direction. He came first to the bodyguard, then the maid, then finally to her. She kept her body perfectly still, except for her heart which beat so hard, she was certain it was sending ripples through the water. He pulled on her hair and lifted up her head, but she quenched every reaction; then he did it a second time so as to satisfy himself.

"Your son said to keep it bloodless," he said with triumph, then called out for his friend.

She struck with savage swiftness, grabbing his own hair, pulling back his head and bringing her knife decisively across the muscles of his throat. Gasping for breath, she screamed, "Don't ever pull on my hair!" She kicked his body from her, and then quickly dog-paddled away from the scene to avoid gagging on the film of bloody water.

Swimming was an impossibility until she calmed down, so she floated on her back until she had regained control of her breathing. Once all was quiet and she was convinced that she was alone, she let the knife slip from her fingers, then stripped off most of what remained of her clothing. With a determined sigh, she kicked towards the mainland, muttering, "I'm sorry to disappoint my son."

*   *   *

A solitary officer kicked up sand as he strode along the beach, criss-crossing between more than a dozen bonfires, around which the survivors of the shipwreck encamped. By late morning, the rain had stopped and the wind was but a ghost of its former self. The sailor found the owner standing alone atop a dune, overlooking the sea which was still a tempest. Fragments of the ship had washed ashore, but other than that, the wreckage had vanished beneath the sea.

"Excuse me, sir," said the officer, standing beside him and rubbing his eyes which were watering from the smoke. "No lives were lost, sir. Everyone was accounted for. All 276 of them."

The owner shook his head. He looked away from the sea and scanned the fires spread out before him until he found the one around which sat Judah, Esther, Paul and their friends. The officer followed the eyes of the owner. "Who are they?" the owner asked. "How did he know? Could their God be real after all?"

"With respect sir," said the officer, "the Jews are Roman subjects. He's a damned peculiar God if he does exist."

The owner dismissed the officer and turned again to face the sea, his own thoughts mirrored in its churning.

*   *   *

Agrippina was picked up by a fishing boat a quarter–mile offshore. She was carried to her resort home, and physicians were called to attend her. News that Lady Agrippina had survived a boating accident quickly spread throughout the region, and hundreds of gawkers flocked to her house. The physicians came and bathed her, and carefully nursed her shoulder which she had injured at some point in her struggle. After they made her as comfortable as possible, she dismissed them. Two slaves remained to attend to her.

She told no one the truth of what had happened, for until she returned to Rome, there was no actual constituency to which she could appeal for protection. She had friends in the Senate and sympathizers in high places, but here she was very much alone. The brilliance of Nero's plan would be cause for admiration had she not been the object of his plot.

She decided her best course of action would be to pretend to remain ignorant of Nero's designs, and leave him with the option of yet withdrawing his hostility. She drew up a hastily composed note to her son telling him that she had survived an unfortunate accident, but assuring him that all was well and she would return to Rome in the morning. He need not bother on her behalf, for he had gone to so much trouble already for which she was thankful. Her hands trembled uncontrollably as she wrote. She then sealed the letter and sent it off immediately through the hands of Agerinus, one of her remaining attendants. Then she waited.

When Agerinus arrived on the island, he was swiftly ushered into Nero's presence. Nero had waited all evening with his friends in nervous anticipation of the news. He neither ate, drank, nor played, but paced about like a caged leopard. When the expected messenger arrived, Nero took a seat, and Tigellinus and Anicetus stood off to either side of him. As Agerinus entered the room, Nero attempted to appear relaxed and unaware, but all the while he fidgeted pathetically.

"So, I understand you come to me with grievous news about my mother," said Nero to the slave.

Agerinus pulled the letter out from a satchel wrapped around his waist. "Yes my lord."

Nero interrupted with contrived grief. "Wait! I don't know if I am quite ready to hear this. Just nod your head slowly if it is true," he sobbed. "Is my mother dead?" He gripped the armrests of his chair to brace himself for the wave of sorrow about to overwhelm him.

Agerinus' eyes widened with a look of puzzled delight, and then with the sweeping smile of one proud to be the bearer of good news, he gladly shook his head vigorously from side to side. Had he not been gripping the chair, Nero would have fallen clean off of it.

"What?" he asked tentatively. "My mother is not dead?"

"No, Lord Caesar!" exclaimed the messenger. "And here is a letter from her own hand, written to set you at ease so that you may sleep fitfully, and not despair."

Nero reached out and snatched the letter from his hands, and opened it. Tigellinus and Anicetus as well peered over his shoulder in utter bewilderment, and read for themselves the note written with handwriting they knew so well.

Nero dropped the note to the ground and slumped in his chair. His head grew light, and he began talking to himself. "By the gods, she's escaped. She lives, and she will fight us. Tigellinus, what are we going to do? Anicetus, you said this would work. How could she have survived!" He stood and flung the chair over in a fit of rage. Agerinus stepped back in complete confusion. He felt an urge to run, but could not explain why. Nero's face was bright red. He turned to look at Agerinus. "You said my mother is alive. Where is she at?"

Agerinus' voice shook. "At her house."

Tigellinus now seized upon a plan to redeem this debacle. He stepped forward and pointed at the servant. "And Agrippina sent you to us. For what purpose?" He shouted the question with the accusatory tone of a prosecutor.

Agerinus shrank back. "To deliver this letter, nothing more. I assure you."

Tigellinus stepped closer to him. "Caesar, look at this man's trembling face. He is hiding the truth from us. I think it is reasonable to conclude that Agrippina has sent him here this evening for only one purpose. She came this afternoon to lull you to sleep, so that now her servant could come tonight and assassinate you."

"No my lord, that's absurd!" screamed Agerinus.

Nero picked up the lead from Tigellinus. "Guards, search this man at once!"

Three soldiers swooped around Agerinus like vultures and forced him to the ground. One of them suddenly stood, holding in his hand a tiny penknife customarily used to break seals. He brought the knife to Nero, and the other two guards forced Agerinus to his knees, pulling back on his head and twisting his arms behind him.

"So this is the tool of an assassin?" Nero asked.

"Caesar, no! I am your humble servant," cried the terrified prisoner. "I couldn't possibly. That knife can barely cut paper."

"Shall we try it on your throat?" threatened Tigellinus. "Caesar, I am reminded that another of Agrippina's bodyguards is yet with us in this very building, perhaps right now planning to join this villain. He should be arrested at once."

Nero beckoned to two more soldiers to carry out the order. Anicetus then spoke. "And what about Agrippina? She may try to flee, or worse yet, may right now be calling for an armed rebellion."

"Yes, she must be stopped at once," Nero said. "Anicetus, I am making my mother your responsibility. Take a detachment of every available soldier, and deal with her as we must deal with every traitor. Go now!" Anicetus bowed, reached for his cloak and left the room.

Anicetus summoned a dozen soldiers to join him, and they rowed to the mainland in three boats. Even as they pulled to shore, they could see that the streets of Misenum were still astir with activity though the hour was late. They marched into town, and when they arrived at Agrippina's home, his worst fears were realized. The house was walled in with people.

Anicetus paused in the street to ponder his choices. He had less than a minute to decide what was in the hearts of this mob that blocked his way. If they were mere curiosity seekers, he could plow through them immediately. But if rebellion were in their bellies, or if Agrippina had aroused their sympathies, then Anicetus and his twelve men would be no match for them. They might riot to protect her, kill the soldiers, and Nero would awaken the next morning to find an empire slipping through his fingers. Tyrants never secure their authority all at once. Their power is acquired one individual skirmish at a time, and in the early days of a dictator's quest for domination, the common people of the streets have the power to overthrow the regime if they would but resist. But with each confrontation that the despot wins, his confidence builds, his support solidifies, and soon the window closes and tyranny is entrenched.

Anicetus, aware of the stakes, opted to gamble and pressed headlong into the crowd. "Let me through!" he shouted. "Let me through!"

Two local officials who had come to offer their services to Agrippina stepped in his way, stopping the wedge of soldiers. "What do you want?" they shouted.

Anicetus met power with power. "Is Agrippina here? You will let us pass. An attempt was made on the life of the Emperor tonight!" He shouted this above the din of the crowd, and immediately gasps and murmuring rippled through it. "Agrippina was behind the plot. You will let me pass, or I assure you, you will face the Emperor's wrath!" The two men hesitated momentarily, then their heads bowed down and they stepped aside. Anicetus charged past. He dispatched three soldiers to the rear of the building, signaled for two to follow him inside, and instructed the rest to push back the people.

When he first came through the door, he saw Agrippina's lone attendant, who screamed and fell back into the corner of the room, begging for her life. Agrippina was lying on her bed in a back room of the house, and her blood chilled as she heard the cry and the rude thumping of the soldiers' feet. She leaped from the bed and ran toward a side exit just as Anicetus burst into the bedroom from the main hallway with his sword unsheathed and extended. He darted after her with the two soldiers coming behind him.

Her only hope was to escape out the back entrance, and as she pulled back the door to flee, she cried out with a hideous howl and fell back onto the floor as she found her way cut off by more soldiers. Anicetus ran into the room and Agrippina kicked her way back along the wall. Her head pounded in pain as the sensation of complete defeat and the fear of death rose up within her soul. Anicetus wasted no time. He stepped toward her and raised his sword.

Just as he was about to attack, she stuck out her hands and implored pitifully, "Wait! Wait!" He heeded her for only a moment, and as he did, she pulled back her robe until the flesh of her stomach was completely exposed. "Strike here," she said pointing to her skin. "This womb bore a monster." She closed her eyes and turned her head away, as Anicetus struck her dead with repeated blows of his sword.

Early the next morning, Nero ordered for her body to be burned on a pyre in a field outside Misenum. He was sullen and silent as the fire was lit, and of all the people who gathered to watch, he stood closest to the flames, staring vacantly at Agrippina's lifeless form as it was consumed.

*   *   *

As the sun rose on the Roman empire that late autumn morning, two fires burned, though hundreds of miles apart—one on a small island in the heart of the Great Sea, and another in an Italian village, far to the north. In time, those two fires would converge, and when they did, thousands throughout the empire would be scorched by the fury of its flames.

Part 2: A.D.60–63

Chapter 6

Despite its 2,000 miles of coastline, Italy had few good natural harbors. The Tiber River ran past Rome and emptied fifteen miles later into the Tuscan Sea at Ostia, but the build-up of silt in its mouth made this spot prohibitive for commercial use until Emperor Claudius dredged it when Nero was a child. Once the Tiber was opened up, smaller merchant ships could sail directly up it and dock alongside of the wharves that had been hastily built at the foot of the Aventine Hill. Nero had plans to continue cutting a channel to the very edge of his new palace, the Domus Aurea, once its construction was complete. But for now, the main business of Rome flowed in and out of the harbors of Tarentum in the south and Puteoli in the west.

When spring came to Italy the following year, the emperor brought a delegation to Puteoli for an annual ceremony which was held to invoke the favor of the Roman gods on the commerce of the coming shipping season. Nero ordinarily gave little interest to such populist rituals, but Rome was still languishing under a famine, and he recognized the value of a carefully timed public appearance. Sharing imperial compassion would boost imperial support, and in Nero's eyes, such support was still in short supply.

After Agrippina's death, Nero initially stayed away from Rome, uncertain of what he would find there. He was convinced that everyone believed he was culpable. Burrus, fearing that Nero might order wholesale changes in the Praetorian Guard to protect himself, convinced his officers to go to Nero and congratulate him on his narrow escape from assassination. Then Seneca urged Caesar to make a statement to the Senate and offered to write the letter for him. To Nero's surprise, the Senate accepted every line of gibberish that Seneca composed and hailed the emperor as a hero.

Only then did he return to the capital and all of Rome filled the streets to greet him, as though Augustus himself had come back to life. This public outpouring of devotion filled Nero with sudden boldness. He struck Agrippina's birthday from the list of public holidays and then released from exile several whom his mother had banished. As each action was endorsed by the Senate and embraced by the public, a burgeoning sense of invincibility came over him. Coming to Puteoli was a simple way to build on this momentum.

Rumors spread that the emperor would sell the grain from the first barges that arrived at a cut-rate price or even give it away. It was not unusual for Caesar to shower unexpected prizes on the citizenry. It was a ritual the people had come to expect since abandoning the republic a century before in exchange for a dictatorship. It was a game they played with their emperor, and in time, they had grown to prefer the pleasures of the game over the privileges of the freedom they had lost.

For Caesar, these tokens of his beneficence were the easiest of narcotics to administer to the people. The slightest unrest could be soothed by simply ordering a three-month reduction in the tax on wine or by opening the Imperial Gardens for an afternoon to the plebs. One simple gesture which cost him nothing could instantly reverse the slightest dip in his popularity. And it was approval which Nero craved most of all.

Each day, he dispatched to the streets groups of young supporters called *Augustiani*, culled from the orders of Roman knights. They walked through the markets and loitered on the Forum, listening to the common gossip of the community, and the reports they brought back to Nero often dictated the shape of public policy. Wherever the emperor went, the *Augustiani* went ahead and behind, mingling in with the crowd to insure that sufficient praise was showered on Caesar. Whenever Nero performed, the *Augustiani* were the first to applaud and the last to sit down, and many a lukewarm observer felt the butt-end of a sword nudged into his side at these events.

The *Augustiani* were in force at Puteoli on the day of the emperor's appearance, sprinkled throughout the massive crowd of people who flocked to the harbor. Nero would not disappoint them. He ordered that the entire load of wheat from the first grain ship that docked was to be emptied out onto one of the harbor's expansive piers. This took several hours and the people buzzed around greedily. Most of them carried empty sacks, unashamedly expecting a handout.

When this laborious task was done, a makeshift stage was erected in front of the pile, and the excitement built. The weather lent to the frivolity for it was a flawless, warm day such as Italy had not seen since before the winter. The *Augustiani* kicked into action, rousing the audience into a frenzy of worship as Nero and his coterie ascended the platform. The mountain of wheat made for a strange backdrop as Nero stood at the edge of the stage. The crowd roared all the louder. He let it continue for ten minutes, and then motioned for quiet. The people quickly obeyed, and soon only the sea gulls could be heard, yet Nero waited a few more minutes as though he expected them also to be silent. At last he spoke.

"Fellow citizens, as we emerge from a long and difficult winter, many are fearful." His voice echoed out across the pier and easily reached those standing 500 feet away. "Some say the days of Roman prosperity are behind us. Too many grain barges have been lost at sea. We are still in the throes of famine. So they say." He was a masterful speaker. His gestures and facial expressions were in perfect resonance with his words and the people stood transfixed to listen to him.

"But I want to assure you that we have never been more secure, that your future has never been more hopeful, and that Rome has never been greater. Roman ingenuity has never been greater. Roman prosperity has never been greater! Roman power has never been greater!" Loud cheering answered the recitation of each line, growing stronger each time. Thousands of cloaks, flowers and empty bags were waved in the air in homage to him.

"To demonstrate our great confidence, we dedicate this entire delivery of wheat to the honor of our gods, who will guarantee our good fortunes. People, you need not be afraid!"

With this, he motioned to the bottom of the stage where more than a dozen guards stood stationed with unlit torches in hand. At his signal, they lit the torches from a large pit of live coals that were burning off to the side, and then the guards walked over to the grain, encircled it, and to the astonishment of the crowd, they set the pile afire with the torches. It took several minutes for the fire to spread over the top peaks, but when it did, the heat was so intense that the delegation on the stage had to beat a swift retreat. Then the stage itself began to burn, so the guards pushed it over into the fire until it was completely engulfed.

Any dismay the people may have felt at seeing the grain destroyed was quickly dissolved by the novelty of the fire. They began to dance and sing around it, and when Nero ordered that steaks and fowl be cooked over the coal pits and the meat given to the people along with wine and bread, the day was completely won. Toasts were raised to the honor of the emperor throughout the day and continued long into the night.

As Nero watched the celebration unfold, he smiled approvingly and fell back into the company of his usual consortium of advisers and attendants. Tigellinus walked up to him with a sneer, and asked, "You enjoy playing with fire, don't you?"

Nero grinned, and looked at Seneca and Burrus who had drawn near. "Seneca, this idea of yours was a masterstroke. With one little fire, we will burn away a winter's worth of discontent. And the beauty of it is we've really changed nothing at all. The famine rages on, but all are happy."

Seneca nodded as he surveyed the jubilation around them. "An able leader soon learns that most people are moved by pictures and shadows. Substance can weigh down a good politician."

"Yes, why be trifled with truth when the people have no interest in it. Look at them," said Nero, surveying the crowd. "Simpletons and buffoons."

As he looked about, relishing the knowledge that he was the source of this gaity, he noticed that another group of several hundred people had congregated at the far breakwater on the other end of the harbor, more than a half mile away. It was a group of people who were taking no apparent interest in the party that he was throwing.

"Now that's peculiar," he said, pointing in that direction. "Is there a dignitary arriving today that I am not aware of?"

"No one that we know of," said Burrus.

"Why, there must be five hundred people over there ignoring all the fun we are having here," Nero said. "This hardly seems right on a day when all of Italy is one big happy family. Find out who they are, Burrus. We must pay our respects. And extend an invitation to them to join us. I don't take kindly to cold shoulders."

As Burrus walked off to investigate, Nero plunged into the crowd to fraternize with his people and milk them of their praise. Occasionally, he stole a glance to the other end of the harbor, and each time, a brief cloud of irritation blew past him but then was quickly gone.

At that moment, several miles out to sea, another grain ship was steering its way into port. It was a vessel from Alexandria and had sailed as far as the small island of Malta before the ravages of winter forced it to dock. There the captain found stranded the entire crew and passenger complement of another Alexandrian barge which had shipwrecked on Malta's rocky perimeter. Out of professional courtesy to his fellow sailors, the captain agreed to bring aboard as many as he could when once he resumed his voyage to Rome. Judah, Paul, Esther and their companions were among those who were granted passage.

As the ship coasted closer to Puteoli, the friends gathered on deck. The sea breeze was rich and invigorating. Gulls were the first to greet them as they approached the land, and the hills behind the shoreline were glowing with greens and yellows.

"Welcome to Italy," Judah said to his friends, breaking the quiet reverie each was enjoying. He placed his arm tenderly around Esther, who betrayed a trace of melancholy through her weak smile.

Julius, the centurion, stood at his other side and Paul was next to him. "Puteoli is beautiful," said Julius. "And spring is the best time to see her."

"It doesn't quite stir the soul as does Jerusalem," Paul said, "but I'll give you the Romans can do amazing things with marble. The harbor sparkles like a jewel from this distance. And look at all the people! What's going on over there?" He pointed in the direction of the wheat fire, which had sent a towering spiral of dark smoke into the air.

"The captain told me that Emperor Nero was planning on making an appearance at the harbor sometime this month," Julius reported. "Perhaps that's what all the commotion is about. Hard to figure what else it might be."

Intrigued, Paul leaned over the rail, as though being two feet closer would bring Nero into view. He turned to Judah.

"Now Judah, you told me it might take up to two years to be heard by Caesar and look! The emperor has come to welcome us in person. What a nice man. I like him already."

Esther brightened a little. "And if Nero hears Paul's case today, we can leave for Jerusalem tomorrow, right?"

Judah sympathetically tightened his embrace around his wife. "My love, I know faith can move mountains, but I wouldn't pack your bags just yet."

The ship sliced ahead, led by the splendid figurehead of the twin gods Castor and Pollux—guardians of the sea—carved into the bow. Paul hovered over the deck's railing like an excited child. For years he had yearned to walk on Italian soil. As they came nearer, noises and voices from the shore could be picked out. Paul pointed to the second group of people that were assembled at the end of the harbor where they would land.

"If those people are here to see the emperor, then who is this group?"

Judah began to salute in the direction of these people, and individual hands lifted up and returned the greeting. Voices could be heard shouting, "It's them!" "There's Esther!" "Judah!" Esther also began to wave, and she turned to Paul and said, "It's our welcoming party."

"It looks as though a good portion of the church has come to meet us," added Luke, who stood nearby.

Julius leaned closer to Paul. "Master Paul, before we arrive, I want you to know that once we are in Rome, I will request that you continue under my care. My family has a small cottage behind our house, and I'd like you to stay there with us. House arrest would certainly be preferable to the emperor's dungeons."

Paul was visibly moved by this act of kindness. He reached out and placed an affirming hand on Julius' shoulder. "Julius, you are very kind. I would be honored to stay with you if it is permitted. Thank you my brother."

"I have much more to thank you for," said Julius who was beaming.

Once the ship landed, and the harried excitement of disembarking was through, the friends joined their party on shore. The emotional fanfare of greetings and introductions went on for some time, and finally, the congregation began to move as one multitude away from the harbor into the town.

Later that day, Burrus took Nero aside to report to him that the smaller group was a gathering of Jews welcoming a notable religious leader who had just arrived from Judea.

"Jews. That stands to reason," humphed Nero. "What a miserable, unhappy race of men. They won't join us at our feasts. Or worship at our shrines. They enjoy all the benefits of our society, but refuse to thank us. Very nearly seditious. Remind me of this someday, Burrus. I would like to show them the back of my hand."

Nero gave no further thought to what he had seen at the harbor, but continued with his revelries for the next few days before sailing back to Ostia in a royal charter. Meanwhile, Judah and his company rested with a group of the disciples for another week in Puteoli before resuming their journey on foot to Rome, which lay 140 miles to the north. Judah's observation would prove prophetic. It would be another two years before their paths would again cross with Caesar.

*   *   *

During the next two years, Nero solidified his grip on power. Publicly, he showed the hand of mercy. When signing warrants for executions ordered by the Senate, he would sigh and mutter, "I wish that I had never learned to write." Privately, his hand was ruthless. With the help of Tigellinus and his *Augustiani*, he systematically weeded out potential threats to his rule. Anyone whose ancestry could be even remotely traced to the Caesar's line risked being crushed under the machinery of terror that Nero was in the process of assembling.

Seneca and Burrus continued as advisers, but their role was now greatly diminished. Nero retained them only because they were esteemed by the public. Their sterling reputations gave the appearance that his administration was seasoned and balanced, when nothing could be further from the truth. He rarely consulted them in political matters and they could no longer restrain his prodigal lusts.

He essentially banished Octavia to her own private residence, which allowed him not only to pursue his affair with Poppaea openly, but at the same time, to experiment with unique forms of debauchery which now became available to him. In exasperation, Seneca quietly withdrew and resumed his writing career which had been prolific before being called into Nero's service. Burrus occupied himself with his Guard, hoping to find at least a few remaining men of valor in whom he could invest his heart.

Nero's love for entertainment expanded. He sponsored an endless variety of athletic and theatrical events. As his boldness grew, the time came when he not only expected men of rank and nobility to attend his shows, but also to participate in them as contestants. He filled Rome with his singing, and went to ridiculous lengths to improve his voice, subjecting himself to dietary restrictions and trying any folk remedy he came across.

He also dabbled in poetry, and occasionally gathered together Italy's finest writers for evenings of verse exchanges—*"word orgies,"* grumbled Seneca's well-known nephew Lucan, who found Nero's parties dreary and his writing unimaginative. Nero composed half-lines of poetry and then challenged his guests to complete the verses, only later to take credit for the finished piece. In virtually every field of endeavor he was a pretender—a master of mediocrity. Because he could not accept criticism, criticism was never offered, and without it, the only thing that ever improved was his vanity.

Of all his endeavors, the one in which Nero truly aspired to excel was the racing of a four-horse chariot, yet the sport was beyond his reach, forbidden as a cultural taboo to those in power. Chariot racing was not far removed in vulgarity from gladiatorial contests, and the thought of an emperor competing on the same sand floor where slaves and pagans spilled their blood seemed beyond reason for the average thinker. But Nero could never chase it from his mind.

"Chariot racing was a skill of ancient rulers and kings," he would argue before his advisers. "It has been honored by the poets and hailed by the masses. Look at how we worship those who triumph in the Circus!"

As emperor, Nero would have his way, but unlike with his singing, he was much more cautious about the steps he took here. He began by constructing a private arena in the Vatican valley, and there he drove his chariots, first to his own amusement, and then over time, he began to allow slaves and commoners to watch him. But eventually, even this grew wearisome and he began to thirst for competition in a real arena. Each day stirred his restlessness more, and finally he decided that the day had come for the public unveiling of his skills. The first completed section of his new palace was soon to be dedicated, and in honor of the occasion, he had commanded for there to be a holiday of amusements in the Circus Maximus. There before all of Rome, he would climb aboard his chariot and ride for glory in the great race.

During these two years, Judah and Paul waited patiently for the case to be heard by Caesar, but the waiting was not without its pleasures. For the two friends, it was a return to their former days of shared labor. Judah still retained the role of chief shepherd of the Roman church, but his responsibilities had long since been delegated to trained and able leaders who would carry on once he returned to Judea. He now was a pastor to the pastors, and spent most of his time in developing the leadership core of the church, imitating the example of Jesus who poured his life into the Twelve that he might more effectively care for the multitudes.

He was not alone in this great work, for Esther was every bit a partner in ministry. She had the ability to listen with both her ears and her heart, and when she spoke, her words were like the proverbial apples of gold on a setting of silver. She was a friend to the weak and wounded, and was deeply loved by all the Roman church. The ache in her heart to be home in Judea was surpassed only by the ache in her heart for any with broken souls, and so she filled the time with fruitful ministry.

Paul was allowed to remain in custody under house arrest, and took up residence in the private cottage provided by Julius. During the day, he worked as a tent-weaver, a trade he learned from his father, and at night he entertained a steady stream of guests. Though his movements were restricted, news of his arrival in Rome sparked great interest in the Jewish community, and before long, Paul was preaching daily to visitors and curiosity seekers who sought him out. Though he couldn't go to the world, the world came to him, and the church in Rome continued to flourish.

So after two winters had come and gone, an uneasiness began to creep into this fellowship of friends as each one sensed that the day of resolution was drawing near. One night late in March, the friends met in Paul's cottage, along with a handful of leaders from the church. The latest of Paul's tents was spread out on a table in the center of a rustic living area and everyone sat stationed around it. Paul and a couple of others were attacking the tent with thread, and the rest leaned back on benches, sipping on cider and enjoying the camaraderie. The door opened and Luke entered, tightly wrapped in a thick cloak. The sound of the wind, moaning through the streets like a dying man, chilled those inside, until Luke pushed the door shut.

"Winter won't go without a fight," Luke muttered as he tossed a packet of thread on the center of the canvas. "This thread should see you through till you're finished with the tent."

"Thank you, brother Luke," said Paul, as he took the packet and cut it open. "You didn't have to interrupt your writing to run that errand for us, but it is appreciated."

"Since I'm not good with my hands in your service, I can at least use my feet," Luke said as he took off his cloak and sat down next to Judah.

Judah grinned. "A physician who is not good with his hands? Isn't that like a carpenter who can't handle a hammer?"

"Or a lawyer who can't get his case heard?" Luke jabbed back in friendly fashion.

"Ouch!" yelped Paul. "The doctor has opened a wound."

"Judah knows that no hurt is intended," said Luke, pulling onto his lap a writing tablet, and spreading a scroll out upon it. "I just wish I could understand Roman law. Its wheels of justice grind with annoying slowness. Two years and still no sign of movement in Paul's case."

Judah looked across the table at Esther who was busily cutting off a stretch of thread. "Believe me, my wife reminds me of that every night."

She tried to ignore him, and said, "Our emperor is a busy man. He has poems to write. Games to play. And a palace to build."

Next to her sat Aquila and Priscilla, an older couple who were among Judah and Esther's first converts in Rome. They were forced to flee when Claudius banished the Jews from the capital, and Judah sent them to Corinth where they joined with Paul during his mission there, and soon they became intimate friends. Aquila spoke up.

"They say the first section of the new palace will be dedicated soon. Complete with a hundred foot statue of Nero himself."

His wife scoffed. "Just what Rome needs—another idol to bow down before."

Paul suddenly put down his thread and reached out a hand to Esther, while drawing Judah's attention. "Judah, your wife here is a gem. She has borne up well with all this uncertainty. You'd hardly know from looking at her that she is languishing inside." Esther shook her head, but he was insistent. "No, dear sister. I know the sorrow you feel, and that same weight hangs over Judah as well. I know how much you two are yearning to see Judea."

He waited for Judah to respond, but he remained quiet, so Paul continued. "What I'm about to say, I've given much thought to. I want you and Esther to return to Jerusalem. Not when the case is over. Who knows when that will be? I want you to return as soon as the shipping lanes are safe to travel."

Esther's eyes brightened hopefully, but Judah shook his head vigorously. "Paul, that's out of the question. I will not back out on you until we've seen this through. As your friend, I think...", but Paul cut him off.

"As *your* friend, I'm telling you that your job is done. You have ministered to me tirelessly these past two years. You have taught me about Roman law. I no doubt will run rings around my opponents' heads, thanks to you and your encouragement. You have allowed me to share with you in the leadership of God's church. And besides, Luke has nearly completed his written defense on my behalf." He pointed to Luke's scroll. "This scroll outlines virtually my entire ministry. These acts of the apostles stand on their own."

Luke broke in. "This record is incomplete, though. Someone insisted that his name not be mentioned," he said with a smirk, looking at Judah.

"And don't you dare," Judah responded. "If I ever fell into disfavor with the Senate, you know what might happen. Once I leave Rome, write anything you want. But for now, my duty is to that man," he said, pointing to Paul.

"And Judah, you have fulfilled your duty beyond anything I could ask or think," Paul answered back. "So as a gift of thanks to you, I myself will purchase your passage on a ship that will take you home." Judah started to protest again, while Esther silently prayed—and for the first time in her life—for her husband to lose his case. "If you love me," Paul continued, "you can only accept this gift of thanks."

Judah rose up from his chair with his limbs tightly clenched, and then he loosened up and sat back down. "You make it difficult to refuse you."

"That's easy when I will not be refused," Paul said. "And besides, an additional point. You are a son of peace. A man of sound judgment. Jerusalem is running short of such people. We've all been following the news from Judea. It is grim. There are so many rebellious voices stirring up discontent. Voices which are begging Rome to silence them. I fear for our people, and for our country. If they insist on war with Rome…"

"They will be destroyed," said Aquila with sad firmness.

There was silence and then Paul resumed. "And so, dear Judah, do not think I am dismissing you and sending you into retirement. I am merely releasing you, that you and Esther might be recommissioned for a higher and needier work."

Again there was silence, and Judah looked away. Luke placed a consoling hand on Judah's back. "It appears that you've won your case, Paul," he said. "You've silenced the lawyer."

Judah threw up his hands. "It appears that I am cornered, and the verdict is rendered. To Jerusalem we shall go."

Paul smiled. "Then if the weather permits, within two weeks the church and I will say our farewells to you. That should give you time to complete one more task."

"And what would that be?" asked Judah, slightly disconsolate.

Paul picked up a corner of the canvas. "Why, help me finish this tent!" Everyone shared in a hearty laugh and the friends continued together late in the night, not wishing for the fellowship to be broken.

*   *   *

Gaius Calpurnius Piso was a well-known aristocrat who lived outside of Rome in an expansive villa which overlooked the city. His family name and wealth insured that he had high connections to men of power in Rome, though he himself had never served in government, except as an occasional consultant to the Senate. He was well-liked by the citizenry and was a rare man of means in that he was both humble and charitable. To add to the richness of his life, he was disarmingly handsome and possessed a commanding presence. He owned property throughout Italy, including a home in Baiae which was famous for the exquisite gardens which surrounded it, and even Nero was known to come to rest in the shade of his villa there.

The day after Paul had released Judah from his obligations, Piso entertained two friends in his home, Flavius Scaevinus and Clodius Thrasea Paetus, both of them well-respected members in the Senate. They spent the afternoon in conversation, sitting atop the flat roof of his home, and from their position which overlooked the western side of the Rome, they began to talk about the city spread before their feet.

"So, has either of you caught a glimpse yet of this hundred–foot *Colossus* that all Rome waits to see unveiled?" asked Piso.

Paetus' face clouded over. "A monstrosity. An eyesore. A blemish on the face of Rome."

"I take that to mean you don't find it attractive?" Piso asked, poking at his friend.

"Gold should be used to replicate objects of beauty, not wasted on the short, paunchy features of the son of Ahenobarbus," Paetus said.

He was an older man, with a long and distinguished career as a senator and enough money to have comfortably retired by now. But since the days of Tiberius, he had watched the Senate slowly deteriorate from a free-thinking body of leaders into an anemic and servile tool of Caesar's, and so he vowed to remain, and represent as best he could the dwindling voice of reason. Nero's ascension only intensified his passion to speak out, but his became an increasingly isolated voice. After Agrippina's death, as the Senate fell over itself in its rush to exalt Nero and condemn his mother, Paetus became so sickened that he had walked from the Senate chambers to the stunned silence of his colleagues.

"As you can tell, our fine Thrasea does not think highly of our emperor," Scaevinus said. He was Piso's age, though not nearly as endowed with the same physical graces of beauty and charm. "And Calpurnius, you should have been in the Senate last week. Did you hear of Thrasea's great coup?" Piso shook his head as Scaevinus roared with laughter, and even Paetus could not suppress an immodest grin. "Well, let me tell you, I've never seen Nero so set back on his heels. And Tigellinus too."

"That's hard to imagine. Tell me about it," Piso pressed, sharing in the hilarity.

"We all know how merciful Caesar is, right?" Scaevinus asked with a hint of irony in his voice.

"Oh, but of course, he is rich in clemency!" Piso went along.

"Or so he wants the world to believe," Scaevinus continued. "Nero sent to the Senate last week an asinine case concerning Antistius Sosianus."

"I've met him before. Not a half bad fellow," remarked Piso. "What did he do?"

Paetus interjected. "He scorned our emperor at a dinner party, slandering him in a poem he wrote."

"Foolish, brave man. I don't suppose you recall the verses?"

Scaevinus tightened his face for a mock recitation. "Something like:
> *The poems that spring from Nero's head*
> *Would make old Homer glad he's dead*
> *The songs that Nero tries to sing*
> *Would e'en dear Circe to madness bring*

Or something like that," he added as Piso nearly fell on the floor, doubled up with laughter.

"Why the Senate should have pinned a literary medal on him!" he said. "But I don't suppose that's what Nero wanted."

"Well, it was all just a set up, really," Scaevinus resumed. "Nero expected the Senate to issue a full condemnation and call for Sosianus' death. Then he would step in and in his own inimitable, merciful style, he would beg the Senate to reduce the sentence, and everyone would hail him as the Caesar the Magnificent, the Lord of Leniency. Tigellinus had it all orchestrated from the start. And sure enough, Quintus Marullus, the consul designate, stood and delivered a passionate oratory in which he demanded Sosianus' execution for treason. And then the whole Senate chirped in with its ready agreement, that is until Thrasea stood up."

Piso was thoroughly drawn in to the story. "What did you say?" he asked Paetus.

"I merely praised our young emperor for demonstrating at such an early stage in his career the fine qualities of statesmanship that few of our most seasoned diplomats possess," Paetus explained. "And I reminded them of our emperor's forward-thinking and innovative leadership, and his proper evaluation of everything which smacks of tradition in our society, and how these laws under which we would condemn Sosianus were themselves a product of an earlier, more barbaric age in our history, and therefore, these laws should be held in contempt for their ruthless nature."

"Brilliant, Thrasea," Piso marveled.

"What Sosianus had done was indeed reprehensible though."

"But of course."

"So the proper course of action would be capital humiliation, not capital punishment," Paetus continued. "Level upon him the severest of fines, take his property, send him into exile where for the remainder of his life, he will awaken each morning to the memory of his pernicious, shameful deed."

"And the Senate agreed?" Piso asked.

Scaevinus jumped in. "Oh Calpurnius, you should have seen it. They were like water in Thrasea's hand. It was like the days of old when the Senate hung on his every word. They overwhelmingly agreed to his proposal. Then Nero and Tigellinus walked in to hear the Senate's verdict, and the look on Caesar's face when it was announced—he tried to hide it, but the way he quivered, you knew he felt betrayed. He muttered something like, *You may as well have acquitted him while you were feeling so generous'* and he stormed out of the room. Calpurnius! It was a moment like this which makes the drudgery of government seem so worthwhile."

The friends enjoyed a moment of silence to sip on wine and savor the pleasure of each other's company. Piso then spoke. "I don't want to cast shadows on your triumph, Thrasea, but you realize that such a victory will not win you friends in the imperial court."

"Since when have I been concerned with Caesar's friendship?" Paetus said coldly. "And the more this man continues in power, the more I despise this whole system of government we have been handed by our fathers. Augustus' greatness has condemned Rome to enduring the lecheries of his children. But this is intolerable. Three generations of idiots is quite enough."

"We need men like yourself in power," said Piso. "Or Seneca."

"Or yourself," Scaevinus uttered, to Piso's shock. "Yes, you my friend. I have no ambition, and have been poisoned by the system. You are uncorrupted by the Roman establishment. As your home here stands outside the city, so you are one who looks on from outside, and you can envision possibilities which those inside cannot, for they have grown blind."

Thrasea nodded his head. "You certainly could do no worse than those we now must submit to. I am too old, and too cynical to be of use. But you are fresh, and unscarred. But listen to us with this foolish banter. It's so easy to see our way when standing on top of the hill. No sooner do we leave the hill than we are lost. We are three dreamers; three *treasonous* dreamers, I might add."

"Then let us dream more treason," offered Scaevinus, leaning forward. "There are many who think as we do. Now Nero has no children. If something were to happen to him…"

Piso interrupted. "Friends, friends! Please, this talk is making me uncomfortable. I enjoy my life as it is, and like you Flavius, have little ambition to see it changed. Life is hard, and could always be improved upon, but I like improving my life in ways where I do not risk losing my life. Enough of this. We're all drunk anyway."

So the conversation drifted away into other areas and interests, but seeds had been sown through their idle chatter and in time, some of those seeds would find fertile soil.

Chapter 7

The day when the Domus Aurea was dedicated was looked to with great expectation by Rome. Nero had purposefully cancelled all holidays and games two months prior to the event to insure that the populace would be more than ready for a party, and when the day broke, the people wasted no time filling the streets to release their pent-up energy. Throughout the morning, the people paraded through the streets eating and drinking from countless booths which had been set up on nearly every corner by eager concessionaires. It was the fastest way to spend the time as they waited for noon to come, the hour when the gates to the Circus Maximus would be thrown open to the fortunate ones who were able to secure tickets for the games.

A visitor to Rome from the south who entered the city on the Appian Way would first see the Circus—more than a quarter–mile in length—stretching out before him between the Palatine and Aventine hills. As it was approached on foot, its magnificent three-story marble arcade towered overhead, but the sensation of being dwarfed did not become acute until one passed through the labyrinth of inner passageways and stepped into the actual arena.

Up to 200,000 spectators could be seated around the arena floor, whose oval track was 570–yards long and 85–yards wide, and separated in the middle by a concrete barrier called the *spina*, which was itself as much a part of the artisanship of the structure as the outer facade, for displayed along its length was an extensive exhibit of statues, obelisks and fountains. The Romans seldom wasted even the smallest cube of marble. Framing the track was a smooth concrete podium wall, which stood ten feet high—just the right height to discourage the wild beasts from jumping when they were let loose in the arena.

Naturally, the best seats were reserved for Roman nobility, and Caesar himself was provided with a spacious, canopied box that seated up to 50 people and directly overlooked the center of the track. From there he could observe and direct the proceedings. Each program began with a libation being poured out in Caesar's honor, and then the games started in earnest, usually with a full slate of gladiatorial contests which filled the first half of the afternoon. During times of intermission, when bodies were removed or the bloodied sand was shoveled out and replenished, wild beasts were put on display, or theatrical troupes performed acts, but if the intermission lingered, the crowd would grow impatient and start to howl their displeasure. Their craving for blood was singular; it was the main attraction that drew them. This they shared with their emperor.

On the day of dedication, Nero waited, as was his habit, until every seat was filled, and then waited even longer until a brooding sense of restlessness had been provoked. Then suddenly, his entourage appeared in his box, and finally, with the blasts of trumpets announcing his entrance, he stepped out in plain view, and the stadium rocked in applause. A chain of whispering also ignited throughout the crowd, for Octavia had appeared standing beside Nero, to everyone's astonishment. They took their seats, and when the obligatory opening rituals were completed, Nero nodded for the first contestants to enter the arena.

The early roots of Rome's gladiatorial contests traced back to the days of the republic more than a century earlier, when wealthy landowners entertained guests by calling for pairs of their slaves to compete in a makeshift ring. The bouts were violent but not mortal, until it was discovered that a fight to the death produced a livelier response in the audience. Just as horse-breeders became attached to a favorite animal who promised success in a race, so the aristocrats began boasting in the notoriety of certain of their slaves who showed ability in the ring. Inevitably, they began to bring their slaves together for intentional competitions, using every festival and holiday as an opportunity to hold games, and soon, a festival was not considered complete without the games. The gladiatorial schools were born.

Certain slaves rose to prominence for their prowess as warriors, and when the Julian monarchy began, Caesar began to bring selected gladiators into his service for his own games. Eventually, the entire system was ratified, then consolidated by the emperor, who in time, made sure the largest, bloodiest and most glamorous games were his own. And as it evolved, the entire beast was fed and empowered by the people, whose blood-lust had been aroused, and now could not be sated. They clamored for more and more games, as drunkards for liquor. So the passion for violence grew and would never be contained, until it had utterly exhausted the moral reserve of the Roman people, and left them in ruins three centuries later.

This same spirit was unleashed again as the first combatants emerged from the tunnels to the deafening roar of the crowd. Most of the early bouts were essentially jerry-rigged executions. Some of Rome's finest fighters—fully armed with shields and weaponry—were pit against a string of condemned criminals, who were virtually naked and unarmed though they each were given small, flimsy spears. The real competition was not between the gladiator and the condemned, but between the gladiators themselves as they raced one another to see who could dispatch of his victim in the swiftest time. An elusive criminal who ran from his fate could induce a shower of catcalls from the stands, as did those who failed to live up to their civic duty to defend themselves.

The second round of fights were more for those who enjoyed the sport of the contests, as warriors with equal strength and equipment fought to the death. Occasionally, if a combatant were severely wounded, the victor would seek the will of the emperor by turning to Caesar as his sword stood poised to kill. Nero relished these moments, for the life of the conquered warrior literally hung in the balance of his thumb, whether it tipped up or down, as was his pleasure. The crowd politely applauded Caesar's mercy when granted, but were far more animated when it wasn't.

On this day, Nero had sequestered his usual battery of attendants in his box with him, including Seneca and Burrus, and the surprising addition of Octavia who had not been seen in public for weeks. They sat side by side in the front row, with Nero hanging ravenously over the wall and Octavia drawn back, looking pale. Tigellinus and Anicetus lurked behind them beneath the canopy, like a pair of twin gargoyles.

"What is it about violence that is so fascinating?" Nero mused, as he watched two of the warriors clash swords.

Octavia continued looking away. She didn't know if Nero was speaking to her or to himself, but she answered anyway, in a bold tone of disgust. "There is nothing fascinating about it. It's offensive. And you've seen so much of it, you've become numb to it." She grabbed the armrests of her chair as though to stand. "I must go, Nero. Please let me leave."

"No!" he said swiftly, reaching out his hand to stop her. "I insist that you stay. The people expect to see us together today as we move house. The people expect to see us in love today, Octavia." He flashed his eyes at her in a lazy, lustful manner that sickened her worse than the violence below. "We must not disappoint the people now." He then turned and caught the attention of Seneca, and shouted back to him, "The people, right Seneca?"

Suddenly a cheer went up from the crowd, and Nero quickly looked back to the contest, and joined in their excitement, for one of the gladiators had brought the other to the ground with a sweeping swing of his sword.

"Nicely done!" the emperor shouted.

The felled warrior however was more stunned than wounded, and with surprising speed, he picked himself up and retrieved his sword, and then to the confusion of the crowd, he began running away from his opponent in the direction of Nero's booth. At first the people booed in displeasure, thinking that he was running to save his life. Nero himself tipped his head in confusion as the man approached. He was accustomed to prisoners making appeals before him, but this warrior seemed to have another purpose.

What happened next was over and done within seconds, but the blur of danger which suddenly overwhelmed those in the box seemed to unfold at half-speed. The man quickened his step as he approached the box, and with a forceful leap, he sprang with one foot onto the podium wall, and with his free left hand, managed to latch on to its top. His grip was sure enough that he was able to bring his sword hurling at Nero, who fell backwards in his chair to the ground to avoid the blow. The blade missed by several inches, and in the split second the gladiator needed to adjust his grip on the wall so as to strike again, Tigellinus bolted to Nero's side with his own sword blazing.

It hissed as it cut through the air, and when it struck the slave, the force was such that it partially severed his left arm and sent him flying back onto the arena floor, where he landed in a stunned and motionless pile. As this happened, Octavia screamed and fled to the rear of the booth. The buzzing of the crowd was the strangest of sounds that had ever been heard in the Circus, as the people waited to see if Nero had been hurt.

Tigellinus leaned over and helped Nero to his feet. His white outer robe was stained with the gladiator's blood, and he shook uncontrollably.

"Nero, are you wounded?" Tigellinus asked.

"No," he said, his voice quivering. He adjusted his garments, pushed Tigellinus aside and approached the edge of the wall. The gladiator was rolling in agony on the sand, with a rapidly growing pool of blood forming under his wounded arm, yet when he saw the emperor's face, he managed to summon his energy long enough to unfurl a string of epithets at him.

"You demon!" he yelled with bitter venom. "You've destroyed my family! You've destroyed my people! May the gods destroy you!"

His head fell back onto the sand in a fog of pain. Nero suppressed his shaking and with quiet authority said to the man, "I'm afraid you have brought destruction only on yourself today."

By this time, the second gladiator had drawn near to this bizarre scene, unsure of what to do but with his sword still firmly in hand. Nero drew his attention and pointed down to the wounded man. "Gladiator, kill this man here and now, and you shall have your freedom."

Hearing this pronouncement along with its promise, the gladiator needed no further incentive. He raised his sword and without hesitation, brought it down on the other's neck, and the beheading was completed with ruthless efficiency. Nero looked at his guards standing behind him. "Release this man at once with a full pardon." Applause began to echo through the stadium as the crowd realized that Caesar had survived. Burrus and Seneca stepped closer to Nero.

"Lord Nero, were you struck?" Burrus asked.

"No," Nero said flatly as he brushed himself off. "Gentlemen, my thanks for your swift and instinctive actions. Tigellinus, again I am in your debt. I do believe you want Burrus' post."

Seneca looked at Burrus who was not amused. "I ought to remind you, Caesar, that we have told you before that your booth was too close to the arena floor," he said.

"Too close?" Nero asked with a slight scoff. "Has anyone been cut or wounded? We've had a bit of drama, that's all. Let's all clean ourselves up and carry on. Octavia and I are moving into our new home, and the people await its dedication. Carry on with the program." He saw Octavia huddled in the back and beckoned for her to come to him. "Octavia, please join me." She shuddered. "*Now!*" he demanded.

She slinked toward him and reluctantly took her seat beside him. Arena attendants brought both a litter and basket out onto the floor to pick up the remains of the dead man, and as they did so, Nero watched with strange fascination.

"Death is so mysterious," he mused to those around him. "What happens when a man draws his last breath? What does he see and feel at the split second when the pain of life and the silence of death intersect? Look at this man. Just seconds ago he was here breathing our air, blinking at our sun, and now in an instant of time, he has traveled to another place. Where does he go? To non-existence? To another life? I'm almost jealous of him. Brave fool, who is now greater than Caesar."

He reached out and tapped Octavia's arm as the dead man's head was picked up by its hair and dropped unceremoniously into the basket. "Octavia, look at the face of this newly crowned god. Oh Octavia, violence is so poetic. It is in its own way beautiful." She ignored his rambling dialectic, and retreated within her own imagination, even wishing that she could die, if only to escape this nightmare existence which her life had become.

The bouts continued for another hour, and then a break was taken for lunch before the chariot race began. At the urging of his friends, Nero had decided not to participate in the race, not because of its impropriety, but because he was still simply unprepared for the arena. Even Tigellinus encouraged him to postpone his plans until he had gained more experience. Nero reluctantly agreed, but only on the condition that an alternative demonstration be made. One way or another, he would introduce his chariot to Rome.

The chariot race was considered by most to be the true highlight of the games. The pounding rhythm of the steeds and the poetic motion of the carriages were irresistible when watched. Not content though with what the Greeks bequeathed them in this sport, the Romans added their own violent innovations. Charioteers were encouraged to eliminate their competition with sudden cut-offs into the wall, intentional sideswipes, or by riding up on their opponents wheels to snap them off. The crowd admired the fast charioteer but adored the ruthless one.

On this day, eight drivers competed for the laurel wreath, and Nero watched them with undiluted envy as they took their stations in preparation for him to drop the handkerchief signaling the race's start. He felt the temptation to throw away the handkerchief, leap over the wall and order one of the charioteers to step aside that he might take the reins, but somehow he was able to admit that this was not his moment to command. Soon his skills would ripen and he would join his brothers in the arena. But not yet. He lifted the handkerchief high, allowed it to dangle for one melodramatic moment, and then let it fall.

The thunder of the horses' hooves was initially drowned out by the thunder of the spectators' cheering, but as the race progressed, they grew quiet to save their throats for the final lap. Like every athlete who had ever been sidelined against his will, Nero saw every mistake that was made and found ample evidence for why he was more deserving to be in action than any of the other drivers. As the race unfolded, he became thoroughly disgusted with the whole field, and considered the front-runner to be so bone-headed, it was beyond reason to understand how he could be in the lead. Nero shouted obscenities at each one as he swept past his booth.

The yells of the people built into a crescendo as the end of the race drew near. Not a person remained seated as the horses cascaded into the final lap, and then furiously bore down on the finish cord that had been stretched across the track from the emperor's seat. Somehow, even Nero forgot himself and was caught up in the simple pleasure of the race, and as they poured past the finish like a rush of wind, for the shortest of seconds he was just a spectator savoring the exhilaration of the moment.

But as the dust of the track settled, this ember of humility also fell to the ground and disappeared. As the winner began to canter once more around the *spina* for his victory lap, Nero thought to himself how ridiculously easy it would be to surpass the ability of this so-called *champion*. And by the time the winner reached Nero's box to receive Caesar's recognition, Nero despised the fortunate bastard outright.

Portable steps were wheeled up to the Caesar's booth, and the victorious charioteer solemnly climbed them and then kneeled before his emperor, who reluctantly placed the wreath upon his head. Nero quickly stifled the eruption of applause which the crowd had begun offering the man, and then with a rude wave of his hand, he prematurely dismissed the odious victor from his presence. The next moment belonged to Caesar.

His own chariot and team of horses were brought into the arena and driven to the emperor's box. Two attendants brought to Nero a bright red and yellow charioteer's cloak and they placed it on him as he stood motionless. Before the day began, rumors had spread through the streets that Caesar would ride his chariot at some point in the festivities, and as the crowd realized that the rumors were true, they began to roar their approval.

Once the garment was securely in place, Nero summoned Octavia to come to his side, and the cheering rang louder yet for they loved her most of all Rome's treasures. The display of affection nearly moved her to tears but the comfort was not lasting. To be a goddess adored by tens of thousands was the loneliest of existences. She did not want to be worshipped, but loved. They praised her for her beauty, but inside she felt as ugly as a leprous hag. They cherished her for her innocence, but no one in that arena felt more fearful of the sword of judgment than she. To them, she was a caricature of virtue and no person at all; to Nero, she was a whore and no woman at all. Her family had been eliminated one by one until she was no longer sister, daughter or cousin to anyone. To her servants she was unknown, for Nero continually rotated her staff of attendants. To all the rest she was mere contagion, who would bring death if they drew too close to her.

Nero did not intend to showcase Octavia, so he drew her to his side and led her down the steps to the floor of the arena. They stepped into the chariot and then Nero took the reins from a slave who had been steadying the horses. With a flick of his wrists, he set the team in motion. He drove them repeatedly around the arena, as the multitudes hailed him as their divine lord. The roar of their worship was like a mighty cataract, and Nero immersed himself in it.

Hundreds of flowers, bushels of fruit, garments and cloaks were all strewn on the sand before them, and when he was fully satisfied with their submission, he directed the chariot into a tunnel which led beneath the Circus and out into the streets. Musicians blasted their trumpets to announce the beginning of the imperial procession which would lead them to the new palace, and those inside the arena rushed as quickly as possible outside to follow.

The journey to the Domus Aurea took nearly an hour. It was built behind the original palaces of the Caesar's (which overlooked the Circus Maximus on the

Palatine Hill) and was accessed by the *Sacra Via*. The main palace rested on forty acres which had formerly been nothing but public warehouses. These Nero purchased and leveled. Surrounding it was a residential district of row after row of privately owned houses. Nero desperately wanted the additional acreage for his palace, but he was unable to convince whole sections of owners to sell and so had to settle for the public lands. In time though, he would get his wish, and the Domus Aurea would be expanded to four times its size. Nero was not one to let his dreams go up in smoke.

Nero drove his chariot up the Capitoline Hill, then through the Forum, and finally along the *Sacra Via* where the first reflections of the late afternoon sun could be seen up ahead, blazing off the gold and bronze roof of the palace (and hence its name Domus Aurea—*Golden House.*) But what caught the eyes of the people first as they began pouring through the massive stone and iron gates which framed the borders of the compound was not the palace, but the towering statue of Nero himself—the *Colossus*—rising up more than a hundred feet from the exotic rock gardens which surrounded the house.

Around it were at least a dozen cherubic fountains, spouting streams of water up to the statue's knees. The water then dribbled down into a crystal pool, which faithfully reflected the splendor of the sculpted marble. Not one pair of eyes which passed through the gates failed to survey the height of the *Colossus*, and it left the viewer blinking and gasping in wonder. Only when one's neck grew tired of craning back to gape at the statue, did the real glory of Caesar's home become evident—the palace itself.

Nothing like it had ever been built. It was an explosion of architectural styles thrust together in one structure. Spread out before the palace were thousands of agate tiles laid delicately into place, like a sheet of ocean water rolled out on a beach, and on each individual tile was chiseled a scene from a story in ancient mythology. Free-standing pillars jutted twenty feet high in front of an ascending staircase, which rose up in groups of five steps each. After every fifth step was a ten-foot long track of granite and positioned along the entire length of the track were sculptures of animals, humans, and mixtures in between, each one lifelike and each one by itself a priceless work of art.

Hundreds lined the steps. Seen from below, the statues seemed to stand guard over the palace like a legion of soldiers, frozen in eerie silence. To walk between their ranks as one climbed up to the palace was intimidating, and that person was exceptionally brave who could do so without at least once looking over his shoulder.

More pillars spread out at the top of the staircase, and these supported a canopied ambulatory which framed the front of the expansive portico, and finally, the palace itself was entered through a set of massive oak doors which had each been coated with gold and silver plating.

Nero escorted the multitude past the *Colossus*, then he and Octavia dismounted and walked across the tiling—he strutting, she dragging. Hundreds of soldiers stood perched as a gauntlet for them to pass through. They walked through the garrison of statues to the top of the staircase where more attendants and dignitaries awaited them. A solitary throne had been placed beneath the center of the portico, and Nero proudly turned to seat himself on it where he could oversee the entire mass of humanity spread out before him. They poured endlessly through the gates and pillars and filled every pocket of space on the grounds below.

Nero motioned for Octavia to stand beside him. Dozens of large oil pots were rolled out in single file and distributed symmetrically across the length of the palace, and then at Caesar's signal, they were all simultaneously set afire. For those below looking up at this surreal scene, it was as though they were looking up into the very throneroom of Olympus, and Nero was Jupiter himself, seated in judgment, ready to hurl lighting bolts from his hand.

Nero never felt more powerful than he did at this moment. He turned to Octavia, who never felt more helpless, and said loudly so as to be heard above the shouting of the people below, "At last I am being housed like a human being."

He thrust his fist up into the air and the shouting reverberated with even greater enthusiasm across the hills of Rome.

*   *   *

The revelry continued long into the night. Nero made sure that his reputation as the finest showman of Rome's Caesars was reinforced. He threw open his private gardens for the citizens and rode among them in his chariot while dressed up in costumes, handing out gifts, money and wine with complete abandonment. Stages were scattered throughout the gardens, where musicians and magicians performed around the clock. People thronged to the zoo which Nero erected and gawked at the panthers, alligators, elephants, apes and other exotic creatures. It was a perfect carnival atmosphere, brought to a close only by a sudden and steady thunderstorm which sent the people scattering to their homes.

When Nero returned to the palace, it was well past midnight. He was alone except for his bodyguards. Octavia had lost her usefulness much earlier and he had dismissed her. The vestibule to the palace was a large, circular room accessible to every floor through interlacing staircases, with a domed ceiling that reached to the palace's highest point. Nero staggered noisily in his wet shoes across the floor, heading toward his private chambers, feeling the effects of the flagon of wine which he dangled carelessly at his side. He heard footsteps up above him, and looked up to see one of Octavia's servants crossing into another wing of the palace. The thought of Octavia aroused him.

"You there," he slurred, and the servant looked down on him. "What is your name?"

"Julia, my lord," the servant timidly responded. She was an older woman with thick, gray hair, bound elegantly with a colorful scarf.

"Julia, of course. You've served in my house for years." The emperor belched. "Is the empress in her chambers?"

"Yes, Lord Nero."

"Have her brought to me at once," and he lowered his head and stumbled toward his own room. His guards took their post at his doorway as he entered the apartment alone. It was divided into three interlocking rooms, the first being a large sitting room, amply and beautifully furnished for the comfort of at least a dozen people. Nero was pleased to see a fire already glowing warmly in the fireplace as walked in.

He stopped to warm himself and stripped off all his drenched clothing which he scattered about the hearth, then walked into his bedroom. After pulling a robe out of a closet, he snatched up his wine and headed into the third room, the sauna, where a walk-in bath was ordered to be kept perpetually filled with hot water. He dipped his leg into the steamy water, and smiled to find it satisfactorily warm. He slithered down into the water and planted himself on a submerged bench with his back to the door.

The warmth, the alcohol, the lateness of the evening combined to overwhelm him with sleepiness, and his eyes closed. The sounds of the day played over in his mind. The swords. The trumpets. The chariot wheels. The screams. Nero's head snapped back involuntarily as he thought of the attack upon him. Octavia's beautiful face then flashed across his mind. Then he heard the chanting of praise which echoed through the arena. "Nero! Nero!" Over and again, he saw their faces, their hands extended in submission to him, and how they rushed after him in the streets as the procession led to the palace. Their nameless faces. "Nero! Nero!" They lined the streets just to catch a glimpse of him. Young and old were there crying out to him. "Nero! Nero!" But it was a solitary voice now. A woman's voice. A voice deep and familiar, and the intonation was somehow off-key, and harsh. His face snapped back again as he traced the crowd of faces. Who said that? "*Nero! Nero!*" It grew louder. The faces rushed by in a blur. His head began to pound to make sense of it. His breath grew short. In a start, his eyes opened.

Agrippina's bloody body was floating in the bath right in front of him. A knife was wedged deeply into her stomach, and her intestines were worming out from the wound. Her eyes were closed, her face was pale with death, but her lips were moving. "*Nero! Nero!*" she moaned. Nero screamed out, his arms flailing wildly in the water, as he struggled to climb out of the bath. He grabbed hold of the edge and frantically pulled out of the water, and rolled away in desperation from its edge, as though his skin were on fire. He managed to scramble to his feet, and looked back at the water, his heart heaving with terror. There was nothing there. The vision was gone.

He inched toward the pool until he was standing above it. The tossing of the bathwater was slowly subsiding, and except for the water he had splashed on the walls and floor, there was no sign of a disturbance. He touched his skin which was still crawling at the thought of the apparition.

"You drunken idiot!" he said to himself. He reached down to pick up the flagon of wine at his feet, and looked tentatively into the cup as though he might see her face even there. He then looked down into the pool again, and suddenly in a fit of anger, as though to exorcise his fear, he whirled around and hurled the flagon from him with such force that it flew out of the sauna, through the bedroom and clattered on the tiled floor out in the lounge. He pulled the robe over his chilled body, and fled the room, only to be startled again, because Octavia was standing before the fire looking at him. The flagon had rolled on the floor to her feet. She reached down, picked it up and held it up to him.

"Nero, you are tired, and drunk apparently," she said. She stood draped in a thick white gown, her hair was slightly disheveled, and her feet were slippered. She set the flagon down on the hearth, and pulled her gown tighter around her, as though to shield her body from Nero's gaze, but his eyes bore into her.

For a moment, he was unsure of what to say. He felt unable to grapple with the cross-current of emotions surging through him. Fear, anger and lust inter-twined together, and he could not get a firm grip on any one of them. Part of him even felt like taking hold of Octavia and weeping like a child at her feet, admitting his vulnerability, confessing his weakness and letting her run her fingers through his hair. But anger was his soul's dominant emotion, and when it was given time to grapple with the weaker spirits within him, it usually brought them to heel, and restored order to his psyche.

And so it happened here. As he looked at her, the tenderness and vulnerability vanished from his eyes. Octavia was no soul-mate or equal. She existed for him and he could do with her as he pleased. What he wanted from her now was not her comfort but her body. And he would have it.

"Empress, I am tired, and only partially drunk," he said. "But what I am most is intoxicated with passion to lie down with you." He held out his hand for her, and she shook with near revulsion. Her hesitation enraged him. "That's not a request!" he barked with fury in his voice.

She looked down, but Nero was only maddened further by this appearance of weakness. Poppaea could stand up to him and mock him to his face, which made her all the more irresistible, and made his conquering of her all the more deli-cious. But Octavia was as frustrating as walking up a sand dune which gives way as soon as it's stepped on. Such wilting, pathetic feebleness. He charged toward her and grabbed her arm, then pulled her forcefully into his bedroom where he whipped her violently onto the bed. "Remove your gown!" he ordered, but she groaned and rolled her head back and forth. He leaned over and caught her cheeks in the vice-like grip of his right hand and shook her face.

"You will freely receive me!" he seethed. "Rome worships me as a god. You will at least receive me as a husband. Why do you always resist me!" He released his hold, and viciously slapped her. "You always resist me!" he roared.

Her gown had risen up on the bed and he saw the bare flesh of her legs exposed beneath him, and immediately his livid face softened. It was for this reason that he needed her. No woman in Rome was as beautiful as she. Each of her physical features was flawless. He knew every curve of her body. Every part of her he had touched and tasted, and if only she would love him and receive him, then this ridiculous warfare could cease, and they could rule Rome together as Caesar and his queen. He placed his hand tenderly on her leg.

"Octavia," he said with softness and regret. "Why can't we just be friends?" His eyes surveyed her body, as his fingers slid down her calf to her feet, where he loosened her slipper and dropped it to the floor. "Friends. Just like we were as children."

His hand now probed higher up her leg beneath the gown, and suddenly, she bolted as though poked with a needle, and scrambled away from him, falling onto the floor in the process. She lay crumbled on the floor, her long hair hanging down like a veil around her head.

"You are not the one I knew as a child," she said with a fatigued voice. "I mean nothing to you. You are drunk with power. Just like your mother."

The mentioning of Agrippina stunned Nero like a hammer-blow between the eyes. At once he was in the bath again, pinned in by her floating corpse. He leaped to his feet. "Do not defame the memory of my mother!" He walked over to her, and pointed his finger like a dagger down on her. "She gave you nurture and care and—"

"She did nothing but ruin my life!" Octavia screamed through her tears, as she rose up on her hands and knees. "And now I am alone in this world."

Nero took a step back, and then his eyes became black. His head began to intently nod in angry agreement. "Yes you are alone, because you wish to be," he slowly said. "And so you deny me affection, when you owe it to me. And you deny me children, when you owe them to me. You are not my wife." His voice was rising in intensity. "You are residue from the house of Claudius which I will wipe from me!"

These last words erupted from his mouth, and came accompanied by a potent kick to her stomach. She screamed and rolled away, but he pursued her and slapped her repeatedly as she held up her hands in front of her face to ward him off. Finally, he reached down and grabbed her by the shoulders and hoisted her to her feet, and with a violent heave, he tossed her from the room so that she dropped sharply onto the hard floor of the sitting room, ripping both knees as she fell. Nero came to the doorway.

"Return to your chambers! You do not belong in this house, and you do not belong to me! Leave. Leave! Before I kill you tonight!"

She pulled herself to her feet and ran from the room, past the guards who stood outside the apartment silent and still, holding back gulps of nervous fear that were welling in their throats. Nero turned to walk back into his bedroom, and in rage, picked up a porcelain vase displayed by the doorway and flung it uncontrollably against the masonry of the fireplace. It exploded into thousands of shards which scattered across the floor. Both guards winced, and stayed motionless at their posts.

Octavia didn't stop running until she was within her own apartment, but even there she felt no safety or comfort. The guards who stood watch outside her door could as easily have been executioners. The room was new and uncertain to her; there was nothing, not even one blanket, which was familiar. Nero refused to allow anything into the *Domus Aurea* which carried even a hint of the old palace. Her wardrobe had been completely replaced. A collection of dolls she had collected since she was a child was auctioned away. He commanded soldiers to ransack her personal effects and burn any correspondence they found. All traces of her past had been eliminated. As she ran into the apartment, she even forgot which chamber her bed was in. Once she found it, she threw herself down upon it and wept inconsolably.

As Octavia tossed on the bed to the point of insensibility, Julia came into the apartment carrying a pitcher of water, and when she heard the sobs coming from the sleeping chambers, she quickly set the pitcher down and hurried toward the room. The sight of Octavia's shaking body filled her heart with pity, and she rushed to her side.

"Empress Octavia, don't cry darling," she said, sitting down on the bed and reaching out to embrace her. Octavia was limp in her arms, and Julia gathered her into her bosom, and gently rocked her. "Don't cry, dear one. Oh child, you are so weary with grief."

There were tears bottled up inside of Octavia that only a mother could bring out, and with Julia there to comfort her, the river of emotion poured out from her as though through a burst dam. Though Nero had tried to stagger Octavia's attendants, he was not able to bring in new servants each and every week. Julia was a faithful slave who had served in Caesar's household since before Octavia was born.

Their relationship had always been special, and somehow it seemed redemptively appropriate that Julia was there on this evening when Octavia needed her most. Slowly, the quaking in Octavia's breast subsided, and she looked up at Julia with eyes so deep and beautiful, that not even the sorrow which had wrenched them could hide the true beauty of a princess which was there.

"My child, you're hurt," Julia said, looking at the two rivulets of blood running down both legs. She rushed off, and brought back some damp cloths, which she used to wash her legs. "Hold these on your knees, dear one, till the bleeding stops," she gently instructed, and Octavia complied. Julia stroked her face and tenderly traced the outlines of Nero's handprint left on her face. Striking her was unnecessary. Nero had been slowly killing her long before he raised his hands against her.

Octavia finally spoke. "Julia. I am alone. Without a friend in the world. He will kill me. I know he will kill me. I cannot pretend to love him, and yet if I refuse him, then he will destroy me."

Julia tightened her embrace. "My child, how my heart has broken for you all these years."

"Oh Julia, you're the only one I have left. And why he has let you stay I cannot imagine. You have loved me as my own mother would have." Julia handed her a kerchief and Octavia wiped her eyes and nose with it. "What can I do? I cannot stay here. And I cannot flee. And there is no place for me to hide. I am cornered and death is all that can deliver me. If you find me a vial of poison, Julia, I would readily drink it."

"Empress, don't mention such things!" said Julia with a start.

"But suicide is a noble way to finish one's life," Octavia continued, though she was hardly convinced by her own words. "And if I take my own life, then at least there will be one thing that he cannot take away from me himself."

"Suicide is the coward's way, child," Julia countered. "It is to spit in the face of God who gives us life."

"But look at the life I have been given! You have told me before that your God is like a father, but what kind of father would give this to his child? This misery! I am damned already. What have I done that I deserve such wretchedness?" Octavia's pain pricked Julia's heart.

"Dear one, life is full of mysteries I cannot explain. But at the heart of our faith is the belief that our God suffers with us. And through his only son Jesus, we believe that God even suffered for us. Maybe that's not an answer, but it is a comfort."

"How is that a comfort, Julia?" Octavia asked. "In your religion, Rome is so powerful, not even your God could stop it from executing his son. That makes me despair all the more."

"But child don't you remember what I've told you? Jesus laid down his life. It wasn't taken from him. He gave it away freely. And his resurrection proves that he has far more power than Rome."

"I'm glad you are happy, my Julia," said Octavia sadly, "but for a Roman princess to find hope in a Jewish carpenter is a bit odd, don't you think? If I want to find comfort in fairy tales, there are plenty of Roman legends to choose from."

"But are any of your legends proven by the testimony of eyewitnesses?" asked Julia, as she checked Octavia's knees and then took away the cloths. "In our community are numerous men and women who have seen the Lord Jesus after his death. Come and talk to them. Come and listen to them. They may help you to understand. They may even be able to help you in this situation."

Octavia shook her head. "Anyone who helps me will risk falling under his wrath. I don't know of anyone who does not tremble before the Emperor."

"I know hundreds who are not afraid of him," Julia quickly retorted. "Hundreds who would gladly risk everything to save you from evil. I know a place where you can still find love and peace. Empress, our people are meeting soon for a special gathering. Let me take you there and show you my people. I'm sure they can help. They can show you that there really is a God who cares."

Octavia wiped her nose again, and feebly nodded her head. In her desert of despair, Julia's invitation was one dry blade of hope yet waving in the wind.

*   *   *

Nero was unable to sleep the rest of the night. He tossed between haunting glimpses of the past and irritating portraits of the present, and when he finally stalked from his bedroom the next morning, he was determined to address both past and present by taking firm control of the future. He convinced himself that Octavia was the remaining burr in his side, and only after she was removed could he find the true glory that awaited him as Caesar. She was the one holding Rome hostage to its past, when a much greater destiny awaited it. Whenever he would take Rome a step forward, one sight of her cast a pall over the people, a spell of brooding reminiscence which sent the nation two steps back. No doubt, she was responsible for the rain that ruined his party the night before.

Nero's first task was to dispatch messengers to go and gather his full assembly of advisers. The matter could not be postponed any longer. He waited impatiently in his counseling room for them to respond, and within an hour, they had each arrived, both the old guard of Seneca and Burrus, and the new guard of Tigellinus, Anicetus and a few others, similarly young and brazen in spirit.

"I will not keep you gentlemen in suspense as to why I have called you here this morning," Nero began. "Last night, my wife Octavia refused me—again. She prefers the solitude of her private chambers to sharing a bed with her husband. I am building for her a palace greater than that which any queen in history has had, and yet on the first night, the very first night we take occupancy of our new home, she does not thank me, she does not show the least bit of appreciation, instead she shuns me! Even at the Circus, she begged to leave my side. And at the dedication following, I had to coerce her to come along to every place we went. She is like a horse who pulls back on the reins at every point. And last night, when I sought her for one gentle touch, one simple token of affection, she refused."

His face sagged with tiredness, his hair was unkempt, his forehead was rigid and red. His body and soul were in perfect alignment.

"My friends, this has gone far enough. And long enough. I have borne with her idiosyncrasies far longer than any ordinary man. Oh, I have looked elsewhere from time to time for relief and companionship. I will not deny you that in moments of impatience, I have turned to other women to give me what Octavia denies. I am more than open about my failings with you all. But the time for change is past. The time for wishful thinking is past. My love for this woman has been utterly quenched. Exhausted, extinguished beyond recovery. And so I have summoned you to ask for your counsel."

Anicetus was quick to speak the words that Nero had planted in his mouth earlier. "Your patience should be rewarded, my lord, and her impertinence should be punished."

"Impertinence? You are too compassionate," Tigellinus remarked. "Her actions are criminal, plainly and simply. Any normal husband would be perfectly justified in putting away a woman such as this. Caesar not only has the right, but the duty to remove her—permanently."

His voice rang cold to the others in the room, especially Burrus. As prefect of the Praetorian Guard, he was sworn to defend the lives and honor of Caesar's household. As Nero had continued his descent into depravity, he gradually forfeited the honor of the leading officers in his Guard, and soon, Burrus found only one member of Caesar's house worthy of defense and protection—Octavia.

Anicetus spoke again. "One is forced to wonder by this behavior if she herself is—how can I put this delicately, Caesar?—*engaged in little side interests*? Her disinterest in you surely means her interests are toward another man, unless of course—but, who am I to imagine such things?"

"Anicetus, your tongue wags," Nero said bluntly. "But in your rambling you speak truth. Adultery is one explanation."

Seneca felt compelled to speak before he lost influence in the conversation altogether. "But can adultery be proven?"

"Has it not been proven already by this mountain of circumstantial evidence?" asked Tigellinus in a condescending tone, and Seneca backed down. "And adultery against the emperor, of all people, is deserving of the severest of penalties. The honor of Caesar's throne must be upheld." He turned to Burrus with the same swaggering air. "Prefect, this situation clearly falls under your jurisdiction. It is your responsibility to bring this matter to the attention of the Senate, and then enact their just decrees."

Burrus did not back down. He was once again a general on the field of battle. "Don't tell me my duties, soldier!" he snapped with such authority that Tigellinus' own throat went temporarily dry at the challenge.

Burrus eyed Nero with a firm and unblinking gaze. "Caesar, the Praetorian Guard will not commit a crime against the empress. We will not raise our hands against a descendant of Germanicus or a daughter of Claudius. The Guard will not be your instrument of execution. And when I have once pronounced on a matter, do not ask me again!"

A stunned silence filled the room. Even Nero was taken back by Burrus' vigor.

"Prefect, would you approve of a divorce?" he asked tentatively.

"Then give her back her dowry!" Burrus shouted.

Tigellinus scoffed. "You mean her throne?" he asked.

No one dared to speak further, until Nero broke the stillness with a surprisingly reserved voice.

"Prefect, your temper borders on insubordination. But I will overlook your emotions. I know that you care for Octavia, as I do. But this is not a situation where emotions matter. We are talking sternly and bold-faced about the political health of the empire. My wife does not love me. And she is unable or unwilling to give me an heir. Simple logic dictates what must happen. Master Seneca, you will agree?"

Seneca struggled with his reply. The absence of children was sadly one reality that stood in Caesar's favor, like a monument of stone which all could see. The public might debate the reasons this was so, but Nero's interpretation would not be seriously challenged. "Yes or no?" the emperor asked sharply as Seneca hesitated.

"Of course, yes," Seneca weakly offered, but he looked down to avoid Burrus' burning stare. "But a trial and execution is overblown. The Senate would unquestionably approve a divorce and exile, but..."

"An exile!" Tigellinus gasped. "Your universal remedy for all of life's problems."

"Eight years of exile did not keep you from returning to power, Seneca," Anicetus said. "And it won't keep her from coming back either."

Burrus' voice rang out again. "She could care less about power and government. Octavia is not a threat."

Tigellinus, recovering his forceful edge and having muted Seneca, now set his sights on conquering Burrus. "But there are those who would use her that are threats," he said. "We have an obligation to eliminate even the hint of temptation from those we might consider enemies. If not legal execution, then there are other ways the state has of defending itself. Ways that are swift and efficient."

Anicetus raised his hand. "Emperor, my men and I are always at your disposal. Give the command, and we will carry out your will."

Burrus could not restrain his disappointment or his distress. He rose to his feet with an exhalation of disgust. "Then let Anicetus fulfill his promise and leave my Guard out of this!" He stormed from the room, slamming the heavy door shut so that every window rattled.

Nero and Tigellinus looked at each other, and in the glance shared a deep understanding of what they both knew to be true but had seldom expressed—Burrus was

a growing, malignant liability. Silence returned to the room, and again Caesar broke it.

"Anicetus, you heard the Prefect. Fulfill your promise. Do it soon. Days not weeks, understood?" Anicetus nodded with a surly, eager grin. Nero began pacing around the room, as he usually did when he was nervous or lost in thought.

"It would be nice if we could one day get beyond these obstacles of power and politics and get down to the business of moving this empire forward. I'm so tired of this," he said, rubbing his throbbing forehead. "There's so much that I want to do, and yet we seem to always be getting bogged down with trivialities. Why does life have to be one battle after another? Why is our history the endless chronicle of one war after another? Life is given to us to be enjoyed. We are put here to drink in of the pleasures the gods pour out on us. But we fritter our time away in conflict. We act as though it is our destiny to be miserable, when happiness should be our aim. The Stoics have had their day in the sun. Let Epicurus now rule! Let our citizens stop to enjoy the fruits of their conquests and labor."

The others knew it was their duty to listen, and so they sat in attentive stillness.

"You all know that next year I plan to host my second *Neronia* in Neapolis, and I intend to pattern my games after the Olympiad of our Grecian brothers, which will be held the following year. Soon, I hope we will put to rest the annual celebrations of our military triumphs, as though these were the highest achievements of our empire, and start celebrating the true triumphs which matter most—the conquests of the Roman spirit. One day I hope we can host such glorious competitions every year! I will lead the way, as Caesar rightfully should. And so I fully intend to compete in our games next year. But now the problem—who has time to devote to training when I must superintend every jot and tittle of the empire's business? Is the Senate incapable of fulfilling its duties? It is such an anemic body!"

As he walked about the room, he passed a small table where several scrolls were piled up in a basket. He looked through the scrolls and then picked one up. "Now look at these Senate cases that I am asked to judge this month. Are our consuls home asleep? Are our praetors lying in sickbeds? Why such inactivity!"

He unfolded the scroll and read from it. "The case of Pratis Andronicus—an inheritance issue. What do I care?" He threw the scroll to the floor and unfolded another. "The case of Gaius Verritus—stirring up sedition in Campania. Enforce our existing laws and be done with it. Why am I needed for this?" He picked up a third scroll. "The case of Paul of Tarsus, defended by Quintus Arrius against the Jews of Judea. A religious squabble! Grown men bickering over imaginary gods. What a pathetic waste of time!" He tossed the scroll back into the basket.

Seneca spoke. "There are solutions, emperor. If you wish, we could—", but Nero suddenly cut him off.

"Wait a minute." He snatched the scroll back up and opened it again. "Quintus Arrius? Wasn't he an advocate in the Senate several years ago?"

The others shrugged their shoulders, but Seneca nodded. "Yes, during the days of Claudius. If it's the same man, he is Quintus Arrius the Younger, having been adopted years before by—", and again Nero interrupted.

"And he was the one who raced chariots early in his career. In fact, he was the champion of the Circus three or four seasons consecutively. He couldn't be beat. A feat that hasn't been equaled since. It's an unprecedented achievement."

"I'm sure it's the same man," Seneca said, with certain relief that the conversation had turned in a more inoffensive direction.

"And to think he is right here in Rome," said Nero, with a sudden spark in his words. "I wouldn't mind visiting with Counsel Arrius and picking his brain about racing. Perhaps I have even found my trainer."

He turned to one of his lesser assistants who had been sitting quietly throughout the consultation. "Send for him."

Chapter 8

In the early days of Christianity, the word *church* referred to people, not buildings. The first Christians were generally poor and owned little property, and so when they met for worship, it was usually in each other's homes. In this way, the church spread throughout the empire as a network of house congregations, and so it was in Rome. However, property outside of the city had been donated to the Roman congregation by one of its members, and in time, a modest amphitheater was built on it which adequately seated the entire congregation of a thousand Christians. With this provision, the church was able to meet peridically for special occasions. The Sunday following the dedication of the Domus Aurea was such a time, as the church was called together as one body to say goodbye to Judah and Esther, who would be boarding a ship for Judea in three days.

The farewell service was to begin at sundown, but the believers started filtering into the wooded sanctuary much earlier in the day. These times of fellowship were sweet to the Christians, who were encouraged to see the sheer numbers of disciples, and to know that they were not solitary pilgrims but part of an ever-increasing family, called out by God to seek holiness in an unholy age.

Laughter and singing echoed throughout the forest that afternoon, as the adults ate and talked and the children played games or waded in a nearby brook. Yet on this occasion, the scent of sorrow hung in the air like smoke, for Judah and Esther were their spiritual parents, and they had never known a time when they were not there. Judah and Esther spent the afternoon circulating among their flock, sharing memories and exchanging tokens of affection with the many they loved, and by the end of the day, every heart had been plucked to the point of exhaustion. It was at that time that the torches were lit and the trumpets blew, summoning the people to gather together.

The amphitheater was built right into a wooded hillside. Enough trees were cleared to provide a suitable number of benches to fill the thirty descending rows that were dug out of the hill in two sections, leading down to a large, open area which had been lined with flat pieces of stone. Judah and Esther slowly made their way down to the front row of benches, and sat beside Paul. Next to him was his guard, who for the last two years had faithfully shadowed Paul as the law required. It was inevitable with such an assignment that the soldier—a young man named Mericus—not only stood over Paul as the arm of Caesar, but now sat under him as a disciple.

Every other bench filled quickly, and in the rush to be seated, few people noticed Julia walk into the sanctuary with another woman who wore a hooded cloak and whose face was shielded by a veil. They sat up on a bench near the back where they could see the entire congregation fanning out beneath them.

As the last ones straggling in took their seats, a group of musicians stood and led the people in a time of singing. It seemed an easy thing to lift praise to the King of heaven as a canopy of stars began to appear in the sky above the forest. When the singing had finished, an older pastor named Andronicus stood and turned to the congregation.

"Beloved family of God," he began, "it is both with joy and grief that we come together tonight. For this evening, we will say goodbye to two of our dearest friends, Judah Ben-Hur and his precious wife Esther, who will be leaving to return to Jerusalem, to begin work among the Lord's people there. We are joyful because we know that this has long been their desire, and so we rejoice with them that God has opened that door. But of course we are sad, because their gain is our loss."

His eyes wandered from one end of the amphitheater to the other as he said this, and many nodded their agreement. "They have nurtured many of us in our faith. They carried us when we were weak. They released us in ministry when we were strong. They will be deeply missed. Judah has a message now to share with us. Let's open our hearts to the Word of God he brings." Andronicus tenderly motioned to Judah who came to the front and stood before his family, and once he had controlled his own emotion, he began to preach his last sermon to his church family.

"My brothers and sisters, as Andronicus has said, this is a time of both joy and sorrow for us all. But isn't this the way it is when you choose to love another? The moment you choose to love is the moment you open yourself up to both intoxi-cating joy and unbearable pain. Both come intertwined together, and if you are to know what love really is then you must accept both. This evening, we are standing at the bitter crossroads where love's joy and love's pain intersect."

He looked down and noticed that Esther was already wiping her eyes. "Let me ask you—is it worth it? Is it worth it to love someone and risk the pain that comes with separation? As followers of Jesus, we must say yes.

"To love is to hurt. When we came here more than fifteen years ago, you could say that we gambled. We risked opening ourselves up to new friends; we risked loving the people we found here. We chose to allow relationships to be born. And something beautiful happened. I found myself loving you, not just as a shepherd loving his flock, but as a father loving his children. We took the risk, we gambled, and now we are going to pay the price for it. We are going to hurt. Was it worth it? What a poor question to ask. Of course it was worth it."

Judah was far less animated than Paul when he spoke, but the people hung on his every word nonetheless, for he spoke not as though to a faceless crowd, but it seemed that he addressed them each individually.

"What is it about love that brings the risk of pain? What is it about love that demands that sorrow tag along behind it? The best way to answer that question is to look at God's love for us. I heard the apostle John once say something simple, yet completely disarming. He said, *Love is of God*. He is right. And so if we want to learn about what love really is, then all we have to do is look at God himself. He's our example. And when we look at God, we can begin to understand why love brings with it joy and pain. You can say of God, that when he created us, he chose the gamble of love.

"See love from God's perspective. He wants to be known, but think of all the people who don't want to know God. All the people who are decidedly irreli-gious. They want nothing to do with God. Think of people who want to relate to God but only on a superficial level. Not one of these people knows God as he wants to be known. They are keeping him at arm's length. That's the risk we take when we choose to love another. There's the risk that you might be rejected. Years ago, I had a childhood friend who turned against me in his adult life, and the pain of that betrayal wounded my heart. Love is a gamble. But is it worth it?

"God thinks so. The reason that Jesus endured the agony of the cross was for the joy that he knew would come after his suffering. The joy of having many come to the Father for forgiveness in his name. The prophet Isaiah told us that the Messiah would *see his offspring*. Think of it! Was the pain of love worth it for Christ? Was it worth it that he allowed people to hate him, to mock him, to spit on him, to pull on his beard, to strip him, to humiliate him, to crucify him? Was it worth it? Yes, Jesus declared, as he looked across time and saw you and me."

Not a sound but Judah's voice rang across that hillside. Even the little toddlers being bounced on their parents' knees seemed unusually quiet, as Judah continued speaking.

"And when you discover love such as this, there comes a time when you find that there's another kind of pain that can occur. This time it's not the pain of rejection or misunderstanding, it's the pain of loss—the pain of being separated from those whom you love. I discovered this as a child when I had pets die. I discovered this in a far more bitter way when our two little ones died."

Judah looked deeply into Esther's eyes as he spoke of the greatest sorrow they had ever shared together.

"Why were our precious Rachel and our innocent little Samuel taken in the budding of their youth? Why did the plague strike them and pass by others? Why were others healed by God, while they were untouched? Many of you remember that time of dark anguish, and many of you lost loved ones of your own. Would we have been better off never marrying so as not to lose our spouses? Would we have been better off sealing up our wombs so as not to bear children who would be taken from us so soon? Certainly I never would have tasted such suffering if I had not become a parent. But what affection, and what hilarity I would have missed if I had never taken the gamble. We bore them to love them, and we can never regret it, even though in the end, we bore them to lose them."

Judah had to momentarily turn away to gather himself and wipe his eyes, which appeared moist and red in the firelight. He sighed and continued.

"It should be comforting for us to realize that God knows as well, not only the pain of rejection, but also the pain of separation. As Jesus served bread and wine to his disciples on the night of his betrayal, he said to them something interesting. He said, *From now on I shall not drink of the fruit of the vine until the kingdom of God comes*. Here he was sharing a meal with his closest friends whom he loved, and he tells them that he will not allow himself to enjoy a moment such as this one until they are all together again at the end of the age. Jesus would feel the pain of separation. Jesus wants to be with us. To see us. To hold us. But until that time comes, there is sorrow, there is longing, and waiting. Jesus understands very well the pain of separation, and that is what Esther and I are feeling today. It is pain that comes when we choose to love, when we take that gamble.

"Is it worth it? Is it worth the pain to choose to love? If there is a heaven—yes! If there is a kingdom to come when we will all sit around a table of fellowship once again—yes! If a day is coming very soon when we will all be together again, and this time, there will be no goodbyes to be said, this time there will be no separation, but perfect, unending fellowship, if that day is coming, then yes, this is worth it!"

A confident sound of triumph now echoed in his words and it stirred up an undeniable response of faith in the hearts of the congregation.

"Fifteen years ago, Esther and I came and took the gamble to love. Today it hurts. Tomorrow it will hurt. But all of us came out better for it. Anyone who chooses to love, who risks the pain and braves the sorrow, will come out better for it. More human, more like God created us to be. Thank you for accepting our love, as imperfect as it was. And dear friends, thank you for loving us. We have grown together. I never thought I would say this, but Rome has been for me a little taste of heaven."

As he finished, Judah no longer held back the full flow of his tears and immediately everyone else released their own sorrow, and soon there was not a dry eye to be found. At Judah's beckoning, Esther came to the front and stood alongside him. Then the applause began, and like a wave, the people stood to their feet, and they poured out their affection on these two whom they loved. As Octavia stood with Julia, she looked with astonishment around her at this showering of spontaneous and sincere affection, and moist patches appeared on her veil. She had never experienced anything like this in her life.

"Julia, to see how these people love each other leaves me breathless!" she marveled.

Julia could only nod at first, for she too was choked with emotion, but when her voice came to her, she turned to her mistress. "His wife, Esther, is the one who brought me to faith. She has the softest, most gentle heart of anyone I know. And she and Judah are two of the ones I was speaking about who saw Jesus after his resurrection."

Paul walked up alongside of Judah and Esther, then hugged them. "And that one there," said Julia, pointing him out. "His name is Paul. He saw Jesus as well. And what's amazing is he used to hate the Christians and persecute them openly."

Octavia pulled back her veil and wiped her face. "So Jesus really lived?"

"He is alive still," said Julia. "Judah's mother and sister used to be lepers, but Jesus healed them, completely."

"Julia, I want to believe you, but it seems so unbelievable. How can a leper be cleansed?"

"The same way a persecutor becomes a preacher," Julia answered. "Or a sinner becomes a saint. With God anything is possible."

"Where are they, his mother and sister?"

"His sister lives in Jerusalem. And his mother went home several years ago."

"To Judea, or was she from someplace else?"

"No child, I mean she died and went home to heaven, to be with Jesus."

Octavia's eyes grew wide in wonder. "Julia, you are sending chills through my body. This seems too good to be true. I've always dreamed that there might be something more to life, but I've convinced myself that there couldn't be. It was just make-believe, like the stories my nursemaids read to me as a child."

Julia placed an affirming arm around her mistress and pulled her close. "Dear one, your dreams might just be coming true tonight." Octavia laughed, then wept, then laughed again. "When the service is over, we will go and talk to the leaders. You'll see that there is still time for hope."

When the applause was hushed, Paul asked the leaders of the church to come to the front. He instructed them to encircle Judah and Esther, lay their hands upon them, and pray for them, and he asked the congregation to bow their heads and pray silently from their seats. Of the thousand pairs of eyes that were in that sanctuary, Octavia's was one of the few that were open, for she was not accustomed to the practice of Christian prayer. But she was profoundly moved by the fervency and spontaneity of these people's intercession.

As she looked around, she saw heads bowed, hands uplifted, and lips moving, as prayers of quiet, respectful agreement were offered up to support the verbal petitions being shared by the leaders. The prayers flowed one into the other, first for the safety of Judah and Esther's travels, then for the success of their mission in Jerusalem, for the prospering of the great work they had begun in Rome, for the increasing fruitfulness of the harvest in all corners of the empire, and then— Octavia's ears burned as she heard it said—for the power of God to be unleashed in the house of Caesar, that Emperor Nero's heart would be turned to the light of the gospel, that heavenly wisdom might crown him and the Senate, but until such a time when these prayers would be fully answered, that God would protect his people living under the shroud of pagan darkness, and help those who might be unjustly molested by Caesar's wickedness. Octavia began to shake.

Finally, the prayers ended, and the service was concluded with the breaking of bread, a ritual which moved Octavia as much as it mystified her. A final hymn was sung and the congregation was dismissed, though people lingered for nearly an hour afterwards in the pleasant afterglow of their time together. Julia and Octavia stayed seated until the crowd of well-wishers around Judah and Esther began to thin out, and then they made their way down the steps to the front.

As they came near, Judah and Esther were both saying goodbye to a giant of a man who towered over them. He had long gray locks of hair, and huge arms, and when he leaned over to hug them, Judah and Esther seemed to disappear momentarily within the folds of his arms.

"Judah of Hur, and Esther his wife," the giant said, "Thord promised himself not to cry when you left, but now you see my eyes. They are wet with grief."

Judah tried to speak, but he couldn't until Thord released his hold on them. "Thord, even our Lord wept at the grave of Lazarus, and he was the strongest of men. Don't be ashamed."

"We will miss you, Thord," Esther added. "I never will be able to drink a glass of wine again without thinking of you and your wine shop."

"Oh! And you have reminded Thord of his gift to you," said the giant. He stooped down and reached into a basket sitting at his feet, and withdrew from it two bottles. "My finest vintage I have bottled for you. Wait until a special time, and drink then in memory of your friend Thord. But not to drink too fast, ha!"

"I will never forget my friend from the north, who taught me how to fight," said Judah, remembering the days when he first met Thord in the Circus shortly after his adoption by Arrius.

"I will never forget my friends, who taught Thord how to love," said Thord, remembering, still with pain, the time when he nearly assassinated Judah as an agent of Judah's enemy, Messala. "But now I fight for the King of kings!"

"And we are soldiers together to the end," said Judah.

Thord picked up his basket. "Thord now goes. I will try to come to the harbor to see my friends off. Rest well till then!" He lumbered away while wiping his eyes, and his shoulders dipped slightly as he climbed the steps. Judah and Esther waved after him as he disappeared over the rise into the forest, and then they turned to Julia who approached, with Octavia behind her. Immediately, Esther and Julia fell on each other with weeping.

"We will miss you, sister," Julia said. "I've known this day was coming for years, but it still has come too soon."

"We never seem to appreciate how wonderful people are until we can't be with them anymore," said Esther.

Judah reached out and touched her head. "I hope you know dear Julia, how much we love you." He then saw Octavia, who stood back with shyness, her face still veiled. "You've brought a friend tonight, Julia?"

Esther stepped toward Octavia, and extended her hands with warmth. "I am Esther. What is your name?"

Julia softly touched Esther's shoulder as Octavia looked down. "Esther, this is my mistress."

Julia gave Octavia an assuring smile, and she slowly pulled back her veil. Esther gasped. "Lady Octavia!"

Judah as well was stunned. By this time, Paul and the other church leaders had recognized Octavia, and drew near in amazement. There was a brief second of uncomfortable silence as each one wondered what might be appropriate to say. Judah finally spoke. "Lady Octavia, I feel embarrassed by the plainness of our surroundings. I wish we could offer you something more comfortable than a wooden bench to sit on, but please come."

"No, don't apologize," Octavia said as she sat down on the bench that Judah offered, while the others sat down around her. "I suffocate in marble. To be here in this place with you tonight has been more refreshing than I could tell you."

Paul moved forward and reached out his hand. "Empress, I am Paul." She looked oddly at the chain draped around his wrist, but accepted his clasp.

"Sometime soon, I hope to have a meeting with your husband." At the mention of Nero, her face fell.

"My husband is not one you would care to meet," she stated sadly.

Julia pointed to the bruising on her face. "Nero has sent the sign of his seal on Lady Octavia's face. And this is why we have come tonight."

Slowly, Octavia unveiled her story to them, with Julia's help at places where she found it too difficult to continue. Every detail which she revealed about Nero's brutality elicited dismay from the Christians, who all had heard rumors of Caesar's cruelty, but were alarmed to find it was worse than imagined. And when she had finished, she lowered her head in despondency and exhaustion. The leaders looked at each other, searching each other's eyes for wisdom.

Judah spoke first. "What you are asking is that we will help you to leave Rome."

Octavia looked up, her eyes red with tears. "It's too much to ask. If it's ever discovered that you helped me, he would stop at nothing to destroy you."

"We believe that evil is to be overcome with good," Judah responded. "What you are asking us is a good thing."

"In the traditions of our faith, provision was made for those were unjustly accused or mistreated," Paul added. "They could seek shelter in a city of refuge. They would be safe there. You have come to us looking for a city of refuge."

"But where could I hide?" Octavia asked in desperation. "I cannot stay in these woods. And my face is known in every city."

"Worshippers of Jesus are all over the empire," Judah said. "You could go virtually anywhere, and be welcomed in a church."

Octavia sighed. "I don't know if it's possible. I don't know if I have the strength."

"It doesn't sound as if you have a choice," said Andronicus, and his simple words drew agreement from the rest. There was a moment of reflection and then Paul spoke with sudden enthusiasm.

"Judah, Esther—the Empress could go with you. You're leaving in three days. Certainly, arrangements can be made to include her in your party, as a servant, or a relative. It seems that Nero could strike at any moment. If we are to help, it should be done expediently." The idea was received with excitement by the others. Paul continued in a more sober voice. "Yet let's be sure we have thought this through. The Empress is right in saying that this could have serious repercussions on the church if somehow this should fail. Are we prepared for what could befall us? Have we counted the cost?"

"Esther and I will assume full responsibility for the Empress' safety," remarked Judah, "and no word of the church ever need reach Nero's ears."

"And if you are caught?"

"Our Lord did not open his mouth during his interrogation. Can we do no less?" Judah said with firm resolve. "There can be no debate here about what is to be done. Don't forget that the Lord Jesus in his infancy was taken to Egypt that he might be saved from the wickedness of Herod. We will help take Octavia into protection as well."

Esther reach out and placed a consoling and tender arm around Octavia. "My child, you must make the choice, but our arms are open wide." Octavia was numbed by the care she felt radiating around her. She leaned her head on Esther's shoulder, and for the first time in as long as she could remember, she felt the sensation of simply resting.

But the sensation did not last long. Sounds of rustling disturbed the wooded silence around them, and they looked to the top of the amphitheater to see what was causing it. Octavia suddenly screamed and fell to the ground in terror as a line of Roman soldiers burst into the clearing.

Chapter 9

Five soldiers emerged on the top step, and one pointed down in the direction of the Christians while looking back at someone else who had not yet appeared. He cried out, "It's her. She's right down there," as the other man came into view. It was Burrus.

Judah stood to his feet as Burrus started down the steps, and Octavia clung tightly to Esther and whimpered, "Oh no! He's found me already."

"Stay still," Judah said calmly. "We'll talk." Burrus and his men approached and Judah held out his hands to them in a gesture of peace. "We welcome you in peace. There's no need for violence."

Burrus stopped, and the two men looked at each. He had learned from his first experience of hand to hand combat that a man's fortitude was usually visible in the hollow of his eyes. Sparks of courage or shadows of cowardice were first revealed there, and as Burrus looked in Judah's eyes he saw a reservoir of bravery which belied his apparent gentleness.

"We do not come in violence," he said, "unless we find it necessary."

Octavia saw that her situation was desperate but she felt a conviction not to further endanger her new friends, so she stood and slowly walked toward Burrus, intending to surrender herself. Loudly, she said, "This is Afranius Burrus, the prefect of the emperor's guards." She walked to within a few feet of him, then stopped. "Have you come to arrest me?"

"What crime have you committed that we would arrest you?" asked Burrus with perfect sincerity, and then while Octavia's heart stood still in suspense, he dropped to one knee before her and bowed his head in a gesture of submission. "We have come to express our allegiance to you, Lady Octavia."

Octavia stepped back, utterly surprised by this unexpected display of loyalty. "Your allegiance?" she asked in shock.

"Yes my Lady," Burrus replied, still kneeling. "Your life is in danger. Your assassination has been ordered."

She shuddered but stood firm. "By Nero. And you are his prefect. You are the one who carries out his will."

Burrus came to his feet and his men behind him remained steady and still, like waxed figures, their swords unsheathed. "I was a soldier long before Nero was born," Burrus said. "I know the difference between legitimate and illegitimate authority. You have done nothing deserving of death. I have sworn myself to your protection and your freedom."

Octavia had never before seen Burrus as she now did. As a child, she feared him for the uniform he wore. As a young girl, she feared him for his sternness. As a woman, she feared him for his closeness to Nero, and it had never occurred to her at all that he might be other than an unswerving subject to the crown. In fact, she found it difficult to believe how she could be the object of anyone's devotion in the court, let alone a man as powerful as Burrus.

"Prefect, your loyalty moves me," she said in simple honesty. She turned to acknowledge Judah and the Christians. "These people too have offered their help."

"I care not who they are, or how you know them," said Burrus soberly. "I only know that you were much too easily followed to this place. My scouts had no difficulty tracing your movements. From here on out, such carelessness could be costly. I also know that time is short. Empress, I hope this does not distress you, but my counsel to you is that you leave Rome."

"I am not distressed, Prefect," said Octavia as she pulled back the hood of her cloak, allowing her long, dark hair to cascade softly around her shoulders, which seemed to magnify her beauty and innocence. "In fact, that is the reason I am here. I know my husband can no longer conceal his hatred of me. These are friends who know my sufferings, and they stand poised to give me shelter."

Paul stepped forward and pointed to Judah. "This man and his wife are leaving the country in three days. We have offered the Empress passage with them."

Burrus looked at Octavia with fatherly concern. "And you trust these people?"

"They risk their lives for me. I need no other proof of their love."

Burrus silently considered these words, and then nodded. "If you will explain the details of your plan to me, I will see to her protection until she is safely out of Italy."

At this, Judah invited Burrus and the others to sit down together. As they huddled together within the shadows cast by the dancing flames of the torches, listening to the steady hum of crickets, and guarded by the citadel of trees, their skin grew chilled and their voices instinctively lowered, as though the forest were teeming with spies, and every star above were a gleaming pupil in Nero's eyes.

*　　　　*　　　　*

Judah awoke the next morning with a start, his body dripping with sweat. The night before seemed like a shadowy dream, and yet as his thoughts began to focus, a heavy pall of dread flooded his spirit. He was chilled by the realization that his world had suddenly changed. With a sigh of resignation, he quietly rose from his bed so as not to disturb Esther, whose deep, rhythmic breathing showed that she was fitfully asleep.

He and Esther lived in an unpretentious home on the outskirts of Rome, considerably removed from the traffic of the city, but now, every clump of horse hooves heard from the road outside echoed with an intimation of danger. The two days before their departure seemed like two millennia, and there was part of Judah's heart that wished to go directly to the harbor at once, and sleep on the pier in blankets if need be, rather than wait here.

After a time of meditation and prayer, his fears softened somewhat and when Esther awoke, he was able to ease some of her own feelings of distress. There was something of the peace of God in all of this, which Judah could not explain in human terms. It was just a sensation of serenity that all would be well, a simple by-product of seeing life through the eyes of faith, and not mere sight. *And what was a man without faith anyway?* Judah thought to himself. Without faith, he would have perished in the slave galleys years before. Without faith, the grief he felt as he laid his lifeless children into graves would have crippled him for good.

Paul, accompanied by Mericus and Luke, arrived a short time later to join Judah and Esther for breakfast and discuss the events of the evening before. Paul alone seemed to have an appetite. While Judah and Esther picked at their bread and fruit, Paul happily gorged himself, seemingly unaffected by what had happened.

The house was simple, though Esther had filled it with a quiet charm over their years, and by its appearance, no visitor could have possibly imagined the substantial wealth which Judah and Esther possessed. They had long since put away the relics of Judah's aristocratic past. His father had been a great man, a true prince of Judea, who even bore gifts from the great Augustus himself, and counted Herod the Great as a patron and friend. Additional wealth had been accrued through wise investments in all manners of shipping and commerce, and it seemed that whatever his father touched was blessed.

Esther's father, Simonides, was brought into the Hur household as a servant, and soon demonstrated such faithfulness in his responsibilities that he became the chief steward of the family of Hur. When Judah's father drowned at sea, Simonides became as a father to Judah, and his daughter Esther became as a sister, and he faithfully managed the family's fortune until such a time as Judah was old enough to assume control of it. After his conversion, Judah poured much of his substance into the needs of the growing church, but it seemed the more he gave, the more his resources grew.

His wealth also expanded exponentially when he was adopted by Quintus Arrius, and as his heir, he came into a massive inheritance when he returned to Rome, and again, much of this he invested into the expanding Christian movement. Congregations from Corinth to Antioch to Alexandria were beneficiaries of Judah's thoughtful benevolence. Yet he was careful not to exhaust his resources, nor did he neglect his relatives. His sister Tirzah and her family still lived in Jerusalem, overseeing the family's property there, and all were well-provided for.

Judah often called to mind Jesus' sober warnings about the rich being unable to inherit God's kingdom without great difficulty, and so from the very beginning of their journey of faith, he and Esther vowed to live in a spirit of simplicity and generosity. No country villa or stately seaside mansion bore their names. They lived in just a small house of modest elegance with a field behind it for the horses and cattle they raised. The residual benefit of so few worldly possessions was the ease with which they could now abandon them. With little care or forethought, they could turn their property over to the church as they returned to Judea, and never entertain another worry about it.

As Judah looked about the room, mulling over these thoughts in his head, the sound of horses again was heard through the open windows, and this time, their hoofbeats did not fade away, but grew louder. Judah looked at Esther, and then leaned back in his chair to look outside. "We have two visitors," he said, and then with a tightening notch of concern on his face, he added, "two soldiers, whom I've not seen before." Esther moaned.

"Now let's look on the bright side," Paul said, as he poured himself a glass of fruit juice. "At least it's not a legion."

They heard every movement of the soldiers' feet as they dismounted and marched up the path to the front entrance, and then came three solid raps on the door. Judah slowly rose, walked across the room and opened the door. One of the soldiers immediately spoke. "Are you Quintus Arrius?" he asked with a stern formality.

"Yes," Judah replied, waiting for what came next.

The soldier reached into a satchel hanging from his side and pulled out a small scroll, bound in wire. "I have an imperial summons here from the emperor."

Judah took the scroll. "Do you need a response?"

"Only your obedience," said the soldier curtly, who then clicked his heels together, saluted, and turned with his companion to return to their horses. Judah stood in the doorway until they had galloped away down the road, and then he turned back inside holding up the scroll.

"You heard it yourself," he said to the others. "A summons from the emperor." He untwisted the wire, while the others waited with tense silence—even Paul, who stopped chewing on a bite of bread to hear the news. Judah grunted as he scanned the message. "It simply says that Caesar wishes to see me this afternoon at his new palace, and to respond only if I am unable to come. It's signed by Seneca."

"Concerning the case?" Luke asked.

"It doesn't say." He tossed the scroll down on the table for the others to look at.

"Is this the first thread of the emperor's web?" asked Esther, feeling constricted by the unexpected melodrama. "Does he know about what happened last night? Was Burrus a spy all along?"

"Now, now, now," Paul muttered as he buttered another slab of bread, "let's not let a little intrigue spoil a perfectly good breakfast." He took a sizeable bite. "Our Burrus seemed a good man. No informant could put on that good a performance. But we'll know soon enough this afternoon, won't we? We'll call the church to pray, and Judah will keep his appointment."

As the morning sun began to fill the room with light and humidity, beads of sweat appeared on their foreheads as they finished breakfast.

                  *   *   *

The afternoon came quickly. Judah finally bid a reluctant farewell to Esther and the friends who had gathered in their home, then saddled his favorite horse and headed into the city. The nearer he drew to the center of Rome, the more depressed his spirit became, not because of anxiety about what awaited him, but simply because of the city's oppressiveness itself. Temples, obelisks and sculpted gods stood on virtually every street corner, competing for the souls of the passersby, and the effect of this religious kaleidoscope was not to foster faith, but to butcher it. Christianity fell on the Roman world like a spring rain, giving its followers order, purpose and hope which were anchored in the objective, historical reality of an empty tomb.

Yet as Judah drew near to the palace, overshadowed on every side by the magnificent buildings of Rome, his own faith seemed for a moment sterile and insignificant. Each plodding step of his horse was like wading headlong up a stream with its current rushing against him. It was easy to understand how a wooden cross on an obscure Judean hillside could pale in comparison to the marbled splendor of this city.

At last, he reached the gates of the new palace, and after telling his business to the guards at the gate, he was ushered inside. The oppressiveness he felt only deepened around him as he stepped into the shadow of the *Colossus*. It awed him and sickened him simultaneously. He was led up the stairs to the palace entrance, and was instructed to wait beneath the portico, where someone would attend to him. He waited at the top of the steps, and gazed out over the horizon of the city. Ten minutes passed, and a voice suddenly spoke from behind him.

"Quintus Arrius." Judah turned and saw Seneca standing behind him, who stepped forward and took his hand. "Welcome. I am Seneca."

"Yes, I recognize you," Judah said, accepting his greeting. "Years ago we crossed paths in the Senate chambers, though infrequently."

"Of course, I remember you now," said Seneca. "We are two grizzled and graying veterans of the Roman court, you and I. Only you have withdrawn from public life. And I cannot seem to extract myself from it."

"I pity you," Judah said with the trace of a smile. "I was summoned to appear this afternoon, as you know. No mention was made of my client, so he has not accompanied me."

"No, that's fine," Seneca replied. "I do not believe the emperor cares to discuss your case in any great detail."

A surge of apprehension welled up inside of Judah. "I am curious why I am here, in that case," he said, trying to repress his alarm.

"Better for the emperor to explain," Seneca said. "Why don't you come with me. Lord Nero is riding in his private circus." Judah drew no comfort from his words, but he was eased by Seneca's excessive cordiality, which seemed unusual if this was the prelude to an interrogation.

Seneca led him into the palace, through the circular narthex, and into a hallway which seemed to be without end. The corridor stretched for more than 200 feet and cut through the heart of the palace leading to its rear side. It was illuminated by panes of glass laid into the vaulted ceiling which stretched thirty feet above the floor. False windows were cut into the walls all along the hallway, and assorted land and seascapes were painted into the openings. And on the walls themselves were painted an incredible menagerie of real and mythological creatures, and no two were repeated.

To walk between this bombastic exhibit of exploding colors and shapes was annoying at first, and dizzying by the time the corridor's end was reached. A door on the other end led out into a courtyard garden, and beyond the garden, the palace grounds opened up into a sweeping meadow. Judah felt relief to be in the open air, taking in the sane and simple colors of God's own creation. As they walked through the courtyard, Seneca drew him into trivial conversation.

"So what has occupied your attention in Rome all these years?" Seneca asked off-handedly.

Judah chose his response carefully. "Religion."

"Are you interested in philosophy?" Seneca appreciated the topic of religion only inasmuch as it led to a discussion of philosophy. Judah appreciated philosophy only if it led to a discussion of religion.

He replied, "Only if it leads to truth."

Seneca laughed apathetically. "I am afraid you're asking a bit much of philosophy then," he said. "Years of studying it still leaves me groping in shadows. Sometimes I wonder if there even is any such thing as *truth*."

Judah pressed him. "Without truth, you then have no basis for morality. And without morality, the world you and I know unravels at the seams."

"You'll get no argument from me," said Seneca. "Morality is the rarest of commodities in the empire today, but—," and he held up his finger triumphantly, "this is what we have armies for. To hold the world together when every other adhesive dissolves."

Judah felt warmly reassured by Seneca's light-hearted banter. Were their efforts to help Octavia known, he wouldn't have been casually escorted to Nero by his chief adviser, but dragged before him in chains. Beyond the courtyard in the heart of the meadow was a huge barn, and Judah surmised that this was their destination, and indeed, Seneca walked in this direction.

"Caesar loves horses then?" asked Judah, sidestepping to avoid scattered piles of horse droppings.

"Our emperor is most renowned for his leisure pursuits," Seneca replied. "And he especially loves his chariot. Am I to understand that you did not see our emperor the other day riding in procession to dedicate his palace?"

"My wife and I find crowds annoying and no longer worth the trouble," said Judah.

"If I were you, I would not let Caesar know that you were one of the few in Rome to miss his celebration," warned Seneca with true concern in his voice. "In fact if he asks you what you thought of it, tell him it was a splendid pageant. That way you need not lie and more importantly, you will not offend him." They passed through the perimeter fencing around the barn. "You, Arrius, were a formidable charioteer in your youth, I understand."

Judah shrugged. "It was a way to pass the time when I first came to Rome. It brought honor to my father and kept me out of trouble."

"You speak modestly. I consulted the records just yesterday. Three consecutive undefeated seasons in the Circus, plus numerous victories in other parts of Italy. And then you took your prowess to Judea where you humbled one of Rome's greatest riders, a tribune named Messala." Seneca looked at him intently. "That must have been a most satisfying triumph." Judah said nothing, but looked at Seneca with a bemused smile. "You'll have to share this fascinating story of yours with me sometime, and fill in some of the gaps that are left in the historical materials I have read. Your life has been an odyssey, Judah Ben-Hur."

"My life is an open book, Master Seneca," Judah finally said. "And I would be more than happy to share its many twists and turns with you. Unfortunately, I am leaving for Judea in two days, so—,"

"Oh you are?" asked Seneca with surprise. "What of your case?"

They walked into the barn, through a small labyrinth of doors and rails. "My client is tended by a team of able hands. I have business in Jerusalem."

"I see," said Seneca, and Judah couldn't help but note the quiet, disturbed lowering of his voice. They walked into the main arena which spread out for 300 feet, and was surrounded by rising bleachers across its length. At the far end of the arena, a lone man in a chariot could be seen driving a team of horses on the sand. Seneca pointed to him. "There is our Caesar now hard at work."

Closer to them was a man dressed in military clothing, leaning over the wood fence and looking out at Nero's chariot. The man turned to them as they drew near, and Judah had to suppress a gasp.

"And here is our Prefect Burrus. I'll pass you onto him for the moment," said Seneca, but then he stopped when he saw Burrus' face collapse into a shocked expression of dismay. Seneca was confused. "Have you two men met before?"

Burrus was swift to answer. "It seems we have but I'm not sure where. You must be Quintus Arrius?" he asked with feigned courtesy.

"Yes, Quintus Arrius," Judah answered. "It is a pleasure to meet you, Prefect."

Seneca was still perplexed but he placed his hands on both men's shoulders. "Gentlemen, I have work in the palace that needs my oversight. I'll leave you two to get acquainted. Or further acquainted, as the case may be. Prefect, you'll see to Arrius' questions?" Burrus nodded and Seneca left the barn.

"*You* are Quintus Arrius?" Burrus asked as soon as he was gone. Judah nodded. "It cannot be. I thought your name was Judah Ben-Hur!"

"Quintus Arrius is my adopted name," Judah explained.

"*You* are the man adopted by the consul, who trained as a charioteer, and served in the Senate? *You*?!"

"The world seems small, does it not?"

"The world seems mad!" Burrus said. "Of all the people in Rome to be summoned to Caesar today, never could I have imagined that it would be you. The gods are playing tricks on us."

"Prefect Burrus, answer me this," Judah said softening his voice. "Does my coming here today have anything to do with what transpired last night? Is this an interrogation?" He gripped Burrus' arm. "Did you deceive us?"

"No!" Burrus answered with conviction. "I assure you that our plans are between us and no one here knows what we have discussed. However—", and he issued a deep and terrible sigh, "I am afraid our plan may not work now."

Judah tightened his grip on his arm. "What do you mean?"

His voice was drowned out by the rattle and clatter of chariot wheels and horse hooves as Nero pulled up to the fence beside them. "Whoa! Whoa there!" Nero shouted as he tried to bring his team to a smooth stop, though unsuccessfully. But once they were controlled and resting in place, he called out, "Burrus, is this our guest?"

"This is Quintus Arrius," Burrus said, though still unconvinced.

"Greetings to you, Counsel Arrius. I'm so glad you've come," Nero said with genuine enthusiasm.

Nero seldom gave inspiring first impressions, as was the case again here. Judah expected something more than this plain-looking man of average height and stocky build, especially with the image of the *Colossus* so freshly impressed in his memory. Judah's first thought was that the sculptor might have erred slightly on the side of exaggeration when creating it. His second thought was informed by his knowledge of scripture—God never looked on the outside of a person but on the heart, and so Judah reminded himself that though here was a man who appeared youthfully naive, he nonetheless was capable of committing great atrocities. He would approach Nero with caution and circumspection.

"Emperor, I am honored to meet you," Judah said, with a respectful tipping of his head. "I don't know quite what to make of your summons. I assumed it had something to do with my case, but I have not brought my client along."

"No, no, no, not a summons," said Nero. "An invitation. I've invited you here. You are my guest. As far as your case goes, don't let it trouble you."

"Then I am at your disposal," said Judah, at last convinced of his safety, but now fully aroused by curiosity. *Why was he here?*

"Come, ride with me," Nero said, as he beckoned Judah to come onto the arena floor. Judah found the request odd, but after sharing a quick glance with Burrus, he walked through a nearby gate and stepped into the chariot behind Nero. Once he had taken hold of the chariot's frame, Nero set the horses into motion and they began a lazy canter around the arena floor. Nero did not say a word for the first hundred feet, but then he turned to Judah and asked, "How do you like my horses?"

"They are beautiful animals," Judah said with perfect honesty. It was a team of Akhal-Tekel horses, each one with a resplendent coat of golden-metallic, and eyes that gleamed with intensity. "They are rarely seen is this part of the world."

"I have imported them from north of Persia," Nero explained. "A fruit of bringing Armenia under our heels finally. But they are like the race who breeds them—temperamental and hard to manage. Perhaps you saw me two days ago as I brought them through the streets to dedicate my palace."

"It was a…splendid pageant," answered Judah, looking away.

"I'm glad you appreciated it," said Nero. "But if you noticed, the horses were much too edgy. I would have run them in the chariot race earlier in the day, but they need more work. Now, you have horses, am I correct?"

"Just a handful of gentle Arabs, as old and gray as I am," Judah replied.

"But you used to be quite an accomplished rider, as I understand. You even rode in our great circus?"

"In the days of Tiberius. It seems so long ago."

"Would you care to lead my team?" asked Nero, and without another word, he suddenly handed both sets of reins to Judah, who took them with reluctance and assumed the lead position in the chariot as Nero nudged him forward. Immediately, Judah could feel the pulse and rhythm of each individual horse through the leather of the reins, and he instinctively made adjustments to give each his proper lead. Nero watched with absorbed fascination as Judah made minute compensations with simple movements of his palms or fingers.

"Yes, I can see in your hands that you are very much at ease with this," Nero marveled.

Judah was quick to mute the praise. "But I hardly know the horses though. It's been so long, my touch has grown dull. A good charioteer must know his animals better than he knows his wife," and as he said this, he quickly regretted his choice of words, but Nero was preoccupied with studying Judah's technique.

"But the knowledge is all there still, wouldn't you say?" Caesar asked eagerly. "The instinct is still in your head?"

Judah returned the reins to Nero. "At my age, Caesar, there is a great gulf between what my mind understands and what my body can carry out."

Nero persisted. "But with someone younger you could transfer that knowledge?"

"I'm not sure I am following your meaning," Judah said, not certain if he wanted to discover Nero's meaning. An unease was starting to come over him. By now they had made several laps in the chariot, and when they reached the opposite end of the barn from where Judah came in, Nero stopped his horses and called for an attendant to come and return the horses to their stables. He and Judah began walking back toward where Burrus was still waiting.

"I'm not sure if you knew of it," Nero began again, "but I happen to have a great love of chariot racing. You could say, in fact, it is a passion."

"You obviously love horses, and I know that you are an accomplished musician," Judah said, knowing that a smattering of praise wouldn't hurt his position.

Nero shrugged his shoulders modestly. "I enjoy music. I am an artist, of course. But an athlete as well. I dabble at so much, and am good at so little. But I want to become good at chariot racing. I want to compete. Like you once did. I want to wear the wreath of a champion. But I want to earn it—not have it pawned off to me because I am Caesar. Now in two years, Greece hosts its glorious Olympic games, but in advance of that event, I intend to offer my own games next year in Neapolis. Have you heard?"

Judah shook his head.

"It is my ambition to ride the chariot to victory first in Neapolis, and then in Greece. But there is my problem. I am inexperienced. My skills are erratic. I need a trained eye to oversee my progress. I need a man such as yourself, Quintus Arrius."

Judah felt coldness creeping up his limbs. The purpose for this visit was no longer hidden in shadows. It suddenly exploded on him in vivid and blinding colors. And he had to find a way to deflect Nero's attention away from himself.

"I am flattered, Emperor, that you see me as one who could help you. However sadly, my obligations to my family and to my work are considerable."

"This case again," Nero said with a sigh. "You are obviously a man of duty. Tell me about this Paul of Tarsus." Judah looked at him, mildly amazed to hear Nero speak so plainly of his friend. "Oh yes, I know all about his squabble with the Jews. Is he the rabble-rouser they claim him to be?"

"He has traveled the empire bearing a message about God's great love for the human race," Judah began.

"God's great love? Or *the gods'* great love?" Nero interrupted.

"The Jews believe that there is one God, Caesar."

"Yes, I know of their peculiar beliefs. How one can look at the variety and disorder of the world and believe there is only one god escapes my ability to reason," said Nero. "But forgive my interruption. You were saying?"

Judah resumed. "Paul has been beaten countless times, though himself having never lifted a hand to anyone. He has been cursed endlessly, though himself never having reviled anyone. He teaches that men ought to support their leaders, and pray for all who are in authority. And he is proud to be a citizen of Rome."

"As he well should. And the Jews are upset because his message, his theology, deviates from theirs?"

"That would seem to be their complaint."

"Well you see then, this is a perfect waste of time. Your time and my time," Nero exclaimed. "For such a complaint falls outside of our jurisdiction. Let them settle such disputes themselves, within their own houses of worship, provided they abide by the civil laws of Rome. We grant freedom to all religions. So Quintus Arrius, you have argued your case well. I pronounce here and now, a complete dismissal of all these charges. Your Paul of Tarsus is a free man and you Quintus Arrius are free to serve me. The time you would have thrown away in defending an inconsequential legal feud can now be invested in a much higher calling."

Judah's mind raced frantically to adjust to all that he had just heard. He felt relief to hear words of acquittal pronounced. He was perturbed that they were pronounced so flippantly. He was alarmed that they were pronounced so as to place a leash of servitude around his own neck. His next words would require all the skill and tact he could summon as a counsel.

"Caesar, I am stunned by your wisdom, by your great generosity, and by the way in which you would honor me by this request. You will appreciate then my grief that I cannot accept your request, for my wife and I have made arrangements to return to our native land of Judea to seek retirement with family we have there."

Nero did not hide his disappointment. "Did you presume upon my generosity that you assumed your case would be so suddenly resolved?"

Judah saw the delicate line he had to tread. "No Lord Nero, not at all. I am but one of a team of counselors, and my services were no longer required for Paul's defense. Our arrangements were made in full recognition of the fact that the case might not be heard for a long time still."

He whispered a silent prayer of thanks that the words came to him so easily and eloquently. Surely, Nero would accept his reasons for declining the offer.

"I would think your wife and family would be thrilled that you had become an object of Caesar's favor," Nero said with an obvious frown, or was it a scowl? "I would think if they truly loved you, that they would he happy to let you take full advantage of this rare opportunity. In fact, I am trying my best to not be offended that you have not immediately entertained the thought of postponing your plans to assist your emperor. You praise me for my generosity, but I find this an odd way of expressing your thanks."

Judah felt the leash tightening. How could he explain to Nero in a word the differences between the generations—that advancement meant nothing for an old man? How could he explain to Nero in a word his own life-story—that ambition and fortune had already allowed him to drink to the full life's glories and splendor, and that now he wanted nothing more than to rest? How could he explain to Nero in a word the convictions of his faith—that a child of God who worshipped the eternal Creator was not overawed by earthly sovereigns, and was not overly impressed by power, rank or wealth? Judah knew that there was nothing he could say that would make this young, self-centered dictator see anything other than his own aspirations.

"I have no desire to offend you, your majesty," Judah said grimly. "The suddenness of your request has caught me unprepared. Might I ask the nature and length of the commitment you are asking?"

Nero smiled approvingly. "I had hoped all the way through the Grecian Olympiad. But let us compromise. Let me again show you my generosity. Serve me through the Neapolis games, and I will release you. Give me one full year to tap from you your wisdom and experience, and you may enter into your retirement."

Judah did not respond except for a slow and heavy nodding of his head. They had now arrived at the other end of the arena. Burrus was waiting, and could see in Judah's face what the outcome had been. Nero reached out and shook Judah's hand. "Master Arrius, thank you for coming. Can you get your house in order and join me in two days?" He gave no time for Judah to reply, but turned at once to Burrus. "Prefect, would you arrange for housing for our esteemed friend here near the palace? Thank you again, Quintus Arrius. I'll eagerly await our first lesson. In two days, first thing in the morning if you please."

Like a whirlwind, Nero hastily marched from the barn, leaving Burrus and Judah occupying an uncomfortable silence. "You understand our problem?" Burrus asked sternly.

"I wasn't given a choice," said Judah, still confounded by what had happened.

"None of us are."

"I've waited years for this moment to leave Rome," Judah continued. "He's taken that away with a sweep of his hand."

"He'll take Octavia's life with a sweep of his hand if *she* doesn't leave Rome," said Burrus with insistence. "Your obligation to him will be completed in a year, so he said. What about our obligation to her now? Is there another way?"

Judah looked at him, freshly burdened by the responsibility for Octavia's safety. "You keep your promise to protect her, and we'll keep our promise to take her to freedom. We'll make any changes we have to. You have my word."

Both men's eyes burned with the fire of a common conviction, enraged by evil and determined to oppose it. Burrus bowed in agreement, and the two men left the arena.

*   *   *

Judah's home was on the southwest edge of Rome, and to return there, he had to take his horse alongside a stretch of the Tiber River which passed by several of the warehouses and wharves erected beneath the Aventine hill. The traffic in this section of the city at this time of day was heavy with merchants, soldiers and sailors, but Judah threaded through them in numb diffidence, completely lost in the catacombs of his thoughts. As such, he failed to notice a young, burly man who hastily crossed the road in front of him, thinly sidestepping his horse by a whisker, and scowling at Judah as he rode by. The man looked nervously around him, and then disappeared into one of the line of offices.

Once inside, he looked about and then called out, "Commander!"

He heard a shuffling off to the side, and emerging from a dimly lit cubicle into the hallway of the office was Anicetus. As commander of the imperial fleet in Misenum, Anicetus maintained quarters in Rome to accommodate his periodic shuffling between the two cities. He motioned for the man to come to him, and then took him into the smaller room.

"You've seen her villa?" Anicetus asked coldly. The man nodded. "You've walked through the woods that surround it?" Again he tipped his head. "She's likely to have a servant with her. Will that be a problem for you?" His head shook firmly from side to side. "The emperor will order his guards withdrawn late tomorrow night. Wait till then, and carry out your orders." He reached into a drawer in his desk and removed a bag of coins. "Here is your first payment. When it's through, return for the remainder. Understood?"

The man took the money and slipped it inside his cloak, nodded and left the office.

Chapter 10

The few leaders who knew of the crisis with Octavia had gathered at Judah and Esther's home to pray while Judah met with Nero, and not one of them could have predicted the news which Judah brought back with him. When she first heard it, Esther was so dismayed that her immediate response was to run outside. Judah followed after her and when he reached her, he wrapped his arms around her to console her. She buried her face in his chest and wept as spasms of grief shook her.

"Oh Judah, we've waited so long to go home," she cried. "How could this have happened? Another two days and we would have been gone! Couldn't you have refused him?"

"I tried my love, but our emperor is a clever and vain man, and dangerous," Judah said. "I sensed he was unaccustomed to not getting his own way."

"He's a spoiled, overgrown boy," Esther fumed.

"With a lot of power," Judah quickly observed. "He thinks he is a god, and unfortunately for us, in a manner of speaking, he is. He could have made things very miserable for us—and Paul."

Esther's grief now gave way to anger, but Judah tightened his hold on her.

"Esther, we must accept what has happened. There are no delays in God's timetable. And for purposes we don't yet appreciate, he has chosen to keep us here longer. It is no harm to us, just an inconvenience, nothing more. Of immediate concern to us is that someone must now take our place for the sake of the empress."

The thought of Octavia instantly softened Esther's heart and calmed her emotions, and she looked up in her husband's eyes. "May God show his pity now on dear Octavia," she said quietly.

They walked back inside the house where their friends were waiting in a subdued and thoughtful silence. "I'm sorry, my friends," said Esther as she wiped her eyes. "It was wrong of me to react so strongly. I should be happy for Paul, and concerned for Octavia, rather than thinking first of myself."

Paul was swift to come up to her and clasp her hands with tender sympathy, borne out of the abundance of his own sufferings. "Dear sister, you will yet make it home. Be of good courage. God knows your heart, and your desires. He pities us as a father his own children. Be patient and wait upon his will." She squeezed his hand and kissed him on his cheek.

Andronicus, Luke, Aquila and Priscilla, along with other leaders and the guard Mericus, were also seated about the room. "So it is true then that Paul's name has been cleared?" asked Andronicus.

Judah pulled a small paper from a pocket in his tunic. "Here is his release, bearing the emperor's seal."

Paul took it and looked it over, and a gleam of hearty satisfaction came over his face. He turned to his guard and disciple Mericus who had stayed hidden off to the side. "Mericus, with this document, you are released from your bondage to me. Take these chains off of my hands—and you may go free!"

Mericus laughed and gladly unlocked the chains. "I should do well to place the chains on my own wrists, Master Paul, for I do not care to ever leave your service."

When the chains fell off Paul's arms, the entire room of saints burst into loud and raucous applause. Aquila stood and proclaimed, "Judah, you are a legend among lawyers. Your abilities will be sung about for generations!"

"And to think of all the time I wasted writing your defense," Luke said with exaggerated lament.

Paul passed the release onto Luke. "Ah, Doctor Luke. Someone will make use of it one day. Don't despair." He clapped his hands together, enjoying the new freedom he had to move his arms about. "I must admit, I had such a strong desire to stand before Nero, that I feel a bit cheated by all of this. What is it that God intends for me?"

Priscilla then spoke. "Paul, we know exactly what God intends here. If you are free, then you must take Judah and Esther's place. You must be the one who will escort Lady Octavia to safety."

"This could be God's provision for you to go to Spain," Luke added. "Perhaps Octavia would not be in as much danger of being recognized in the West."

"But there are no churches in Spain," said Esther. "And our ship is bound for Judea."

"Hmm," Paul muttered, scratching his beard. "The first thing I shall do is shave. A new life demands a new face. But then friends, I think you are right," he said, with rising enthusiasm. "This indeed could be the very door which God has opened for the spread of the gospel in Spain. I could take the empress to Asia. Your ship is scheduled to stop there first?" Judah nodded. "I could see that she is welcomed into the church family, and then turn to the West before winter. What do the rest of you think?"

There was eager and unanimous agreement between them.

"Then let us pray and turn our hearts to sorting out the details that yet remain to be put in order," Paul instructed. "We don't have much time."

*   *   *

The following day, it seemed that all of Rome was on pins and needles. Nero was agitated by the knowledge of Anicetus' plan, and he lashed out at his attendants throughout the day in anxiety of what was to come. Irritability spread over the palace like a mist until it seemed that everyone, from the guards to the cooks to the very pets that roamed the grounds, were snapping at each other.

The Christians were likewise on edge. News of Paul's sudden acquittal, coupled with Judah's unexpected appointment, spread through the congregation, as did the announcement that Paul would sail for Asia at once. In a whirlwind of surprises, only the slightest of stray gusts can cause a person to stumble, and the concern of the leaders was that the stray gust might come from the church itself. The severest threat to the rescue attempt was, ironically, the church's greatest characteristic—its love.

Hundreds of believers had planned to come to Ostia harbor to see Judah and Esther off. All would be equally motivated to bid farewell to the great apostle. Yet the quieter and less visible their departure was, the better for all concerned. So the message was quickly filtered through the congregation that Paul desired an exit from Rome without fanfare. His Jewish enemies would not yet have heard of his release, but would be incensed—perhaps to the point of murder—once they had. He must leave Rome quietly. A sword forever hung over Paul's head, and with the removal of his personal guard, the danger would be greater.

However, one provision was made for the protection of Paul's party. The church had originally assigned two of its members to accompany Judah and Esther on their voyage home, so two tickets remained unclaimed. One naturally fell to Julia whose life would be endangered by the disappearance of her mistress. As a widow, she was free to leave Rome.

One more companion needed to be chosen—someone with the strength of a protector and the heart of a servant, who had few attachments to Rome. The leaders thought of him simultaneously—Thord. When the gentle giant was asked, he needed no time to ponder his decision, but agreed at once, and that afternoon, a sign appeared in his wineshop's window: *Closed for the summer, that Thord might rest.*

Octavia also spent the day in nervous apprehension. She had been banished from the Domus Aurea, and so returned to her private residence in the heavily wooded hills east of the city—a place that had belonged to the family of Claudius for generations. Nero did not allow any attendants except Julia to serve her, and forbade any callers but himself to see her. A small retinue of guards kept post outside of the villa, but she did not know whether these were Nero's assassins or Burrus' deliverers. She couldn't avoid peaking out of the corners of her windows at them throughout that tense day of anguished waiting.

Only Julia was with her inside the vast mansion, and without the usual noises of servants and visitors trafficking in and out, the house was a cold and lifeless mausoleum. Julia tried her best to soothe her mistress, but she too was wracked with misgivings and doubts.

So the evening finally fell on that long day, and appropriately, it rained and thundered all through the night, and no one who had a stake in what the morning light would bring was able to sleep. As morning approached, the storms blew out to sea, and in their place, rolled a thick bank of fog which descended on Rome as the first threads of light began to pierce through the darkness.

Paul and Luke spent the night with Judah and Esther, and before dawn, the four friends rose together and ate a hasty, unenjoyable breakfast, before Judah had to leave. Nero expected him early. They walked outside together, and Judah turned to Paul.

"So it is goodbye again, dear brother. It seems that every ten or fifteen years, God sees fit to bring us together for awhile. I'm glad for it."

"As am I, Judah," said Paul, with a tear in his eyes. "But maybe next time we won't have to wait quite so long. In fact, as ancient as we are, next time might just be in the kingdom of our Lord. And then we can stop this nasty habit of saying goodbye."

"You can't imagine how much I look forward to that day," Judah replied.

The friends embraced with a warmth that only thirty years of friendship could bring, and as they pulled apart, Paul said, "As you teach Nero how to ride horses, teach him love and mercy as well."

Judah shrugged with a smile. He then drew near to Esther, and no words needed to be shared between them. They kissed with a yearning that only thirty years of marriage could bring. He squeezed her tightly.

"I'll see you tonight, my love," he whispered. "And to you brother Luke," he said turning to his friend, "don't let Paul miss his boat!"

Luke nodded as Judah walked to his horse, which he mounted with some stiffness. He waved, then led the horse onto the road, and he vanished at once within the darkness. Soon the sound of the horse's feet died away.

The three returned inside. A half-hour passed and again, the clatter of horses was heard, with the creaking wheels of a wagon mingled in with the echo. The early light was of little help for visibility because of the thickness of the fog, but out of the mist came Thord, driving a worn and rickety wagon, pulled by two horses in nearly the same condition.

"Halloa!" the giant bellowed, as his friends came out to greet him. "Thord has come, dependable as the sunrise."

"Thord, that I will never doubt, but is your wagon as dependable as you?" Paul asked, slapping the flimsy sides of the wagon. It was essentially a long cart which Thord had converted into a makeshift carriage by inserting benches, sideboards and a canopied cover.

"If my cart dies on the way, then we ride my horses," Thord said with a wide smile which revealed a crooked range of yellow or missing teeth. "If my horses die on the way, then Thord will carry you all himself!"

"Very good," laughed Paul, who had grown to love this faithful man during his time in Rome. "Then let us be off at once. Julia and the empress will be waiting to meet us." They loaded a small collection of bags onto the coach, then Paul reached out to Esther. "Be courageous and be patient, my sister. Run the race well, and you will be rewarded!" he said.

He and Luke jumped into the wagon, and with a shout, Thord set the team into motion, and the three men rocked and jolted their way down the road and disappeared. Esther folded her hands beneath her chin and exhaled deeply, as the lonely fog enveloped her.

*   *   *

The arena was dark when Nero and his two guards pushed open its doors and walked inside. What was visible of the barn looked like the empty hull of a ship. Nero left his guards and walked out onto the middle of the arena floor, disappearing into the gloomy void. As he stirred up sand and sawdust on the floor, he disturbed the early meditations of numerous doves nesting in the rafters.

He did not enjoy silence. Voices came to him in the quiet which he heard at no other time. Whispers from another world echoed in his soul telling him he was lost. Telling him he was vain. That he was just a prideful, little man, who would have a short, pitiful life. *Humble yourself.* What was the presence that overshadowed him in the stillness? Nero hated the silence and he hated the voices. They were surely evil, he thought, and so whenever he could, he filled the gaps of empty space with noise, movement and sound. That way he would not have to hear them.

"The empress dies this morning, my lord," came another deeper voice, and Nero jumped as he heard it. It was Tigellinus who had walked out on the arena floor after him.

"Tigellinus, you approach with the stealth of a demon," Nero angrily complained. "And you scare me like one as well. Have the decency to announce your coming next time."

"I apologize Caesar. You are on edge?"

"I'm sure I will sleep better tonight. This will not fail, Tigellinus?"

"It cannot fail, Caesar."

"Don't speak to me of certainties after the last time!" snapped Nero. "What a botched spectacle that was."

"Anicetus set that debacle right, and he is in charge of this from the first," assured Tigellinus. "And please Lord Nero, Octavia is *not* Agrippina."

Nero grunted. "A pitiful end to the house of Claudius. But bramble must be cleared to make room for new growth." He brushed his hands together as though to warm himself. "Tigellinus, would you see that my servants are awake. I want my horses bridled and ready when Arrius arrives." He began to walk off but then turned back around. "And I want to know once it is over. Come as soon as you hear." Tigellinus saluted.

*   *   *

"It's chilly this morning, Lady Octavia," said Julia as she pushed down a few articles of clothing into a travel purse that was already busting at the seams. "It might be wise to wear an extra cloak over our clothes."

Octavia was also stuffing a bag, and she grunted in frustration that it repelled her efforts, like an infant refusing to be fed. "Oh Julia, what good is this!" she exclaimed in aggravation, as she pushed the bag aside and dropped down onto a nearby chair, covering her eyes as though to hold back tears. "Why are we doing this? It seems like I'm dreaming. I can't believe this is happening. I keep telling myself that this situation is not so bad. Nero was just drunk and thoughtless."

Julia kneeled down beside her and laid a sympathetic hand upon her leg. "Dear one, I'm sure Agrippina thought the same thing. If anything, your situation is more desperate than you can imagine. If your life were not in danger, Burrus would not have come to you."

Octavia looked with misty eyes toward the room's window which was milky with the heavy morning fog. The light was sufficient to illuminate the silhouettes of trees hidden outside within the fog, and Octavia thought to herself that they looked like a group of curious giants leaning over and peaking inside the window. She smiled at such a childlike thought.

"There was a time when I was young, Julia, when monsters were just imaginary villains in the nursery stories I was told. The world seemed so safe then. And innocent. Can you imagine how disappointed I was when I discovered that there really are monsters in the world? Oh, if only I could find some peace! If only I could wake up as a child in my bed again and discover that this has all just been a dream."

"My daughter, maybe tonight when you lay your head on your pillow you'll find some of that peace again, hmm?" asked Julia, and Octavia nodded with a reluctant, but hopeful sigh. She stood back up, leaned over her clothes and made one more attempt at conquering her bag.

"I'm used to having fifty pairs of shoes in my closet to choose from," she said in bewilderment. "I wonder how I will manage with just four?"

Julia fastened her own bag and then came over to Octavia. She looked down at her purse, and shook her head in parental exasperation. "Four pair? How about two?" she corrected, plucking four shoes from the bag and dropping them onto the floor. With that accomplished, she pushed on the bag and easily fastened its hooks. "I believe you'll find it liberating, empress. Jesus taught us that life is not found in the abundance of possessions."

"Or shoes?" Octavia asked with a blush and a giggle.

"Or shoes!" Julia agreed. "We should go, child. They'll be meeting us at the crossroads soon."

"What if the guards don't let us go?"

"They let us walk yesterday, exactly as we are dressed now. Why wouldn't they today? We carry more with us for a visit to the hairdresser than we have with us now! We must trust that Burrus will get us to the crossroads as he promised."

They slipped on their cloaks and slung their travel bags over their shoulders, and thus equipped, they did not appear overly conspicuous. The least suspicion of anyone who saw them would be that they were fleeing the country. They walked through the house, and as they stood at the door, Octavia took one final look around her at possessions and rooms that she would not see again. Though every part of her cringed with a strange anxiety, she at last said, "Here we go."

She pulled open the door and they stepped outside. The sensation of walking through the fog was like walking inside a moving bubble. They could see fifty feet in any direction around them but at the perimeter of the bubble was a solid wall of white, and objects inside the bubble seemed to glow with a dull shimmer. They inched forward along a path that led to the front gates of the property, and once they reached the gates they stopped and looked at each other.

"Where are the guards?" Octavia asked in a whisper.

They looked on all sides of the stone pillars and iron railings, and even glanced inside the hedges that spread out from the gates and lined the road ahead. There was no question about it—they were very much alone.

"Are we safe?" Octavia asked.

"Jesus is with us," answered Julia. "Let's go for our walk."

They stepped forward onto the road, walking side by side directly down its center, with the hedges ten feet away on either side of them, six feet high, and thick with new foliage, stretching as far as they could see like a gauntlet of green stone. Within the artificial bubble of the fog, the sounds of the forest seemed amplified around them, and they jumped at each one. The birds were not chirping but trumpeting. The crackling of a twig was not a deer gliding through the woods, but the trampling of an elephant. The bubbling of a nearby stream was like the roar of a cataract. And their own breathing seemed to echo like a cry in a canyon.

Octavia reached out in a reflex of fear and took Julia's hand, and so they proceeded, step by step, twitching nervously like frightened ground squirrels. Soon they were far enough down the path that the gate and the villa disappeared from sight and all that stretched behind and before them was the road, the hedges and the canopy of trees.

"I wish we didn't have to walk so far," Octavia bemoaned, looking behind her, wishing the house were still in sight.

"It's less than a mile now, child," said Julia, her eyes riveted straight ahead. All at once, she stopped and put out her hand to Octavia, who immediately wheeled her head forwards and gasped. Up ahead in the distance, barely visible in the cloud, was the shadowy form of a large man. They stood frozen in place, watching the man's own motionless form.

"Who is that?" Octavia whimpered to her servant.

"It could be one of Burrus' men," Julia replied.

"Then why doesn't he call out to us?"

The man said nothing and did nothing. "Who are you?" Octavia called out, and her words seemed to trigger something within the man, for no sooner was the question asked, than he began to walk toward them with the stride of a soldier. As he stepped into the bubble of visibility, his hand reached purposefully to the hilt of his sword.

*   *   *

Judah arrived at the Domus Aurea and guided his horse along a side street which Seneca promised would take him to a back entrance of the palace grounds, and bring him more directly to the arena. He felt relieved that he did not have to hike up the palace's front steps and traverse the length of its gaudy central corridor. When he announced who he was, the guards greeted him with an unmistakable flourish of honor, which would have flattered someone else, but scarcely impressed Judah.

He knew intimately the deceitfulness of power and saw its poison at work in full measure when he had walked the hallways of the Senate. To watch lesser men fawn over their superiors in the hope of advancement, to see greater men exhibit inexcusable condescension with those beneath them, to see young and eager reformers begin their careers with high idealism which they so readily set aside that they might profit from the established system—it was a stench in his nostrils. The words of his Lord, *It shall not be so with you,* rang in his head every dreary day he served in the Senate.

He was swiftly ushered inside, and an escort rode with him to the arena. He dismounted and as he walked into the barn, disgusted with the turn his life had taken, he muttered a short prayer which the escort could not hear. "God give me the strength to endure this misery. Make me usable."

Nero was standing near his chariot with Tigellinus. He was dressed in a garish charioteer's cloak, and looked more like an actor than a rider. When he saw Judah enter, he quickly walked up to him and shook his hand with eagerness.

"Good morning Master Arrius. My thanks to you that you have come in such a timely fashion. We will of course set you up with additional housing near to the palace so that you won't be inconvenienced with long rides every day."

"Caesar, thank you for your thoughtfulness," Judah said dryly. *I'm glad you wouldn't want to inconvenience me any more than you have,* he thought.

They walked over to the chariot, where Nero pointed to Tigellinus. "This is Tigellinus, a friend from childhood. He thinks my thoughts after me."

In that case, avoid him, Judah thought, as the two men saluted each other.

"And here, of course, are my horses," Nero continued, circling his animals, then rubbing the outside horse on its side. "You met them the other day. So where does one begin in this process of becoming a champion of the great Circus?"

"Perhaps it would be good if you allow me to observe your horses for awhile at work while you drive them," Judah said. "That way I can acquaint myself with their abilities and temperaments."

"Very well," Nero said. "We'll make them earn their morning oats."

He stepped up into his chariot, and then looked over at Tigellinus. "I'll be in the arena most of the morning. Don't disturb me Tigellinus, unless something urgent should arise." He said the words slowly, and the intonation was not lost on Judah.

*　　　　　　*　　　　　　*

Neither Octavia nor Julia recognized the man as he walked out of the mist. As the stranger drew nearer, Julia instinctively began to recite words of comfort she had learned as a child. "*The Lord is my shepherd, I shall not be in need. He makes me to lie down in green pastures.*"

The man was dressed in a dark, ordinary cloak and his faced registered no emotion except sinister determination. The women's feet seemed anchored into the ground, though both of them looked frantically about them.

"Who are you?" Octavia called out. *Where was Burrus?* When the man was thirty feet away, he suddenly withdrew his sword with a smooth, precise motion, and raised it to attack.

"Julia run!" Octavia cried, dropping her satchel, and both women turned to flee. But then Octavia screamed all the louder and stopped in her tracks. Barricading the road behind them were two other men, both soldiers, and both armed with bows. With their escape blocked off on all sides, Octavia dropped to the ground in paralyzed fright and Julia fell down over her as though to protect her, though she knew nothing could help them now.

When they fell to the ground, the man with the sword stopped, for he had not seen the soldiers until that moment. A puzzled look came over his face. And then his eyes tightened in fear as the soldiers dropped to their knees and with one rapid, polished movement, they drew their bows and in dramatic unison, fired their arrows within an inch of each other into the man's chest. The women's eyes were closed and they gasped in horror to listen to the feathered hiss of the arrows pass over their heads. No sooner had the soldiers fired their arrows, than a flurry was heard in the hedges, and four more arrows exploded out of the greenery and each found their mark in the torso of the man, who was dead before he fell to the gravel.

The women waited for an eternal moment with their eyes shut, and their breath suspended, but then slowly they looked up. The assassin was sprawled out lifelessly before them like a pin cushion. They looked behind them to see the soldiers, but to their surprise, the road was deserted. They looked into the hedges on either side of the road, but they saw nothing and heard nothing. Even the birds had grown silent. The woods were gripped in an eerie stillness.

"Let's keep walking, child," Julia said. Octavia picked up her purse, and the two women crept past the dead man, and then hurried down the road, not looking behind them even once. "*The Lord is my shepherd, I shall not be in need...*," Julia repeated as they disappeared into the fog.

*   *   *

Nero ran the horses for nearly an hour, and Judah had to force himself to be observant, for his mind was racing with anxiety over Octavia's rescue. But Caesar was equally distracted, and the entire session was marked by almost comical gaps of inattentiveness by both mentor and pupil.

After the hour, Caesar stopped to rest the horses, and walked over to Judah to ask for his evaluation. But before Judah could begin speaking, he was interrupted by a line of servants who descended on Nero like buzzards. One with a towel wiped Caesar's face and attacked each bead of sweat as though it were a cancerous mole, all the while shaking his head in apparent offense that perspiration would even dare appear on Nero's divine head. One brought water, and hovered over Nero with such apoplectic urgency on her face, that one would believe Nero to be near death. Another brought a fresh pair of sandals, but first, the servant washed the emperor's holy feet of each speck of dust which had defiled them.

Judah looked on, shielding his disdain for this pathetic sycophancy. This was not a man who had just completed several dozen laps in a practice arena; this was Hannibal the Great descending from the Alps, or Octavius returning to Rome after crushing Antony's army. He was unsure who sickened him more—the unctuous servants or their puerile master.

When these ablutions were completed, Judah himself was offered a glass of water which he begrudgingly accepted, and finally they were left alone again. "So what are your first impressions, Master Arrius?" Nero asked.

I think you're a vain, pampered ass. "I think you have some very fine horses, Caesar," Judah replied. "It would seem that the first one in from the left is...," but again he was interrupted, this time by Nero's own wandering eyes, which had turned suddenly toward one of the entrances in the arena where Tigellinus had appeared.

"Excuse me for a minute Arrius," and Nero stepped away with rude abruptness. He marched hurriedly across the floor, and then leaned expectantly over the fence where Tigellinus stood. "Well? Is there any news?"

"Nothing yet, Lord Nero. I thought we might have heard something by now, but then again, Anicetus was not certain on the exact timing of events. It all depends on circumstances, you understand."

"You have not eased my anxiety," huffed Nero. "Anicetus better not disappoint me." He stomped away and returned to Judah, and once at his side, tried to cover up his agitation. "So Counsel, you were saying the first horse in is…what? Fast, slow, beautiful, ornery? What do you think?"

"She seemed the strongest of the four," Judah began, "and if so, we might want to consider…," but now his own voice trailed off, for away on the other side of the arena he saw one of Burrus' men enter, striding alone along the fence and then disappearing into another hallway. "…consider harnessing her on the inside."

So the morning pressed on, with both men playing at cooperation but riddled with an uneasiness borne of being passive combatants in the fierce struggle then being waged outside the arena.

*　　　*　　　*

Julia and Octavia arrived at the crossroads without further incident but they were utterly exhausted by the suspense that weighed upon them. Their hearts pounded like war drums within them, and their legs seemed as heavy as iron pillars. To know they were protected but yet not see their defenders enticed them with comfort but did not give it entirely. They were being carried along blind and naked on the rushing tide of fate—so Octavia felt, or faith—so Julia felt.

When they reached the crossroads, they stood in the center of the intersection, and looked out in all four directions but saw nothing. The temptation to run and hide in the woods surged through them both and just as they were ready to give in to the thought, they heard the clattering of horses' hooves start up from a distance. Out of the fog came Thord, driving his two horses slowly along.

Julia clutched at Octavia in relief. "It's them!" and for the first time, the women felt a true sense of safety. When the wagon pulled up alongside of them, Thord greeted them loudly. "Good morning! Thord's caravan is here to serve you."

"Why Thord, these two ladies should not be walking alone on such a miserable morning as this," Paul declared as he and Luke jumped off the back of the wagon. "Do we have room in your fine carriage to bring them along?"

"Ha! Thord will make room for them," the giant bellowed. "If Thord must cut down a tree and make a new wagon, I will do so."

Paul and Luke took the women's bags off their shoulders and then led them to the back of the cart. "Right this way, dear ladies," Paul said. "It's not quite the litter of a queen, but it's the finest escort in the east woods. Watch your step."

They helped the women climb up into the wagon, and while Luke adjusted the canopy which was stretched over the rear half, he asked, "Was your trip uneventful?"

The women looked at each other and shuddered simultaneously. "We entertained one visitor," Octavia replied quietly.

"Oh dear. A friendly one, I hope," Paul said.

"Not exactly, but thankfully he was detained, and won't be bothering us again," Julia explained.

"Let's be on our way then with due speed," Luke urged. "In case their visitor has friends of his own."

"Ride on, Brother Thord!" Paul yelled out. "The morning hours are wasting!"

Thord snapped his reins and the horses plodded on. Their destination was Ostia harbor, newly refurbished as part of Nero's extensive building program, and now an expanding hub of international travel and trade. The ride lasted three tense hours. As the sun rose up over the hills, the fog burned away, and traffic increased on the roads as the city of Rome gradually sprang to life.

The closer they drew to the harbor, the worse the congestion became which was both a blessing and curse, for they easily blended into the cluttered mass of humanity. But whenever Thord was forced to slow the wagon down or stop it altogether, the travelers held their collective breath, until he resumed.

Worst of all were the soldiers, who were scattered everywhere. It seemed to them that every third person wore a uniform and carried a sword, and most unnerving was that at any given moment, any one of these soldiers could suddenly scream out, "Stop that wagon!" Octavia trembled to be standing so near a precipice of disaster, but Paul's unflagging confidence seemed reassuring, and Julia's own face was steady with hope.

As they drew within a mile of Ostia, Paul began to fidget some himself. "Well friends, this is the part of our little adventure that will be most interesting. But the less of an adventure this is, the better for all of us. Empress, we cannot call you by your title any longer. Even your name is a harbinger of danger to us. Might I suggest that you now adopt the name of Mary, and if you do not find it offensive, might I additionally request that you see yourself as our daughter. Julia will be my wife, Thord will be our servant, and together we might suitably pass for an extremely dull Jewish family, making our way slowly back home to Judea."

Luke laughed. "I knew you'd settle down and marry one day, Paul."

Paul smirked. "God pity the woman who would ever truly become my wife. I don't think she could keep up with me! Now then, before we arrive, I feel a need to unburden myself with prayer. May we join hands within this circle and commit this journey into our Savior's hands?"

He reached out his hand to Octavia who took it tentatively, and Julia took her other hand. What little she had experienced of the prayers of these people in the past few days she found slightly odd but strangely comforting. They spoke to their God in a tone of familiarity, as though he were standing right beside them, as though they actually expected to be heard. Seeing the others bow their heads and close their eyes, she imitated them in an awkward, childlike fashion, and listened with fascination as Paul poured out his soul to the God he called *Father*.

Scarcely had the "Amens" been uttered when Thord announced that the harbor was in sight. "Julia, my wife, and my daughter Mary, it's time for you both to don your veils," Paul said. "Thankfully, your modesty and our safety go hand in hand."

Julia assisted her mistress in wrapping her head in a Jewish shawl, which when in place covered the lower half of her face. Beneath this, dropped a silken netting to shield her eyes from view. Julia then securely fastened her own veil, and once it was in place, Paul announced, "And now we are ready. Hopefully, our ship will be ready as well."

Indeed, their ship had been docked for two days and was ready to be boarded, and at the direction of the harbor officials, Thord guided the wagon to the appropriate pier and within minutes, pulled to a stop.

"No hesitations, no doubts, no stammering," Paul reminded everyone as he pulled back the canvas. "Just a simple, dull Jewish family."

As they stepped down out of the wagon, Andronicus walked up to them, and with him was Aquila and Priscilla. "Greetings Andronicus. How have things been at the harbor?" asked Paul.

"We've had to send home maybe fifty or so who hadn't heard all the news, but other than that, your sending-off party is the committee of three you see standing before you, and Luke as well."

"Very good. I can't tell you how much my family and I have enjoyed your Roman hospitality. And you have our other belongings for the voyage?"

Andronicus pointed to two large crates that had been stacked up on the pier. "Everything you need to make your trip home a pleasant one."

Paul nodded approvingly. "My daughter especially thanks you for your generous provision." Andronicus smiled at Octavia who nodded politely through her veil. "Now if you'll help us get situated on our vessel, we will bid you farewell. We're all quite tired from this hectic morning and I'm sure my family could use the rest."

Before boarding, Paul had to show himself to the customs agent assigned to the ship, but since he carried all of his necessary documentation, including the diptych bearing the seal of his Roman citizenship, the interview was a brief formality, and they boarded the ship without incident. After situating the two women, Paul and Thord returned to their friends for a final word of goodbye.

Paul took Andronicus by the arms, and looked up in his bright and zealous eyes. "Andronicus, you have tremendous shepherding gifts which God has given you. Use them in full measure and don't be afraid to make mistakes, for his grace is stronger than our failings." He turned to Luke. "You are a faithful companion, Doctor Luke. I hope you will come and visit me, and continue your chronicles of our work together. I can speak, but you can write, and so yours is the more lasting and greater gift. Use it well. But...," and he waved his finger in front of Luke's nose, "...no mention of this event anywhere!"

"We shall laugh of it in heaven," Luke said. "Not a word of it to anyone until then. Take care my brother. And if you make it to Spain, I will indeed visit you there. And Thord, I will take good care of your horses," and the giant beamed to hear this. "Your wagon, however, I may burn."

"And with my blessings!" Paul added, and Thord made a mock protest, but hugged Luke in the end. Paul then embraced Aquila and Priscilla with deep affection. "Encourage Judah and Esther, will you? They are strong, but even the strong ones need to be lifted up."

"This moment doesn't seem right without them here," said Priscilla.

"No, it doesn't. These have been strange days. Friends, thank you for your own encouragement. So many dark moments in my life that you have brightened. Just be yourselves, and all will be well."

Such was their parting, and the fellowship was again broken. At the sounding of the noon bells, the ship pulled in its anchor, set its sails, and slowly pulled out to sea, and within an hour, it was but a speck on the blue horizon, and then suddenly it was gone, drowned out by the glare of the afternoon sun. Only then did the Christians on shore retreat from the harbor, and if they had been looking up into the hills at that moment, they would have seen an aging soldier sitting straight and stoic upon his horse at the edge of an overhanging bluff, also looking out to sea. As the ship vanished from sight, the soldier reached up to his eyes and wiped away a solitary tear with the skin of his crippled hand.

*   *   *

Nero finally tired of his lessons by the early afternoon, and as Judah prepared to go, the emperor thanked him. "You have underestimated your abilities as a trainer, Counsel Arrius. Already I can feel improvement in the areas we have worked on."

Judah was exhausted, hungry, and desperate for news, but he tried to be diplomatic. "The horses respond to very subtle differences in their handling. If you work on turning the reins as I showed you, you'll find yourself with more command."

"Thankfully, you'll be here to oversee my progress," Nero said, fully intending his words to be complimentary, and never guessing that to Judah's ears they were a curse. "Our time has been profitably spent. I will see you again two mornings from now, and every other morning after that."

It was less a request than a command and with that, Nero turned and left the arena. Judah's first thought was that, in respect to the hour, whatever the outcome was, it was over and had already been decided. God had rendered his verdict, and there was no use wasting any more time worrying about it. To be anxious about the future might be mildly justifiable from a human point of view, but to agonize over events that were over was futile. So he resolved to be at peace as he journeyed back home. The ship had sailed and what was done was done.

Judah splashed his face with water from a nearby bucket and as he turned to go, a voice suddenly called out, "Arrius."

He looked up and saw nothing, but then in scanning the length of the arena, he saw across the track a man's silhouette standing in the shadows beyond the fence. As the man stepped forward into the light, Judah held his breath when he saw that it was Burrus. Neither man walked toward the other, and neither man spoke. Burrus' only movement was to nod his head in a slow, decisive fashion, and the satisfaction that shined from his face told all.

The weight on Judah's shoulders slipped off in an instant, and he acknowledged Burrus' message with a respectful tipping of his head. In that silent exchange, each man saluted the other, and then Burrus withdrew into the shadows and disappeared. For the moment at least, Judah felt young again.

Chapter 11

Anicetus was more than twice Nero's age, overshadowed him in physical strength, and was ten times the warrior. But he was not Caesar, and so as he sat before Nero early that evening, he shook violently as he reported that Octavia had disappeared. The last thing any man wanted was to pique the emperor. As the day wore on and still no news had come, Nero suspected that something had gone wrong, so by the time Anicetus arrived at the palace, the magma was already hot and in need of only a fissure. The intensity of the eruption startled even Tigellinus. Once the announcement was made, Nero's first response was to take a leather racing helmet that was upon his desk and fling it with the force of a catapult against the closest wall.

"Anicetus! What do you mean she has disappeared?"

Anicetus looked down and could not suppress the trembling in his voice. "She and her servant are gone. And Cassius, the man I hired, has not reported back to me."

"Caesar, we searched the house this afternoon," Tigellinus added, "and they are not there."

"What does that mean, they are not there!" Nero thundered. "Are you saying they have run away? Are you saying they are spending the day at the beach? Where are they?"

"We didn't see any signs that Octavia had packed up an unusual amount of her clothes. The bed had been slept in, the wardrobe was full, a few pair of shoes were on the floor. All of her personal effects seemed in place."

"I thought she was being watched. How could she have gone anywhere at all in the first place?"

"Cassius was to have been keeping watch from the time the soldiers withdrew," Anicetus tried to explain. "If he was delayed, there may have been a gap of time in which they could have left without being seen. But it would have been well past midnight. And it was of course foggy this morning."

Nero scowled. "Enough of your petty excuses. Was there no one with this Cassius?"

"He was meant to be a lone assassin. How many men are needed to kill a woman?"

"Correction, Anicetus—how many of *your* men are needed to kill a woman," the emperor sneered. "You forget, we've been down this road before, and again, you have taken a simple task and made it complicated. You redeemed yourself last time. What do you intend to do now?"

"Emperor, I am subject to your command. I will strangle her myself if that will make you happy."

"Yes, strangle the wench yourself," Nero mused as he paced behind his desk. "That only seems fair. A man should be responsible for his own mistakes. Curse you, Anicetus, why did you botch this up!"

Nero reached over and picked up the racing helmet, crumpled by the wall. He held it up to Anicetus. "I'd like to do this with your head right about now." He reshaped the helmet into its original form and brushed at where the leather had been marred. "The beauty of a rogue assassin is that it is all so secretive," he said, more calmly now, "and we can all then mourn the tragic loss of dear Octavia, while the killer is never found. But why would you, my trusted friend, slay the empress? What reason would you have?"

There was a lengthy silence. "Lover's quarrels often end with someone dead," Tigellinus slowly said to break the stillness. "We all know that Octavia loves to vacation in Misenum."

Both men's minds were sparked by the suggestion. Nero came around the desk and stood above Anicetus. "Anicetus."

"Caesar?"

"Have you slept with your emperor's wife?" There was a playfulness in his voice now though he spoke as an inquisitor.

Anicetus smirked. "I am a handsome dog, you know."

"An irresistible devil," Tigellinus muttered. "I wouldn't doubt you've slept with half the women in Italy by now."

"I would of course deserve to die for such adultery," said Anicetus.

"Yes, you would deserve to die," Nero proceeded. "But does Caesar want to lose both his precious wife and a trusted friend all at once? The loss would be too grievous. More than I could bear. Though betrayed and wounded by a friend, I can still show mercy."

Nero returned to his desk and sat down upon his chair. He leaned forward, his hands folded in front of him. "So Anicetus, choose the site of your banishment now, and I will commute your sentence."

"How swift is Caesar's justice, how inscrutable his adjudications, that they are given even before the crime is committed!" said Tigellinus, with as much spiritedness as he could muster. "There is yet one problem with this scheme. Where is the one against whom Anicetus will commit his crime?"

"There are but two alternatives here, each with its own set of possibilities," Nero said. "She has either fled, and so knows something of our intent. Or she is just away from her house for a time, visiting a friend, shopping, still knowing nothing of our plan. If the latter, we wait for her return and Anicetus fulfills his duties. If the former..."

"Why would she have fled? How would she have known that her life was in danger?" Anicetus asked.

"You probably threatened her yourself that night," Tigellinus said to Nero.

"I was drunk! I don't know what I said. Besides, she doesn't have the stomach for running away. Someone has helped her."

"She might have offered Cassius a greater reward, and they both have fled."

"I find that hard to imagine. She also lacks the brains for running away. No, if she has fled, then someone has helped her, and it is someone who feels great loyalty to her. Someone who feels great loyalty to the descendants of Germanicus." The others immediately understood his meaning. "It is someone we must watch carefully. And if the empress does not in fact return, then it is someone we will eliminate. Tigellinus, you have been long overdue for a promotion."

*   *   *

Octavia did not return. She and her servant disappeared; neither was Cassius seen again. Nero ordered for a full investigation, and grieved aloud over her disappearance, but still the rumor spread through the streets that Nero himself had disposed of her, which so alarmed the emperor that he demanded of Anicetus that he at once make public his confession.

The event was played up like a Greek tragedy. Anicetus was bound in chains and brought before the Senate. His face was bruised from his interrogation, and Nero nearly swooned to hear Anicetus say the words that Octavia had been his lover. Anicetus confessed that he had threatened to kill her when she suggested ending the affair, and in her fear, she had fled knowing she could not face Nero, nor could she remain with Anicetus, but where she had gone was a mystery. Smitten with remorse for offending his emperor and betraying his friendship, Anicetus repented of his adulteries and pleaded with Nero for mercy.

Remarkably, Caesar granted it, and the people marveled at the forbearance of their great leader, who even in the face of unconscionable malice, could yet be forgiving. And even generous. Anicetus was banished to the resort island of Sardinia, condemned to a punishing life of wandering beaches with vacationing nobility by day, and being entertained at the dinner parties of retired senators by night.

Judah watched this charade of justice from a distance. His contact with the emperor was limited to several hours on alternating mornings, usually three times a week, and although Caesar was often chatty during their sessions together, the affairs of the state only rarely filtered into their conversation. Nero usually spoke only of himself, seldom inquired into Judah's own life, and in fact, was interested in Judah only insofar as his expertise in horses ran. Once the sessions had finished, he quickly left the arena, and after the first two weeks, he abandoned the cordial pleasantries of saying goodbye altogether.

To be brushed off in such a cavalier fashion was of little consequence to Judah; in fact, he preferred it that way. If he procured more favorable attention from Nero, more obligations were likely to follow, and the last thing he wanted was to be drawn further into Caesar's web. Yet it was distressing to watch how Nero acted toward others, especially his servants, whom he treated like insects.

On one occasion, he was brought drinking water which was too warm, and he splashed it immediately in the servant's face, followed by cutting slaps of his hand. Another servant accidentally sneezed on the emperor's foot. Caesar erupted into a rage and demanded that the servant kneel before him with an open mouth and remain that way while Nero spat down his throat. He verbally accosted each one, and struck them all as a matter of course, no matter their age or size.

Judah had to walk away during the breaks in their sessions, because he could not tolerate seeing such relentless abuse. Most painful of all was when children fell under the shadow of his wrath. One child who had the misfortune of passing gas in the emperor's presence was forced to stand still while Nero coated his body with fresh manure, and the mother could only look on helplessly, holding back her tears for fear that Nero would see them and make the situation worse.

There were moments when Judah's grief and anger were so kindled that he thought of driving Nero through with a pitchfork and accepting the consequences. Any hopes he entertained of being used by God to bring Nero to faith were rapidly crushed beneath the weight of Caesar's unrestrained depravity. Slowly, Judah sank into a murky depression, for he could find no purpose for why he had been thrust into this position, and the heavens seemed like brass to him when he looked upward for answers.

The only worthwhile moments for him were found in Burrus' company. Though Judah seldom stayed in the small house provided for him by Caesar, when he did so for reason of bad weather or weariness, Burrus often sought him out. The first few times, he came ostensibly to ask if word had come concerning Octavia's fate. (Eventually a letter came from Paul indicating that all was well with his daughter Mary. She had ended up somewhere in Asia—Paul was careful not to say where—and he was preparing to embark for Spain.)

In time, Burrus came just because he found Judah's company refreshing, and the two men soon discovered that they were exploring the frontiers of a genuine friendship. But then came the day when a sharp pain arose within Burrus' throat. Physicians spotted a noticeable swelling which they feared was a tumor. Several weeks later, it was confirmed. Burrus was dying.

Nero made no secret of the fact that Burrus was now *persona non grata*. He no longer solicited him for counsel, he ignored him in public, and Tigellinus was asked to schedule the rotation of guards in the Domus Aurea. Burrus bore this ostracism with dignity, but as his illness intensified, Nero found a new way to strike at him. Making public declarations of concern for his prefect, Nero offered

Burrus the services of his own private physician. Privately, he commanded his physician to mix poison in with the medicinal salve that was applied to the lining of Burrus' throat.

As Burrus' duties were reduced, Nero quelled the murmuring of the Guard by promoting as acting prefect a popular soldier, Faenius Rufus, but secretly, Tigellinus was being groomed as Burrus' successor. Nero had become the supreme actor, keeping the mask always to the audience, whether an audience of citizens or soldiers. Only in private did the mask come off, and the contrast was alarming to those, like Judah and Burrus, who saw it.

Judah maintained a cordial distance from Seneca. Something about the philosopher disturbed him. Seneca seemed to recognize the evil that was polluting Nero's court, and at times appeared genuinely distressed by it, but there was something lacking in his spirit which created a check in Judah's heart and prompted him to be cautious around him.

As Burrus' health declined, the time came when he no longer could come to Judah, so Judah went to him instead. Judah knew death well. As a young prince in Jerusalem, he saw men die in the stoning pit and on Roman crosses. While chained as a prisoner in a Roman galley, he saw men die of exhaustion and disease. And he was there at the foot of the cross as the Son of God cried out, "It is finished!" Death could not be hidden in this age. Life was fragile and death was ordinary, and yet everytime Judah saw its face, it sickened him. Now to see this noble man, emaciated and pale, caused a hollow of grief to grow within him.

"Judah Ben-Hur, I have fought with soldiers my entire life," Burrus said to him one evening, in a voice marred by the enlarging tumor. "I have discovered in you the soul of a true warrior. And I do not admit this easily, but I have also found in you the heart of a friend."

He sat upright, but stiffly, in a large chair with Judah across the room from him. The nights were again turning cold after the long summer, and logs blazed near them in the fireplace.

"Burrus, I likewise value the man you are, and the friend you have become," said Judah. "I know that I have shared with you many things about Jesus Christ, so I trust that you will receive what I now say with the full honor with which it is intended. I have seen in you more of the spirit of Jesus, and more of his character and strength, than in many of my brothers and sisters who bear his name."

"I am honored Judah, that you think so," responded Burrus. "I have come to admire this Jesus you have spoken of so highly. If all the things you have said of him are true, then he is undeniably the greatest warrior of all. But I am of earth, and he is of heaven, and so there must forever be a gulf between us. If he is as you claim, a man without evil, then I will never be worthy to stand before him."

"None of us is worthy to stand before him, Burrus. He came that we might be made worthy. And his death is the passageway. His resurrection is the proof. All he asks is that we cast our lot with him."

Burrus was not convinced by Judah's argument. "I have spent my life despising soldiers and politicians who switch allegiances on the field of battle once the tide has turned against them," he said. "Once we put on a uniform, we declare our colors, and a real man will stay true to the end. He will accept the consequences. If victory, then he shares in the spoils. If defeat, then he shares in the ignominy. The tide has turned against me, Judah, and defeat approaches. Shall I now in the waning moments of my life seek asylum with your God, having spurned him my whole life? What I find unacceptable about your faith is that your God would still find a man like me acceptable."

"Now you're sounding like Seneca," Judah said, shaking his head. "God is moved by humility, not proud arguments."

"Please, Judah. Accuse me of being a magician or an actor, but not a philosopher. I have seen how little philosophy has done for poor Seneca."

Burrus suddenly leaned forward, gripping his throat as it seized with pain. Judah sat by helplessly until it passed. "I don't know what is worse—my illness, or the cure which Nero sends me. Oh Judah, I am tired. Who or what can defeat someone like the son of Ahenobarbus? Seneca keeps hoping that words will win the day, but Nero has ruined our language. I used to think that if enough legions could be rallied against him, he would crumble, but he has appointed his own generals and scattered them across the empire, so who will march against him? He has corrupted words and co-opted power. And he dazzles the people with smoke and mirrors. What is left to defeat him? I am tired of it all. I long for a simple world, where honor and valor and truth mean something."

Judah looked tenderly upon his friend. "I share your frustrations Burrus, but not your despair. When words and power and politics and all else have failed, there is one thing that can yet defeat evil," he said. "Evil can be overcome by love.

Maybe not all at once. But every selfless act of love performed in defiance of evil is one step closer to defeating evil. Thousands may need to suffer. Years may pass. But one day love will triumph."

Burrus stared into the fire and pondered Judah's words. A look of satisfaction came over his countenance. "I have one single consolation in this world. That I came to my senses in time to help at least one person. If that is what you mean Judah, then I fully agree with you."

After another pause, Judah spoke again. "Tell me about Seneca. I can't read him. In private, he talks like you, Burrus. In public, he speaks another language."

"Seneca was the first to realize that Nero was slipping away from us," Burrus explained, with a touch of melancholy. "He dreamed once that Nero was Caligula—our worst emperor—come back to life, and he wasn't far off the mark. He warned me that we might have to oppose him. But at some point he lost his boldness. Maybe when Agrippina was killed, he lost his nerve. He kept insisting that it wasn't time yet, that there was still a chance for Nero to change. I don't think he still believes that, but the moment has been lost, and he finds himself trapped, forced to be a mouthpiece of a regime he hates. I used to think Seneca was a better man than this. But who am I to boast, for I am just as responsible as he for unleashing this monster on our people."

Judah looked down at the flickering shadows on the floor. "My father died when I was young, but he said one thing to me that I will always remember. *You can never tell the worth of a man until he is tested.* If Seneca is a good man, he will yet find a way to pass the test, as you have my friend."

Judah looked at Burrus, and saw an ocean of anguish and regret tossing in his eyes. But Burrus could not let it go. He stared into the fire, and sighed from the depths of his fatigued soul.

·*   *   *

Shortly after Octavia's disappearance, the emperor requested that the Senate sanction the annulment of his marriage, and outsiders marveled when the Senate boldly ruled that the annulment be delayed. What outsiders did not know was that this was just another ploy of Caesar's to sway public opinion in his favor. By appearing submissive, Nero would quiet alarmists who observed him siphoning power away from the Senate. He would also win sympathy from the Roman citizenry who would see him enduring insult at the hands of a harsh Senate at a time when he was already suffering.

But all along at the time of Nero's choosing, he would have his annulment. That time had now come and he commissioned Seneca with the task of directing the Senate to act on his behalf. The cackling hum of nearly 600 men filled the Senate chambers on the day Nero selected. Chronic absenteeism had plagued the Senate in the years following Nero's ascension. But not on this day. A nervous energy hovered in the air.

The auditorium was an octagonally shaped hall with a domed roof. The senators sat on rows of cold marble that bent in a semi-circle around the central platform, where the emperor sat with Tigellinus, Seneca and the presiding consul. The consul brought the Senate to order, then nodded to Seneca, who stood and walked to the podium. "Esteemed colleagues, we must now direct our attention to the matter of Lady Octavia," he began. "Lord Nero has approached us now a second time and offered us his request for the annulment of his marriage, on the grounds of adultery and desertion. Is there any discussion on this matter?"

A senator stood. "With respect to our emperor, Roman law demands that there be some evidence before such a ruling be made. May we have a review of this evidence?"

"The evidence is two-fold," Seneca replied. "You have heard direct testimony given to you in the confession of the former commander Anicetus, who swore to you under oath that he had committed adultery with the empress. He has been duly sentenced by this body and is now serving his just punishment. That alone is sufficient evidence to warrant annulment, and it should have been granted at the very time of Anicetus' conviction. The second piece of evidence is circumstantial in nature but is more convincing still. Octavia has been missing for the past six months. That alone ought to constitute some measure of proof. Her unfaithfulness is suggested by the very act of desertion."

This comment stirred up the pot, and pockets of mumbled conversation boiled up around the room. One senator turned to another and whispered, "Or it suggests that she has been disposed of," drawing nods of agreement from the other. "I want to know why she was so unhappy," could also be heard amidst the muttering. The consul stood and called the assembly back to order. When the room quieted, another senator stood.

"Is there any correspondence which has come to our attention in the past several months which might reveal her intentions? Have any witnesses come forward to testify to her plans? Surely, she confided in someone. What of her servants?" and again echoes of assent rose up among the body.

Seneca waved them silent. "As you know, everyone has been thoroughly questioned as to her disappearance," he explained. "She has covered her tracks well. The fact that her closest servant also vanished into thin air suggests that there was some planning behind this disappearance. She did not go alone. Did she have help? We can only speculate.

"The Senate is also very much aware of the growing distance between the emperor and his wife. Her melancholy was perpetually on display. And we must consider this: however personal her depression was, it had political ramifications in that it has prevented the conception of heirs. Our political stability requires the smooth transference of power from one generation to the next. The emperor is deeply grieved that his private life has failed in this area."

As he said this, Nero winced and looked down, to illustrate Seneca's point.

"His concern for Octavia remains unwavering."

Compassion filled Nero's face.

"But for the good of the empire, he has resolved to move forward. He has resolved to put this behind him. The Senate must reward Lord Nero's good will by granting this annulment. Gentlemen, you are wearying the emperor with this hesitation!"

Nero cocked his head to the side and tightened his eyes with a look of exasperation.

"Hesitate no longer. I ask you now to indicate with your applause that the emperor has suffered long enough. I ask you, I implore you, to indicate with your applause that the empire can now move forward and be healed of this tragic and painful episode!"

The intensity of Seneca's eloquent voice was rising to match the urgency of his plea. As he spoke, applause rang out from around the chambers, and senators began coming to their feet, first singly, then in groups, then in entire rows. Seneca now had to shout to be heard over their cheering.

"Assure Caesar of your loyalty, of your support, of your allegiance, of your unwavering *worship!*"

His final admonition brought the rest of the house to its feet, and their cacophonous cheering went on unabated until Nero finally stood and advanced to the podium to acknowledge them, his face dipped slightly in a pose of humility.

Tigellinus leaned his head over to the consul, and while both men showered their own praise on Nero, said, "Seneca can still be of some use to us."

The consul nodded. "Yes, he can still raise the roof, Prefect."

*   *   *

Nero announced his marriage to Poppaea Sabina that very day. Within a week she was securely ensconced within the Domus Aurea, and within a month she was pregnant and the city began to feel a sense of closure over its loss of Octavia.

Nero's attitude became increasingly bold and malignant. He ordered for a new wave of ambitious building projects to begin, in disregard of the weakened state of the treasury. At Tigellinus' prompting, he ordered the assassinations of two of the governors he feared most. When their heads were brought to him, he joked of one that the governor had gone prematurely gray, and Tigellinus picked the other head up by its nose and commented, "Emperor, how could such a long-nosed man have scared you?"

Nero's one habit that remained unchanged during this time was his devotion to mastering the chariot, and to Judah's chagrin, Nero faithfully maintained his sessions with him. With no reprieve in sight, Judah's heart became sullen and calloused. Only twice before in his life had Judah experienced such depths of despondency—when chained to an oar in the belly of a Roman galley, and much later when his two children died. The thirst for vengeance preserved him the first time; his passion to see the church established carried him through the next valley.

Now only a faithful wife and a dying friend kept him from sinking. Were it not for the ballast of Esther's cheerful forbearance and the friendship of Burrus, Judah felt certain that he could fall apart at any time. And then came the day when a messenger ran breathlessly to his door with a word from Burrus. *Judah, please come now.*

*   *   *

When Judah entered the room, he found Burrus lying supine on his bed, wrapped in blankets. His face was ashen, his eyes were closed and his body shook in erratic waves of pain. The smell and darkness of death filled the house. Judah approached the bed and touched Burrus' trembling hand. His eyes opened at once, and though the interruption created an unsteadiness in his already labored breathing, his face immediately brightened.

"Judah, you have come. Thank you, my friend. I have sent for both you and Seneca. I know death well, and it is close. It is very close. The emperor's poison has been slow to act, but deadly."

"Are you certain Nero has done this?" Judah asked, and Burrus lifted his shaking hand off the bed as though to exhibit it.

"This is not the work of a tumor," he said in a weak, raspy voice. "Ahenobarbus is not patient to let nature take its course with me. He is a viper. And when you walk with vipers, as I have, you will one day be bitten." He took hold of Judah's arm with his hand. "Beware when Nero raises a toast to you in honor. Throw the glass far from you!"

Judah was stung to see Burrus' sinewy arm withered to a feeble limb of skin and bone. Death was so ugly and abhorrent. It was an utter desecration of what God intended for humanity, and was the surest sign of its fall from grace.

"I promise you Burrus, I will never drink from the emperor's table," Judah said. "What he offers can never quench my thirst."

"That is good! You will live long then," Burrus added. He closed his eyes and waited for a billow of discomfort to pass by. "My obligation is nearly over. Yours too will thankfully be finished in due time. Be patient my friend. The winter is long and bitter, but soon comes the summer and Nero will play his games and you will be released."

"That time cannot come too soon, but Esther says that I have become cynical. I brood, fearing that something else may yet keep us from going home. We have a proverb which says, *Deferred hope sickens the heart.*"

"Be hopeful yet, Judah. Caesar has a short attention span. He will soon tire of horses and move on to find other worlds to conquer, and you will be dropped with unceremonious abruptness."

"Thank God."

"Tell me, Judah. Is Octavia well?"

Judah nodded and smiled to assure him. "Be at peace. She is safe, and she is happy."

"It would be for the first time in her life. I'm not sure how I would have helped her without you. Your example has not been lost on me, Judah. Your people have something that the rest of us seem to be missing. You are either fools, or the most fortunate people on earth."

"Burrus, you too could share in our good fortune," Judah said. "It is a gift for the asking."

"After a wasted life such as mine? How many times have I told you, an honorable soldier must fight the battle to enjoy the spoils of victory!"

"And how often have I told you, my friend—not in this war," Judah said with urgency. "Our Supreme Commander has done all the fighting for us. Believe me, Burrus, I know. I watched him die. I watched him die in my place. I watched him die for you. You could not add one good deed to his sacrifice. God will forgive you, but only through him. You cannot earn what is a gift. You can only receive it."

Burrus closed his eyes, and his body shook, but this time it was not in pain, but deep and bitter anguish. Weeping came over him like a storm, and he could not hold back the relentlessness of his tears.

"My life has been so wasted!" he cried out, convulsing with self-reproach. "It has all been in vain!"

Judah leaned over his friend and silently prayed for him, as Burrus shook with the birth-pangs of contrition. Still more tears flowed from him, and then Burrus summoned the strength to speak again.

"But if your God will still receive a wretch such as me, then I will lay down my sword at his feet." He reached out and clutched desperately at Judah's hand. "My life has been so wasted! O God of Ben-Hur, have mercy on me! Take pity on this twisted, foolish soul! Have mercy! I am in agony. Forgive, O Jesus, the evil I have done. Undo the evil I have done. So wasted. So wasted!"

In the moment of silence which followed, Judah now spoke aloud the words circulating in his heart. "Father in heaven, hear the prayer of my friend. Give him eyes of faith to receive your love, and release him from this burden of sin and remorse."

Slowly, the shaking in Burrus' frame ebbed, and an aura of peace came over the two men. Burrus' head fell back into his pillow, and within moments, he was asleep, succumbing to the exhaustion that consumed him. Judah sat silently in the chair beside his bed until he awoke, at which point they resumed their conversation.

As evening shadows began to darken the room, Judah's thoughts turned to Esther and he slowly rose to leave. "I will come tomorrow when Nero is through with me."

Burrus lay weakly in his bed but his bearded face registered contentment and rest. "Peace to you, Judah. If Nero grants me another day, I will be happy to see you."

With sadness, Judah turned to go. As he left the house, he met Seneca at the gate coming in. "Seneca, Burrus is expecting you," Judah said.

"How is our friend?"

"The shadow of death is on him," Judah answered grimly. "Rome may soon claim another casualty."

Seneca's eyebrows raised slightly. "One who suckles at the breast of the mother must be prepared to accept her discipline as well. Burrus understands that. I understand that. You also have been nourished from Rome's bounty. You should speak less disparagingly, Arrius."

"Rome is no mother, she is a whore!" Judah bellowed angrily. "And I have seen her destroy everyone who has slept with her. Check your bed, tonight Seneca. Soon, it may be your turn."

Judah turned and walked away, leaving Seneca slightly unsettled by the exchange, but he gathered himself, and entered the house. He found Burrus as Judah had left him, and when Burrus saw him, he laughed. "Seneca, come in my philosopher friend while I yet have strength to endure your rhetoric."

Seneca approached the bed and stood over him. "You sent for me. And you have tasted of the emperor's poison, you say."

Burrus looked at Seneca with a penetrating stare. "Seneca—we *all* have been poisoned, haven't we?" The sensation of discomfort again came over Seneca. "I regret that I will be unable to serve with you any longer. Give my apologies to Nero. I'm sure he's fully absorbed with his new wife, not to mention his training for the Olympiad. Quintus Arrius is quite spent with the emperor's demands. I'm sure you also are weary."

"I am planning to inform the emperor soon of my desire to retire. My usefulness seems to have reached its end."

"A few years ago you told me that our tutelage was not useful at all, but was in vain. Wasted!" Burrus added. "I must confess to you Seneca, it seems that you have softened your position considerably. It seems that you are more steeped than ever in his plans."

Seneca was pricked by Burrus' criticism and reacted defensively. "My thinking about this has not changed, Burrus. We are dealing with an evil that is subtle, and not easily exposed, and furthermore…"

But Burrus cut him off. "*Subtle!*"

He spoke with such vehemence that it twinged his throat and caused him to wince in pain. When the throbbing subsided, he glared at the philosopher. "Seneca, you are making me nauseous. Philosophy has ruined your head and removed your stomach. Have you no heart for doing what is right? Is saving your short, pitiful life all that matters to you? This evil is not subtle! It must be resisted. I'm going to tell you something Seneca, that I have hidden from you because at some point I lost your trust." Seneca's expression remained unchanged. "Octavia is alive!"

Now Seneca's stoic mask dropped to the floor. He could not hide the sensation of stupefied amazement which came over him. "I helped to save her life from this subtle evil of yours. She is alive! Others must be saved from him. Seneca, summon your courage. I can do no more. You alone are left to stop him!"

Burrus' revelation was like a cuff to Seneca's face. To discover that Burrus had done what he himself had failed to do aroused a pang of guilt within him. To then find that his friend had hidden his heroics from him because he doubted his trustworthiness was the sharpest of rebukes imaginable. Seneca was stunned and speechless.

He now saw for the first time the anemia of his moral philosophy. Prior to this moment, he had felt uneasy by some of his actions. But now standing above this dying soldier, confronted by his simple virtue, Seneca felt dark and ugly shame. He wanted to praise Burrus and run from him at the same time.

Finally, thinking of nothing better to say, he asked with unconvincing poise, "Do you have a message for the emperor? He asks about your condition."

The irony of Seneca's question struck Burrus as absurdly amusing and he started laughing, again to the point where the pain became excruciating.

"Please Seneca, don't make me laugh! It hurts too much." He calmed himself and then placed a finger on Seneca's hand. "Seneca, you tell Ahenobarbus not to worry, for I am now well." He took a firm grip on his hand. "Remember Seneca, you alone are left."

*   *   *

Later that night, a knock came on Judah and Esther's door. It was a man Judah did not recognize. "I am a servant of my master Seneca, with a message from him for Quintus Arrius," the man said.

"I am he," Judah said simply, and the man quickly handed him a small scroll, saluted and turned to leave. Esther was in a chair beside the fireplace, and she looked with concern as Judah came and sat beside her. He opened the seal and read the note, though he already knew its contents. He sighed heavily and looked into her eyes.

"Burrus is dead."

She leaned over and put her arms around him, and they remained frozen in the embrace for several minutes. "Judah, I feel suffocated," she said. "I feel that a rope is tightening around us. I just want to leave here, today—now."

"I don't think we would make it very far, my love," Judah said, leaning back. His face was wet, and he wiped it with the edge of his sleeve. "Nero is bent on winning his chariot race, and I think he would stop us. And then what would we do? Better to wait. It will be over soon. The new year is coming, and then summer is not too far around the corner. And when the *Neronia* is over and the emperor has had his fun, we will be free."

"I'll believe it when we are together on that ship. Until then, I am afraid. Judah, I feel as though storm clouds are gathering over us. If you offend Nero, or disappoint him, or look cross-eyed at him, he might turn on you. Every day you are away, I fear for you."

"Don't worry about me offending Caesar," Judah said to soothe her. "I may kill him, but I will not offend him." She didn't appreciate his attempt at humor. "You know Esther, Judea will not be a panacea either. All the news from Jerusalem is troubling. There's much unrest."

"We don't need to live in Jerusalem," she said. "Let's find a cottage near the sea, or live in the countryside. But whatever we do, let's leave here and go home!"

"Just a little while longer," Judah said softly, holding her again.

Chapter 12

Nero made sure that Burrus' funeral was offered with full honors. He praised him with emotional speeches, publicly mourned his loss and decorated him with numerous imperial awards. Poppaea chastised him for his excessive pageantry the evening after the funeral but he reproached her.

"Poppy, I always love a show, and besides, I will never forget what Seneca once taught me. It is customary for leaders to insult the living and praise the dead. It is especially fitting that we honor the virtuous dead for speaking the truth to us in life, since of course we no longer have to hear it from them."

Poppaea marveled at the wisdom of her husband and loved him all the more, and he naturally cherished her because of her teachable spirit.

The following week broke hard on Judah. Winter descended on Italy and covered it with sleet and murky gray, perfectly matching his disposition. Esther tried to convince him to pick up a few of the duties in the church which he had relinquished in anticipation of leaving Rome, but he felt unable or unwilling to do so. Andronicus spent much time with him trying to encourage him. He also arranged for small groups of younger Christians to accompany Judah on his journeys into Rome, ostensibly that he might disciple them, but more so for the benefit of Judah himself.

Indeed, Judah found himself enjoying the enthusiasm of the young believers, and it proved a pleasant diversion from the dreariness of Nero's world which remained unchanging, especially his foul treatment of the servants. The more Judah watched this recurring cycle of condescension and abuse, the more he realized that the ones who needed his ministry were not Nero and his cronies, but the pool of miserable slaves that served them.

And so it was that the more Nero harangued his slaves, the more Judah sought to comfort them afterwards. At first the servants were suspicious that a man of rank and nobility would even speak to them, let alone with tenderness. But soon they discerned his sincerity, and after the sessions with Nero were through, Judah found himself becoming a pastor again to a new congregation of hungry souls who sought him out for words of hope and consolation. He quickly came to know them by name, and learned of their backgrounds and families, but as he grew in his knowledge of their humanity, he also found himself growing more intolerant of Caesar's mistreatment of them.

One morning late in winter, Judah returned to the arena after a break in the session and heard the emperor barking out for the towel boy, who had failed to come at the designated time. The boy, who was maybe ten at most, suddenly appeared from the other end of the barn and ran up to Nero with a towel in hand, but his body trembled in terror. Nero snatched the towel away from him.

"Damn you boy, why weren't you here when I needed you?" he shouted. The boy wouldn't answer for fear. "What makes you think you're so important that you can waste my time?" he raged on. "Let me write the lesson on your back for everyone to learn."

Nero stood up and grabbed the boy by his robe and threw him against a pole. "Hug that pole with your arms like its your mother, boy!" and the boy, while crying, placed his arms around the pole.

Nero then made several twists of the towel and with a violent cock of his wrist, snapped the end of it on the boy's back. The boy cried out as it cut him. Again Nero whipped it across his body. Then a third time. He raised the towel a fourth time but as he brought his arm forward, he felt the towel suddenly jerk backwards in his hands, which twisted his arm and forced him to release it.

Judah was actually surprised by how easy it was to strip the towel from Nero's hands. He had guessed that Nero's arms were rather weak from the sorry way he usually commanded the team of horses, but now he knew it. Nero spun around like a top and looked up in Judah's red eyes, and at first he was filled with bewilderment, for resistance of any kind was something he was unaccustomed to. Judah handed the towel back to Nero.

"The boy was not late, Caesar. He was with me," Judah said with firmness, but yet respect. "He is undeserving of this punishment. I'll offer you my own back if you like."

In the arena, Judah had considerable leeway in giving correction to the emperor, for Nero was sincere in his quest to become a charioteer, and aggressiveness gave Judah credibility in his eyes. He saw Judah as a legendary charioteer of high repute whom he respected and desired to emulate. But he saw something other than a charioteer here and it perplexed him. He didn't know whether to be angry or apologetic. At last he chose the path of restraint.

"The boy should have told me," he said demurely. "I would have readily pardoned him. I'm sure you know Arrius how vigilant we must be in watching our servants."

Nero assumed that Judah, like all great men, was attended to by a body of slaves. Judah had in fact freed his slaves years before.

"Slaves are like race horses, Caesar," Judah said carefully. "They work better when treated with respect. So shall we resume our lesson?" Nero nodded, still taken back by this peculiar intervention. When the session was over, Judah sought out the boy, who was bringing feed to horses in another barn. The boy looked down when he saw Judah come.

"Silanus, you must be more careful my son," Judah said with fatherly compassion, turning the boy around to gently inspect the wounds on his back. "I won't be able to help you every time."

"I'm sorry Master Arrius," the boy said contritely. "I had been playing."

"As you serve the emperor, remember to keep your eyes on God our Father, and all will be well, Silanus," Judah continued. "Do all your work to please him, and you won't have to worry about pleasing Caesar." The boy nodded. "How is your sister? I did not see her today."

"She is ill," the boy answered.

"Tell Livia that Arrius is praying for her," said Judah gently. Silanus and his older sister Livia were two children whose parents had died a year earlier, and now they were stranded within Caesar's household, watched by an aunt, but in reality, surviving no better than orphaned mice in the barn. Judah's heart bled for them the most, and he ached for a way to help them, but how he could not say.

*   *   *

"Lord Nero, I have served you now faithfully for fourteen years, eight since you have become emperor."

Seneca sat in a chair across from Nero, who was pushed back from his desk, staring at his tutor thoughtfully.

The philosopher continued. "During this time, you have poured out upon me such riches and honor that the only thing I now lack is the time to suitably enjoy them. Every man longs for the day when he can retire from his duties so that he might relish the fruits of his labor, and live out his days in peace."

Nero did not say a word, so Seneca resumed.

"But what have I actually done Caesar, that I have been worthy of such high distinction? I have merely assisted in the education of a young man who was already gifted with an incomparable measure of wit and wisdom from the very womb. My task was easy. Scarcely to teach, than to direct. To merely channel the abundance of your abilities. And look what you have given me Caesar, for this simple labor of mine! Often I ask myself—is this the son of a simple knight, who is now regarded as a leader of the nation? How could my unknown name have come to sparkle so with notoriety? What happened to the old Seneca, or rather the young Seneca from so long ago, that used to be content with so little? I used to delight in the simplest of gardens, and now I find myself the overseer of multiple estates. It is too much, Caesar. Far more than I deserve, and certainly far more than I desire."

Nero leaned forward and at last spoke. "What can I do for you, my tutor?"

"I am now old, as is readily apparent, and the simplest tasks I now find burdensome. To maintain the cottage of my fathers is more than enough work for me. I am no longer equal to the vastness of my wealth. What I ask you to do for me is to take this burden off of my hands. Reclaim all of my property for your own, and grant me but the pleasures of my ancestral estate, and the time I used to expend on maintaining mansions and gardens will now be invested in what I love best—the pursuit of the mind. Allow me to step aside from my duties that I might fade into the background and be thought of no more. When one has reached my age, all that is needed is rest. Relieve me of my property, release me from my duties and grant liberty to my soul. And all will redound to your glory, Caesar. This is what I ask."

Nero smiled, and at once addressed Seneca's request. "I first owe you thanks Seneca for giving me the ability to respond to your premeditated speech with an impromptu reply, for you are the one who taught me how to speak, both with carefully crafted oratory and, when need arose, with spontaneous precision. Now as you know, Seneca, my forefathers were all known for their great generosity with their counselors, especially those who advised them in times of warfare."

He stood and walked slowly around his desk, pausing to look at a painting that hung from his wall of Julius Caesar in his Pontic triumph. Having brought another of Rome's enemies to heel, Julius was walking between two lines of elephants, preparing to accept the honors of the Senate. Off to the side was a line of war wagons, one with the words *I came, I saw, I conquered!* painted on it. Nero pointed to the painting.

"If I had been born in a time of war, you would, no doubt, have fought for me, but instead, you have given me what the times demanded—your wisdom and your philosophy. What you have given me can never be taken from me, unless my mind can somehow be stolen from me. What I have given you is trivial in comparison and can be lost by fire or storm. And so my gifts to you may seem excessive, but I assure you, I have far more to give you, dear friend."

He came to the front of the desk and sat on its edge, looking intently at Seneca. "How can you plead weakness with me! You are yet sharp as a razor and ready for all affairs of the state which I assign to you, and ready as well to reap in their rewards. Seneca, do you forget? I am young! My reign is scarcely dawning. I need you now as much as ever. You prepared me for manhood; I now insist that you play a part in guiding it."

Nero then reached over and embraced Seneca, and the philosopher thanked him, but as he left the palace he was unconvinced by Nero's stirring rhetoric. Yes, he had taught him well—maybe too well. Burrus was right. They had all been poisoned.

*　　　　　*　　　　　*

Several weeks passed, and the Mediterranean breezes turned warm giving intimations of the coming spring. Judah and Esther's spirits began to lift with the thought that warm weather would eventually bring the Neapolis games, and afterwards their freedom. Letters arrived from Jerusalem where Judah's sister Tirzah and her husband John lived, enjoying retirement, grandchildren and the heavenly hills and valleys of Ephraim—all the pleasures which eluded Judah and Esther but now dangled before them with tantalizing nearness.

One afternoon, Judah left the palace and began his ride home, only to realize as he looked up at the threatening skies, that he had left his rain cloak behind. He turned around and plodded back to the arena. He thought the barn was empty, but when he entered it, he heard the muffled sound of voices coming from one of the stalls, and then to his dismay, he heard the cries of a young girl.

He quickly walked in the direction of the voices along the sawdust path that encompassed the arena floor, and then another scream compelled him to break into a run. When he reached the stall, he saw Livia, Silanus' teenage sister, fighting off a stable-hand who had wrestled her to the straw floor and had ripped down the top half of her tunic. As the man tried to lick at her bare chest, Judah was filled with such rage that he immediately reached down and grabbed the stable-hand by the hair. With a powerful wrenching of his arms, he threw the man forcefully against the wooden wall of the stall, and the man collapsed in a stunned heap on the floor. Judah's heart sank in disbelief. It was Nero.

The warm weather had also worked to arouse Nero's irrepressible passions. Lust ran through him like a flooded river. It had washed away his inhibitions, his modesty and shame long before he left adolescence. He was addicted to the sexual experience, and enslaved to every sexual impulse. Having never refused even one of his desires, he was now unable to resist any of them. He had reached the point where one arousing sight or one erotic thought was sufficient to provoke a chain of lewd behavior. The demon at work inside of him imprisoned his soul behind a wall of stone which Nero himself laid, one brick at a time, with every immoral choice he made throughout his life.

Nero revealed little of this side of himself when he was with Judah, though his language was often vulgar. But from the servants, Judah heard disturbing stories of nighttime orgies and ribald parties that usually degenerated into licentious experimentation, and there were mornings when Judah could hardly stand to look at Caesar's face without feeling revolted by the scattered emptiness he saw in his eyes. And now as he looked into Nero's eyes, which were glazed by the impact of hitting the wall, that same revulsion swept through him.

He reached down and gave his hand to Livia, who had pulled up her tunic with a blush of humiliation. "Livia, go," Judah instructed. "Find your brother and go home now." She whimpered weakly and ran from the stable. Judah looked at Nero who had pushed himself up onto his hands, but it was clear that he was shaken. He slowly lifted his head up and looked at Judah. A cloud of anger began to swirl on his expression, but Judah did not give it time to materialize.

"Caesar, if you are to retain my services, then I insist that you channel your energies into training. Otherwise I will not waste my time here."

"Who are you to tell me what I am going to do!" barked Caesar as he struggled to his feet. "No one lifts a hand to me!"

"Your back was turned to me. I did not realize it was you, Caesar," Judah said with intensity. "And of course, I did not expect that it would be you. In my world Caesar, only a depraved coward would assault a powerless young girl. Why would I possibly think to see you doing such a thing? It is unbecoming for one who aspires to be a charioteer."

The words and the authority with which he spoke silenced Nero. He looked at Judah's eyes, but it was like looking into the sun, and he turned away.

"You are confusing your duties, Arrius. You think to be a counsel again, but you are my trainer. Nothing more. I advise you not to meddle in my affairs again." With that, Nero pulled tight his loosened garments, and stormed out of the stable, brushing Judah sharply as he walked by.

Judah now realized that he had one more obligation to perform amidst his other duties. Within the church, he knew of countless people whose hearts ached for the weak and wounded members of Roman society. In fact, the church was like a net thrown under the Roman world, and many of those who had been discarded and left for dead by the insensitivities of the culture were caught in it. As Judah stood alone in the musty stall, he vowed that two others would now find the safety of the net.

Two weeks later, Silanus and Livia were sent into the city's marketplace to purchase food for their aunt's table, as they did nearly every afternoon. Standing near the vegetable stands, they were approached by two men and greeted by name. No one saw the children slip away silently with the men, no one saw them walk to the outskirts of the city, and no one saw them climb aboard horses and disappear into the evening shadows of the surrounding countryside.

When they failed to return that night, the aunt told the others not to worry, for the children had been threatening to run away in the silly way that children do, but once they were chased by the first tramp or gripped by the first pang of hunger, they would be back. More than likely, they'd be found in their own beds by morning. But they weren't. The steward of Caesar's household was told about the runaway barn slaves, who reported it to Caesar, who shrugged it off as a reason why young servants shouldn't be given too many responsibilities. Silanus and Livia never did return.

*   *   *

Judah and Esther took frequent walks together in the forest that surrounded their home. The world always seemed more sane and liveable after a walk. Problems seemed less overbearing. And all of the urgent demands of life were always exposed as fraudulent whenever the two of them joined hands and headed up any of the many trails that spread out from their property. With the coming of spring, their walks became especially delicious, for life was bursting out all around them, and they looked upon every budding leaf and flower with the awe of a child.

"I've seen more than 65 springs come in my life," Judah said to Esther one day, as they emerged from the woods after a morning together, "and each time it's as fresh and marvelous as the first time."

Esther stopped him and wrapped her arms around him. "Are my kisses still as sweet as the first time?" she asked. He laughed and kissed her tenderly.

"Even with lips as old and wrinkled as yours, I'll never grow tired of kissing them!"

She hit him playfully, and they continued their walk to the front of the house, and were at once surprised to find a strange horse tied up to one of their trees. They looked around the stony garden, and then out from behind one of the trellises walked Seneca, who smiled warmly upon seeing them.

"I hope you don't mind. I was taking a leisurely stroll through your garden," he said. "I'm sure it will be quite lovely in just a few more weeks."

"Why Seneca, you surprise me. You must have taken quite a wrong turn today," said Judah. "But you are welcome. This is our home. And this is my wife Esther." Seneca cordially took her hand and kissed it.

"Your husband cannot stop speaking of you in the fondest ways," he said warmly. "I simply could not believe that such a woman as he described even existed, so I finally had to meet her. I see though already, that Arrius does not exaggerate."

Esther accepted his compliment with modesty. "Thank you Master Seneca. You are a famous man and my husband speaks of you also with great respect. May I offer you a drink?" Seneca accepted her hospitality, and while Esther went into the house, Judah directed him to a set of chairs in the garden.

As Seneca sat down, he said, "To answer your question, Arrius—no, I did not take a wrong turn. I have sought you intentionally and would have been disappointed if I had failed in my search. Tell me, by which name do you prefer to be called—Arrius, or Ben-Hur? You are a man of many identities."

Judah shrugged. "Sometimes even I am not sure who I am. Call me as you wish. My appearance is Roman, my heart is Jewish, my citizenship is of earth, my allegiance is to heaven."

"Very well then, I am a lover of simplicity, I shall continue to speak to you as a Roman. And as a Roman, I know Arrius that you will understand the gravity of what I share with you now. It has been my observation of late, in conversations I have overheard with the emperor, that he suddenly looks on you with disfavor. This concerns me, because I am fond of you Arrius. Surely you know that it is not a prescription for a happy life to irritate Caesar."

At this, Judah briefly recounted the incident in the stable to Seneca, who frowned when he was through.

"That is grievous. Unfortunate, that you should have been at the wrong place at the wrong time."

"I don't see it that way, Seneca. I came at precisely the right time. Who knows what he would have done to that girl."

"That girl was just a slave, which brings to mind another thing that concerns me," Seneca continued. "You have made no secret of your affection for the slaves. I would advise you to be more cautious. Is it a coincidence that the girl you saved from Nero's prodigal lusts also disappeared a short time later?"

Judah bristled with suspicion. "It was my understanding that she ran away, and who will blame her? If you suspect that I have helped her, search my home, turn over my property, if this why you have come!"

Seneca raised his hand to assure Judah. "Arrius no, you need not fear me. In fact, if you told me that you had helped the children, I only would have respected you more. My concern is genuinely for you and your wife. A man needs to choose his battles carefully, and your sympathy for those whom fate has selected for poverty and servility may give them momentary happiness but bring upon you lasting grief."

"I do not believe that fate selects a man for destitution," Judah said. "Only men in their arrogance do this to other men. And when a man is weak, then it is up to the strong to bear him up, for who is to say when the strong man might himself become weak? Only pride keeps us from seeing that all men are equal in the eyes of God."

At that moment, Esther walked out with a tray of glasses filled with wine, and she handed one to each of them, but sensing the tenseness of the conversation, she quickly excused herself.

"I find much worth in your philosophy, Arrius," Seneca said. "It's your politics I question. I have devoted much of my life to the service of this boy who has become king. I have come to you as a friend simply to urge you to be cautious. The *Neronia* approaches in less than a month. Keep your highest objectives in mind with every word you speak, and every action you engage in. If you truly want to return to Judea, then leave Caesar's redemption to others, and forget about his slaves. Perform the duties that are asked of you, and soon you will be home."

"And this is why you have come? To bring me this message?"

"It is from my heart, Arrius. I do not want to hide from you the danger you are in if you do otherwise. If your destiny is Jerusalem, then I wish to help you to achieve it."

Judah could not dismiss the sincerity written in Seneca's face, and he felt humbled that he would make the considerable journey to his home to share this admonition with him in person.

"Seneca, I apologize for mistrusting you. I am appreciative that you would go out of your way to share your concerns with me. I assure you, I will give each of your thoughts careful consideration." Seneca raised his glass as a gesture of friendship, and then drank from it.

"Perhaps this would be as good a time as any to brief you on what to expect during Caesar's Games," Seneca suggested, and Judah indicated that he was ready to listen.

The two men continued in conversation throughout the afternoon. Esther later joined them, and before the day was through, she and Judah invited Seneca to honor their new level of friendship with a ritual that symbolized their growing bond—they invited him to join them on a walk.

Chapter 13

Neapolis, or *New City*, (and later Naples) was founded by Greek colonists around 600 BC, then was conquered by the Romans three centuries later. The city continued to prosper, but maintained its Greek ambience, which may have explained its great popularity with Nero, and why it was chosen as the location for his second *Neronia*. Nero came to Neapolis with a flotilla of two dozen ships, which resembled a veritable invasion force to those who watched them sail in from the surrounding hillsides. From there, Nero marched on the city with great pomp, bringing in his train a massive army of athletes, musicians, politicians, soldiers, slaves and even elephants. It was a spectacle unlike anything the people had ever seen, but then again, it was something they had come to expect from Caesar, whom they esteemed as the greatest showman of all. He did not disappoint them.

The imperial caravan stretched for several miles, and Nero commanded that it give the appearance of a military triumph. Citizens came by the tens of thousands, walking from Pompeii, riding from Calabria, sailing from Sicily, and Nero even imported a thousand knights from Alexandria because he enjoyed the robust way the Egyptians applauded. They lined the roads to catch just a glimpse of the emperor, which was easy because he rode with Poppaea in a royal litter mounted on an elephant. He was dressed in the full regalia of a general, and he saluted the crowds with a sword that he swung awkwardly about in the air.

When he arrived at the city, he ordered that a ceremonial breach be opened up in the city walls, which was a ritual the Romans observed to honor a victorious general who had returned from a great conquest. Nero passed through the breach, and then stood atop the walls while the minions below hailed him as their god, and their shouts cascaded down the surrounding valleys and were heard by farmers miles away.

While Nero may not have outwardly looked the part of a great leader, he possessed something which no one else could duplicate—the command of the people. It was more than charisma. It was felt when he spoke. There was something about his words which left those who heard him spellbound, as though a spiritual force were projected from his mouth. And when he combined his speech with a visual spectacle, his power was complete. Even later, after he was dead, the spell would not perish. The belief circulated among many that Nero would appear again and many clung to that hope with cultish fervor.

After the ceremony at the wall, Caesar entered the city. A thousand-voice choir welcomed him with an anthem sung to the accompaniment of hundreds of horns and cymbals, sounding together in majestic unison. Teams of dancers filled the streets around them, waving banners and brightly colored ribbons around their heads. The dancers led the procession up Neapolis' ascending streets to the center of the city where the main temples and governor's palace rose up in splendor, mimicking the great Athenian Acropolis. At the palace, Nero was greeted by a sizeable convocation from the city. A company of soldiers stood at full attention behind them, stretched out in two ranks leading up to the palace steps. The governor stepped forward and bowed before Nero.

"Caesar, the citizens of Neapolis welcome you to our great city. We are deeply honored that you have chosen our city for the site of the *Neronia*, and that you have graced our region with your divine presence. We are your servants."

"Rise, my friend," Nero said, bringing him to his feet. "Your greeting is acceptable. I am well pleased with our reception." He brought Poppaea forward with his hand. Her pregnancy was advanced and obvious. "This is my wife Poppaea, the goddess whom I worship. You will esteem her as you would Diana."

The governor bowed submissively to her. "Lady Poppaea, we rejoice that you are here and pray the favor of the gods over the child you carry. Our finest sculptors await to capture your beauty in marble. We hope you will oblige them with a sitting sometime this week." Poppaea smiled as best she could, for she was still recovering from the elephant ride which had nearly sent her into labor. "Lord Nero, our palace, our city is yours. As we proceed to your apartment, please honor us with a review of your soldiers which have prepared tirelessly for your arrival."

"*That* is always a waste of time. Soldiers and legions are the same in every province," Nero said, puzzling the governor. "But let's humor them, shall we?

What I desire most of all is to review my wife, in a bath. And afterwards, I would like to inspect some of the facilities for the Games. So lead on."

He beckoned for the governor to proceed, and they turned and marched between the ranks of soldiers up into the palace. The afternoon was used to rest, the evening was filled with state dinners, the following day was for tours of the city, and the next night the opening ceremonies of the Games were held. The program lacked nothing of the extravagance of the Greek Olympiad, for Nero had brought over a delegation from Greece and gave them the responsibility of converting his Games into a mirror image of their own, and Nero was satisfied with the result.

When the opening ceremonies were completed, Nero hosted a party in his own apartment, and at midnight he promptly dismissed his guests. The competitions began at noon the following day, and for once, Nero's mind was on something other than frivolity. Tigellinus and Poppaea remained behind as the last guests excused themselves. The three of them stood together on a veranda which overlooked the city. The sheen of the full moon lit up the marble buildings that stretched out beneath them and Nero marveled to drink it in.

"The competition begins tomorrow Caesar. Are you prepared to conquer?" Tigellinus asked.

"I've waited a long time for this," Nero answered, still gazing out over the city. "No Caesar has done what I am about to do. This is our defining moment Tigellinus. Julius, Octavius, Tiberius—we leave them now to lie in the dust. From here on out the empire will be shaped and molded by me. Historians will see this moment we are now in as the inauguration of the Neronian era. The golden age truly begins now. Let the doors of the Temple Janus be locked shut and the keys thrown away. Let our armies disband and soldiers learn honorable trades. Let art and sport flourish. And let me be the general to bring in this new millennium."

"I see you are not flagging in confidence," Tigellinus mused in response to Nero's dreamy soliloquy.

Poppaea slid up to him and placed her arms around him. "I know that he is nervous. He tossed all night."

Nero ignored her. "Look at this magnificent city! The daughter of Athens. Greek architecture is flawless. It is as though the gods designed this city themselves and lowered it here straight out of the heavens."

"You sound as though it is a pity that Greece does not still rule the earth," Tigellinus said.

"She still rules, Tigellinus," Nero continued. "We conquered a people. But their culture, their language, their spirit still rule our empire. We cannot compete with her. Rome is an ordinary, dirty city."

Nero's eyes had been riveted on the vista of the city but now he broke his quixotic reverie and looked directly at Tigellinus.

"It ought to be burned to the ground. Reduce it to ashes and begin again."

Tigellinus stared back at Caesar to measure his thoughts, and while this silent exchange occurred, Poppaea tightened her hold on Nero. "And afterwards we could rename Rome, Neropolis. And people will travel from all nations to Neropolis to offer sacrifices to its god."

As she attempted to kiss him, Nero became annoyed and abruptly pushed her aside. "Poppaea, your worship is not required tonight."

Her face fell at the unexpected scorn and she walked off in a snit, saying, "Don't come sniffing for any sacrifices in my bed tonight."

Nero watched her go and rubbed his face in irritation. "Why would I want to roll around with a fat woman anyway?" he asked sarcastically of Tigellinus, who said nothing. "What I need more than anything is sleep. Tigellinus, one favor if you would please. I wish to drive my horses first thing tomorrow. Would you see that Quintus Arrius is brought to the arena before breakfast?"

"Certainly," Tigellinus replied with his customary brevity. Then looking after Poppaea he added, "And sweet dreams, Caesar."

*   *   *

The next morning broke early for Judah, who found it difficult to sleep in the provisional housing provided by the city as part of its hospitality. As Esther lay in bed, he whispered in her ear that he would return soon, and walked outside to seek a place to pray. He could find no privacy in the compound, for already there was frenzied activity all around, though the sun had scarcely risen. He could find no pleasure in praying within the city, for its temples and brothels seemed to desacralize the very air. So he kept walking until he came to the gates of the city and then passed through them to the outside, finally finding a place of solitude in a grove of trees which lined a nearby stream. There he poured out his soul before God.

For Judah, prayer was more necessary than his daily food. Much earlier in his life, he had observed that there was an almost uncanny parallel between the nourishment of his body and his soul. Just as his body became unruly and weak if the day continued without food, so his spirit began to harden and wither with just one day without the bread of prayer. Without prayer, the winds of temptation blew harder and the annoying foothills of life became alpine peaks. Prayer calmed the storms and made passable the mountains. *I am the vine, you are the branches; apart from me you can do nothing,* Jesus had said, and Judah knew this full well.

When Judah had finished, he returned to his apartment, and found Esther awake and a message waiting for him from Caesar. Judah was to come at once to the chariot track.

Judah scowled, then sighed. "It's a good thing I've prayed this morning."

"One more week and it's over Judah," Esther said, adding a comforting hug.

Judah set out at once for the stadium, buying a biscuit and cheese from a vendor along the way. The Neapolis circus paled in comparison with its prototype in Rome, but it ran a full track, seated 70,000 spectators, and provided adequate entertainment for the citizens who felt out of touch with the capital city.

The area around the stadium was deserted when Judah arrived except for a few guards posted about the entrance, who gave him ready clearance to pass inside. The empty corridors beneath the circus were like catacombs, and except for an occasional servant hustling past like a ghost, Judah was alone. The smell of hay and horses hung in the air. Beneath the floor of the stadium was carved out a labyrinth of stalls and chambers, used to cage wild animals for shows and exhibits, or prisoners for the gladiatorial contests, or horses when the chariots were run. Judah bypassed the stalls and proceeded directly out onto the circus floor.

The sun was just then high enough to poke through the latticework of the marbled crown of the stadium, and it scattered a kaleidoscope of shadows on the sand. A few feathery clouds skittered across the sky which otherwise was clear. Judah walked slowly out onto the middle of the track and felt dwarfed by

the carved mountains of stone around him—the beautiful masonry and artwork of the *spina* and the cascading tiers of empty seats which rose up on all
sides. He felt insignificant and ordinary, but then he realized that it was not he
that was insignificant, but this monument of granite and marble that encompassed him. In fact, the whole monolithic culture which had created this structure was insignificant.

The behemoth of Rome was a myth. One day all of this would crumble into
dust, while God's kingdom would continue on, relentlessly filling the earth until
time itself would be swallowed up by eternity. Judah thought of the psalm which
declared that God sits in the heavens and laughs at those who think to defy him,
trusting in their own autonomy. Not a scornful laugh. But a laugh of irony. The
way a father laughs at his little child who wrestles with him on the floor and
would think to pin him down. And in God's case, it was a laugh mixed with pain,
because most of his children had pressed on with the delusion that they could
live apart from him.

As Judah looked out over this glorious but empty splendor, the sound of
applause suddenly burst upon his contemplation. He heard in his mind voices
and shouts from his past, he saw the stadium filled with a cheering throng, he
sensed the rush of the chariot beneath him, and felt the dust sticking to his sweat
strewn skin. Then a face came across this line of illusion—a face he remembered
well, that beautiful face ruined by arrogance, of the one who had once been his
friend. Heaviness and grief flooded Judah's spirit as he looked out over that
empty track, and his head lowered.

"Messala, Messala," he whispered in a voice broken by sorrow.

In that instant, his reflection was rudely shattered by the echoes of a real
chariot that was just then driven out onto the track from a ramp on the far end
of the circus, and without delay, the driver drove the horses directly toward
Judah. He assumed it was Nero, and when a dozen or more servants and soldiers
materialized in the stands around him, as if out of thin air, he knew it was. Caesar
was shouting exuberantly as he approached, and he swept by Judah as though to
show himself off, but Judah only coughed at the dust that was kicked up around
him. Nero slowed his horses and came back around.

"Arrius!" he shouted excitedly. "Arrius, a final training run is in order." He
brought the horses to an unsteady stop beside Judah. "You would agree?"

Judah stepped toward the horses and patted them gently. "It might help settle the horses some after the voyage. But with due respect Emperor, you have tapped from me all I can give you. From here on out, your own instinct will be your best ally."

"Do not minimize your contribution, Arrius," Nero praised him. "I have hung on your every word. May I now ride in the greatness of your shadow."

A servant walked up to Nero and handed him a large, clear glass filled with black liquid. Nero took the glass and held it up to Judah as if for his inspection. "You did keep one little secret from me."

"What might that be?" Judah asked.

"You never told me that a mixture of water and boar's dung was therapeutic for the muscles. I spoke with the Greek riders this morning. They all swore by it."

"Caesar, that would be a secret also to me," Judah replied, but Nero ignored him, and proudly brought the glass to his lips and drank half of the fluid while his eyes squeezed shut in apparent nausea. When he finished the draught, he coughed, and then slowly opened his eyes, while wiping the black phlegm off his mouth. Then issuing a deep sigh, he held out the glass to Judah, offering him a taste, but he respectfully declined. Nero handed it back to the servant.

"Yes, I can see how that might stimulate the muscles," he said. He then wrapped the reins tightly around his wrist and waist, and before turning the horses onto the track, said, "Well Arrius, I will welcome your observations as I ride this morning."

He snapped the reins and the horses pulled out, and with another shake of his wrists, they broke into a canter. Judah walked off the track and climbed up a narrow stairwell that was cut into the arena wall. He then proceeded to a viewing platform in the governor's box on the main level, reserved for royalty and dignitaries. To his surprise, Seneca was already seated in the box, watching Nero. The two men greeted each other, and then Judah sat beside him.

"Caesar has invested much time in this event, in comparison to all the other competitions he has entered," Seneca said as they watched Nero disappear behind the *spina* to the other side of the track.

Judah looked surprised. "I knew Nero is singing. He is doing other events as well?"

Seneca laughed. "Didn't you know? He is competing in every event. He'll ride, he'll sing, he'll wrestle, he'll run, he'll recite poetry. You Arrius are one of

many trainers he has assembled to take him on to greatness and immortality."
Judah shook his head in derision. "Of course he won't succeed at everything. But
then he is young and has not learned that bitter lesson of life. What do you feel
are his chances of success here?"

"You want a serious appraisal?" he asked, and Seneca nodded. "He has good
horses. He handles them with average competence. He is competitive enough."

"But is he a champion?"

"He is untested in the circus," Judah answered. "Only in the past few months
has he begun racing against other drivers at smaller events. But this is different.
Very few do well at first."

Seneca looked out as Nero came into view again. "Arrius, I want you to
understand something. Our emperor must do well at first. This is Caesar who is
out in that chariot. And Caesar cannot fail."

Judah scoffed. "What do you mean, Caesar cannot fail? Only God cannot fail.
Caesar is human, with all the frailties of being human."

"You and I may see that in him. But the vast majority of people see divinity
in him."

"Don't get me started, Seneca," Judah said angrily. "There is divinity in only
one man."

"Yes, you've told me about your Jewish Messiah. But Jesus I do not see, and
Caesar I do see. He is flesh and blood for the empire. And he must not fail."
Judah reacted again, but Seneca was quick to continue. "Arrius, you remember
our recent visit together? We are not talking about philosophy here, nor does this
have to do with theology. This is politics. Simple politics."

Judah was unconvinced, but decided against pushing the argument further.
"Unless you eliminate his competition, you cannot guarantee the outcome of a
chariot race."

"Speaking politically, Arrius, there is. There is a more dignified approach to
address this dilemma. An approach which rewards the spirit of the competition
inherent in these games, and also which rewards the noble competitors themselves."

"*Bribery?*" Judah asked with astonishment. "Seneca, what are you thinking
about? You want to pay his opponents to throw the race?"

Seneca raised his hand to mute Judah's anger. "Arrius, this is not competition.
Not the way you and I understand it. I want you to see this whole Olympiad as

theater. As a stage. And we are the stage-managers who must do everything we can to see that Caesar occupies center-stage. The other athletes will have later opportunities to test their true abilities. But this event is unique because Caesar is here. And so, we must reward the actors and actresses who are part of this theater. What I am asking you is that you merely compensate our performers for being part of this spectacle. Nothing more. Your conscience need not be offended by this."

"You misjudge me, Seneca," Judah said resolutely. "I did not give a year of my life away to become a stage-manager for that arrogant ass of a boy out there. Look, your god has just lost his reins!"

Judah stood to walk away, and as he did, he pointed out onto the track where Nero had just crashed his chariot into the wall while attempting to turn. The horses jumped and kicked in confusion as he tried to regain control of them, and all the while, echoes of Caesar's profane shouting could be heard bouncing around the circus.

*   *   *

The Olympic games officially began sometime in the eighth century before Christ at Olympia on the Peloponnesian peninsula of Greece. The earliest Olympiads were primarily religious festivals held in honor of Zeus, and the athletic competition consisted of a lone foot race, 183 meters in length. Only later were additional events included. The eighteenth Olympiad included a pentathlon of spear and discus throwing, wrestling, running and jumping. Boxing was added later, as was chariot racing, and eventually, the festival was expanded to an entire week of competition, and in time, Zeus and his pantheon of gods had to share the glory intended for them with the human champions who supplanted them in popularity.

It was the fame associated with competition which enthralled Nero more than sport itself. Early as a boy, he went to the Circus whenever he could, and he stood in awe of the champions as they stood atop the victory podium. He saw the way people marveled at the bulging arms and scarred faces of the gladiators. He saw the popularity ascribed to the charioteers and the honor showered on the fastest runners. But it was not their skill he admired, or the exhilaration of the games he thirsted for. What he envied most in these athletes was the praise they received.

His earliest toys were miniaturized clay figurines of circus performers, which he used in make-believe games where he conquered in an imaginary arena to the delight of an adoring world. The illusions of grandeur which all children inevitably hold are eventually tempered by the realities of life as they grow up. But Nero never escaped his childhood, nor was he ever forced to abandon it. No one ever asked him to grow up. Rome was ruled by a boy animated with adolescent desires, equipped with the strength of an adult, and empowered with the authority of a king. The empire was his playground and its people were his playmates, compelled to play whichever game he chose by whatever rules he dictated.

The *Neronia* was now his latest game, and as Seneca had informed Judah, Caesar was a contestant in virtually each event. The competitions were set to begin at noon with wrestling, and as the hour approached, thousands had already gathered around the wrestling pits to catch a glimpse of the emperor. The opening bouts came and went, and when the time arrived for Nero's scheduled match, the crowd began to chatter in nervous expectation. Nero's opponent walked out and stood beside the ring, looking lonely and nervous, but Caesar himself had not yet appeared.

Suddenly, the applause broke out, for the emperor had arrived. A path opened up in the mass of people, and Nero emerged, surrounded by four soldiers and a coterie of attendants. The ever-present *Augustiani* fanned out secretly into the crowd. The umpire called Nero and his opponent to the center of the ring and gave them their instructions, and then they were sent back to their positions to prepare. Nero's attendants had already erected a spacious pavilion of purple and yellow velvet over Nero's corner, like a general's tent on the field of battle.

Nero stood stiff and proud beneath the canopy, looking out over the ring at his opponent, who also faced him but looked down at the sand while a lone assistant whispered in his ears. Meanwhile, Nero's servants engulfed him, giving him sips of water, rubbing his arms and loosening his sandals. His own wrestling mentor offered some final words.

Both men were clad in loose tunics, and at a signal given by the judge, they disrobed. Even the commoners in the crowd felt uncomfortable to see their divine Caesar standing naked at the edge of the ring and the aristocrats among them were positively ashamed, for it was the shared belief among most of the gentry that nude wrestling promoted debased sexual practices which weakened the moral health of the nation. Generals forbade their men to wrestle, fearing it would strip them of the fortitude they needed to fight as good soldiers. For those who did look, it was immediately apparent that Nero's opponent was a much finer physical specimen than he. His stomach was rippled and firm, where Nero's sagged slightly, and his arms and legs were anchored by defined muscle, which Nero lacked.

At a second signal from the judge, the men approached each other and immediately locked arms, and circled around each other for several tentative seconds. The crowd now began to cheer, and after a moment the chant of *Caesar!* began resonating above the din. Nero's opponent had not come without his supporters, and those who knew him were surprised that he had not yet made a charge for Nero's legs. Caesar had made several attempts of his own which he easily shrugged off, but the man showed no offensive vigor and seemed to be dancing more than wrestling. Few of them realized that he was in fact dancing, swaying at that moment to the tune which a messenger from Tigellinus had whispered in his ears the day before.

If Nero were an ordinary person, the match would have been finished within the first minute. The man resisted Nero long enough to discover that the emperor's skills and instincts were deficient. Satisfied with this knowledge, the man stopped resisting altogether. He dropped his arms and allowed Nero to cradle him. Nero wobbled a bit, and then clumsily dropped his opponent to the sand, and after a few seconds—during which the man flopped like a dying fish—Nero managed to secure a pin position and the match was over. The crowd exploded in delight as the judge took Caesar's hand and thrust it high in the air, proclaiming, "Nero Caesar wins this contest and crowns the Roman people and his world empire!"

Time and time again over the next week, those words would be pronounced with almost religious fervor. Nero proved to be Italy's most amazing wrestler, its finest archer, its fastest sprinter, its most enduring runner. Though he was forced to take several rest breaks during the marathon, inexplicable injuries and sudden illness thinned out the field as the race was run, and Caesar remarkably placed first.

At Caesar's insistence, the *Neronia* included competitions in music, poetry and oratory, and he showed the world his well-rounded abilities by capturing the championship wreaths in each event. He won wreaths as a singer and instrumentalist, as a composer and bard, for extemporaneous speech and debate. An entire committee of servants was needed to collect, label and crate all of Caesar's wreaths and awards. The exhibition of Caesar's prodigious talents left observers breathless. They worshipped him every place he went, and he accepted it with the humble dignity befitting his role as *the First Citizen*.

In keeping with Nero's request, and as was often customary with festivals and competitions, the chariot race was scheduled as the final event. On the night before the great race, Nero attended a dinner hosted in his honor by the Greek delegation. When the dinner was through, he mingled with the guests who fawned over him. The ubiquitous Tigellinus stood nearby, helping preserve a pocket of space around the emperor, and whenever a person came too close or spoke too long to Nero, one scowl or an acerbic cough was enough to dispatch him.

As they stood along the wall admiring the well-dressed guests, one of the Greek dignitaries approached and bowed low to Nero.

"Caesar, your gifts, your talents, your abilities are beyond measure. The powers of all the gods are in you. You have restored glory to Greece by instituting these games, and I assure you that our entire nation will eagerly anticipate your visit to Greece next year. Thank you for inviting us to share in this glorious event." He bowed again and walked off. Nero smiled with unabashed pleasure.

"The Greeks alone know how to appreciate me and my art," he said quietly to Tigellinus.

"The *Neronia* has been a great success," Tigellinus replied. "Run the chariot to victory tomorrow and your triumph will be complete."

"That reminds me that I have not seen the old man Arrius around here tonight," said Nero, looking about the crowded room. "I wonder where he is. I expected him here to be honored with me."

"He is probably praying in his room," Tigellinus sneered. "He can't quite shake his Jewish superstitions."

"Let him pray as long as he saves a little worship for his emperor," Nero said in a distracted voice, as his eyes fell upon a youthful, clean-shaven man standing across the room with a group of other young men. He pointed to him. "Who is that—the one in the red toga?"

Tigellinus looked where Nero was pointing. "Some young Greek freeman. Sporus, I think, is his name. He's been around most of the week."

"He has very striking features," Nero said admiringly. "I've been watching him tonight. You know, Tigellinus, these Greeks are a very erotic race. They have much to teach us about our passions. Fewer sexual boundaries to hem them in." Nero paused, but Tigellinus understood the direction this was going, so he was not surprised by Nero's next request. "Go and invite young Sporus to my chambers in a half-hour, would you Tigellinus? And make sure my Poppy is busy doing something else."

*   *   *

The day which Judah and Esther had yearned for arrived at last. They could hardly sleep the night before in excitement at the thought of being free, and Esther was so giddy that Judah wondered if she might run to the sea once the race was finished and start swimming for Judea right then. As it was, fortuitous scheduling insured that they wouldn't have to wait long. A vessel bound for Judea was leaving Puteoli, a mere ten miles from Neapolis, in three days.

A large segment of the Roman church was already in Neapolis to say farewell to Judah and Esther, and a great many other believers from the surrounding area would be there in force to send them off. Judah could care less about the chariot race, which he assumed was a formality after watching Nero amass his treasury of prizes from the earlier contests. He would sit with Caesar, oblige him with a few words, watch him race and be done with it. What he longed for most was to have time with his friends, and then head for home. His real home.

Andronicus and several other families had arrived in the middle of the week and Esther decided to spend the day with them rather than subject herself to a tedious afternoon in the arena. The friends enjoyed breakfast together, and then Judah set off for the circus for the last time. The stadium was nearly filled when he arrived, for the great race was preceded by several hours of preliminary entertainment. Judah passed directly to Nero's quarters, and found him pacing anxiously, with two guards at the door and a pack of his friends drinking and playing dice around a table.

"Good, Arrius, you're here," said Nero with unconventional warmth. "It's an hour before the race begins. I thought you had abandoned me."

"Would I work so hard and then miss the day of reward, Caesar?" Judah responded. "This is your day, emperor. A day charioteers will remember throughout history." Judah then swallowed hard. "Thank you for giving me this opportunity to serve you."

"The honor has been mine, Arrius. May I now do justice to the training you have given me. Please tell me again of your rituals before racing. My mind is a blur and I cannot keep my thoughts in focus."

Judah looked around at the roomful of people. "For one, I spent my last hour alone. Others cannot help you focus your thoughts. And I always ate a good meal a couple hours before the race. Considerable energy is expended in the race. One wants to be neither sluggish with a full stomach or weak with an empty one."

"Which reminds me," said Nero excitedly, and he walked over to the table where his friends were sitting and picked up a glass of the black boar's liquid. "I dared my companions to share in this elixir with me, but I see none have taken the challenge. Too bad."

His friends shrank from the glass as Nero took it away, but he gallantly held it up in front of them and began to drink from it without reservation. Once again came the deep, hesitant breaths and the wave of nausea, but when it passed, he proudly deposited the empty glass on the table, as they gawked at his accomplishment.

"Arrius, I can't believe you've never heard of this. It's very enlivening. The Greeks said it keeps your limbs alert and your vision sharp," he exclaimed.

"Is that why your eyes are watering?" asked one of his friends, and the others laughed.

Judah nodded, scarcely amused. "If you'll excuse me emperor, I shall check on the horses and make sure they are properly equipped. If you have need of me further, I'll be in the governor's box. Just remember, keep the horses working together. One horse alone will not win the race."

"Yes Arrius, thank you. And for the rest of you, I shall dismiss you as well. Please go and take your assigned seats. My mentor suggests that I need time alone to rein in my thoughts before I rein in my horses. So please." His hand pointed firmly to the door, and the others mumbled begrudgingly but obeyed. "Guards, you as well may step outside," and they followed after.

Nero sat down and closed his eyes but he could not relax. The moment he stilled his arms, his feet began to tap on the floor. When he stopped his feet, his fingers began to pick on the thread of his racing tights. When all his limbs were motionless, his eyes began to twitch. He reached out and picked up his racing helmet and began to fidget with its strap.

An onrush of thoughts poured through his mind. Images, faces, voices. He saw Octavia, Poppaea, a snakeskin his mother had made into a charm bracelet when he was a boy. Assassins had come into his bedroom when he was toddler but were chased off by the snake on his floor. Or so Agrippina had told him, but he was too young to remember. The image of Sporus crossed his thoughts, and the twitching started up again in earnest.

He placed the helmet over his head and then stood up and wrapped himself in his racing cloak. A mirror with a bronze-backing hung from the wall and he walked over to it to inspect his appearance. The helmet needed straightening so he leaned closer to the glass to adjust its positioning. When he craned his neck to tighten the strap, the room came into view and that was when Nero saw that he was not alone.

Seated in one of the chairs was a teen-aged boy with jaundiced skin and red eyes which bore angrily into Nero's back. The sight of the boy caused every inch of Nero's skin to crawl and his breath to constrict in raw horror. He whipped around in a reflex of terror, pressing his back against the wall and knocking the mirror to the floor, where it shattered in a piercing explosion of glass. But when he turned, the boy was gone, and he was by himself.

"Brittanicus!" Nero uttered with a shiver.

The door opened and a guard looked into the room. "Caesar?" he asked, perplexed to see Nero frozen and pale against the wall, his racing helmet cocked sidewise on his head as though someone had struck him. Slowly, Nero recovered himself and he looked at the guard.

"I thought I…I thought I…," he stuttered, and then waved him off with his hand. "I'm fine. Continue waiting outside. I pinched myself with my racing strap."

The guard nodded and pulled the door shut. Nero sank down into one of the chairs and buried his head into his trembling hands.

*   *   *

When Judah reached the stables underneath the circus floor, he found Nero's servants swarming over the horses as they did to Caesar himself, but the horses seemed in no mood to be treated like their master.

"Let them breathe, let them breathe," Judah said to the cluster of servants standing about the horses' heads, tending to the braids in their manes. "This is too much. You'll unsettle the horses before the race. All of you leave except for the harness team," he ordered tenderly, and the servants bowed respectfully and left. Judah stroked the horses' heads, and each of the animals responded as if in gratitude for him sending away their tormentors. "Race well, my friends," he said. "I am tired and I want to go home."

Judah sighed and walked away, but before he could leave the stables, he heard his named called out. He turned and saw a man striding up to him, dressed as a charioteer in bright green riding vestments. His face was stern and he spoke in a foreign accent. "Are you Quintus Arrius, the emperor's racing adviser?"

"Yes," Judah replied carefully.

The man held up a pouch that appeared to be bulging with coins. "What is the meaning of this?"

Judah looked at the pouch and shook his head. "I don't know what you mean."

"This is silver, which one of your messengers brought to my quarters this morning," the man said with accusatory firmness.

"I sent you no messenger."

The man ignored him. "And he told me this was my reward for racing against Caesar, and that more would follow if I allowed him place."

Judah's face clouded over. "I sent you no messenger. I assure you it was someone else."

"He said he was your servant. This is dishonorable and I will not race at all if this is the price of victory."

"But I'm telling you…," Judah began, but the man threw down the pouch at Judah's feet and stormed off, dropping his helmet and racing sash into the sawdust as he went. Judah's face burned with indignation that his name had been used to buy off the charioteers. He reached down and picked up the pouch, and squeezed it tightly in his fingers as though he could melt down the silver with the heat of his anger.

The sound of applause and cheering filtered down into the caverns beneath the stadium indicating that the entertainment had begun. Judah found the steps which took him up to the main level and slowly worked his way to the stands, though he entertained the idea of remaining in the stables, thinking that the company of the horses might be preferable to the company he would find in the governor's box. Judah found that most of those whom Caesar surrounded himself with were either villains or knaves. He had been unable to develop relationships with any of them, and he sensed that they viewed him with curiosity at best, as one regards a worthless relic.

As he entered the box, none but Seneca and his wife stood to greet him. Judah took a seat beside them. "The program has begun," Seneca said. "I was growing concerned about you. Where is your wife? We have saved her a seat."

Judah could not shield his disdain. "Like me, she is sickened by this entire affair." He leaned closer to the philosopher and said quietly, "You bribed them all anyway. And you sent your messengers in my name. How dare you soil my reputation."

Seneca looked down. "No Judah, you're wrong. Caesar has been watching you to see to see if you are for him or against him. This way he believes that you support him. I did it for your sake, Judah. Soon, you and I can wash our hands of all of this."

Judah's whispering now became louder. "No, Seneca, you're the one who's wrong!"

The intensity of his voice brought a troubled look from Seneca's wife, who could scarcely hear their conversation.

"There is no washing of your hands from this until you choose to stop giving in to him. But you keep telling yourself, *Just one more compromise. One more concession. Then it will all go away.* But it's not going to go away! You have to choose which world you want to live in. Sooner or later you must make your stand!"

Seneca turned away, unable to bear the weight of Judah's logic and zeal, while Judah sat back and tried to quell the angry trembling of his body. No one around them could hear their exchange, for everyone else in the box found amusement in the antics they saw on the track below.

Three chariots had each been harnessed to teams of ostriches and their drivers were attempting to direct them forwards, but with comical results. When chariot racing was the central theme of an event, the Romans found creative ways to weave entertainment out of it. Chariots pulled by anything that breathed— camels, dogs, slaves—ran against each other in mock races that left the crowd laughing in the aisles. The featured race was customarily preceded by numerous heats, usually between four or five chariots. During the height of its racing season,

the Circus Maximus ran as many as 24 heats a day, but thankfully for Judah, Nero
was eager to appear before his people, so he ordered that only four heats be run
before his race. Judah endured all of the preliminary events in brooding silence,
and finally the heats began.

As the four races unfolded, several collisions and a spilled charioteer helped
stir up the savage juices of the crowd, though they hissed their displeasure when
the fallen driver successfully avoided getting trampled. Judah felt a tenseness
building up within him as the final heat was run, and it seemed the more he tried
to ignore the dryness in his throat, the more it tightened up. He tried to dismiss
the thought creeping up in his head, but there it was anyway—part of him was
now thankful that Seneca had purchased the race. Nero's abilities were inferior
even to these lesser drivers he saw racing before him. To race against the fiercest
and best in the Great Race was laughable. And should Nero lose the race, who
could imagine what the bruising of his fragile ego might produce?

The final heat finished, and the restless crowd, sensing that its crowning
moment had arrived, stood to its feet and began to chant in unison *Caesar!* and
soon they added the rhythm of their pounding feet to the echo. But Nero was
not one to appear without an glorious entrance. The final contestants drove onto
the field in their chariots, and most of the spectators were confused why Nero
did not accompany them. They soon found out the reason.

At that moment, a steady cavalcade of horses poured out of the tunnels and
ramps of the circus, many with painted coats, ornately braided manes and tails,
and all of them splashed with plumes. The riders of one group of ten horses
brought their animals into a horizontal line, and as soon as the animals were in
formation, the riders leaped atop their backs and to the delight of the crowd,
began sidestepping back and forth across the horses.

Still the horses came, and now there were several hundred orbiting the track.
Some pulled *carrucas*, long elegant wagons on which were displayed large images
of the gods and the imperial family, carved from ivory or molded from gold.
Groups of jugglers walked between the horses, interspersed with teams of musicians who blew upon their horns though they could barely be heard over the
cheers of the awed spectators. Finally, when the performers had nearly covered
the entire track, came Nero himself driving his chariot, and he acknowledged his
worshippers with dramatic flourishes of his hands.

The spectacle was well choreographed, and by the time Nero emerged, his opponents had already circled the track, and they promptly fell into rank behind him, while the horses which had first paraded into the circus left the same way they had entered. By the time Nero had driven around the track, all that remained on the field were the charioteers, who brought their teams into the starting position in front of the governor's box.

Judah sat forward in his seat, and even Seneca seemed mildly intrigued. A priest stood and poured out obligatory oblations to the Roman gods, and then pronounced the litany of *Hail Caesar!* which the crowd repeated with robust enthusiasm, and then to Judah's astonishment, each of Nero's opponents swung their horses into a circle around him, and lifted their arms in obeisance to him. Victory was conceded in their submission.

With these rituals and gimmicks completed, nothing yet remained but for the presiding official of the games to call the racers to order and begin the race. The drivers aligned their horses beneath the starting cord and tightened their reins around the waists. Nero checked to see that his knife was snug in its casing. Each charioteer carried one so that in the event of a pile-up they could cut themselves free—and perhaps the throat of whoever caused the wreck as well. Each man steadied himself, and kept a steely eye on the official. And then, the flag was dropped.

The horses exploded into motion, kicking up a whirlwind of dust as they sprang from the starting line. Judah and Seneca looked at each other. "Seven laps to freedom, Arrius," Seneca said in an affirming voice.

"If you say so," Judah remarked. "You're the stage-manager."

He looked down on the track, and the only point of interest for him in the race was in discovering how a grand spectacle such as this could possibly be orchestrated. In the second lap he saw a demonstration. Judah watched as Nero came around the *spina* in possession of the inside lane. It had obviously been given to him right away. But as they sped to the next turn, his nearest opponent held a horse-length lead over Nero on the outside and was in clear position to drive him into the concrete if he chose. Nero should have recognized the danger and slowed down defensively, but he pressed on wildly, and was ripe for disaster. Instead, his opponent took the turn wide, and allowed Nero to pass around the corner unscathed. Nero shouted deliriously as it happened, thinking that he had shaken off the rider with his own cleverness.

So the race continued. It was as though there were an invisible wall around Nero which none of the other drivers would breach. As soon as they drew near to Nero, they bounced off to the left or right. If Nero pulled up behind them, they cordially pulled aside as though he had called out pleasantly, "Excuse me! Pardon!" instead of the shower of profanity that he spewed out on each of them.

The racers did not even bother to interfere with each other, for they knew it was pointless to risk injury for a race which meant nothing, and halfway through the contest, the crowd grew agitated with the apparent absence of bravado on the track. Judah yawned. Maybe one day he would write Caesar a letter from Judea and tell him the truth about his racing. But in the end, he thought better of it. It wasn't worth his time. Better to spill his blood for other causes.

Nero was such a poor charioteer that it forced the other drivers to tap all of their superior skills just to keep the emperor in a position where he could win the race. Several times, Nero allowed his team to wander to the outside of the track, and those in front would have to slow down to give him time to catch up. They ran at such a restrained pace, that one charioteer regretted not bringing his wife and children along for the ride. But in the end, it was their efforts at keeping the race at an artificial speed that led to disaster.

With two laps to go, Nero again drifted off the beaten path, and two charioteers found themselves—to their dismay—side by side in the lead. They both looked at each other with exasperation, and simultaneously tightened their leads to slow the horses. Nero recovered himself and charged down upon them. As the turn approached, the two charioteers attempted to separate and create a path between them through which the emperor could pass to victory, but Nero was too impatient to allow the opening to develop. He ran recklessly forward.

His horses managed to squeeze into the gap, but as they entered the corner, he was unable to adjust the reins in time, and his carriage slammed into the side of the chariot to his outside. Their wheels bounced off of each other, sending Nero's chariot rocking to the side. The outside charioteer managed to pull away, but Nero could not control his weaving, and when his horses veered to make the turn, the force drove his chariot onto its outside wheels. Suddenly to the alarm of all who watched, it tipped over altogether, violently spilling Nero onto the arena floor and sending him rolling like a log into the podium, where he stopped with rude abruptness.

Thousands stood to their feet, and an odd wave of murmurs and whispers swept through the circus. Judah and Seneca stood in a synchronized reflex of horror as they watched the catastrophe unfold before them, and both hurried to the brass railing in front of the box and leaned out over it. Nero moved once, and then fell motionless into the sand. Seneca's eyes remained riveted upon Nero's crumpled form as he spoke quietly under his breath for none but Judah to hear.

"Better for all of us if he is dead."

*   *   *

News of the accident spread swiftly through Neapolis and the surrounding region, and people came by the thousands and enveloped the circus, waiting for word of the emperor's condition. Caesar was taken by stretcher to an infirmary within the compound of the circus. His left arm was broken, his face was bruised, and he was unconscious from the concussion, which allowed his physicians to set the fracture. But they could do little else until he regained consciousness.

When Esther heard of what happened, she hurried frantically to the arena but was not allowed inside, so she asked that Judah be sent for, and when he appeared through the mass of people, she ran up to him and clasped her arms around him. Judah led her away from the crowd, and explained what happened as they walked. The question most pressing on her heart was also the question she was most afraid to ask, but the oppressive cloud overhanging them could not be ignored, and Judah finally spoke of it.

"Esther, I fear for what is about to happen. When he awakes—," and he paused to evaluate his choice of words. "The emperor is capricious and vain. If this turns out badly, you must leave without me."

Esther's protest was immediate. "Judah, no! I cannot—,"

"*Esther!*" said Judah firmly. "Listen to me. Our arrangements are made. If something happens to me, the only thing that will keep me alive is knowing you are safe. If he decides to turn against me, he could also strike at you, and that would be more than I could bear."

"Judah, can't you understand?" Esther cried. "I watched Messala take you away from me, and the pain nearly killed me. You want me to stand by and let it happen all over again? How could I do that? How could I live again without you?"

"I'm not saying this is how it will happen, Esther," Judah said, feeling the bitter grief of Esther's words. "But if it should, then I want you to leave at once for Judea. Not a day's delay. If you are alive I will find a way to come to you, I swear it!" She began weeping in his arms and he pulled her tightly to him and stroked softly at her hair. "I love you, Esther."

They limped back to the compound on the other end of the city and met Andronicus and several others waiting there. Judah repeated for them his instructions to Esther, and they all reluctantly agreed that should the situation become desperate, they would do what they could to save Esther. The evening fell, and the troubled friends went to their beds with their minds churning with anxious prayer.

The next morning they all awoke at sunrise, as Romans customarily did, but Judah had been up much earlier and was intent on returning to the infirmary as soon as possible to learn of any news. Instead, the news came to him. As the friends were finishing breakfast and Judah was preparing to leave the compound, a knock came at the door of their apartment. Judah opened the door and found one of Seneca's young servants standing there.

"Good morning, Fabius," Judah said warmly. "You've come with a message from your master?" The servant nodded with urgency. "What is it, my child?"

"Lord Nero is no longer unconscious." He paused.

"And? That is good. Is there anything else?"

"He has called for you by name."

"Is that the message?" The servant again nodded. "Tell your master I will come shortly."

The servant stepped back to leave but Judah called out to him again. "Fabius, come and take some food before you leave. You look hungry and I doubt you've eaten."

The slave looked astonished, and sheepishly followed Judah into the apartment, where he was offered some bread and fruit in the presence of the others. But to find himself treated as an equal by those he knew exceeded him in status made him feel awkward, as though he were standing there naked, and so he quickly snatched at the food and excused himself. When he was gone, Judah turned to Esther and his friends.

"So Caesar has called for me by name. Do you suppose he wishes to thank me for my service?"

Esther reached out and took his hand. "Let me go with you, Judah."

"No, my love," Judah replied earnestly. "But do prepare your things. If the Lord sends me back to you, we'll leave this forsaken city today. And if the Lord does not send me back to you," and he looked deeply into her eyes which were searching his own face with dispirited heaviness, "then you fly from here, and Andronicus will be the bridge which will keep us together."

Esther's tears came without restraint and she clung to him with desperation. "But what if he kills you? Judah, don't leave me!"

"Not even Caesar can make a capital offense out of being an incompetent horse trainer. Don't be afraid, Esther." He smiled down upon her and brushed her face tenderly with his fingers. "We're probably all worrying for nothing. Just be ready. And be strong. Nothing will keep me away from you." Her face dipped down in discouragement but he raised her chin so that their eyes met again. His own eyes burned with determination.

"*Nothing* will keep me away from you."

Esther could not answer him. She buried her head in his chest and trembled, and then after a moment, she controlled her sobbing and pulled away from him.

"I will be waiting for you, Judah," she said in a broken voice. Judah waved to his friends and then gave Esther one more kiss. He looked at her as though to engrave her face into his memory, and finally left the apartment, looking behind him just once as he crossed the threshold and closed the door. Only as he left the grounds of the compound did he allow himself to weep, and as he walked toward the circus he had to wipe his face more than once.

Though the hour was yet early, the crowd around the circus was already building, humming with the rumor that Nero was awake and might soon appear before them. Judah passed through them and proceeded directly to the infirmary. Guards and attendants stood nervously around the doorway, and when they saw Judah approach, their quiet voices grew more subdued still. Seneca stood there among them and his grave expression offered no solace. They opened up a path through which Judah could walk, and as he entered the room, Judah could not have found a more ominous collection of souls.

Poppaea and Tigellinus stood above Nero who lay on his back upon a bed, and standing along the walls around the room were several more of his young and sinister friends. Nero saw him enter and his face immediately clouded over.

Poppaea and Tigellinus mimicked the look, as though they were puppets. While Seneca remained in the doorway, Judah stepped forward to the bed.

"What do you have to say for yourself, Quintus Arrius?" Nero asked. His left arm was tightly wrapped in bandages. Abrasions and bruises marred the rest of what Judah could see of his body which was covered by a sheet from the waist down.

"Is there anything to say except that I am glad to see that Caesar is recovering?" Judah responded delicately, but Nero did not appreciate his tact.

"Stop your pleasantries," he spat. "Spare me your sympathy. My arm is broken. My back is out of place. Look at my face! I have been humiliated in the eyes of the Roman world."

Judah felt that he must at least attempt a defense. "An accident is no cause for humiliation."

"An accident! An accident that my chariot tipped over at the slightest imbalance? You accuse *me* of ineptness? I called you into my service to prepare me for such moments. The ineptness is not mine, it is yours. You have failed me, Arrius. And now I must suffer for you negligence."

Poppaea leaned over him and cradled his head as though to comfort him and protect him from Judah's malevolence.

"If those were your expectations Caesar, then I never would have accepted this commission," Judah said soberly. "No mentor can be asked to guarantee the performance of his athletes. Mistakes and unforeseen events are a part of competition. Even champions must continue to learn."

Seneca looked on with admiration for his friend and chose to intercede. "Caesar, we have questioned each of the drivers in the race, and to a man, they marveled at your obvious abilities and praised the training you have received from Arrius. Charioteers are bred, not born, and yet you have reached in but one year a level of skill that would take the most gifted of men five years to achieve. You ought not be ashamed of your performance, and Arrius ought not be rebuked."

"But I am ashamed!" Nero stormed back. "There I was, spilled upon the track like a clumsy toddler learning how to walk. Is that the posture of a champion, Arrius? Lying face down in the dust? I agree with you, Arrius. You are not negligent at all. You knew full well that my chariot was unstable. This was no accident. This smacks of sabotage!" Judah's eyes grew black in disbelief.

"You were the one overseeing the equipping of the horse team," Nero continued. "You were the one in charge of the racing crew. Plenty of opportunity to loosen a bolt or crack a frame."

"Caesar, how can you possibly accuse me of this?" Judah protested.

"How can I accuse you of this?" Nero mocked. "How can I not, Arrius? Twice during our training, you deliberately resisted me. And once you did that which is inconceivable—you struck me! You struck Caesar!"

Gasps issued from those around the bed.

"All along, you have shown yourself to be my enemy. You do not lack for motives either. Were you angry that I detained you and kept you from your precious Judea? Were you jealous of my youth, seeing in me the abilities which you had lost? Or was it your love of the slaves which sent you to strike at their master? Which is it, Arrius? Personal vendetta? Political conspiracy?"

"I rearranged my life to serve you," Judah argued. "I gave you completely of my time and efforts. I showed you loyalty. And I did it all without complaint."

"Exactly. Why complain when all along you knew how this would conclude? And to the end, you continued to reveal your hostility to me. Refusing to give my imperial reward to the other drivers."

Judah's eyes widened as though he had been slapped in the face.

"Oh yes, Arrius. Seneca would not say that you refused to help me, and Seneca would not tell me that he tried to cover for your uncooperativeness. But I could see. I have many eyes and many ears. And it doesn't stop there. You also refuse to honor me by your absence at state dinners. Such loyalty, Arrius. Well, I have beaten you. I have beaten you by surviving your plot, and now I will beat your further by taking your freedom—permanently!"

He now looked past Judah and Seneca to the guards peering in from the door. "Guards, take this loyal and dedicated man, and place him in custody. A jail cell awaits him in Rome."

The guards came obediently into the room and stood on either side of Judah. As they took his arms and ushered him out of the room, Judah glared down on Nero and uttered with severity, "May God have mercy on your soul, Nero, for your crimes will surely bring your guilty head down to hell!"

Poppaea clung tightly to Nero to ward off the barbs of Judah's cruel tongue. Seneca walked out ahead of the guards, and once they were out of the room,

Judah suddenly broke free of the soldiers, grabbed Seneca and pushed him against the wall.

"Seneca, I implore you," he quickly whispered in his ears. "For the love of all that is right, save Esther. Get my wife out of here!"

The guards angrily snatched at Judah and jerked him away from Seneca, and pushed him down the corridor. Judah looked back, his eyes pleading with desperation. "Send her to Jerusalem! Don't let her stay behind." They turned a corner. "To Jerusalem!" Judah shouted. "Seneca—remember Burrus!"

Seneca looked after them as they disappeared from sight, and then stood there until the echoes of their footsteps died away. He sighed, then turned and walked the other way.

Part 3: A.D.63–68

Chapter 14

Plautius Lateranus walked about the circuit of small rooms and chambers and gawked at the selection of statues and paintings that adorned each nook and cranny. Hardly a pocket of sizeable space existed that was not ornamented by marble, amber, ivory or brass. As he continued walking, he came into a spacious parlor, where four men sat around an oak table, eagerly gorging themselves from a bountiful selection of fowl and fish heaped high upon a platter. Behind them was a circular stove filled with coals, and on the iron grating above the stove cooked still more meat. Empty plates and glasses waited on a hutch, and beside them were ripe vegetables and fruit arrayed handsomely in bowls, looking like another art display.

As he walked into the parlor, the men around the table hailed him with friendly greetings, among them Calpurnius Piso and Thrasea Paetus. Piso stood and walked over to him, offering him a warm handshake.

"Plautius, welcome! I see my doorman left you to wander aimlessly through my house, but you have found us."

"I only had to follow my nose," laughed Lateranus. "The aroma brought me directly to you."

He was in his forties, and of all the men in the room, was the only equal to Piso in stature and appearance. Because he was a senator, he exceeded Piso in position, but Piso was wealthier and so exceeded him in influence. In observing the two men's comradery, it seemed that they enjoyed a cordial rivalry.

"And by all means, take a plate and please join us before the food disappears," Piso invited him with an outstretched hand, while returning to his seat. Lateranus quickly reached for a plate and began disassembling the fruit sculpture in search of the pieces he desired. "When you walked in, we were just discussing Thrasea's latest entanglement with the emperor."

"Good night, Paetus, what on earth have you done now?" asked Lateranus, inspecting several strawberries in his hand as though they were diamonds.

"It's what Caesar did for Thrasea last week," said another man, Antonius Natalis, a respected knight, and close friend of Piso.

"In forbidding him to come to Antium?" Lateranus asked. "Yes, I know all about that. Don't forget, I was there."

As Poppaea had advanced to the end of her pregnancy, Nero demanded that she make an uncomfortable journey to Antium, to insure that his child would be brought to birth in the very city where he had been born. Nero's mind was forever active in creating symbolic visual expressions to portray his greatness before the nation. When Poppaea gave birth to a daughter, the Senate was then compelled to come to Antium to celebrate with an official thanksgiving—all except Paetus, whom Nero specifically forbade from attending.

Paetus now spoke as Laternus took a chair around the table. "Let the record show that I consider it the highest honor I have ever received to be singled out by the divine Caesar in this fashion. In the eyes of the gods, whose praise I esteem most, to be rebuked by a spineless and depraved man is the surety that I am living my life as virtuously as I ought. I will slit my throat the day Nero speaks one favorable word about me."

The others around the table boldly nodded in admiration of their noble friend. The fourth man, Afranius Quintianus, also a senator, seemed shamed by Paetus' words. "Thrasea, you are a father to me in the senate and I regret that I did not stand up for you by refusing to come to Antium. I pray that you forgive me."

Paetus smiled. "But there is nothing to forgive, Afranius. What I do, I do for conscience, not conspiracy, and so I do not expect others to share in my actions, or the consequences my actions bring."

"But my conscience condemns me. I should have stood with you."

"Then it is your conscience which should forgive you, not I," Paetus continued. "Or else, it is your conscience which should move you to further action. But fear not, my friend. You can be assured that with Caesar, your conscience will be given many more opportunities to be aroused. We live in days when virtue lies dormant.

Gray areas have vanished in our time and all is either black or white. Don't worry, Afranius, you will have other chances to declare which color you are."

Lateranus now spoke. "It is interesting that you mention conspiracy in the same breath as conscience, Paetus. For does there not come a time when one's conscience is offended so frequently that conspiracy becomes the logical and necessary direction in which conscience leads?"

Paetus took a bite out of an apple and stared solemnly at his friend. "There are some whose consciences automatically rule out conspiracy as a method for resolving injustices. Some who are peace lovers, who trust in the gods to restore balance to the moral universe."

"But the gods do not send lightning bolts from heaven to weed out evil men!" Lateranus said with exasperation. "Their instruments are righteous men wielding swords. But if the righteous fail to raise their swords, then not even the gods can intervene, and the wicked continue in power. Tell me, Paetus, are you a lover of peace or a lover of justice?"

The atmosphere was growing tense, and the others nibbled nervously at their food. Paetus answered quietly, but with an unmistakable authority. "And tell me, Plautius, I didn't hear you earlier. Were you in Antium?" Lateranus felt the sting of Paetus' rebuke and looked down. "The way to resist those without principles is to never compromise your own. Never give them the pleasure of seeing you stoop to their level. Evil cannot be extinguished with more evil, anymore than a fire can be put out with torches. Violence is the cheapest form of resistance. And how often has it been seen that conspirators soon become as oppressive as the tyrants they replace?"

"Meanwhile, noble men continue to be forced into hiding, thrown into prison, or are slaughtered outright," said Lateranus, not wishing to yield the argument. "Sulla dies, then Plautus, who's next? Your turn cannot be far off, Paetus. Did you see what was done to Quintus Arrius? An old man with distinguished service—accused of masterminding a plot on the emperor's life! His trial was a sham—a circus! Anyone with half a brain knows the truth of what happened."

Quintianus sighed. "Thank you, Plautius. My conscience just managed to forgive me for being in Antium, and you have to mention that shameful incident. Now I feel wretched all over again."

"And what speeches did you make to plead for his deliverance?" Paetus asked. "What challenges did you offer to the evidence brought before us? Where was your voice when the vote was cast?"

"I did not vote for his death with the majority!" Lateranus shouted.

"No, but you abstained, as did you Afranius," said Paetus, his own voice rising in intensity. "Whose voice echoed with mine asking for his pardon? Not one. And so, forgive me if I doubt your courage for carrying out grand designs when it fails so easily in the simpler ones." He tipped a glass of wine to his lips with a decisive snap of his wrist, as though to signal that the argument was won. Looking at Laternus, he asked, "Tell me, what exactly would you propose be done with the emperor?"

"The bastard should be murdered," answered Lateranus.

"You would wish the death of the man who freed you from exile?"

"Why should that matter? Do you think I exchanged one form of slavery for another?"

Paetus continued his assault. "And in a year or so, you are likely to be appointed to a consul seat. Why would you place that in jeopardy?"

Piso now intervened. "Goodness, Thrasea. You are relentless tonight. I can't tell if the excessive heat in this room is from the oven or from you. Please gentlemen, I expect political banter when I invite senators into my home, but why every time we gather must we plot the emperor's death? Soon my name will be circulating on the Capitoline Hill as an arch-conspirator. And I hardly say ten words when we are together!"

Paetus and Lateranus looked at each other and their eyes brightened, signaling a momentary truce. Piso restocked the platter of meat, and the five men continued picking at it, and each other, on into the early hours of the morning.

*   *   *

Nero walked swiftly down a side hallway through the senate chambers, while Tigellinus struggled to keep pace with him. His arm was yet strapped in a sling, and his face still bore traces of bruising, but there was an excitement, even a wildness, about his countenance.

"Tigellinus, this is a most unbelievable turn of events!" he exclaimed. "And the entire Senate has been summoned?"

"As soon as we heard, Lord Nero," replied Tigellinus. "Of course, we knew you were out of the city, and so we have waited for your arrival. All of the city is astir with the news."

"Why weren't we told earlier?"

"The prisoner was fitted for transport at once and brought to Italy. No messenger could have arrived any earlier. It is naturally what you would have wanted."

Nero smiled. "Finally, those who serve me are learning how I think." They turned into a receiving room which led directly into the main hall of the Senate. "Can it really be after all this time? Ah, my curiosity, my passion, my wrath have all been unleashed at once. Let us welcome home our wandering child."

They strode directly into the chambers, and a torrent of clamorous chatter immediately drowned them out. Every senator was in his seat, and hundreds of smaller inquiries and discussions were taking place in groups of two or three. As the emperor entered, these smaller tribunals gradually disbanded, and all eyes were drawn down in Caesar's direction, as he sat anxiously upon his throne.

The consul called for order and then motioned to Nero, who sat up in his seat and bellowed out with his most formal, official voice. "Distinguished senators, you all know the purpose for this unscheduled gathering. I know you have been waiting with great patience. We shall not delay any longer. Let us bring out our guest of honor. Usher in the prisoner!"

With a flourish, he motioned to soldiers stationed on the other side of the podium who withdrew behind the stage and then re-emerged a moment later, leading in a small, thin prisoner whose arms were bound and head cloaked. The murmuring among the Senate kicked in once again, and Nero stood up as the prisoner was brought before him. His lips seemed to quiver, and a thin strand of saliva dripped from them.

Suddenly, one of the soldiers reached up and roughly stripped the cloak from off the prisoner's head. Nero wiped his mouth and his eyes narrowed with intense pleasure as he found Octavia standing three feet away from him.

*   *   *

The first thing Judah noticed when the cell door was opened was the smell. The odor of urine was immediately apparent. But before he had time to make any mental adjustments to this new environment, the guard pushed him inside the cell, so hard that he fell to the floor and his face rubbed up against the brown, damp straw that covered it. He pushed himself slowly up on his forearms, and turned to see the door pushed shut.

The assault on his senses at that moment was profound. His nose stung with the smell. His eyes batted in vain to make use of the thin sheet of gray light that came under the door. His ears were pricked by the turning of the guard's key in the lock, and the sound of his footsteps drifting away. His tongue craved water, a feeling made all the worse because there was no water. In the prostrate position he found himself in, Judah sighed, let his head sag slightly and moaned a few simple words.

"Oh God, I yield myself to your will. Give me your strength."

Once his head had cleared, he stood and paced off the dimensions of the cell. Ten by ten. The Romans were a geometric people, giving thought to aesthetics even in their brutality. There was no bench or cot on which to sit—just a stone floor covered with dirty straw not fit for a barn animal. He kicked away the straw from a section of the floor and dropped his weary body down. He closed his eyes.

This was now the third jail cell he had occupied since his arrest. After a week in Neapolis, he was brought to Rome and held for trial, though not once was he brought before the Senate for questioning. He only heard rumors through his guards that his case was being tried. Now he was transferred once again, either to await for execution or to rot for the rest of his life. All he knew for sure was that the conditions of his incarceration were rapidly deteriorating with each transfer. The one treasure he had been able to thank God for up until now was simple light. But now that too was gone.

Even so, God answered Judah's prayer, and his spirit remained resilient in the early part of his captivity. He sang hymns, recited long portions of scriptures which he had committed to memory, and spent hours in prayer, and there were moments when the presence of God seemed to fill the cell. The knowledge of Jesus' promise that he would always be with his disciples was now more than a tenet of faith, but a reality which Judah experienced, a grace that had been uniquely provided at the moment it was needed.

The only thought which unsettled the confidence he felt was his ignorance of Esther's fate. Not knowing what had happened to her was like a dagger to his faith, and when his mind wandered into careless speculation, his heart sank and the Presence within his cell grew faint.

"Father, give me one sign. One word. One spark of hope that I can cling to." Over and over, this prayer fell from his lips. And finally, the prayer was answered.

Several weeks after being brought to this third cell, the door opened at an uncustomary hour. Judah looked up and saw the silhouette of a man standing there, illuminated by the light of two torches. Judah sat and waited with his eyes squinting, but the man said nothing. Finally, he stepped closer and Judah could see his face. It was Seneca. Immediately, he sat up.

"Why Seneca, come in. What a surprise," said Judah with friendliness. "I'd offer you a seat, but…I don't have one."

Seneca came into the cell with an attendant standing behind him.

"I expected you to come earlier," Judah then said.

"I could not," Seneca replied soberly. "If I were to be of real help to you, I had to wait until things had calmed. Now that we are back in Rome, I thought you might be interested in knowing that the Senate has already taken up your case."

"I wasn't aware there was a case against me. And what kind of trial is this where the defendant is not allowed to speak in his defense?"

"Those who make an attempt on the emperor's life are given no hearing," he said, and Judah laughed scornfully. "The Senate asked for your death. But Nero pleaded for clemency, and commuted your sentence to life in his dungeons, which is where you are now."

Seneca said all of this without any inflection in his voice. He announced it as though he were describing the weather. "So you intend to help me?" Judah asked. "What help can you give me now?"

"I already have helped you," said Seneca.

Judah's eyes narrowed and his ears perked up. "What about my wife? What about Esther? Where is she?"

"The emperor wanted her found."

Seneca paused between sentences, as though to deliberately annoy Judah by holding back the news he bore. Intended or not, the effect worked. Judah grabbed his arm. "Seneca, you didn't let it happen! I trusted you."

"I placed her on the ship for Judea that night. My contacts told me the other day that she has arrived safely, and was heading for Jerusalem. And so I already have helped you."

Judah's head sank low below his shoulders, and Seneca could see his body start to heave with sobbing. Through his tears, Judah squeezed Seneca's arm in a gesture of gratitude and said quietly, "Thank you. Seneca, thank you. She is safe."

"I fail to see how Jerusalem will afford her safety," Seneca said. "Judea is a violent province filled with unruly people. Even now, Nero is preparing to appoint another in a never-ending string of governors, and you can be sure he will be commissioned to use all measures to preserve order."

"We have family there who will care for her better than I can now." Judah wiped his face with his arm, then looked up and stared into Seneca's eyes. "You're always concerned for safety, Seneca. Speak to me honestly, how safe do you feel right now? Don't you feel his breath on your neck even as we speak? I've read some of your writings, Seneca. You write of goodness and truth and courage, and then the same hands which create such gallant words turn around and distribute bribes. Who are you, Seneca?"

Seneca sighed. "You are right, Arrius. I am not the man of my writings. I am not a good man. Goodness is proven by actions, not words, and I have failed. You are a freer man, Arrius. You always have been free. I have watched you with envy. I thought I once knew what freedom was, but now I am hemmed in on every side. And even should I free myself from these earthly tyrants, the tyranny of my natural mortality will soon claim me."

"Death is a doorway, Seneca," Judah replied. "Like all earthly tyrants, it too pretends to be more powerful than it really is. Jesus taught his followers to see death as a defeated foe. It no longer needs to be feared."

"Your philosophy suits you well, Arrius. I am happy for you."

"Do you know the difference between a man of philosophy and a man of faith, Seneca?" Seneca shrugged his shoulders. "The man of faith believes in the words he speaks."

"So there is the problem, Arrius. I have nothing to believe in."

The men observed an uncomfortable silence, while Judah remained sitting in the straw and Seneca stood in the shadows. Seneca then spoke. "I will do what I can to provide some comforts for you. A cot. Fresh straw. Perhaps a window cut into the door. Be patient with me for all must be done without Nero's knowledge. I am more deserving of this dung heap than you. But if you will believe me, I shall suffer with you."

"All I hope for, my friend, is that you will come to share in the redemption I already enjoy," Judah said. "With the God I serve, there is forgiveness for failed tests and life that outlasts the grave. Surely a man of philosophy must hunger for these."

Seneca sighed. "As I said, Arrius, your philosophy suits you well." He turned to go. "I will visit with you again." He then reached out to his attendant who handed him an object, which he in turn held out to Judah—a blanket.

*   *   *

"Well, well, well," Nero began, conjuring up the most condescending tone possible. He began to walk around her, as a lion sizing up its prey. "Look who has come home. Can it be my dear Octavia?"

He waited to see what effect his words would have on her. It used to give him twisted pleasure to see her tremble just at the sound of his voice. Nero was a pathetic soldier. The only combat he would ever know was on the battlefield of the human psyche. He was a soldier of the mind and he took pride in his ability to break a person's spirit. But Octavia's lovely face showed nothing of the old fear. She looked straight ahead, and his ranting and pacing seemed scarcely able to affect her at all.

Nero stopped in front of her and jabbed her with an icy glare. She met the gaze directly without flinching, and as he looked full into her deep, beautiful eyes, he saw his own wraith-like face staring back in the reflection, and quickly resumed his pacing.

"So where in the world have we been hiding?" Nero asked. Knowing that she was unlikely to answer, his question was directed more at an interrogator who stood nearby, looking pompous and important.

"Ephesus, Lord Nero," responded the interrogator.

"Ephesus. Such a long way away," Nero said contemplatively. "Octavia, did you take a wrong turn one night on your way home? You always were easily distracted, but—Ephesus!" Suddenly, he turned on her again, and his voice cut with sharp rancor, as he screamed in her ear. "Who helped you?"

Deep within her spirit, a tremor shook through her, but she cloaked it well, and gave no hint that Nero's loathsome presence unnerved her. She refused to speak. The interrogator resumed his testimony.

"She was found within a religious community, Emperor, of those that call themselves *Christians*. The slave of a senator who was vacationing in Ephesus pointed her out in the crowd. She was followed to the home of a freeman, who turned out to be a leader of this Jewish sect."

"Has this ringleader been questioned?" asked Nero, making sure his voice carried to every corner of the auditorium.

"Both he and Octavia's own female servant were questioned. All they would say is that she had come to Ephesus of her own free will with no assistance, and had joined this community while there."

"Yes, but were they *questioned?*"

"Octavia's servant died while being questioned, Caesar."

Again, Nero could not see it, but Octavia's spirit cried out in pain when this was said. What remained visible was a stoic strength unlike anything Nero had ever seen in her before. But something else now gnawed at him.

"Octavia, you were in the home of a freeman. Was this your lover? Did you sleep with this man?" The more he thought of it, the more irritated he became. "You allowed the temple of your body, consecrated by Caesar, to be defiled by other worshippers? You are no princess. You are filthy slut!"

As he said this, he spat upon her face. She looked down, unable to wipe her face because her hands were bound, but the wall of strength around her heart would not crumble.

"There is no evidence, Caesar, that this man was her lover," interjected the interrogator. "He was a very old man."

"That changes little of the fact that this is someone who spurned my love, and could not wait to desert me," Nero pined in syllables broken by grief. "That she has had other lovers is beyond question. Old or young it doesn't matter to her. Anyone but Nero is the sole criteria. The question yet to be explored is how did you leave us? Who helped you? And please, spare me the nonsense that this was the achievement of you and your servant! I know you much better than that. I expect an answer. Who helped you? Who are these Christians?"

Octavia's heart jumped. She did not want her friends subjected to imperial scrutiny. She spoke to refract the light away from them. "Burrus helped me."

"So you can speak?" Nero said with satisfaction. "Burrus. That stands to reason. I might have guessed. Anyone else? Seneca, perhaps?"

She shook her head. "Only two of Burrus' servants who accompanied me on the ship in which I fled."

"I should have known that Burrus was up to no good," Caesar muttered. "But then, the gods, who see into the hearts of men, meted out a painful judgment to him, so justice has yet been served. But tell me, how exactly did he help you?"

"I'll tell you why he helped me," Octavia answered. "You threatened to kill me."

Nero laughed. "The Senate does not want to hear about our bedroom quarrels, Octavia. All of that is old news. I have since gone on with my life."

"Then why can't you allow me to go on with my life?"

Octavia's bold and simple question drew a muffled reaction from the congregation of senators. Nero spoke swiftly in order to quell it.

"Because you are a threat. Wherever you go, crowds gather. A simple slave can pick you out of a crowd. Already, this building is surrounded by thousands of people ready to worship you all over again. Ready to undo all the good things we have done in your absence. Ready to open up old and painful wounds. You are a threat."

He now turned to the senators.

"Senators, you must agree with me! What we have represented here in this small, frail package is dissension. Disunity! Instability and rebellion! We must not be fooled by outward appearances. We must push back the feelings of sentiment and compassion which are right now forcing their way into us. And we must deal with this threat as we would any other. Shall we allow this empire to rip apart into sentimental factions? Shall we confuse the nation with the illusion that some mythical past can be recreated? We must not allow this to happen. And so, after examining the prisoner, there can be only one resolution, one punishment, one just and right course of action!"

He extended his arm to the Senate to allow them to render their verdict, and pronounce the word that he would not say. A few seconds of silence slipped by and then a lone voice rang out from the chambers.

"Death!"

Soon afterwards, an echo was heard.

"Death!"

Then two or three other voices offered the cry, and suddenly, like the bursting of a rain cloud, dozens of additional voices shouted until the entire assembly pronounced in repetitive unison the cry of "*Death! Death!*" The cacophony of voices was like the pelting of stones down upon Octavia, and she lowered her head and shuddered. Nero finally raised up his hands to quiet them.

"As always, the Senate is swift to enact justice to preserve the stability of the realm. As always, I am merciful, when the situation warrants it. Octavia, I hereby order with the Senate's approval, in light of the love we once shared, that you be confined in permanent exile to the penal islands off our coast."

The Senate at once broke into applause, and cries of "Merciful Caesar!", "Nero is great!" rose up above the noise. When the sound faded, Nero turned once again to Octavia.

"Do you have anything to say to us in response to this just sentence of the court?"

She looked up at him, with eyes that were steady and bright. "Lord Jesus, do not hold this sin against them."

"Lord *Jesus*?" Nero asked. "Octavia, have you been away from Rome so long that you have forgotten? *Caesar* is Lord." He motioned to the interrogator and to the guards. "Take her away for more questioning before she is deported." He waved at the Senate. "Thank you senators for your swift and decisive attention given to this matter."

He walked off the platform, and as Tigellinus drew close behind him, Nero leaned over to him and whispered. "See that her exile is not long, Tigellinus. And send me evidence."

*　　　　　　*　　　　　　*

Two months later, Nero sat alone at his desk in his private quarters, working on a speech he was to deliver for the honoring of a newly retired general. Two raps sounded out from the door.

"Come!" Nero yelled.

An attendant entered the room, bearing in his hand a small, wooden crate. He marched up to Nero. "Lord Nero, Prefect Tigellinus instructed me to bring you this box. He said you would have great interest in its contents."

Nero nodded and the man placed the box down upon the desk, saluted and swiftly left the room. Nero's eyes widened with curiosity. He reached out and drew the box to him, and then lifted up the lid which was secured by a sliding hook. What he saw inside compelled him to suddenly stand up with a start.

He looked down into the box in fascination, and then reached into it and withdrew both a large, braided clump of dark hair and a knife with a simple wooden handle and a blade stained with dried blood. Nero turned the knife over in his hands several times before returning it to the box, and then he raised the hair to his nose and allowed its strands to run along his nostrils. He fingered it with a certain tenderness, even reverence, and then spoke as though lost in a poetic reverie.

"How many times I stroked this silken hair. How many times I kissed this virgin neck. How short our exile in life can be."

Again, he smelled the hair, closing his eyes, which twitched uncontrollably.

Chapter 15

Winter came upon Italy with gray and icy fierceness. A melancholy descended upon Rome, deepened by the sudden death of Nero's daughter, who was sickly at birth and was quickly finished off by the brutal weather. Just as his joy at her birth was amplified with theatrical fervor, so Nero's lamentation at her death became a spectacle in itself. He declared his Augusta to be a goddess and the Senate agreed to finance the erection of a shrine in her honor, and a new order of priests was ordained to attend to her worship.

Burrus' property was declared forfeit to the state, and those that survived him of his household were driven from Rome, penniless and persecuted. The Guard was purged of those who were known to be Burrus' closest supporters. Seneca was further isolated from the court, yet when he requested a second time to resign his post, Nero refused him, preferring to keep a threatening, tormenting shadow hanging over the philosopher.

As spring came, the public brooded over the dwindling corn supply, and the restlessness became so acute that Nero postponed his plans of traveling to Greece. Publicly, he claimed that the gods' omens of his tour were unfavorable. Additionally, he had seen the sorrow in the people's faces whenever he spoke of leaving and so, for their sakes, he would not leave the country. The discerning ones among the Senate knew better. The restive murmurs bubbling up among the citizenry could only be contained by Nero remaining in Rome.

Judah bore his imprisonment with a resiliency that amazed his guards, and strengthened the Christians who visited him. Aquila and Priscilla attended to him faithfully, and Andronicus came often to uplift his mentor, but usually he received more encouragement from Judah than he himself was able to give. Seneca as well found pleasure and sanity in Judah's company, but aside from having a window cut into the door and providing him with a cot, he found little he could do to offer Judah relief.

Judah was comforted most by letters he received from Esther, delivered through Andronicus' hands, which chronicled her voyage to Judea and assured him that she had safely arrived at Tirzah and John's home. He hid the letters under the straw of his cell, for they were his bridge to hope which kept him confident that he would outlast Nero's vengeance. He was also buoyed by the memory of another dark time in his life when he was condemned to die, chained to an oar, again as Rome's prisoner and again unjustly, but God intervened and overturned Rome's verdict. Judah never lost his faith that God would do so again.

And then Judah's hope was fortified by an unexpected visitor. One day, his cell door opened slightly, and a guard whom Judah had befriended stepped inside.

"Master Hur," he said.

"Yes, Cestius," answered Judah weakly, for he had been sleeping.

"Your advocate is here to see you."

Judah sat up wearily. "My advocate? I don't have an advocate."

The door opened wider, and from behind Cestius appeared a clean-shaven face, beaming like a summer day.

"Oh, you must be joking!" Judah cried out, quickly standing to his feet and embracing the visitor. "Paul, you old dog, what are you doing here?"

"Judah!" Paul exclaimed with joy, and the two men squeezed each other with great tenderness. Cestius politely pulled back out of the cell. Paul pushed away from his friend momentarily to take a good look at him. He reached out and tickled Judah's chin which was covered with an unkempt beard.

"Now, the last time I saw you, you had the smooth face and I was the bearded one with the chains."

"Our world has turned upside down, hasn't it?" said Judah with a smile. "Please sit down, let's talk."

He motioned for Paul to sit by him on the cot. As Paul did so, he kicked at the floor. "They've given you straw. I used to dream of having straw in my cell. The floors could be so cold."

"Rome spares no expense for her prisoners," Judah said sarcastically.

"Well, news travels slowly in the West, Judah," Paul explained, his voice becoming more serious. "I came as soon as I heard what happened. This is not how I anticipated things would work out for you."

"I can't say that this was on my wish list either," Judah responded. "We serve a mysterious God, who is full of surprises. But who am I to question the one who sees further than I? So tell me, Paul, how is the West?"

"Truthfully? It's been quite challenging. The soil of Spain is hard and fallow. The heat oppressive. The seeds that are planted will be hard-pressed to mature. More than once, Brother Thord delivered us from the mouth of mortal danger."

"Has he returned with you?"

"Yes, and wishes to see you as soon as he is strong enough. Bandits and violent mobs could not stop him. It took the tossing of the sea to slow him down. He proved to be a most faithful friend in my travels. But I needed spiritual strength alongside of me as well. I missed the partnership of strong companions like you. But now, we are drawn together once again. As you served me during my time of captivity, so I will serve you here until the Lord makes plain his will."

"You commit yourself to an uncertain task then."

"So be it. Though I must tell you, Judah, my spirit is deeply troubled with foreboding of what the future holds."

"Ah, you've been dreaming again."

"More than dreams. The Lord is speaking to many, not just to me, that a fearful time of testing is about to fall upon the church here. Even Peter has sensed the urgency of this moment, and he is right now on his way here from Judea."

"I too have been unsettled in my prayers," said Judah. "Of course, you have heard that Octavia is dead."

Paul nodded solemnly. "I am afraid the princess is the first fruits of many martyrs to come. But this conflagration is not for Rome alone. Jerusalem too will soon be swallowed up by it. These next years will be very dark."

Judah had often feared this, but hearing the words spoken by so trusted a friend, and knowing that he was separated from Esther by an impossible gulf, struck him as a piercing dart to his soul. He lowered his head in his hands.

"I miss her, Paul."

Paul reached out and placed a consoling arm around his friend.

"There have been many times in my life when I have envied those of you who were married. You have known pleasures that are foreign to me. But you also experience pain that I am spared. Take courage, Judah. Dear Esther is certainly not alone. And if God wills for you to be with her again, then not even a demon like Nero can prevent it. Be strong, my brother."

Judah looked up and saw in the dim, gray light that his friend's cheeks were streaked with tears. Judah sighed.

"Once Seneca told me that my life was an odyssey. He couldn't have been more right. For me, it has been either elation or despair. Prosperity or poverty. Unbridled success or utter disaster. I'm either a prince or a prisoner. I can never seem to find the middle ground. Never find that place of just simple, ordinary peace. Oh Paul, I am so tired. I just want to rest."

His head fell into his hands once again. Paul placed a palm upon Judah's head and silently prayed for him and Judah bowed limply before him and received the blessing. "Summon your strength one final time, Judah," Paul urged when he was through praying. "We were together at the beginning, and apparently, we will be together at the end. I will race you to the finish line, my brother. Let's see which one of us makes it to heaven first."

Judah looked up and then laughed. He reached out and firmly grasped Paul's hand as though to accept the challenge. "Don't think for a minute I am going to give up now. Besides, I already have a step on you. I'm the one in prison."

Paul smiled. "Don't count me out, Judah. I'm not through irritating Caesar yet!"

*   *   *

Each time the senators met with Piso, the room seemed to grow darker. Torches and lamps were replaced by candlelight. The raucous laughter and vigorous debate which used to characterize their times together were gradually replaced by long periods of whisperings or angry, restless silence. The talk of conspiracy and assassination had seasoned with time, evolving from foolish banter and frustrated ranting into sober and deliberate discussion, and finally reaching the level of orchestrated planning.

Other senators and leading citizens joined the circle of conspirators, and it was not surprising to find that the intensity of discontent was epidemic in scope, spanning every level of Roman society—civilian and military. Faenius Rufus, the commander of the Praetorian guard and an equal to Tigellinus in authority, joined the movement, along with two of his colonels, Subrius Flavus and Gaius Silvanus.

Thrasea Paetus, in keeping with his principles, soon withdrew himself from the company of his friends, but he was replaced by one who was an equal in wisdom and stature—Seneca. Seneca's intellectual vigor provided the group with a coherent shape and direction. The history of Rome had already provided them with examples of bungled assassinations, and Seneca urged the men to apply the lessons of the past to their plans for the future.

The architects of Emperor Gaius' assassination more than twenty years before had succeeded in murdering the hated *Caligula* but failed to devise an effective plan for what to do once the deed was done. As the confused conspirators scrambled about to secure a preferred replacement, Claudius was found hiding behind curtains in the emperor's palace by ignorant members of the Praetorian guard, and was bearing Caesar's mantle by nightfall. Because of this, twenty years later *Caligula* lived again in Nero.

Seneca thus counseled patience, and his was the steady hand which guided them as the summer began. It was agreed that Piso would serve as the rallying point for the new republic which would arise after Nero's death. Time would be taken to insure the support of the military, the Senate and the praetorian guard, and once all had been secured, the assassination would expediently follow.

As the meeting where the final plans were agreed upon drew to a close, Plautius Lateranus excitedly rose to his feet and addressed his colleagues. "Then gentlemen, let the signal be given. The gods only know what else Nero can destroy if he is given the time."

*   *   *

Rome was an overcrowded and ugly city. One of its writers described Rome as a city "filled up rather than laid out." Its streets were narrow and crooked, hemmed in by cheap, wooden houses crammed together in an uneven, unsightly fashion. Many of its fourteen districts were veritable slums. Rodents were as common as the residents, and took boldly to the streets even in daylight. It was no wonder that the wealthy all owned vast estates outside of Rome, and they gladly fled the city in their leisure time, spending as much time as possible away from its oppressive stranglehold.

The summers were especially intolerable, and when the weather was hot and dry, steaming piles of uncollected garbage lay strewn on the corners of most streets, and the houses could almost be heard rotting and cracking under the baking sun. Built mainly of timber, the city was a tinderbox waiting to ignite. Fires were not uncommon, but none had been widespread. However, Rome's system of fire-fighting was crude and inefficient, and city planners knew that it was only a matter of time before real disaster befell the city.

Because of the heat and the general distress, the city came to a standstill during July and all who could afford it took to the countryside. So it was that Nero was vacationing in Antium when the urgent message came to him one morning from a sweating, exhausted messenger that Rome was burning. With six soldiers to accompany him, Caesar at once mounted his horse and rode toward the capital, forty miles away. He changed horses several times, and refused to stop, treating the guards worse than his animals, and finally toward sunset, they reached the southwestern hills on the outskirts of the city, though the soldiers were now in two groups for one of the horses had come up lame.

Nero had ridden several hundred yards ahead of the soldiers, and so he was the first at arrive at the ridge overlooking the capital. Even before he broke free of the trees into the clearing, the air was heavily sifted with the stinging smell of smoke, though they were still several miles away from the city. But none of this could prepare Nero for the surreal sight that unfolded before him as he came to the ridge and looked down into the valley.

Coils of smoke rose up from what seemed to be the entire city, like slithering giant serpents weaving through every street and building, driven on by a most unfortuitous wind. Between the smoke rose massive columns of flames, lashing upwards for a hundred feet or more in places. If hell itself had opened up its jaws to devour the city whole, the effect would not have been any more dramatic. The initial reaction of horror which overwhelmed Nero was quickly replaced by a sensation of reverent awe, such as a novice sea voyager feels when encountering his first whale—first fear, then amazement. Nero, ever the artist, found the panorama before him breathtaking.

The first group of three soldiers came into the clearing behind Nero, and were likewise astonished by the vision. "Caesar, the entire city!" cried out one. "How can it be?"

Nero felt a need to be alone to savor this moment and so he called out, "Soldiers! Move on to Rome now with all speed and offer your help wherever it is needed. I will wait here for the others. Now—fly!"

Obediently, they drove their horses over the crest of the hill, following the road down into the abyss beneath them. Nero stepped down from his horse, and then placed his hands on his hips and scanned the horizon from one end to the other, marveling at the uncontrolled fury of the fire. "Tigellinus, my creative friend," he said under his breath, as though in appreciation. And then he continued to talk to himself.

"Somehow this moment demands a response, which is always the trouble with the awe which nature inspires. The beauty of a woman can be tasted; the arousal she brings can be consummated. But nature arouses feelings for which there is no perfect satisfaction. She leaves us hanging, wanting more. How can I complete this moment where nature's passion is so visible? How can I bring to a climax this beautiful seduction?"

He continued his reflections for a moment more, and then reached for a satchel hanging on his horse's side and removed from it his lyre which he usually carried with him wherever he went. He then stood atop a boulder on the precipice of the hillside and began to sing:

> *"You too, O Troy, raise your sacred ashes to the stars*
> *And show the work to Agamemnon's Mycenae*
> *Now has the reward for disaster proved great!*
> *Rejoice, you ruins and praise your pyres*
> *Your own son raises you higher!"*

He continued singing and never did notice the second group of soldiers emerge into the clearing. The leader of the group motioned for the others to stop before they came up behind Nero, and the three of them looked at each other, perplexed, as they watched their emperor serenade the fiery inferno engulfing Rome.

*   *   *

Deep within the emperor's dungeons, the smoke which was filling the caverns began slowly and decisively to choke out the breathable air the prisoners needed. Their cries for help went unheeded however, for every guard had fled to save his life. Those trapped in the prison were essentially doubly confined, by walls of both iron and fire. The heat created by the fire turned the upper cell blocks into a furnace, and those prisoners died first, being incinerated in the flames. Those in the underground cells were more fortunate; they would die choking on the smoke before the flames would reach them.

Judah stretched out upon his cot with his head buried in his arms, feeling nauseous and light-headed as he gasped for pure air, but every breath he drew was contaminated by smoke, which twinged his throat and lungs. His head throbbed as the noxious fumes slowly overcame him, and his headache was made worse by the piercing cries of helpless victims who were right then perishing on the floor above him. He had tried to pray, but his thoughts were now scattered, and as he fought to keep conscious, even the memory of Esther seemed vague and shadowy.

A sense of betrayal and abandonment washed over him in that moment, for he was convinced that he was now to die, and to lose his life in this way, after surviving in so many other impossible situations, seemed ignominious and divinely irrational. But gradually, his breaths drew fainter, his thoughts darkened, and somehow death now made sense. It seemed acceptable, even easy.

Judah soon lost consciousness, so he failed to hear the sound of keys clanging in his celldoor's lock, and he failed to see the door driven open by two men whose heads were shrouded with wet towels. They rushed to the cot, and after turning Judah over, one nodded his head at the other, and they draped another damp cloth around his face. Then together, they lifted Judah up to his feet and dragged his limp body out of the cell.

Their journey up and out of the web of dark corridors was treacherous since they could barely see their way, and several times they became disoriented and had to retrace their steps. Once they had climbed out of the lower levels, the mounting heat became their next enemy, but they readjusted the towels about their faces, and plunged ahead, ignoring the stretched out hands of several prisoners who were yet coherent enough to reach out through the bars and cry for mercy.

Finally, they burst out into the open streets, which was scarcely an improvement, but a literal jumping from the frying pan into the fire. Sweeping toward them on one end of the road was a massive wall of flame thirty feet high, and a virtual burning maze blocked every other possible exit. Waiting tentatively for them in the street were two other men on horseback, and they were struggling to restrain three other anxious horses. In their desperation, the men dragged

Judah—much less gingerly now than at first—toward the horses. With some struggle, they and their partners hoisted him up onto a horse, then the others mounted their steeds, and the party moved quickly but delicately through the fiery labyrinth to safety.

The riders wound their way through the city past sections in full blaze where teams of frantic people worked together to form water lines, but their efforts were pathetic and useless, and the sulfurous hissing of the fire seemed to mock them for even trying. Other sections of the city were already burned out, littered with smoldering hulks of stone buildings, and mountainous piles of ash. Among the ruins sat survivors, like living corpses, with their empty, red eyes staring out through soot-streaked faces. Some of them limped through the streets completely naked, wandering like drunken fools, talking to themselves. The men pressed on, driving their horses through the city, heading toward the nearest road that would take them out of it.

As they slowly climbed the hills away from the inferno, the fresher air began to revive Judah. He coughed and spat, and slowly lifted his head. It seemed so like a dream to find himself bobbing up and down upon a horse surrounded by masked men, barely cognizant and scarcely alive. But he had no strength to question nor resist, so he simply tried to rest as the dizzying journey continued.

They rode on for another hour. By this time, the sun had set and the city was now far behind them, but parts of it glowed in the darkness, like embers in a campfire. Then the caravan turned into a forest, and Rome disappeared from sight entirely. A short while later, they came to a wide stream, and to Judah's relief, the front rider signaled for the others to stop, and all of the men fell off their horses in weariness. One of them came to Judah and held out his hand, and helped him off.

"Who are you?" asked Judah, burning now with curiosity. The man pulled the cloth off of his face. It was Seneca.

Seneca smiled and took the hand of his friend. "We couldn't risk having someone recognize us as we left the city. Forgive our abruptness with you. It is a shame Quintus Arrius—excuse me, *Judah Ben-Hur*—it is a shame that you perished in this damnable fire. Nero will be quite distressed to have lost one of his more notable prisoners. He took a certain pleasure in knowing that you were rotting away under his thumb."

Judah was moved. "Seneca, I owe you much thanks."

"I would do much more for a man of honor such as yourself." He then held out his hand toward the stream, where the other men were already gulping in water. "Come, drink, and be refreshed. We'll talk again after we have rested."

The other men were three of Seneca's servants, and when they were finished drinking, bathing, playing in and otherwise making love to the water, they dutifully went about setting up a camp beneath the canopy of trees. Seneca and Judah washed in the stream, and for Judah, the feeling of running water washing over his skin was ethereal. As he stepped out of the stream, his only regret was that he would have to cover himself with the foul prison rags which had been his only clothing for months. But then Seneca displayed his thoughtfulness again, pulling a fresh tunic out of a canvas sack which he handed to Judah.

"There are two or three other tunics in the bag," said Seneca, "along with sandals and countless other items my wife packed for you. I told her to think like a man on a journey, not a woman. You may feel free to lighten your purse if you desire."

Judah laughed. "Why Seneca, you've misjudged yourself. You've told me that philosophers only talk about goodness, but here you are doing it. You ought to be careful. The next thing you know, you might accidentally run into truth."

"There's little danger of that," said Seneca with a smile.

"You've run a great risk coming to save me."

"There's actually very little risk involved here, provided tomorrow morning you head to the north, keep going until you reach the Alps, cross the mountains heading east, and follow the coastline. I believe when you arrive in Judea, you can then find your way to Jerusalem if you ask directions of the native Jewish populace."

Judah drew near to the fire that the servants had started and stared into its flames, as he pondered Seneca's proposal. "So I really am free from this moment on, and I can go home."

"It is as I said to you—Judah," and Seneca used this name tentatively. "Nero will think you are dead, but to assure that he is never suspicious, your Roman friends must also think you are dead. You are now free to begin your new life. Your wife awaits you in Jerusalem. Tomorrow morning after we have rested here, you must go and find her."

While speaking, Seneca reached into another bag and pulled out a loaf of bread. He tore off a piece for himself, then handed the rest to Judah, whose hunger was so intense, he wanted to cast off civility and sink his teeth right into the loaf.

"I fear though if you travel by sea, you will run too great a risk of being recognized," Seneca continued. "Such is the man you are. There are too many harbors and too many soldiers to face before you are out of Italian waters. So I counsel you to go north through the mountains and across by land. I release into your service three of my fittest servants who will go with you."

The three men stopped their work momentarily to look at Judah. Seneca pointed to each one in turn. "This is Julius, the wise. Urbanus, the strong. And Catus, the swift. They would die for me, and they would die for you. I have provided you with ample provisions for some time, and plenty of silver."

Judah broke off some bread and tossed the loaf to Julius, who caught it and shared it with the other two. While chewing ravenously on his first mouthful, Judah said, "Seneca, again, I am awed by your kindness, but you ought to come with us. This is your chance to leave this nightmare behind."

Seneca shook his head and his bald crown glowed in the firelight.

"No. My family is here. Your family is in Judea. I am part of this tragedy. Right now another tragedy is about to unfold in Jerusalem. Caesar is soon to appoint another governor. Rumor has it that he shall select Gessius Florus, who is a disciple of the emperor, and every bit as much a self-absorbed imbecile as Nero himself. It is not a promising omen for your people. They have not been submissive to the fair and competent rulers placed over them. How can they live in peace with one who is cruel and incompetent? If you can, you must do what is possible to head off your people's impending rush to disaster. You must be there in Jerusalem. Meanwhile, I shall remain here and fight the battles appointed for me. My destiny is tied to Rome."

Judah nodded, silently acknowledging the wisdom of Seneca's reply. Only then did he become aware of the mystical sounds of the forest providing the backdrop for their conversation. A choir of crickets sang over the music of the stream, while the crackling of the fire offered the necessary percussion, and the wind blowing through the trees was the low droning of strings. He thought of Esther in that moment, and his heart swelled with longing. His aging body suddenly felt young again, and when he closed his eyes, he could nearly feel her embrace, her tender skin pressing against him, her breath on his face as she kissed him.

Thousands of miles lay between them, but with the intoxication of liberty filling his spirit, Judah felt that he could traverse them in a day. A younger, more
foolish man would have left at once, but Judah knew that emotion would
scarcely carry him over the next hill. He would need to rest.

Another image of Esther crossed the vision of his thoughts. She was standing
alone in the doorway of Tirzah's house, looking out longingly down a road, waiting for him to come. The road was empty and despair was in her eyes. Judah
turned to Seneca.

"There must be a way to tell my Roman friends the truth of my deliverance.
If they hear that I have perished, they will send word to my wife, and I must
spare her the torment of thinking I am dead."

"Yes, I can see how that would be grievous," Seneca agreed, after some
thought. "Telling your friends though still strikes me as being dangerous. Nero
has very large ears, as you now know."

He rubbed his face for a moment as he puzzled over a solution, then looked at
Judah. "Allow me to perform one more favor. I will dispatch another messenger
to Jerusalem, who will arrive there first, bearing a note written in your hand.
Assure your wife that all is well with you, that she is to disregard any future
notices to the contrary, and that you will join her as soon as you are able. Would
that set you at ease?"

Judah nodded.

"It is obvious that you are cared for by a great many people," Seneca continued. "You are part of an unusual community. Your Jesus, whoever he was, has
managed to bring the best out in those who follow him. If philosophy is known
by its fruits, then yours has much to commend it."

"But as I have told you before, my friend, the Christian is not motivated by a
philosophy, but by a person," said Judah. "A philosopher can teach us how to live
rightly, but can give us neither the power or reason for doing so. Jesus gave all
this. He lived to teach us how to live rightly. He died to give us the power to live
rightly. And he rose from the dead to give us the reason to live rightly. Why
should one be virtuous if there is no heaven? Why spend your life contemplating
the good if there is no God to take note?"

Seneca stared vacantly at the ground having nothing to say.

"Seneca, all of your philosophy comes down to answering one question: is there a God or not? If there is no God, then there can be no heaven. And if there is no heaven, then there is nothing lasting about life, and therefore no real meaning to life. And if there is no real meaning to life, then you and I who contemplate the good are fools, and Nero is the wisest and most fortunate man on earth."

Seneca scoffed at this. "Heaven forbid the thought! Judah Ben-Hur, your passion is unmistakable. Please believe me, I am no atheist. Nature alone convinced me there was a Creator long ago. But whether there is one god or many, whether this god is good or evil, whether this god is alert or asleep, are questions that nature and philosophy will not answer. I am left with the need for faith, but I have none. I have spent my life looking for the footprints of the gods, but my search so far has been in vain. Moses, Socrates, Virgil have each brought me to the foot of the mountain, but the mountain is always shrouded in darkness and I can climb no further. Now comes the most ridiculous assertion of all. You tell me that God has left footprints in a Jew named Jesus who was crucified. If he has done a miracle for you to convince you, then you are blessed and I rejoice with you. But I again am in darkness."

"If a miracle were all that was needed to convince you, Seneca, then God would surely grant it."

"What other obstacle would stand in my way then?" Seneca objected.

"It is the obstacle that stands in the way of us all—our pride."

Seneca's brow furled with a trace of offense.

"To enter heaven, Jesus said we must humble ourselves like a little child. A little child can admit that he is weak. Admit that his own resources are inadequate. And that he has made mistakes. This is where the quest for God really begins. The barriers that keep us from God are seldom of the intellect. Those are easily bridged. I have all night, Seneca. I could easily show you the prophecies of our scriptures handed down centuries ago that foretold of our Messiah, and all are fulfilled in Jesus. I can introduce you to dozens of eyewitnesses who will corroborate my assertion that Jesus is alive, including a man who once openly persecuted us. Spend time in our community, and soon you will see with your own eyes the power of answered prayer. Barriers of the intellect are seldom what keeps a man from knowing God. Ultimately, Seneca, it is the barrier of the will which keeps us from God. Our greatest problem is pride."

"You are harsh to your friend and emancipator," said Seneca, but not angrily. "I suppose with reflection though, that your words are not far off the mark. Still, yours is a strange deity who would allow his son to die while an infidel like Nero goes on unpunished."

"If heaven is watching, he will not go unpunished."

Seneca reached down to the ground and picked up a stick with which he began to probe into the fire. He looked around to make certain that his servants were occupied elsewhere, and then spoke quietly.

"I hope your God will forgive us if we do not wait upon his justice. Even now as we speak, plans are being laid for Caesar's removal. If your God answers your prayers, then I ask you to intercede for us. If in the end it turns out that Nero is to blame for this disastrous fire, then we've already hesitated too long." He looked up at Judah with black, mournful eyes. "The cost of cowardice is great. It is a lesson Burrus was trying to teach me. I think now I am finally learning it."

At the mention of Burrus, Judah's heart was warmed. "Burrus would be the first to say that it is never too late to learn one's lessons."

Seneca jabbed at the fire again as though poking at a snake, and then released the stick into the heart of the flames.

*   *   *

By the time the early morning light began fingering through the trees, the five men had already risen from their sleep and had broken apart their camp. Two of the servants then rode out to the edge of the woods and returned with the news that the fire in Rome was still raging unabated. In the meantime, Judah sat down and composed his letter to Esther.

My dearest wife and friend,

Grace to you from our Savior, under whose wings we rest together even though we are separated for a time. I think of you constantly, my love, and my prayers for you never cease. There are times as I kneel in prayer before sleeping at night when I am certain you are right there beside me, as you have been for so many years, and it hurts to look up and find myself alone (even though I know we are never alone!)

For reasons I cannot explain, this letter must of necessity be sparing of details. But I want you to know that I am coming home to you! God has intervened—as we knew he would—and even as you read this, I am drawing closer to you step by step. The reason I am writing now is to assure you of my safety, no matter what else you may hear. Rome has been partially destroyed by a tragic fire, and some have heard that I am dead. Do not be alarmed or succumb to despair if you are told this. For the safety of all, the others must—for a time—believe I am gone. But rest assured that I am very much alive and will soon be by your side. I will keep the pledge I made to you on the beach in Myra several years ago. We will end our days together in our homeland, side by side.

Be patient for my arrival, and keep the fire of your faith burning bright.

With all my love, I am yours forever.

"Would you feel comfortable sending a messenger bearing this note?" asked Judah, handing the small scroll to Seneca. Seneca read it, and nodded.

"No one is compromised and your Esther is set at peace," he answered. "I will dispatch this by sea as soon as possible. In the meantime, your own trek must now begin. Your three servants will know the way through the northland, but once you have crossed the mountains you will have to find your own way through Macedonia and beyond."

Seneca shared some final words with his servants, and then each of the men mounted their horses. They rode along silently to the edge of the woods where the road began.

"Here is where we part," said Seneca. He looked at Judah, and the two men reached out between their horses and locked arms in a bond of friendship.

"May your God show his mercy to you, Judah Ben-Hur."

"And you, Seneca. Thank you for all you have done," said Judah. "May you yet find something to believe in."

Seneca nodded, though not without some faraway pain written in his face. With reluctance, he released his grip on Judah's arm, then turned his horse and slowly pushed down the road. Even his horse seemed to be limping under the heaviness of his spirit. Judah watched until the philosopher disappeared, and then he motioned to the servants to lead him forward to the north.

Chapter 16

The fire devoured the city for six days, and once it was contained and nearly extinguished, a second, hungrier fire broke out in another section of the city which blazed for three more days. Augustus had divided the city into fourteen districts during his reign. The fire failed to reach only four of them. Three districts were completely decimated, and the others survived in various degrees of ruin. Thousands of people were left destitute and homeless, and though the poor suffered most—as they always do—the wealthy were not unscathed. The mountains of charred remains that it left behind were from tenements and private estates, shops and temples, private galleries and government offices.

Even Nero suffered. The Domus Transitoria was destroyed, and one wing of the *Golden House* was damaged, though the core of the house was preserved along with the gardens that surrounded it. Everything else in the vicinity was reduced to ashes, including each parcel of property which ringed Nero's estate— property which Nero had been unsuccessful in wooing from its owners before the fire. That area in particular was thoroughly and surgically erased, as though it had been cleared for construction.

Nero's response to the disaster was swift. He opened up his private gardens to the mass of refugees which milled about the city. He slashed the price of grain to a third of its market value. Once emptied, the grain ships were brought from Ostia harbor up to the center of the city, and their empty cargo bays were filled with debris which was then hauled out to sea and dumped. The emperor made sure that he was seen offering sacrifices of appeasement in the temples, and more importantly, that he was seen comforting his people.

A commission was appointed to oversee Rome's rebuilding, and new plans for the reconstruction appeared seemingly overnight, which some felt was a sign of efficiency, and others a cause for suspicion. To encourage private investment in the work, Nero ordered that automatic citizenship be conferred on anyone contributing at least 100,000 sesterces to any building project. The emperor wasted no time setting into motion the repair and expansion of his palace. Naturally, the landowners who had formerly refused to sell their property now accepted Nero's offer of complete imperial compensation for rebuilding their homes, provided they did so in another location. The *Golden House* suddenly found itself part of a sprawling 200 acre estate.

Speculation ran wild about how the fire might have started. Some were certain that they had seen lightning strike the city, and since the skies had been clear, the theologically-minded thought it was plain that the gods were expressing their displeasure by sending fire. The clumsy knew how easy it was to leave a cooking fire unattended, and return to find it burning more than food. The lawless and the law-keepers alike knew the simplicity of arson. Before long, the observation was made that the fire began on the exact day that Rome had been sacked and burned by Gallic invaders 454 years earlier. And then an even more improbable discovery was made (by one of those persons who lives in every age and culture, who has far too much leisure time at his disposal)—the fire began 418 years, 418 months and 418 days after the earlier disaster.

Nero's name began to be whispered in the city streets. Didn't the emperor aspire to enlarge his palace? Didn't he publicly express his disdain for the architecture of the city and long to leave his own mark on Rome? Didn't the second fire—which broke out inexplicably after the first had been contained—begin on Tigellinus' own property? Still, Caesar remained oblivious to the mood of his people until the day when he saw it written on a wall in front of him.

Several days after the fire was finally extinguished, Nero was walking through his gardens among the countless numbers of homeless victims who were given sanctuary there. Poppaea and Tigellinus flanked him on either side, and a wall of soldiers surrounded them. They moved like an untouchable mass through the desolate humanity that hobbled around aimlessly. Those who were fortunate found shadowy relief from the scorching sun by staking out some ground beneath the winding laurels or the groves of myrtle that dotted the garden. Nero wiped his forehead, which was creased with perspiration.

"Poppy, remind me to take my walks in the morning from here on out," he murmured. "I hope the people take note how their emperor has skipped his summer holiday to suffer with them."

"How could they not see all you are doing for them?" his wife answered with a submissive echo.

Caesar curled his nose with a scowl. "I don't know which is worse. The lingering smell of smoke which hangs in the air, or the odor of all these unwashed bodies wafting in my private garden." He raised his finger and adopted the poise of command. "Tigellinus, see that our guests are ushered to the lake, and insist that they bathe. We are Romans after all. The fire need not have burned away our dignity as well."

"In the annals of military history, I don't believe soldiers have ever been ordered to give baths before," Tigellinus responded acidly.

"If we grant the soldiers liberty to watch, do you think you will have difficulty finding volunteers?" Nero retorted, and Tigellinus cracked a depraved grin.

"No, my lord, I think you will find this the cleanest camp in the city by tomorrow afternoon."

Nero caught a glance of a young woman sleeping on the grass, wearing only a thin, smoke-smeared gown, torn nearly to her waist. "As emperor, perhaps I shall show them my sympathy by bathing with them," Nero announced, slapping Tigellinus on the arm and pointing out the woman. Poppaea bit her lip and looked down, as the two men erupted in bawdy laughter.

As they continued walking, they suddenly heard a loud cry rise up from off to the side, and another young woman ran from the faceless crowd, burst through the soldiers and fell at Nero's feet. She clutched at his legs and moaned pitifully. Nero waved off the soldiers who instinctively turned to pull her off.

"Lord Nero! Lord Nero!" she cried with a voice that stuttered in between her sobs. "The fire has destroyed everything. My husband and children are all...dead! Everything is gone. Our house is destroyed. I have nothing. I don't want to live. I just want to die. Caesar, why did this happen?"

Poppaea placed her hands over her mouth to hold back her own emotion. Tigellinus scowled. Nero appeared mildly annoyed, but he caught himself quickly, and his eyes suddenly lightened, his forehead softened, and in a smooth, fluid motion, he reached out his hand and placed it tenderly on the top of her head.

"Woman, I weep for you," he said softly. "I weep *with* you. We have all suffered greatly through this. I cannot give you back your husband and children.
But I will give you back your home, your property, and if you believe in me, I
will give you back your hope." He touched her face with his fingers and tenderly
raised her head so that their eyes met, and she marveled at his compassion, for his
own eyes were filled with tears.

"Believe in me," Nero repeated with persuasive insistence. "Drink this bitter
cup of sorrow, as we all must drink it. In time, we will all learn to live again."

Her disjointed breathing slowly calmed, and her quivering lips even managed
to smile faintly. He patted her head, and helped her to her feet, and the soldiers
cleared a path through which she returned and disappeared into the throng. The
soldiers closed the path, and the imperial bubble began moving through the garden again. Tigellinus leaned toward the emperor.

"Tears, Caesar? Do my eyes deceive me?"

Poppaea was dabbing at her own moist eyes. "Who wouldn't be moved?" she
asked. "The poor woman."

"A disaster is great political capital for a leader, Tigellinus," Nero lectured
under his breath, while letting his manufactured tears run freely down his face. "I
can generate more loyalty with a few carefully placed tears, than with a thousand
of the most eloquent speeches."

"Your tears aren't real?" asked Poppaea with disappointment. "There wasn't
even a part of your heart that was touched by her anguish?"

Nero looked straight ahead, but Tigellinus answered in his place. "Lady
Poppaea, have you never placed your head on your husband's chest? You'd find
that Caesar has no heart," and the emperor howled in laughter at the joke.

"Then my husband, you are a better actor than I thought," replied Poppaea
with disappointment.

The garden stretched on in a rectangular shape from north to south for a little
more than a half mile. Its southern gate opened directly onto the *Sacra Via* which
took the traveler back toward the Capitoline Hill. As they approached the
southern gate, Nero saw that the roadway seemed unusually busy for the height
of the afternoon. There seemed to be an agitation in the air as they inched out
into the streets, and then their progress was stopped altogether. One of the

soldiers posted at the gate approached Nero's guards and whispered an earnest message into their ears.

"What's that?" Nero called out to them. "Guards, why have we stopped? Move ahead!"

He waved them forward, but one of his guards turned back and shouted above the din of the crowd, "Caesar, there's been an incident outside the gate. It's best we return to the palace through the garden."

"An incident!" Nero barked. "But I must be with the people today. Press forward at once. We'll stop whatever incident is taking place."

The guard frowned, then turned around and with his fellow soldiers, forcefully pushed ahead into the street, while Nero looked left and right to catch a glimpse of whatever disturbance had taken place. The noise of the crowd grew louder as word was passed that Caesar was coming into the street. Tigellinus' nose flared with the scent of danger.

The mob seemed thickest to the left of the gate along the stone wall which encompassed the garden. The wall rose up to a height of ten feet and was framed at the top with iron latticework. It was normally covered with ivy at this time of year, but the first thing Nero could see over the top of the guards' shoulders was that the ivy on this section of the wall had been torn down. He caught a glimpse of what seemed to be some writing along the top section of the wall.

"Let me through!" he shouted, prying apart two of the guards and forging his way through to the wall. At the sight of the emperor, the people in the street pulled back in alarm, and a pocket of space was opened up at the front of the wall. As he stepped into it, Nero saw at once what the clamor was about. Printed in letters which filled the entire height of the wall were two words which screamed from the white stone masonry: *Nero Arsonist!*

His reflexive reaction to the graffito was one which he had reinforced repeatedly since his childhood whenever he was accused of wrongdoing.

"It's not true," he whispered. He said it once again, only a little louder as though to convince himself, and then he trumpeted it to the crowd. "*It's not true!*" he cried as loud as he could.

He swung around and stared at the people, and for an instant, as he stood there in isolation with his back against the wall, it was as though he stood in a courtroom facing a multitude of accusers. Caesar staggered back defensively against the wall, with his eyes darting back and forth across the empty faces that confronted him.

"This is the slander of criminals and vandals!" he shouted, trying to gather himself together. "People, look behind these very walls. I have opened my own home to you! I have wept with you." He touched his cheeks hoping some evidence of his crying was yet visible. "I will rebuild your homes and your businesses. We will work side by side. Rome will rise up from the ashes greater than ever in her history, and you shall all rise with her. Do not be fooled by these lies. We will find the real lawbreakers who have dared to torch our holy city. They will be punished!"

A smattering of applause was heard echoing in the street, but hardly the enthusiastic support Nero anticipated. Instead, most looked at him as though he had just addressed them in a foreign tongue. He quickly beckoned to Tigellinus to come to him, and grabbing his arm when he drew near, he whispered firmly, "By the gods, Tigellinus, dispatch a crew at once to erase this slander."

Suddenly, his mouth went dry, and a gasp of fright pursed his lips. He clutched at Tigellinus frantically. There among the faces watching him, five or six rows back, was Octavia, with red damning eyes glaring at him. Her skin was white and covered with dust, as though she had just clawed her way out of her grave.

"Tigellinus, it's her!" he uttered in stark horror.

"Who, Caesar?" Tigellinus whispered, scanning the crowd which had begun to disperse. Nero's reaction was so strong as to be embarrassing, and the prefect tried to shield the emperor from the onlookers. "I don't see anyone."

Caesar's hands began to tremble. She still looked at him, frozen in place as the others walked past. And then a red line appeared on her throat, and Nero watched in horror as tiny rivulets of blood began to run down her neck. She didn't react at all. Her face remained emotionless and still, as though she felt nothing, and then the blood poured like a fountain from her neck, soaking her toga and collecting in a pool at her feet. Nero was now shaking violently, and he started to drop to his knees. Tigellinus braced him by the arm.

"Nero, what's happening to you?" He spoke with authoritative fervor. "Come to your senses! You're being watched." He summoned the guards to surround them, and ordered one to bring water.

Poppaea rushed to Nero's side and embraced him. "Nero, what's wrong?" she pleaded with him. "You look as though you've seen a ghost."

Nero dropped to the ground trembling, but as he fell, his eyes searched through the legs of those that surrounded him. The part of the street where she had been standing was now deserted and the dust was dry.

*   *   *

Nero spent the rest of the day tossing in his bed with a fever. He spoke to no one concerning the vision, and both Tigellinus and Poppaea assumed his condition stemmed solely from being accused of burning Rome. He took to criticism like an emetic. And without approval, he wilted. Tigellinus discerned the impending crisis from afar. Caesar or not, the government would unravel if the accusation of imperial arson could somehow be attached to Nero. Suspicion would have to be diverted.

The next morning, the prefect reported to Nero while he was eating breakfast with his wife. Caesar picked sullenly at his food, and when Tigellinus entered, his face brightened momentarily.

"Good, it's you Tigellinus. I want you to come and encourage me with the news you bring."

Tigellinus hesitated. "Shall I lie to you, or do you wish to hear the truth?"

Nero stabbed at the melon on his plate before him, and he spoke with a low, listless voice. "Then at least have the civility to say something positive before you dampen my mood. Tell me what is going right. You can be so depressing sometimes."

"You want something positive?" asked the prefect, stepping toward them and taking a chair. "The sun rose in the east once again this morning. You have air to breathe, food to eat and clothes to cover yourself with. You are 27 years old, rather than 72. You're a Roman rather than a Celt. And you don't seem to be too much overweight. Shall I go on?"

"Tigellinus, why do I endure you?" spat the emperor. "Everyday, you give me something more about you to hate." His face curled as he swallowed a section of fruit. "This fruit is bitter. Just as well. Fitting for the news you bring me." He motioned for Tigellinus to continue.

"Caesar, the talk is everywhere that you…rather, that *we*…were responsible for the fire."

Nero slammed the gold fork he had been holding down onto his plate. "No!" he yelled, pushing back in his chair and beginning a nervous pace about the room. "I am speechless. I am astounded. How could this be believed? We must squelch these rumors at once. The Senate must be summoned. A royal proclamation must be issued."

"Caesar, that will not do," Tigellinus countered. "If the people don't believe your words, merely speaking louder will not change their minds."

"Then what can we do?" said Nero, and the desperation in his voice was obvious.

"You can only clear your name by finding the real perpetrators."

"You wish to turn yourself in, Prefect?" asked Nero with a pathetic laugh.

Tigellinus reacted to this with an icy scowl which unnerved even Caesar. But the look softened, and he said, "Now if I were the arsonist, Emperor, would I have been such an idiot as to start it on my own property? Obviously, someone has tried to impugn us with guilt. Our task is thereby made easier. The list of those we might suspect is narrowed to those who hate us."

"Yes, we must find the real arsonists," Nero said, falling in step with Tigellinus' reasoning. "Obviously, it was arson. The fire was much too widespread."

"Obviously," the prefect agreed.

"So who did it?" Nero continued, still pacing. "Who had reason for such a crime? Who hates Caesar with such venom? Who hates Rome? A group of escaped slaves? Some of our disenchanted senators? This could be our chance to purge the Senate of those who oppose us."

Poppaea had remained silent throughout this entire exchange, but the game being played intrigued her, and finally she spoke, answering her husband's question.

"Christians."

The word came forth so unexpectedly, that the conversation stopped and Nero halted in his tracks. The word had never aroused any interest in Caesar before. He lumped the word along with every other religious sect he knew of, and branded them all as essentially irrelevant. Poppaea on the other hand hated Octavia, and even after her death, could never seem to escape from her shadow. Her execution had been labeled a martyrdom by the many who loved her, and so now her memory was like a fly which Poppaea could never fully brush away.

She pressed her case. "Octavia joined with the Christians. Octavia was executed as an enemy of the State. Quintus Arrius was a Christian, and was imprisoned for his attempt on your life. The Christians have ample reason to hate Caesar."

"But who are they, really?" Nero asked. "How many of them are there? Other than Arrius, I never have met any, and he is dead."

"If what I have heard of them is true, then they're a pestilent group, my lord," Tigellinus reported. "They're atheists, you know. They refuse to worship any of our gods."

"I've heard far worse," Poppaea said. "They're cannibals."

"Cannibals!" scoffed Nero. "Please Poppaea, if we're to convince the Senate of their guilt, we mustn't stoop to ridiculous charges like that. Simple sedition is an ample accusation."

Poppaea would not be deterred. "But I've heard more than one person tell me that Christians eat flesh and drink blood in honor of their Christ."

Nero looked to Tigellinus for some confirmation of this, but the prefect shrugged his shoulders. "It is possible. They have secretive meetings at night, and refuse to participate in any of our festivals, and snub their noses at our games. Clearly, they are up to no good."

Persuaded by their arguments, Caesar nodded vigorously and clapped his hands together.

"So there we have it. With a little inductive reasoning, we have solved this crime. How could we have endured this sect for so long? And now it comes to this. Look at how they have repaid us for our tolerance. We must act swiftly and decisively, and stamp them out from our midst. Tigellinus, begin tracking down these Christians at once. All of Rome must see with their own eyes that we have found our arsonists!"

Tigellinus dipped his head in a bow of obeisance and left the room, while Nero pulled up to his breakfast table with renewed energy and resumed his meal.

Smiling at Poppaea, he grunted approvingly and said, "This melon is exquisite. Fruit seldom tastes so rich and ripe this early in the summer."

Juice from the fruit drooled down his face. Poppaea leaned over to him, and dabbed at his mouth with a napkin.

"I'm glad it pleases you," she said, then kissed him lustily.

*   *   *

Judah needed no motivation but the thought of Esther's face to propel him forward to the northern reaches of Italy. But if there were one other incentive that helped quicken his pace, it was the thought that within a few months, winter could come early to the Alps, and he might find any of the eastern passages cut off with snow until the spring. Despite the urge to move swiftly along, they were slowed by the decision to travel only at night, and seek remote spots to bivouac during the day. The liability of Quintus Arrius' fame was very real, and all might be lost if he were recognized.

His legendary stature worked one positive effect: it insured that his new servants quickly bound themselves to him in heart and spirit. Judah partially expected to wake up one morning and find himself deserted, for slaves were known to escape when given far less liberty than Julius, Urbanus and Catus now enjoyed. The open countryside, and the deep, hidden recesses of the Apennine mountains which cut through the heart of Italy were formidable temptations to overcome, but they soon grew to revere and love this aging hero, and they vowed between themselves to serve him to the end of his quest. He treated them as freemen, and spoke to them as sons. When Catus fell ill shortly before they had reached the banks of the Po River, Judah refused to break camp and move forward until he had recovered, even though it magnified the odds of the upcoming winter slamming its door shut on them.

They avoided traveling through larger towns, and when provisions were needed, two of the servants would be sent into any nearby village while the third remained with Judah. So they continued forward, creeping north, then east, and finally reaching the Adriatic Sea. They hugged its coastline as it curled like a shepherd's crook beneath the southernmost slopes of the Alps, and by the time winter broke out around them, they had safely passed out of Italy into the hill country of Illyricum.

It seemed that once they had slipped out of Nero's immediate shadow, a certain emotional burden was lifted. But with the easing of the strain, and the achieving of their most pressing goal, Judah's own physical resources waned, and he succumbed to a severe and extended fever. The servants could not have imagined the immense physical toll that Judah's sufferings had taken on his body. They could not have understood the emotional weight of defending a philosophical view of the world so contrary to the spirits of the age. They did not perceive that Judah had reached the point where the surge of adrenalin had stopped its flow and all of his being was demanding rest and renewal.

Judah found his rest in a homely, remote hostel, built of weather-beaten granite into the mountainside of a solitary village, whose proprietors were an old retired shepherd and his wife, both of whom appeared as worn and ancient as their property. The rooms they offered were nothing more than a string of stone cottages, each furnished primitively with a fireplace, a cot covered with a mattress of straw, and stone benches along the walls. It was so much stone that the servants expected to pick out gravel from the bread which the innkeeper's wife baked each morning. There the men waited while Judah convalesced.

At times, the three servants feared for the life of their new master, as he drifted in and out of consciousness over a period of weeks. Slowly, he began to recover, but by the time he was fit to travel again, a powerful winter storm descended from the Alps and threw up walls of snow and ice around them. Their way was blocked until the first thaw of the new year.

It was a desolate place. Their only diversion was the entertainment provided by a herd of goats which performed daily on the stage of ice and rock. Each morning, the men were awakened by the clopping echo of the animals dancing on the roof timbers, and on more than one occasion, a clever beast would nudge its way into one of the cottages and greet the unsuspecting sleeper with a hospitable kiss. The servants were quite beside themselves to be holed up in this barren wasteland and it prompted them to remember the luxuries they had left behind in service to Seneca.

They then began to complain. It was a trickle at first, the sort of grumbling pets give when held against their wishes. But then the trickle became a torrent, and the mumbles gave way to howls of discontent. It became the servants' favorite hobby each day, and soon Judah grew exasperated with their whining.

Each night, the men took their dinner in the proprietor's tavern, along with usually a few dozen other local people who seemed to appear by magic out of the crevices of the mountain, for it didn't seem possible that the terrain could support any sizeable population. But still they came each night and filled the inn, and to a man, they boasted that the innkeeper's wife was the finest cook in the region, which caused the servants to pity the natives and despair for themselves.

It seemed that she had an affinity toward cabbage, and the servants came to the point of gnashing their teeth as they learned that cabbage could be stewed, steamed, fried, baked, battered, boiled and broiled. It could be pureed into porridge, folded into bread, whipped into potatoes, minced into sausage, sliced into cakes, chilled into jelly and fermented into beer. With cabbage, she left nothing to the imagination, for she had exhausted every possible use for it, except perhaps to make soap from it. And though each night, the new entree was spelled out with exotic and tantalizing detail, the end result inevitably turned out to be a dish with cabbage as its main ingredient.

Even Judah found it to be a test of his endurance, but he brought to mind the Israelites love affair with manna, and chose to suppress his murmuring. Besides, he felt it best to model for his servants a better way of handling dissatisfaction, for they continued to spiral downwards into newer forms of lamentation.

One night, the four men left their cottages and scurried across the frozen ground to the tavern. The wind was bitter, and it reminded each of them why they had chosen not to continue south just yet. They opened the door to the tavern and braced themselves for the aroma of cooked cabbage, and once again, it slapped them smartly across their faces, stinging their noses, watering their eyes, and nearly giving them the courage to turn around and start walking toward Macedonia. The place was filled and lively, and Judah marveled again to wonder where they all came from. They found an empty table, and it was not long before the proprietor crossed the floor to greet them.

"Welcome friends!" he said robustly, as he dangled a filled water pitcher from his hand, not minding that water was spilling out onto the floor. He was a short man, less than five feet tall, with long, gray locks of tangled hair falling like willow branches off of his wrinkled head. It was so tousled and matted that the men had to wonder if the goats found a way to lick and gnaw on his scalp each day. "You got your strength again, eh?" he asked Judah as he filled his glass.

"I'm feeling much better, thank you," Judah replied, saluting his host.

"And now comes the snow," the innkeeper said. "Bad for you, good for me. It means you stay awhile longer?"

"But why is it bad for us when we have the pleasure of your hospitality, and your wife's fine cooking?" said Judah, nearly sending the servants falling off their chairs. But the innkeeper beamed at the compliment. "And what will be served tonight? Let me guess. Could that be soup I smell, made of—"

"Cabbage," said all three servants in droll unison.

"And fish," the innkeeper proudly announced. "Fish soup made with our native sturgeon, lightly creamed with goats' milk. The sturgeon's eggs are especially good when eaten raw, but I'm afraid my wife lays claim to them, and I have none to offer you."

"Well, four large bowls of your fish soup then," Judah said, and then scattering a glance at each of the servants, added, "and four heels of bread to soak up the broth. We don't want to miss a drop." The innkeeper bowed and scurried off, while the servants' faces turned various shades of color.

"If even one flake of fish turns up in the cabbage soup he brings us, I will take off my clothes and dance upon the table," announced Urbanus.

"That will make me more sick than the soup," moaned Julius.

"And fish eggs!" piped in Catus. "Master Seneca would have to barter away a grandchild to put caviar on his table. This cretin acts as though he finds them under rocks."

"Just imagine what we might be eating tonight at Seneca's table," said Urbanus and the others sighed in agreement.

Judah had heard enough. He slapped his hand down on the table, rattling the glasses, and startling some of the nearby guests.

"The next one of you who so much as breathes a complaint will sleep outside tonight." He looked at Urbanus and said, "Naked!"

The slaves had never heard Judah raise his voice before and were stunned by his outburst.

"With me, you live as freemen, and yet you prefer the comforts of slavery. What a pack of fools you are. At the end of our journey together, I am ready to release you men of all your obligations to me. That means freedom for you! Yet you make me doubt that you are even ready for such a gift. My people were once slaves in Egypt and no sooner did they taste the challenges which came with freedom, than they began to wish for their slavery back, and they complained of every little hardship they encountered. They walked in freedom but there was still slavery in their hearts. Get rid of it, gentlemen. Burn it out of you. If you want freedom, then show me that you deserve it."

His words were met with stone-cold silence. On the one hand, the servants were shamed by his reproach, for it cut with precision. On the other hand, their hearts were suddenly swelled with joy by the words of promise he spoke. That he treated them with dignity was rare enough; that he stood poised to emancipate them was almost unheard of. All at once, the sounds, shadows and smells of the tavern seemed different to the men. Even the smell of cabbage had a new appeal to it, and when the soup came, though it took faith and imagination, it tasted like *fish* soup.

When the meal was through, the innkeeper brought cups of steaming cider and set one before each of the men. "Put a cup of this in your bellies before bed, and you'll never feel the cold, even if the wind blows off the roof!" he said with cheery laughter.

The servants looked down into their mugs, searching for floating vegetables. A young man and woman had walked behind the innkeeper, and followed him to Judah's table.

"I thought you might like to meet two of our new guests," said the innkeeper, drawing them forward. "They came over the pass with the storm on their heels. And they are from Rome, so perhaps you have met."

Judah smiled at the innkeeper, whose innocent naivete kept him from picturing a world larger than his own, and so he assumed that Rome was like any other village, where everyone knew everyone else. The couple looked down with shyness at the floor. Judah saw that they were in their twenties or early thirties, and assumed that they were married. They were bundled in well-worn coats made from skins which seemed hastily woven together, for some of the seams were unraveling. There was scarcely any color to their faces, and Judah discerned a pall of melancholy overhanging them, and his heart was moved with pity.

"You are welcome to join us," Judah said with warmth, extending his hand toward two empty chairs at the table behind them. "We're enjoying some of our host's fine cider." Judah signaled to the innkeeper. "Two more for our friends from Rome."

The innkeeper nodded vigorously and hurried off. The servants pushed back in their own chairs to make room around the table for the couple, who reluctantly joined the circle.

"I feel awkward crowding in on your company," the man finally said apologetically. "The host was insistent we would know you. My name is Persius, and this is my wife Antonia."

"No need to apologize," Judah replied. "We four have been bottled up with each other for weeks now, and our conversation has deteriorated into drivel and complaining. We could stand hearing some fresh voices."

"You are very kind," said Antonia in a timid, tired voice, but she kept her head tilted down.

"How long have you been here?" asked Urbanus, who was the most forthright of the three servants.

"We arrived last week," Persius answered.

"Barely," his wife added. "The blizzard nearly swallowed us alive."

"You're fortunate to have made it this far," said Judah.

"These mountains have become many a man's tomb," ventured Catus but the other servants shook their heads at him, as Antonia shivered.

"So you are from Rome, the innkeeper says?" Judah asked. "What brings you so far from home?"

Tears appeared at once in both their eyes, as though Judah had punctured a blister with his question. The man wiped his nose. "Rome is no longer our home. It is to us a dead city. Filled with the dead. There is no life in it."

"I see that the Great Fire has claimed you as one of its victims," Judah said with the full empathy of his shepherd's heart.

"Our daughter! Our little girl!" the woman suddenly cried out, looking up. "We lost everything!" and she broke down sobbing. Each man felt his own throat choke up with emotion at this unexpected display of pain.

"Ariella was our littlest treasure," the man tried to explain through his own sorrow. "We couldn't get our little daughter out of our house in time. She was three years old. She was already gone when I opened her door." His voice shook erratically with mounting agony. "Her room was an inferno, and she was laying on the floor. It was too late. I came too late!"

Judah reached out and placed his arm around the man's back in consolation. For an instant, his own mind took him back to a bedroom many years before, where he sat on a bed and clutched the lifeless bodies of his own little children, one after the other, as they died a week apart. No test of his faith was as severe as beholding the suffering of innocent children. Heaven never seemed as silent and God never seemed as uncaring as then.

"I know the bitterness of your pain all too well," he said. "I laid my own little ones in the ground long ago, and there was nothing I could do but watch as the plague took them from me. And I didn't know why. And still I fail to understand. But life continues, and though it hurts, you must go on living."

Silence fell on the little party, disturbed only by the innkeeper bringing the additional mugs of cider. Taking note of the quietness and the tear-streaked faces, he quickly retreated. Then the woman said something which astonished the men. "But at least the ones who started the fire have been caught and punished."

At this, her husband shook his head and his voice rose in protest. "No Antonia! Those people could not have done it. They were wrongly accused. I know it!"

Judah leaned forward with an peculiar queasiness rising up in his belly. "What people? Who was punished?"

"You've not heard?" Persius asked, and Judah shook his head. "Nero blamed those who call themselves *Christians* for starting the fire."

The servants gasped and Judah suddenly pitched forward as though he had been hit from behind. His head grew faint, and for a moment, he seemed to be listing.

"O dear God," he muttered, though it seemed incoherently. "O dear God." He looked up at the man and took hold of his hand. "You say they were punished. Tell me what happened. How did Nero punish them? Are you sure they were Christians?" His voice intensified with each question, and his grip on the man's hand tightened like a vise. "Tell me! What did that butcher do to them?"

Persius was unnerved by Judah's response, so he drew back in his chair, but he began to share what he knew.

"It was awful. For the last few weeks before we left, Nero turned his gardens into a tribunal. And hundreds of these Christians—I don't know who they are, some kind of Jewish sect I've heard—they were arrested and brought to the gardens. There was a mock trial. It was a farce, as far as any thinking man could see."

Persius stared into Judah's eyes which seemed to be pleading with him through a cloud of pain and unbelief, and so what he said next, he said carefully. "And then the executions began." Judah trembled. "Ruthlessly, as though it were all a dramatic production of some kind."

Judah rubbed his temples which were now pounding with incredible pain. "Tell me how they died," he requested, with his voice subdued.

The man was hesitant to continue, but he looked at the servants and they nodded. "Many of them died in the arena. They were bound up in animal skins, and then led blindly out onto the floor. Nero released the wild animals to attack them. They were forced into gladiator fights. But none of them would pick up their swords. They refused to fight. Not one of them resisted."

"Did you see this?"

"No," Persius answered. "I had friends who went to the arena. They told me what happened. I did go to the gardens though. I had to see these so-called criminals myself."

"What happened in the gardens?"

"They were tried before Caesar's tribunal, and then he executed them there."

"How?" Judah pressed him.

"He waited until night and then they were bound to poles and he set them afire."

"Alive?"

The man nodded, biting his lip, and Judah nearly became nauseous.

"He would drive between them in his chariot, mocking them. I know they were innocent though. I know it!" He looked at his wife with a look of reproach. "The night I went to the gardens, I was standing there with the crowd watching, and suddenly, one of the Christians who had been set afire began to sing." The man's eyes started to moisten again with tears. "He began to sing! And then twenty feet away from him, the next in line joined him in song, and soon the entire row of them were singing out at the top of their voices, while they were burning. Nero drove up to them in his chariot. He heard them singing, and you could see that it disturbed him. He yelled out, *'There will be no singing in my gardens tonight! Infidels—go and meet your god.'* But they kept it up, louder and stronger. They wouldn't scream. They just sang. And Nero became furious. He demanded that they stop at once. *'Stop it!'* he yelled. *'Don't you know you are dying!'* The song only grew quieter as the fire killed them off one by one. Nero drove off in a rage, and that's when I knew they were innocent."

"How many of them died?" Judah asked after a few moments of tense silence.

"He killed hundreds of them. He just went on and on until even the people felt sorry for the Christians. And anyone with half a brain knew that Nero killed them to cover up for his own crimes. The Christians could not have done this. And I know it is so, because one of the leaders of the Christians cast a spell on Nero and caused his voice to become grotesque."

"By the gods man, what are you talking about?" asked Urbanus somewhat callously.

"Nero found one of their chiefs. His name I think was…," and as his voice tailed off, Judah spoke with a bitter finality.

"Paul."

"Yes," the man said nodding. "Well, then you know of them."

Judah looked into the man's eyes. "I am a Christian. I know these people well. And yes, they are innocent."

Persius and Antonia both stared at each other with astonishment. Up until this time, Judah's shock had thwarted any tears from coming, but now as anger and grief circulated in his soul, it churned up a surge of emotion within him, and he began to weep. "What happened to Paul?" he asked, his voice shaking.

Persius, moved by pity and respect for Judah, answered quietly. "Nero arrested him. He was brought out the night I was in the gardens, and Nero tried him before a quorum of the Senate that was present. He wanted information from Paul, but he refused to speak. He didn't even attempt to defend himself."

"Like his Savior," Judah whispered to himself. "He wouldn't allow himself to be a freak in Nero's circus."

"He wouldn't give Caesar any information," Persius continued. "Nero became angry and began to rail against him. *'Haven't you anything to say for yourself? Aren't you afraid of me?'* Paul stared directly into Caesar's face, without so much as flinching. You could see fire in his eyes. And Nero turned away from him, as though he were afraid of Paul! And then Paul spoke so calmly, with such authority. He said to Nero, *'I pity you. Even now the flames of hell are licking at your feet.'*

"This enraged Caesar. He flew at Paul and spat on him, and slapped his face. *'You threaten me!'* he said. *'A Jew in chains has the audacity to threaten the divine Caesar?'* I could see the veins in Paul's arms bulging out as though he could burst the cords from off his wrists. And then the most incredible thing happened. Paul shouted back. *'Do not blaspheme the living God, Caesar!'* he commanded with such force, I thought he must be a king. *'You are a man of dust. And for attempting to silence his people, God will now silence you!'* And when he said that, Caesar fell backwards onto the ground as though he had been run over by a bull, and he grasped at his throat. When he tried to speak, his voice was raspy, like an old man's voice. I've never seen anything like it. The crowd was frightened. The soldiers didn't know what to do. They finally picked up Caesar and helped him to his chariot, and as he was escorted away, he barked out to one of his officers, *'Kill the sorcerer!'* Soldiers threw Paul to the ground right then and there, and..." Persius' head looked down at the table. "That's what I can tell you."

Judah wiped his eyes. "Paul was my friend."

There was more silence, allowing the noises of the other people in the tavern to drift back into the hearing of this dismal circle. Persius exchanged a glance with his wife. "We have worn out our welcome here. I have spoken too much."

"No," countered Judah with forcefulness. "You are a messenger sent from God." Then with solemn firmness, he said, "I must go back to Rome."

His servants reacted to the unexpected announcement with alarm. "Go back?" said Catus. "Master, you heard his tale!"

Judah nodded his head. "The church has been scattered. I must go and gather the survivors."

"Is there a church left?" asked Julius.

"God always leaves a remnant," Judah answered. "Evil cannot exterminate good. We must go back."

"But your wife!" said Catus, as though Judah had not already considered the cost of his decision.

"Esther would be the first to tell me to go back," he replied, bravely covering up the wretched hollowness growing like a cancer inside of him.

"You will face almost certain death," warned Persius.

"So be it," said Judah. "A death sentence hangs over us all in the end, doesn't it?" At this, Judah stood and leaned over the candle flickering tenuously at the center of the table. "Even the divine Caesar lives in its shadow."

With a single puff of air, Judah extinguished the flame, then closed his eyes as the blue smoke coiled around his face.

Chapter 17

My dearest Esther,

Grace to you and peace from our loving Father, whose unseen hands always sustain us through these desperate and lonely days.

How my heart aches to be with you! You are my dearest friend and the one with whom I can share all that I am. Each night, my dreams are filled with visions of your face. In those mystical moments between sleep and awakening, I hear your voice call to me, and there for awhile, I am happy and undisturbed. How I wish my life as it is now were really the dream, and I could open my eyes and find myself with you.

But it cannot be just yet. By now you have heard of the disaster in Rome. The days of grace are over for the church, and a terrible season of persecution has begun. I have no doubt that these are the beginnings of the birth-pangs of suffering which the Lord warned us of, and that soon, he will return as he promised. But until that time, the sun will be darkened and the moon will not give its light, and so we must set our faces like flint, and endure till the end. What are these temporary hardships we must now endure compared to the glory that awaits us? And so where the Lord calls us, we will follow. Those who seek to save their lives will lose them, but those who hate their lives in this world, will preserve them unto eternity.

It is with these thoughts anchoring my soul that I have made a difficult decision. No doubt, as you have prayed, the Lord has already spoken these things into your spirit, so I hope you are not devastated. I must return to Rome, my love. Our precious flock has been decimated, and those who have survived are no doubt scattered and wounded. I cannot believe that all which we have labored for so mightily could be so easily destroyed. I cannot believe the Lord would allow it. So I must return to gather the remnant and rebuild what has been torn down.

How long this will take is unclear, but what is clear is that our dreams for rest and retirement must be sacrificed. Not our will, but His be done. Wait in Jerusalem until I write again. Perhaps in the end, I will return to you yet. Or perhaps I will send for you and we will finish what we started here. I will pray for you each day at sundown, my love. Join me in that hour, and we will fellowship together in our spirits.

I send this by the hand of a trusted servant named Catus. Treat him well, and when he has rested, send him back to Rome with a letter from your hand. How I long to hear from you!

Your companion in love, hope and faith,
Judah

           *   *   *   **

In late winter, a restlessness fell on the Roman world. Nowhere was this so evident as at the seaside, where mariners and dreamers gathered to look out over the water and wait for spring. They listened for the bickering of gulls, or the mournful cry of the whale. They waited to feel the first blowing of the southern breezes which was when bare chested sailors would begin to sing and hoist up sails on barren masts, and soon, the ships would awaken and every harbor would be filled with activity and life.

And women. The return of the sailing vessels to their sea channels brought out the lonely phantom figures who loitered in the shadows of the wharves, waiting to put out the fires of coarse and hungry sailors for a nugget of silver. The harbor at Misenum, where Caesar docked his imperial fleet, was no exception. Here, the whores walked about openly with nearly as much official recognition as the customs agents, and the joke among the officers was that with Nero as Caesar, it was only a matter of time before the whole lot of them would be commissioned. In fact, mock ranks were parceled out to certain local favorites.

Late in February, a woman appeared at the Misenum docks asking for Volusius Proculus, the rear admiral of Nero's navy. Those who had been with Proculus for some time recognized her as a prostitute—a *lieutenant commander*—from several years before. She was taken to his office and told to wait, and when her escorts shut the door behind them, she could hear them break into sniggering as they left. Fifteen minutes passed, and the door opened again. Proculus entered, dressed ready for war. He wore his full uniform, missing only his shield and helmet.

He was in his forties, and was heavy, made so by what had become a desk job. The woman looked at him at once but he did not return the glance, nor said a word until he had crossed the room and positioned himself securely behind his desk. The nervous way in which he situated his chair, gripped tightly on its armrests and checked to see that he sat erect upon it, gave the appearance that he was securing a battle station. Finally, he glanced up at her, and she looked just as he anticipated, though a little older. Her long dark hair was streaked now with silver; her face, once smooth, was creased with several noticeable wrinkles, but her form was as feminine as ever. Time had not shorn her of her beauty. He rested his thumbs behind the straps of his vest, as though to check that they were still attached.

"Epicharis," he then said. "Yours is the last face I would have expected to see today. What has it been—five years? I must say, your visit has stirred up the men, and if word gets round to my wife, she will never let me hear the end of it."

"Your wife can rest," Epicharis answered. "I am not the same woman I was."

"You have made use of your freedom to do better things then?" said Proculus, leaning forward. This woman he once knew as a tigress appeared mellow and tame. "That's a shame. What else has freedom given you?"

"An understanding of myself. It has shown me how despised and mistreated I was as a slave. How those who have power abuse those beneath them."

"But my dear, this is the way of the world," he said, more at ease now. "And as I recall, you seemed quite content in your former life. You certainly made many a man content."

She suddenly lunged out of her chair and before he could draw another breath, she was behind him with her arms groping beneath his vest, and he felt her breath on his neck. All of his flippant bravado suddenly evaporated and he felt his heart pulsating with an old but familiar rhythm, as he found himself at the crossroads of passion and danger.

She drew him along for a few seconds and then whispered in his right ear. "I was never content." She licked the lobe of the ear, and he was unable to move. "I hated myself." She kissed his cheek. "And I hated you. As I hate you now." Her fingers were stroking his skin now and still he froze. "Remember the next time you lay with a whore how much she really hates you." Her words slipped out with sultry softness. She engulfed his lips within hers. "But you are the bigger fool because you don't understand this. Even now you don't understand." She suddenly clamped down on his lips with the razor's edge of her teeth, and he cried out in pain, as she spun away from him to the other side of the room.

"You slut!" he yelled, holding his fingers up to his bleeding lips.

"I'm sorry, did you bite your lip, darling?" Epicharis asked with feigned concern. "Shall I tell your wife that you're still a weak, unfaithful man? I had hoped better. I think I shall go."

"Why did you come?" he asked spitefully, searching for a cloth with which to nurse his lip.

"The world is filled with weak men. I came to test you, but you have failed the test. I thought you might be the one to turn to, but you have given me reason to doubt."

"Turn to for what?"

She hesitated, then leaned low over his desk, allowing him a tempting view of what lay beneath her cloak. "Do you still hate Nero?"

His head tipped back. "What do you mean, hate Nero? When did I ever say I hated the emperor?"

She straightened up and laughed, and then sat—or posed—at the edge of his desk. "Oh please, Volusius. Did you ever receive the credit that was due you for building the boat which sent Agrippina to her death? No, it was Anicetus who took all the glory. Anicetus who was promoted. Anicetus who was showered with all the emperor's favor."

"The emperor can dispense his blessings on whomever he pleases."

"Meanwhile, here you rot in Misenum. Whatever became of your dreams, Volusius? Don't tell me you have no more ambition! Has every part of your manhood died?" He scowled. "Tell me, what are the odds of your advancement now? Do they not plummet more each year? Have you not noticed how Nero now looks to those who are younger and more energetic to fill the key posts of his empire? Has your turn not already slipped past with him?"

"Epicharis, what do you want with me?" he suddenly bellowed.

Having achieved the response she wanted, she continued. "I want to know if you are still hungry." She moistened a finger and tenderly wiped the wound on his lip. "That's all. If not, I will be on my way." She stood up and began to walk about the room. "But if you are still hungry, then I have come to help you be satisfied, as I have satisfied you so many times."

"Tell me what you have to say and be done with it," he barked, as though to a foot soldier.

"Can't you feel the ground trembling beneath your feet, rear admiral? All of Italy is now being shaken. There is soon to be a shift in power, and where will you be when the changes come?"

"What changes are coming?"

"Do you have any idea how many people out there hate Nero?" she asked, pointing to the window.

"I have never assumed that everyone would like the emperor."

"Hundreds! Thousands if you move to the streets and villages. But those that hate him most are powerful people. Organized people," she added, with emphasis.

Proculus frowned. "Tell me, how does a former slave woman come by such astounding information that remains hidden from the rest of us?"

"You insult me, Volusius. I have always made it my business to know. It is part of my compensation. Besides, you flatter yourself. I think you and Nero are the only two in Italy who do not see it coming. Did Nero honestly expect the world to believe his explanation for Rome's burning? How many more innocent people have to die at his hands? But soon he will be stopped. All that remains is for the time and place of his execution to be chosen."

"So a high level conspiracy of powerful men is about to sweep Nero from power. If this is so, why have you come to me?"

"But isn't this what friends are for? When opportunity calls, we want others to share our good fortune with us. You know how Nero loves to play with his ships in Misenum. This very spot could be the site of Italy's redemption. Think of the honor that would be yours. You are worthy of this, Volusius. And my friends are worthy of you. You have strength and leadership to lend to this noble cause."

"Maybe they are not worthy of me. Who are they? Give me the names of these noble conspirators."

"Now Volusius, that's not how this works." Her back was turned to him as she surveyed a shelf on the wall which held a collection of sea creatures carved from wood. She picked up a dolphin and ran her fingers along its smoothly varnished side. "I want to give you time to think this over, and count the cost of your involvement. There are so many already enlisted in this cause, that should you even think of betraying us, you would die. So we give you three days."

She returned the dolphin to the shelf and withdrew a small parchment from a pocket in her cloak which she handed to Proculus.

"If you choose to join us, come to this apartment three evenings from now. From there I will take you to meet some of the leaders and you will learn more."

As he took the parchment, she stroked his hand with a tender caress. "I have missed you Volusius. I hope we can work together again. Side by side." His hand shook slightly as she withdrew. She tightened her cloak about her and went to the door. "Three days, my love." She smiled and was gone, like the ending of a vision. He took the note and held it up to his nose which quivered as the fragrance of her skin still lingered.

*   *   *

Proculus did indeed count the cost for three days. In the end, he could not believe that a circle of notable and powerful conspirators would stoop to send out a former slave and prostitute as one of its emissaries. He convinced himself into feeling insulted that no one of worth or rank had approached him. *"You have leadership to lend to the cause,"* she had said. This conspiracy was obviously a plebeian band of malcontents.

What Proculus did not know was that Ephicharis was no emissary but had come to him on her own volition. She had stumbled onto the plot months before by accident, then used her considerable charm to slip inside the inner band of conspirators. But she grew tired of their ceaseless discussions and postponements. They were weak men making grandiose plans of a glorious future. She saw in it possibilities for her own ascension, but as they fidgeted and stalled through the winter, she grew frustrated and decided that a prod would be needed. If a contingent of the naval command could be recruited, she felt certain that this would provide the final push needed to move this boulder of treason forward. And so she came to Misenum.

On the third day, she waited anxiously for Proculus to come. When the knock came at the appointed time, she opened the door excitedly, but at once her heart sank. Three soldiers waited outside with their swords drawn. With swift efficiency, they bound her and threw her roughly into a barred prisoner carriage, and without delay, the carriage was dispatched to Rome.

News of the arrest came to the conspirators through one of their own—Faenius Rufus, the commander of Nero's Guard. It sent a tremor through the entire community, but in the end, their immediate fears were unrealized. At Nero's bidding, Proculus appeared at the interrogation and he laced Epicharis with accusations which she easily repelled by simply appealing to her lowly station in life.

"Caesar, who am I but a former slavewoman, and in my freedom, I now live worse than when I was a slave," she said in her defense. "I am scarcely able to stay alive, and in time's past, I made my living—I am ashamed to say—by selling my body and my dignity to men such as this. At one time years ago I was this man's mistress, and in recent days he approached me, wishing it to be all over again. I resisted him, and in his anger, he has invented these fables. I am nothing Caesar, and I prostrate myself before you, and appeal to you to save me from this demon!"

It was a moving performance which confounded the interrogators and humiliated Proculus in Caesar's sight. Proculus' inability to produce any names or reveal the smallest detail of the plot further shamed him, and when it was over, the rear-admiral was sent from Rome with his ears ringing from an imperial tongue-lashing.

Even so, Nero ordered that Epicharis be kept in custody for awhile. A trace of suspicion yet lurked in his mind, and an attraction as well. "It's for your protection," he assured her, but heavier on his mind was the thought that this seasoned woman might be able to add a certain spice to his own life.

This near disaster was enough to summon the conspirators to action, and within days after the interrogation, seven leaders of the plot gathered at Piso's villa in Baiae.

"When and where, gentlemen? That is the only question before us today, and if we dabble in other matters, I will pick up my coat and be gone," said Plautius Lateranus, rapping his knuckles impatiently on the table to call the meeting to order. "If Epicharis was motivated by our inactivity, then who can blame her?"

"And look what our delay has cost us!" remarked the knight Antonius Natalis. "Lady Poppaea is pregnant again and after the summer, an heir will be born."

"And each day the Senate is drained of more and more of its power, and the treasury is drained of more and more of its money," said Flavius Scaevinus. "The city is in ruins and all Nero can do is add wing after wing to his *Golden House*."

Subrius Flavus, one of Nero's colonels, frowned. "Last week I stood fifteen feet from Nero while he sang at the theater on the Esquiline. I could scarcely resist ramming him through with my sword right then and there."

"He has his voice back then?" asked Piso. "The magician's curse has worn off?"

"Since when did he ever have a voice?" asked Rufus, who stood lurking in the background, and the others murmured in agreement.

Seneca lifted his hand to draw the others to attention. "Gentlemen, let's not be so harsh on ourselves. There has been no delay. And Epicharis' presumptuous impatience nearly unraveled in one afternoon months of delicate planning. We are still waiting for words of support from our legions in Gaul and Africa."

Lateranus slapped his hand on the table. "Pardon me Seneca, but screw the military! If the Guard and Senate are behind us then the generals will fall in line. We have waited too long. When and where? That's all we're here for. And if no one has the guts to draw a battle line, then here it is. Piso, invite Nero to your gardens two weeks from now. He loves to come here in the spring. We'll butcher the bastard while he's smelling your flowers. Rufus and Flavus will dispatch of Tigellinus, and I'll slit the throat of Ahenobarbus myself. We then escort Piso to Rome and our new leader is in place by sundown."

His proposal drew nothing but silent stares. Then Flavus began to nod, and Scaevinus as well, but all were waiting for Piso to react, for it had become his movement to command.

"I have one objection, my friend Plautius," he finally said. "As detested as Caesar has become in our eyes, to spill his blood on this soil under the pretense of extending hospitality to him is ignoble. This ground is too sacred to me to so profane it. Rome is better. Let him choke on the ashes of the ruins he created. In his vanity, Nero will provide us with endless opportunities to catch him in public, especially as he puts on display the fat belly of his wife. Is not the nineteenth of April the festival dedicated to Ceres? Will there not be games in the Circus? I propose that we give the people something to truly celebrate on that day."

Lateranus paused, then nodded in vigorous agreement. "By Jupiter, Piso, you speak with the voice of Caesar already. I submit to your plan, if the others agree. But with one condition. I get the first blow. In fact, I will petition the emperor when he takes his judgment seat." He stood and swung around to Piso who sat on the other side of the table. "I will kneel before Caesar—," and he dropped to one knee before Piso, dipping his head in submission. "When Caesar lowers his ear to hear my petition—," and Piso, playing along with the game, obediently lowered his head, "I will snag him by his throat, and hold him down—," and he latched onto Piso's neck, "while the rest of you converge on him and show him what you think of him." With a feigned uppercut, Lateranus thrust an imaginary knife into Piso's heart.

Scaevinus applauded. "Well done, gentlemen. But let me add one condition more. I want to provide the knife you use, Lateranus. Let mine be the first blade to pierce his body."

Rufus now came forward and he reached down onto the table and picked up a real knife. "This rehearsal is flawed though, my friends." He walked up to Lateranus and placed a hand on his head, while extending the knife toward his chest. "If your first thrust is to his chest, you will fail. Drive it through his throat first." He pulled down on Lateranus head until his neck grazed the tip of the knife. "Caesar always wears armor in public."

He threw the knife back down onto the table and walked back to where he had been standing, leaving Lateranus slightly ruffled by the gruffness of his demonstration.

Piso smiled. "Are there any other conditions or corrections, gentlemen?" No one spoke. "When—is the nineteenth of April. Where—is Rome. What—is the liberation of our empire!" This brought a clamor of excitement from the others, as they all stood to their feet and shook one another's hands.

*   *   *

Nero's furious extermination of the Christians was shortlived and restricted to Rome and its vicinity. It was more precisely a prosecution than a persecution, for the reason he targeted them was to single out a scapegoat for the fire. In no other province were Christians harassed, though their sudden notoriety aroused curiosity, even suspicion, from the general populace.

Nonetheless, the precedent of animosity had been set by Nero, and later emperors would hunt down Christians solely for their religious convictions. For the next two and a half centuries, random outbursts of persecution broke like unexpected storms over the church, such that the complaint of a later Christian writer was that if the Tiber was too high or too low, the public would cry out for the blood of Christians. No one could have imagined, least of all Nero, that the boulder he set in motion would eventually roll back over Caesar's throne, and Christianity would become the dominant philosophical force in the empire, snuffing out the very vestige of Greek and Roman paganism.

For now though, it was a mere nuisance, and once the messy task of punishing the Christians was over, Nero and the empire washed their hands of them and went on with their business. And so, as Judah returned to Italy expecting an open season on Christians, he found instead that they and the atrocities committed against them were hardly talked about at all.

To Urbanus and Julius, coming back to Rome seemed the height of absurdity. To throw away all the ground they had gained, and more so, for Judah to place his life at certain risk for uncertain gain, could not be fathomed. But they obeyed their master in blind obedience, and though neither of them realized it, Judah also was blindly following his own Master.

He had no clear plan in mind except to begin gathering his scattered sheep together wherever he found them, and he thought it best to begin with those believers who lived furthest from Rome. He knew of a family of believers who lived forty miles from the city—Persis, a retired merchant and his wife Marcia. Persis had been a tireless leader in the church, but five years earlier, his health failed and he was compelled to move to the country.

The sun had just set by the time they approached Persis' small estate. The first frogs of spring were filling the surrounding marshes with music, and the glowing orange rim behind the western horizon was a transfixing sight for the weary travellers. The road they walked was empty except for a stray dog which Julius chased away with a stone, and when they turned to pass down the path leading to Persis' home, Judah at once stopped. Something did not feel right. He quickly discerned the reason for his discomfort. The path was ungroomed and overrun with weeds.

"Let's light some torches," said Judah, with a dryness spreading through his throat. Once done, Judah sighed and pressed on down the path with Urbanus and Julius quickly following after, not wanting to be left alone in the gathering darkness. The first true sign of disaster came a hundred yards down the path at the front gate of the property.

Large ribbons of colored cloth spread across the entrance from pillar to pillar like a web, and each of the men recognized at once the distinct markings of

Caesar's seal. A large notice accompanying the seal spelled out that the property was forfeit to the Senate and all trespassers would be arrested on sight. Through the gate, the men could see the outline of the house, and there was yet enough light to observe that every door and window was boarded up.

Judah looked at Urbanus. "Give me your sword," he demanded, stretching out his hand. In all their travels, Judah had never carried a weapon, but he allowed the servants to each carry a short-handled sword as a deterrent to beasts and robbers.

"Master?" Urbanus asked, suspecting what his master intended.

"Your sword, I said!"

The grim determination in Judah's voice was not to be questioned. Without another word, Urbanus slowly unsheathed his sword and laid its handle on Judah's open palm. Without hesitation, Judah raised the sword above his head and sliced down on the seal, ripping through the cloth with ease. He struck the seal for Esther, for Burrus, for Persis and Marcia, and for all the saints who had likewise suffered. He swung the sword with such vigor, that if ten Neros had been stacked beneath the blade, ten heads would have been rolling on the road. Living under Seneca's docile rule, the servants had seldom seen authority even questioned. This act of defiance simultaneously alarmed and excited them.

"Master, you've committed a capital offense!" gasped Julius, and the two servants looked around in dread, expecting a cohort of soldiers to suddenly appear out of thin air and surround them.

Judah returned the sword to Urbanus. "And what would you call the robbing of this man's property and the taking of his life?"

He stormed through the gate and marched up to the house. He easily pried the boards away from the door frame, and when he found the door locked, he beckoned for Urbanus to come. "Seneca called you the *Strong.* Kick in this door." Urbanus' stomach was twisting in knots but he obeyed, and with one measured kick he broke open the door as easily as Judah cut the seal. Judah slapped him on the back. "That wasn't so difficult, was it?"

The signature of Roman soldiers was immediately evident inside the house. The furniture had been tipped over, storage chests were ransacked, and most of the artwork was defaced or ruined, and covering it all was a macabre layer of dust and cobwebs. They inspected the rest of the house and found that the loft where the bedrooms were situated was undisturbed, so Judah surmised that the wreck-age was created for no other purpose than to terrorize Persis and Marcia before they were taken away.

"Forgive your enemies and pray for those who persecute you." As Judah stood amidst the ruins of the house, the words of Jesus seemed preposterous, and they would have seemed impossible had he not heard the Lord pronounce the absolu-tion of his executioners *from the cross itself.* It defied reason. Such a feeble response all but assured that evil men would win the day, and in fact, would lead to the annihilation of those who were good. The evidence was strewn out on the floor before him. Judah's soldier's heart could reach no other conclusion, but his shepherd's heart knew better. The one hanging from the cross who said from his heart, *Father forgive them, they don't know what they are doing,* was the one who spoke the truth. Judah's soldier's heart was noble but misguided.

There was a deeper, more ominous thought churning in Judah's mind, that was interrupted by Julius. "Master, we shouldn't stay here. If we are found, your quest will end and nothing will be accomplished."

Judah ignored him, and spoke his thought out loud. "You understand what is most disturbing about this, don't you?" They shrugged their shoulders in igno-rance. "The soldiers would never have come here on their own. It's too far from Rome. Someone had to have told them that they were here. Told them that they were Christians." His voice rose with anger. "Someone gave Nero names. God help us if someone bearing the name of Christ betrayed his family of faith!" As he said this, he kicked at the pile of rubble beneath him with a reflex of disgust. The clatter of Judah's unexpected outburst alarmed the servants, but not nearly as much as the voice that now called out to them from the shadows in the loft.

"Judah?!"

The servants bolted like frightened cats, and even Judah jumped at the sound. At the top of the stairs was a young woman whom Judah recognized at once.

"Sarah, is that you?"

The woman nodded, placing her hands to her mouth as though holding back tears, and then she ran toward the staircase and flew down it, finally falling at Judah's feet, where she began sobbing bitterly. Judah knelt beside her and tenderly embraced her. Urbanus and Julius slowly crept back into the room and hovered silently over them, looking like angels as they stood in the soft light of the torches which they held aloft. As the woman's crying began to ebb, she raised her head, and looked in Judah's eyes.

"What happened?" he asked tenderly. "Why are you here alone?"

The heaving of her chest made it difficult for her to talk, but she drew a deep breath and began to speak. "I was there when it started. The soldiers came one afternoon when the church was meeting in the glade. I had taken some time to be by myself and was on a walk in the woods and heard them come, so I hid. They just appeared at the top of the hill, a hundred or more of them. And dozens of wagons. And before anyone knew what was happening, they just started rounding everyone up. They forced the women into the wagons. They chained up the men and boys in long lines and then marched them out of the woods back to the city. They threw them into prison like criminals, and they accused us of being arsonists, and then—," she clung tighter to Judah and shuddered. "Why did it happen, Judah?"

"I can't answer that question, dear one." Judah looked up at the two servants and quietly said to them, "This is Sarah—Persis and Marcia's oldest daughter."

They nodded sympathetically. "We'll go and bring some water, Master," said Julius, and they walked outside after lighting a set of candles they found near the door.

Judah brushed some of the wetness off of Sarah's face. "Sarah, how did you get away? What happened to your own family, to Gaius and the children?"

She shook her head and looked up at him with eyes wrung out by sorrow, eyes which seemed to desperately implore him for answers, but he had none to give, so she looked down again. When she spoke again, her words were listless. "They're all gone, Judah. We were separated, and they were taken away. I never saw them again. I tried to find them, but I was so scared. Judah they killed so many!" She started shaking as another wave of grief broke over her. "I thought you were dead, Judah. We thought you were killed in the fire."

"For some reason, God kept me alive." He couldn't disguise the emptiness in his voice. "I was on my way to Jerusalem when I heard what happened. By that time it was too late to do anything about it. I wish I had been here."

"They would have killed you too, Judah. Just as they did to Paul, Peter, Andronicus. All of the leaders are dead."

"Luke? Aquila and Priscilla?" She nodded at each name, and Judah felt his body start to shake. *My God, My God, why have you forsaken me?* The words welled up within him so strongly that he whispered them aloud. "What about your parents, Sarah? What happened here?"

She laid her head on his shoulder. "I'm not sure. But I think they came to Rome to find me, and if they did…," her voice trailed off. "I came home as soon as I could, and this is what I found. I have been living with my aunt and uncle who live several miles from here. Every so often I come and see if something has happened with the house. I was here today, and was sleeping upstairs when you came in. I'm sorry if I scared you."

"Scared us? We must have frightened you silly," Judah said with a fatherly smile. "Sarah, how many others are left?"

"The rest went into hiding. Meeting in homes mainly. I saw maybe three hundred believers at a prayer gathering before I left Rome. Clement and Linus were helping with the shepherding duties. There are many still left, Judah. Nero did not find us all."

These words were the first ray of hope to fall on Judah's dark spirit since the night he was told of the disaster, and he was immediately encouraged.

"God be praised that the emperor remains as incompetent as ever." He lifted Sarah to her feet. "Still, even an incompetent dog can wound if it lands a bite. But I will not allow Nero to push us back. He isn't rid of me yet."

The servants returned, bringing buckets of water with them. Judah took a long draught, then washed his face, and when he pulled the towel away from his face, both Julius and Urbanus noticed a burning intensity in his eyes that they had never seen before.

*   *   *

A week before he was to die, Nero remained happily unaware of the threatening forces preparing to converge on him. His wife was advancing in her pregnancy, the reconstruction of Rome was moving steadily forward, and the empire was quiet with the exception of tremors of unrest felt in Judea (and there was nothing unusual in that.) In one week, the Festival of Ceres—the goddess of the harvest—would come. Ceres strode over the earth, scattering seeds and blessing the soil, when she wasn't quibbling with her mischievous brother Poseidon who flooded the coastal plains on a whim just to irritate her. Nero cared little for the theology of the story, but only its theatrics, and at the festival he and a local acting troupe would perform a dramatic tribute to the goddess.

The only time Caesar even thought of religion any more was when he was on stage portraying one god or another, but as soon as his mask was off, so was the charade of piety. He had reached this point of irreligion through literal thoughtlessness. It was not as though he had at one time meditated upon the plausibility of the spiritual side of humanity and then rejected it after a period of agonized reflection. He had never wrestled at all with life's great questions. When he was a student learning at Seneca's feet, he acquired the habit of regurgitating his tutor's philosophical drivel merely to please him, but he himself had never once mused intently over God's existence, or the possibility of a divine claim on his life. He had never once seriously wondered about heaven, or the immortality of the soul, or eternal judgment. He was a man of enlarged appetites and limited vision—an utterly carnal man, little more than an animal with human intelligence.

As Nero continued on his self-absorbed path, the assorted pieces of the plot against him each fell into place with such ease that the conspirators felt all but assured of their success. They met one last time several days before the festival to choreograph the particular steps they would take to complete their mission. Each man then returned home to await the hour of decision.

Seneca retired to his family villa and spent the time writing letters and walking in his gardens with his wife Pompeia. Piso also spent the time in his own home outside of Rome. Each time he found himself alone, he began to sweat profusely, and so to quell the growing anxiety quaking in his breast, he hosted an endless progression of parties. Rufus and Flavus resumed their duties in the Praetorian Guard, and Rufus laughed to himself when Nero assigned him the responsibility of arranging for security at the festival.

"Does the chicken know whom he just hired to guard the henhouse?" Flavus whispered to him in a hallway later that day.

The others spent the days following normal routines as best they were able, but as the festival drew close, each man was gnawed by a restlessness which gradually became unbearable.

On the eve of the celebration, Scaevinus invited Natalis to his home for lunch, and the two men burned away the hours of the afternoon by drinking and

sharing in jittery conversation. As a checkerboard of shadows began to drift over
the patio where they sat, Natalis stood to dismiss himself, declining an invitation
to stay for a dinner party. "You know me, Flavius. I like to throw myself headlong
into a festival, so I'd best rest up."

"You won't sleep an hour tonight," scoffed Scaevinus, rising to escort his
friend to the door. "But suit yourself. As for me, the best way to prepare for a
party is to get drunk the night before."

"Keep your wits about you tonight," Natalis exhorted. "There'll be plenty of
parties yet to be celebrated if all goes well."

Scaevinus slapped him on the back. "Fear not, my friend. When I'm drunk
I'm more coherent than most senators are sober. But there'll be no drinking to
excess tonight."

As they walked through the house toward the front door, they passed a display
case of handsomely dressed oak. Inside was a collection of swords and knives.
"Oh Antonius. Before I forget—have I ever shown you my collection of
weaponry?" He reached over to the case and removed a bronzed dagger. "I'm
especially fond of this piece," he said, handing it to Natalis, who pulled it from
its leather sheath and inspected it thoughtfully.

"The molding is exquisite," he said, sliding his fingers along the gold handle.
"An antique."

"It was a gift from the curate of the Shrine of Fortune. It dates back to the
Republic." Natalis handed it back, as a servant walked by them in the hallway
from another room. Scaevinus leaned toward Natalis so as not to be overheard.
"And will be the instrument to take us back to the Republic."

He then called out to the servant. "Milichus! One second please." The servant
stopped and quickly returned. Scaevinus held out the knife to him. "I wish to
wear this knife tomorrow for the festival, but the blade is dirty and dull. Hardly
presentable. Would you see that it's properly cleaned and sharpened?" The slave
bowed his head and left with the knife. Scaevinus then extended a hand to his
friend. "A good evening then to you, Antonius. Rest well." He laughed. "But
when you find yourself tossing at midnight, pay us a visit."

"Don't hold your breath," smirked Natalis, as he saluted his friend. "We'll see
you in the morning."

Scaevinus retreated back into the house and checked on the preparations being made for the dinner, afterwards pouring himself a glass of wine and sitting down at a table in his library, where he pulled out a box containing all of his financial records. When Milichus came in an hour later to announce that the first guests had arrived, the table was strewn with documents, and Scaevinus was busily poring over his will, which Milichus felt was odd. His master seldom paid attention to the finances of his estate, and reviewed his will only at the end of the year. Scaevinus quickly gathered up the documents and returned them to the box.

"See that these get put back in their proper place, Milichus—would you, my boy?" he asked, whisking by the servant to go and greet his guests. One paper had fallen to the floor, and Milichus picked it up to return it to the box, but seeing the other papyri scrolls proved irresistible, so he rummaged through the box until he found the will. But before he could unroll it, a sudden noise in the hallway startled him, and he quickly resealed the band around the scroll and closed up the box, chastising himself for being so inquisitive.

Scaevinus was habitually grand and pretentious, but throughout the evening he was excessively so, to the bewilderment of his guests and the embarrassment of his servants. He gave away gifts recklessly, right and left. Finding a friend admiring one of his flowering bushes in his garden, he ordered it dug up at once and transplanted to the friend's property. When the sun had set, he called together his corps of servants—more than twenty in all—and with his guests as witnesses, went through an elaborate ceremony in which he granted freedom to several of them, and gave allowances of silver to the rest. Most of the servants were ecstatic, and the guests politely applauded though they were uncomfortable by the frivolous display.

By the end of the night, Scaevinus grew weary of carrying a glass of wine around with him, and so he exchanged it for a decanter, and continued to drink from it. To the dismay of those around him, he only grew louder with drunkenness. And when he began raising crass toasts to the emperor, his guests began to excuse themselves *en masse*.

When it was over, it was past midnight, and Scaevinus sat alone out on his patio, nearly naked except for a linen wrapping around his waist. He dangled the decanter between his legs, allowing its lips to rock back and forth on his fingers. All of the servants had retired for the night, except Milichus who waited for his master to be done with the day. When he saw his servant, Scaevinus called out, "Milichus, my fine boy. Have you tended to my knife yet?" He voice drawled with his intoxication.

"No, Master Scaevinus," the servant answered. He was hardly a boy, but was in fact a married man of nearly forty. "I was planning to send it out at daybreak. I shall see to it now it you like."

"No, that's all right, morning will be fine," Scaevinus replied. His head was dizzy from the mixture of drowsiness and drunkenness, and it bobbed up and down upon his chest. "I want to show it to Caesar tomorrow afternoon."

He suddenly broke out in a fit of childish giggling, and couldn't suppress drooling as he laughed. "Show it to Caesar! Ha!" he cried out again.

Milichus' face showed no emotion at all. While his master's head was spinning from the effects of alcohol, his own mind was racing with burning, treacherous thoughts aroused by his master's behavior of the past month, and reinforced by the odd events he had witnessed throughout the evening.

Scaevinus struggled to stand up and once he was erect, he started to sway which prompted Milichus to rush to his side to offer support. "I'm fine, boy. I'm fine," he said, waving the servant off. He began to take very tentative steps, but then stopped himself. "Oh, one other thing, Milichus. Would you put together a package for me tomorrow."

Milichus waited for more details, but his master had a vacant look on his face, as though he had fallen off a horse. "What would you like in the package, master?"

Scaevinus belched and scratched his nose. "Bandages and styptics. Put in the package a roll of bandages, and styptics. I'll take them with me to the circus tomorrow." Milichus' face grew dark as this order was given, and as he watched Scaevinus continue his awkward dance to the house, a furrow of contempt appeared on his forehead.

The next morning before the sunrise, Milichus slipped out of the front gate of Scaevinus' estate, clutching a package under his arm. He headed toward the center of the city, joining hundreds of servants who were already hustling through the streets, tending to the business of their households. He marched into the Forum and turned toward the marketplace, but then walked straight past the shops where he might have been expected to transact his business. Instead he proceeded straight through to the end of the Forum and stepped out upon the *Sacra Via*, where he continued walking, in the direction of Nero's palace.

Chapter 18

Judah looked out at the faces staring back at him of those he had known and loved for years. Their expressions bore the scars of sadness and survival. Their eyes told the tale of the bitter events that had engulfed them. Some of the eyes Judah looked into were dark and empty. Some radiated gentleness and hope. Some flashed with anger and others were red with sorrow. But behind their expressions, Judah saw the fire of faith still burning bright, and he found his flock more eager than ever to follow after the One who had suffered and died for them.

Inspired by Sarah's report that hundreds of believers had escaped Nero's wrath, Judah and his servants had pressed on to Rome, though Sarah declined Judah's invitation to come along with them. He skirted around the city, and came first to the home of a young, enthusiastic disciple named Clement, whom Paul had won to Christ in the early days of his time in Rome. Both Judah and Paul had seen in him the seeds of leadership, and now Judah was greatly encouraged to see that his young friend had not only endured the test, but had risen to the demands of helping in the church's recovery. As for Clement, one sight of Judah standing at his doorway seemed like a visitation from heaven.

Most uplifting for Judah was the discovery that the church had not only survived, but was growing. Nero's sword cutting at the church was like a plow cutting into the soil, sowing more and more seed. The example of those Christians who suffered martyrdom—their courage under persecution and their tranquility facing death—moved the hearts of hundreds who watched, and when the storm had passed, many of these sought out the Christians. And the church was ready to receive them.

With any other organization, the evisceration of its leadership would have been like the cutting of an artery, leading to slow but certain death. Not so with the church. Jesus had instilled in his followers an extraordinary idea—that they were each like branches attached to himself, the vine. As long as each remained connected to the vine through meditation, prayer and obedience, they would become increasingly fruitful. Therefore, great worth and potential was ascribed to each disciple.

God's Spirit was poured out liberally on every believer, irrespective of economic status, gender or race. Each member had gifts to use for the good of the community. Leaders existed not as taskmasters, but as servants, to help the others reach maturity. The Christians' passion for reaching the world with the message of God's love, teaching those who became disciples, and unleashing those who reached maturity was what drove the church forward in the generation after Christ, and enabled them to lay down roots at every corner of the empire.

It was this passion which insured that the church would continue to flourish even when persecution came. Striking at its core of leaders was as ineffective as lopping off a branch from a vine. New leaders were already growing to take their place, and they in turn were already training those beneath them. What Judah had received from the apostles, he had passed on to his flock in Rome, and now as he returned, he found that the work had not been curtailed at all.

The news of Judah's return to Rome swept through the church like a flash of lightning, and a meeting was announced where he could address the congregation as a whole, though not at the former site, for now the Christians had to be particularly cautious about where they met. So the following Sunday, the Christians came by the hundreds to a hillside five miles south of Rome. A few were so excited, they ran the entire way. Others had come the day before, and slept all night on the grass, so eager were they to see their beloved pastor. Many believed a rumor that Judah had in fact resurrected from the dead, and so the fervor that spread over the whole assembly was both sentimental and apocalyptic.

Four to five hundred of them were waiting when Judah arrived with Clement and other leaders, and as Judah walked up the grass toward them, whispers of excitement bounced through the congregation. A silent awe filled the hillside sanctuary, broken only by the cry of a hawk overhead. Then as Judah approached, they solemnly stood, each one in a quiet gesture of honor. Seeing them, Judah stopped and at once began to weep. He began to mouth the names of those he recognized, and as he stared out over that multitude, in that moment he saw his life as he had never seen it before.

The strange events of his life—the loose tile on his roof which accidentally fell and struck the Roman governor, Messala's betrayal, his years wasted as a galley slave, the leprosy of his mother and sister, Saul's persecution, the death of his children, Nero's untimely call to service and the mishap at Neapolis, his separation from Esther—all of it somehow fit together in light of this moment, in the shadow of these faces whose lives had intersected with his. Somehow he could now accept it as being part of some overarching plan. Not that God wanted these evil events to occur–God was no sadistic puppetmaster. But he took these events, intended for evil, and made them conform to his redemptive purposes. He would never have chosen this life for himself. But as he stood and looked at the canvas of his life, he now could discern the brush of the Divine Artist at work.

Judah could hold back no longer. He threw himself into the crowd and began to touch the skin and feel the breath of these people whom he loved. For the next hour, heaven broke out upon that hillside, and in those moments, healing came to the Roman church and hope came to Judah.

When the emotion had finally died down, Judah moved to the front of the congregation and stepped up onto a ledge that jutted up from the soil. From this natural platform, he gazed out over his family.

Then he began to sing. It was a serene and beautiful hymn they had sung together for years. The others joined him in the song, and the harmony of their voices carried down into the valley below as a blessing to the ground.

Throughout the centuries that followed, as wars and suffering came to Italy, that plot of sacred ground was never blemished by the stomping hooves of war horses or the boots of soldiers. No blood was ever shed upon it. No instrument of human hatred ever scarred it. And those who sit upon that hill to this day and listen to the wind rustling through the grass often think to themselves that they hear the sound of people singing.

*   *   *

"This is a beautiful knife," said Nero, turning over in his hand Scaevinus' dagger, while Milichus sat before him in a chair, fidgeting nervously as though a bug were crawling beneath his undergarments.

Tigellinus and Rufus stood behind him, and both were as still as stone, but Rufus could feel sweat streaming down his back. He looked down once, as though expecting a pool of perspiration to be building at his feet.

"Senator Scaevinus has always had exquisite and expensive tastes," Nero added. He suddenly turned to Milichus and pointed the tip of the dagger's blade just under the slave's nose. "If you are lying to me, this blade will be used to disembowel you while you are still alive! Slaves are always looking to advance their position."

"No, Lord Caesar. I swear I am telling the truth." Milichus body shook as he looked down on the ominous blade.

"But what is the significance of your truth?" asked Nero looking at his prefect and commander. His voice had a noticeable raspiness to it. "Wills and bandages hardly constitute evidence of a conspiracy. You have no names. You've overheard no conversations. All you've heard is the eccentric babblings of your eccentric master, and quite frankly, I find this all a waste of time. I woke up this morning looking forward to a festival. Right now I should be preparing for a party, but instead here I am mulling over threats and innuendoes. I am so irritated I should like to kill you right now. What do you think, gentlemen? Is there any credence to this slave's tale?"

Tigellinus spoke at once. "The word of an informant must never be summarily dismissed, Caesar."

Nero nodded. "True. A lone fissure on a mountainside may be the one warning that an eruption is forthcoming. Ignore it at the risk of your own destruction, I suppose? What do you say, Rufus?"

Based on what he had heard from Milichus, Rufus felt confident that Scaevinus could dispatch of the accusations. "To my knowledge, Senator Scaevinus has never had a quarrel with Caesar. He has fully supported your initiatives. I have no doubt that he could quickly offer up a satisfactory explanation for each of these accusations. The only proper thing to do is to have him come to the palace to speak in his defense. The sooner the better, Caesar. The festival must go on."

"Yes, of course," agreed Nero. "Let's not waste anymore of this day's precious time. Let's have the Senator brought at once." He again pointed the knife at Milichus. "If you have wasted my time, I shall make an example of you before every slave in the kingdom."

When the guards came to summon Scaevinus to the Domus Aurea, he quickly surmised from Milichus' absence what had happened. His head ached from the previous night, and he cursed himself that he had not curbed his ardor. He asked the soldiers for time to finish some correspondence, and then quickly wrote a message to Piso to alert him to the crisis.

Piso: I have been summoned to the Domus Aurea and will be unable to keep our appointment. A servant of mine turned up missing this morning. If you find him, send him back to me at once. In the meantime, we should be prepared to reschedule our engagement. Scaevinus.

Once he had entrusted the message to a servant, he followed the soldiers to the palace, and as they walked, his active mind assembled the layers of argument he would use in response to an assortment of possible questions. By the time they were climbing the steps of the Domus Aurea, he had erased even the possibility of guilt from his mind.

The proceedings had been moved to an interrogation room within the palace. As they entered, Scaevinus first saw a battery of soldiers posted along the walls. A chair was positioned in the center of the room and off to the side was a table where Nero sat with Tigellinus and Rufus. Another line of chairs stretched across the room, where a number of Caesar's officers sat, among them Subrius Flavus. At the end of the row sat Milichus, looking horribly out of place. When Scaevinus strode into the room, Nero stood to greet him.

"Senator, I'm sorry to disturb you this morning but news of a distressing nature has come to us, and we are compelled to ask you a few questions. I am sure you understand."

As Scaevinus passed Milichus, he acted surprised.

"Milichus? This is why you have not returned home this morning?" Nero gestured to the lone chair, and Scaevinus sat down. "So what has my faithless, truant servant been telling you? That last night I was drunk and said some uncomplimentary things of my Lord Caesar. That would be regrettable if it were true. There were plenty of witnesses with me last night who will readily verify—"

"Yes, that would be regrettable, Senator," Nero interrupted. "But your servant accuses you of far worse than slander. He claims that you are plotting my death."

Scaevinus' mouth dropped opened in a brilliant pose of dumbfounded amazement. "Caesar, I am speechless. And I am utterly curious as to how this uneducated slave could possibly arrive at that conclusion."

Nero walked to the table and pulled out the knife from underneath a cloth that had concealed it. "He showed us this knife. Do you recognize it?"

"Of course I recognize it. It is a priceless, family heirloom, and I specifically asked my servant, my *soon-to-be-dead* servant, to have it sharpened and cleaned for the festival. And I am grieved that this has happened because, Caesar, this knife was to be a gift which I was going to present to you at the Circus this afternoon." He glared at Milichus who managed to sustain the eye contact. "By the gods man, how could you possibly deduce from my simple request that I would assassinate my Lord Caesar!"

"He says you were reviewing your will yesterday afternoon, and he found that unusual. Why would he find this suspicious?" Rufus asked, knowing his friend could handle the question.

"What of it? I will review the finances of my estate whenever I choose. This man is a domestic steward, nothing more. No matter what grandiose schemes are running through his head, he is not a probate officer or my financial counselor. He is in no position to offer comment about my fiscal habits." He began shaking his head, and a slight blushing overcame his face. "Oh Caesar, I am so sorry for not attending to my servants as I should have. I am embarrassed that someone from my household should dare to come to you in such a manner. I regret this incredible waste of your time."

Nero waved his hand. "If we expose a traitor within your household, why would that be a waste of time, Senator?"

Scaevinus wasn't certain how to interpret this remark. Nero resumed.

"And I'm sure you can understand our need to take precautions. Your slave also mentioned that you asked for a package of bandages to be prepared. Were you planning on being hurt today?"

Scaevinus scoffed. "I made no such request. He's concocted a lie to strengthen his accusation, which makes sense for him. I know this man." He pointed a finger at Milichus. "He has lied himself in and out of trouble time and time again. It's a wonder I have endured this slave. Which reminds me, I did grant freedom to a handful of my slaves last night. It's a tradition within our family to express our generosity to our more faithful servants in this manner. Milichus no doubt feels overlooked and slighted, and is enacting his revenge."

Nero seemed convinced, Scaevinus appeared vindicated, and Milichus squirmed in desperation, but he boldly spoke out. "I am not inventing this, Caesar. He did ask for bandages! And he has been having long and secretive meetings with people for months now. Even yesterday, he spoke with a strange man I have never seen before throughout the afternoon. They talked for hours!"

"The gall of this man to assume he understands the details of my finances and my social life!" thundered Scaevinus. "Can he produce one word of treason from any of my meetings or conversations?"

"With whom did you meet yesterday?" asked Tigellinus, whose own curiosity was all but dead.

"A man I have come to know in the past year. A freeman named Natalis, enlisted now in an order of knights. We share a common interest in wine and women."

"What did you talk about with your friend, Natalis?" Nero asked.

They had spent the afternoon discussing little else but the plot. Scaevinus would have to be cautiously inventive. "Mainly of the festival, and of the debaucheries we would amuse ourselves with. I'm embarrassed to say it was mainly debased boy talk. One begins to feel less inhibited during festivals, you know."

Precisely, Nero thought to himself, thinking of the sexual entertainments he had planned for the festival.

"Anything else that comes to mind?"

Nero threw the question out as more of a rhetorical formality than anything else. It was just a bridge to pronouncing the inquiry closed. He didn't expect an answer, and wished to be done with this diversion. Nor did Scaevinus need to answer. A casual shrug of his shoulders would have satisfied Nero. But he answered anyway.

"There's always Senate chit-chat to be hashed over. We talked a little about Seneca."

Scaevinus would not have known that Seneca was right then the most detested name in Nero's head. He could not have guessed that even as he spoke, Nero was devising a way to be rid of the philosopher, as part of his ongoing campaign to eliminate all his rivals, real or imaginary. Rather than dying on the vine, the inquiry took on new life.

"What has my old friend been up to, of late? It's been awhile since I have seen him."

"I've seen very little of him myself. He seems to be drifting back into his private life."

"Yes, and neglecting his public duties," Nero said spitefully. "When did you see him last?"

Scaevinus now seemed to be on uncharted water. He had to navigate carefully. Should he tell Nero that he had seen Seneca only a few days earlier? *"And what were you doing?" "It was a clandestine meeting where we finished plotting your assassination. Nothing more."*

"I saw him just last week, as a matter of fact."

"And what were you doing? Where were you?"

"It was just a social gathering at Calpurnius Piso's villa. A dinner party of senators and friends."

"Why wasn't I invited?" Nero mused.

I wonder.

"Who else was there?"

Damn this scrutiny! Scaevinus looked at Flavus who was nervously rubbing his temples at the officers' table. "A...let's see, Plautius Lateranus, Afranius Quintianus."

"Your friend Natalis?"

"Yes, he came. As I said, we've become quite the pals lately."

"Did Seneca say anything? Was he talkative?"

"When isn't he?" responded Scaevinus, laughing slightly.

"Hmm," was all Nero said. He eagerly wanted something to pin against Seneca. "Did he say anything unusual?"

"Frankly, most of what Seneca says I find tedious. I try to avoid listening to him." Scaevinus stole a glance at Rufus whose foot was tapping rhythmically on the floor.

"So you have no recollection of your conversation."

"No, Lord Caesar. Nothing stands out in my memory of being of any significance. No doubt, I was drunk half the evening."

"You need to check this habit of yours, Senator," Nero mildly chastised.

"Yes, my lord."

Nero paused and looked at Tigellinus, then turned back to Scaevinus. "Before we are through this morning, I would like to meet this freeman Natalis, just to find out what he remembers of that evening with Seneca. You wouldn't mind, Senator?"

"Of course not, Caesar," Scaevinus said calmly, while his intestines twisted into knots. By now, conspiracy was the last thing on Nero's mind. He only wanted to ruin Seneca. So while the others waited, Natalis was sent for.

Scaevinus had correctly prophesied over Natalis that he wouldn't sleep. He had tossed in his bed all night, and was so unsettled, he even threw up once. He was in the process of dressing when the guards came to his house to bring him to Nero. As a politician, Scaevinus was well trained in the art of duplicity and could spin convincing lies, but Natalis had no knack for subterfuge. His mind was undisciplined and his heart was weak for so great an enterprise as this.

Whereas Scaevinus arrived at the palace in firm control of his faculties, Natalis scarcely had the strength to climb the steps. It seemed to him that the dozens of statues that lined the staircase were each looking at him with accusatory eyes and the gargoyles that stood watch over the ambulatory seemed to be spitting at him, hissing the word *Conspirator!* over and over again.

As he came inside the Domus Aurea, he managed with one Herculean effort to suppress the panic welling inside of him, and as he entered the ready room, his countenance somehow appeared unruffled, though this composure hung in place by the thinnest of threads.

"Ah, here is our friend at last," Nero said with cordial impatience. He directed Natalis to the center chair. As the knight sat down, he quickly scanned the room. Seeing Flavus and Rufus at their assigned posts gave him immediate assurance that all was not lost, and Scaevinus was sitting proud and erect among the officers. Their eyes met, and Scaevinus tipped his head just slightly.

"You are Antonius Natalis, a freeman, a knight and a friend of this man over here?" Nero began, pointing at Scaevinus.

"Yes, Lord Caesar," Natalis replied quietly.

"The reason we have asked you to come this morning is to help us sort out a few simple details pertaining to some recent events. You were with Senator Scaevinus just yesterday, I understand." Natalis nodded. "How long have you known the Senator?"

"We met last year."

"It's good to have friends in high places. You must feel gratified to have made such an acquaintance."

"He's a man whose company I have come to enjoy."

"He drinks a bit much though, doesn't he?" Nero asked with a smirk.

"We all have our areas of excess, I suppose," answered Natalis.

"Do you have other high and influential friends? Do you know other senators?"

"I have met others." Nero held out his hands in a gesture of curiosity, inviting Natalis to continue. "Marcus Atticus. Plautius Lateranus. Junius Marinus."

"Well done! Such an aspiring knight you are. With such connections, it appears that one day your star too shall rise over the Senate. And the great one, himself—have you met Seneca?" Nero ventured.

"I've had the privilege of meeting Seneca."

"Be careful of what you describe as privilege, my young friend," warned Nero, wagging his finger. "Few know it, but Seneca and I are not as close as we once were. In fact, we have been at odds lately. I need to find out why he has grown . cold to me. When was the last time you saw Seneca?"

Natalis sensed hostility where there was none. The emperor's slight conde-scension cut at the thin veneer of confidence that covered him. Why was Caesar poking and prying at him in no certain direction? Should he tell of the meeting the week before? A line of sweat appeared on his forehead, and he was unable to keep himself from gnawing anxiously on his knuckles. Nausea was building inside him. None of this was lost on Tigellinus, who had been all but asleep but now something in him was aroused. He bore his eyes into Natalis and studied his every movement and every breath.

"*Tell the truth!*" Scaevinus urged him on with invisible fervor.

Natalis spoke. "I saw him just last week. We had dinner together at Calpurnius Piso's invitation. Flavius was there with us."

Scaevinus sighed in relief. Tigellinus though sat forward, and then inter-rupted. "Wait a minute. Senator Scaevinus specifically told us that Seneca was *not* at that dinner engagement."

Scaevinus blanched. The liar! *Tell the truth, Natalis!*

If Natalis had looked at Scaevinus in that moment he would have read in his eyes which way to turn, but a paralysis of fear came over him, and his head throbbed to decide what to say next. *Conspirator!*

"Well, then it must have been the week before," came his stammering reply. "It seems there have been so many parties of late."

Tigellinus stood, like an awakened giant. "Did you see Seneca in Piso's home last week? Yes or no!" he boomed.

Natalis looked from one side of the room to the other, then buried his head in his hands. "I don't know. Why are you asking me these questions?"

Nero's eyes grew wide in amazement. The knight was hiding something. Somehow he himself had missed it, but with one shrewd maneuver, Tigellinus has brought the deceit to the surface.

"We can help you remember," Tigellinus muttered, reaching into a crate that sat on the floor near his feet. From the crate he pulled out an iron ball which he grasped in the palm of his hand. "Guards, stretch out his hand upon this table," the prefect ordered. The ball would be used to crush each of his fingers one at a time until he spoke.

As three guards moved toward Natalis, Nero suddenly grabbed him by the chin, and jerked his head back. "Antonius, what are you hiding? Confess to your emperor immediately and I will exempt you from prosecution!" he shouted.

Natalis fell on his feet before Nero and sobbed, "I confess! Caesar, I confess!"

At once, Scaevinus jumped to his feet. "Natalis, you fool! Do you realize what you're doing?"

But the knight was blubbering like a frightened child now, and spouting off a chain of scarcely comprehensible words. "We were together. We were planning your assassination. I confess. Oh Caesar, take pity on me. I am foolish!"

Every man stood and gasped at the astonishing revelation they had just heard. From across the room, Flavus and Rufus looked at each other, and for an instant in that pocket of space, the fate of the empire hung in the balance. At first Flavus waited for some indication from his superior officer, but seeing only indecisiveness, he finally drew his sword, and in the confusion of that moment, he raised it toward Caesar.

*   *   *

"Some people would think it peculiar that we choose to worship when we are hurting so much."

The song had finished, and Judah had motioned for the congregation to be seated. When all was again quiet, he started speaking.

"Most people would say to us at this moment, *Just curse God and die. You've suffered so much. He's obviously deserted you.* But remember what our brother Peter wrote to us before he died. He told us not to be surprised by painful trials when they come as though something unusual were happening. He told us to be glad, for in fact, in the moment of trial we are actually sharing in Christ's own sufferings. And Paul reminded us many times that the righteous will be persecuted by the unrighteous, and his chains and scars bore eloquent testimony to that truth. Suffering does not mean we have been abandoned.

"We are standing today in a long line of the Lord's suffering servants which can be traced all the way back to Abel, who was murdered by Cain for his righteousness. And since that time, the sons of Cain have hated the sons of Abel. There is nothing surprising in this. Our Lord himself warned us of the price to be paid for being his disciples. *If they hate me, they will hate you,* he taught us. *A servant is not greater than his master. If they persecuted me, they will persecute you,* he said.

"If God has not abandoned us, then perhaps some might say that all of this is a sign that God is just not as powerful as we make him out to be. Maybe this proves that God has somehow lost his grip on the universe, and that there are forces of evil which even he cannot stop. The unrighteous seem to be forever trampling on the righteous. Obviously, evil must be stronger than good.

"Dear ones, we must not be tempted to think in this way. It is the wicked who will fade like the grass, David said. It is the wicked who will wither and be no more. The wicked will not inherit the earth—the righteous shall. In the end, creation belongs to God's children!"

Judah spoke with an uncustomary zeal which stirred the hearts of his listeners, and as often happened when he preached, he sensed the very wind of heaven blowing on his lips.

"But we are not at the end yet, though I can scarcely imagine that this age will endure much longer. We find ourselves in that period of history when kingdoms are in conflict. God's kingdom has broken in, and the enemies of darkness are in confusion and disarray, but the war is not yet won. And as this conflict unfolds to its inevitable conclusion, there will be setbacks and casualties and suffering. Heaven will not be won without a cross.

"And my friends, the cross is how you and I will conquer. At first glance, it might appear as though the wicked are stronger than we, because we will not engage them on their level. We will not use their weapons. Our implements of battle are utterly foreign to them. They come at us with spears and swords, and what we hold in our hands are mere pebbles by comparison. They strike us on the cheek, we turn the other. They steal our shirt, we give them our cloak. They curse us, we bless them. They mow us down, we sing. They hate, we love. Our weapons are the word of God, prayer, and a message of forgiveness. How can we possibly win with these, let alone survive?

"We win as our Lord Jesus won—with a cross. On the cross, he absorbed within himself all the hatred and evil of men. He took the fiercest blow the world could muster, and on the third day, he was still standing. By his resurrection, Jesus proved that love conquers evil. Love swallows evil whole. Love drains evil dry of its power and destroys it. What seemed like defeat was instead complete and total victory. The resurrection changes it all!

"Jesus' resurrection came so soon on the third day to show us what our destiny is. We, on the other hand, must wait for our resurrection. It lingers over the horizon. But it is coming, dear ones. Our loved ones who were so needlessly slaughtered on Nero's altar are alive still, and one day we shall join them, and on that day, no one will be able to separate us from them again.

"And so if this life gives us blessings and prosperity and health, we thank the Lord for showering his bounty on us, and giving us a small foretaste of the glories to come. Yet we never place our hope in the world's uncertain riches, and we never forget that we are but stewards of things we cannot keep.

"And if this life turns its back on us and strips us naked, we thank the Lord still, for a better life awaits us, a better kingdom is coming, and there is nothing on earth we would keep in exchange for that hope. If the season of grace is taken from us and the night comes when no man can work, then we shall seek him all the more, and set ourselves like flint against all who oppose us. And we shall never compromise or disown the name that is above all names. Let them do what they will to our bodies, for our spirits are secure and our destiny is sure.

"We will stand, now and in the end. No intimidation will make us waver. Be courageous beloved of God. Those who acknowledge him before men, he will acknowledge before the Father in heaven. Live your lives with one goal in mind, that you might hear him say on that day, *Well done, good and faithful servant of the Most High!*"

Now the multitude stood again, aroused to full conviction by the inspired words of encouragement which Judah spoke. Across the field, scores of arms lifted to the heavens and waved in the wind like sheaves of wheat. They cried aloud and prayed to God in response to Judah's challenge. Some fell on their faces and shed tears of repentance for daring to drift away in the moment of their pain. Some joined hands with their neighbors and offered up intercession.

It was a spontaneous, Spirit-led outcry of prayer, and though no one could see the impact of this moment on the physical world, a convulsion right then ripped through the realm of the spirit which utterly confounded the principalities and powers in control of the Roman government.

*   *   *

In the parade of empires that dominated the Mediterranean basin over the centuries, there was one thing besides land which was bequeathed from one conquering race to the next. It was one constant that linked the Assyrian to the Babylonian to the Persian to the Greek to the Roman: torture.

Cruelty begat cruelty, and the only thing which changed from one regime to the next were the innovations made upon earlier forms of barbarisms. The Persians took impalement from the Assyrians and invented crucifixion which the Romans took and converted into a sort of sidestreet theater, where executioners could play dice at the feet of the condemned. Daniel was thrown to lions in a pit in the ground while the guards turned their backs, intending to pick up his bones in the morning. The Romans sewed the Christians in animal skins and fed them to the lions before cheering throngs, as musicians played their instruments in the background and royalty stretched out on velvet cushions. The Romans legitimized torture by making it into an art form, and so her citizens became desensitized to the screams of the victims and thought little of the practice—at least until such time as the inquisitor turned on them.

At the point Natalis crumbled, Scaevinus felt all of his bravado run to his feet. His world fell apart in an instant, as though he stood on a bridge which had given way without warning. His able mind had no reserve of insight to draw on once his valor drained out of him, and all he could think of was that his body was soon to be subjected to unspeakable torment. At the moment of the confession, Nero lost command of himself and the situation. He fell back, stunned by the revelation, unable to decide what to do. So Tigellinus stepped forward and ordered that chains be brought and that both men be bound.

By now, the whole room was a mass of confusion, and as Flavus looked to Rufus for direction, his own mind had determined that this was the moment to act. Nero had fallen back against a chair less than five feet from him and with one swing of his sword, he could end this nightmare. No one but Rufus saw the colonel pull out his sword. He slowly, deliberately raised it, with the blade parallel to the floor and on line with Nero's neck. He looked once at Rufus before swinging, and in that one look, Nero was given three more years of life.

Seeing the intent of his officer, Rufus lifted his hand and shook his head firmly from side to side. Reluctantly, Flavus lowered his sword. He would not be given the chance again. The next time he stood before Nero at arm's length, he would be without his sword.

The dignity of the ready room was unsuitable for what would take place next. Tigellinus commanded that the men be taken to the dungeons of the palace, where they would be compelled to share their secrets. They were dragged off screaming, and the sound of their anguish stung Flavus' ears.

Scaevinus' written warning to Piso reached him a full two hours before the plot was uncovered, as he sat at his breakfast table with four of his co-conspirators, among them Plautius Lateranus. The news was met with stone-cold silence.

"What should we do?" asked Piso finally, and the color of his skin betrayed a growing paleness. "We didn't prepare for this! Nothing was to take place until this afternoon."

"Maybe it's nothing and we're alarmed for no reason," said one. "It doesn't say he's been arrested. He's just being questioned."

Lateranus slapped his fist upon the table. "The tongue of every slave in the empire should be ripped out! We would be fools to sit here and wait. The moment is not of our choosing, but the time for us is now."

Piso's heart sank. "Nero will not come out in public after this. What are we going to do? Storm the palace?"

"Calpurnius, you're not thinking," said Lateranus. "Sometime this morning, if it hasn't happened already, your name will be mentioned to Caesar by someone alleging that you have committed treason. Five minutes later, soldiers will be sent out to look for you. Calpurnius, we are dead already in the eyes of Caesar. The die is cast. Shouldn't we use our freedom, at least while we have it, to fight for what we believe in?"

"What is your suggestion?"

"We send out word right now to all our friends. Rufus must address the Praetorian. Quintianus the Senate. The rest of us gather at the Forum, and Piso, you will speak to Italy from the platform and summon your countrymen to freedom. Once we make a move, the public will rally behind us. Once they see how many of us there are, it will be like a flood sweeping Nero away. He has no plans to stop something like this. He's just an actor, surrounded by degenerates and the fraud Tigellinus."

But Piso was unconvinced, as fearful men usually are when given reasons to be courageous, and from the beginning, Piso had a weak stomach. The conspiracy never was his idea, but as it evolved, his name became attached to it, though quite by accident. His home had been the seedbed of the plot. His money and charisma stood out as other people came into the circle, and they naturally assumed he was the driving force behind it all. Only later as men of power and influence attached themselves to the plot were Piso's deficiencies called to attention, but by then it was too late. He had become the figurehead, and the ultimate success of the plan rested on his shoulders. But it was a weight he was unable to bear.

Lateranus managed to convince him to send out a handful of messages, and then they set out for the Forum. Merrymakers for the festival filled the streets, and many of them joined Piso's procession, some because it looked like a parade, and others because they had heard a rumor that sedition was in the air. No matter, the more the numbers around Piso swelled, the more intimidated he became, despite Lateranus' best efforts to whisper encouragements in his ear. Before they reached the Forum, Piso felt it necessary to stop. A makeshift platform was created for him on the street corner and he stood to speak to the hundred or so people that surrounded him.

To Lateranus' dismay, Piso wilted before his very eyes. His speech was not a call to revolt, but a call to enjoy the blessing of Ceres, and after he had tossed out a few additional meandering words, he invited his listeners back to his home where he would provide free wine and cheese to any who would raise a toast to

Nero. The crowd cheered, and as they dispersed, Piso stepped down from the stage and stood before his companions. If Lateranus had been armed, he would have stabbed Piso on the spot, but all he could do was look into his hollow, frightened eyes and despise him.

Piso looked away. "I'm sorry," he said weakly. "This was never my plan in the first place. I can't go through with this."

He walked away and disappeared within the crowd that was already streaming toward his home. With his pathetic retreat, the conspiracy died a swift and efficient death, which was more than the conspirators could hope for.

As Lateranus predicted, the soldiers arrived at Piso's villa early in the afternoon. By then, the games in the circus had been postponed, and the news had filtered through the streets that a plot against the emperor had been exposed. Piso had taken time to amend his will while awaiting the soldiers, taking great pains to insert a variety of clauses flattering Caesar, in the hopes that when Nero declared his property forfeit to the state—as happened with all traitors—he would yet show beneficence for his surviving family. Mercy though was not available for Piso. After being given time to speak with his family, he was taken outside and bound to a chair in view of the hundreds who had drunk to his honor an hour before, and then his wrists were slashed, and after ten excruciating minutes, he bled to death.

Lateranus was killed even more ruthlessly. He was dragged from his house like a common slave while his children howled with tears and chased after him down the road. He was taken to a common grave where slaves' corpses were disposed of, and there was executed by the hand of a Statius Proxumus, a Praetorian colonel like Flavus, who was also a consenting participant in the conspiracy. Proxumus' arm trembled as he raised his sword, but Lateranus knelt and stared stoically into the trees. He died, refusing to say a single word against him.

Proxumus was not the only conspirator to find himself in the delicate position of prosecuting his own allies. Both Rufus and Flavus were given authority to conduct interrogations. At first both men tried to conciliate between their two identities, but it was impossible to sustain—Flavus because he was betrayed by his conscience and Rufus because he was betrayed by those he questioned.

Toward evening of the first day, Rufus was together with Nero and Tigellinus, when Scaevinus was brought out again from his cell. Two soldiers had to support

him as he limped into the chamber. The chains around his ankles were unnecessary because he could scarcely walk, and his face was bruised almost beyond
recognition. Both Scaevinus and Natalis had already surrendered names under
the duress of the earlier interrogation, but their lists differed, and Nero wanted
them to be tested again.

Earlier in the day, Scaevinus thought that Rufus might still use his position to
move against Nero, but now it was plain that his only thought was to save his
own life. Scaevinus was too broken in pain to endure the charade any longer.
When Rufus approached him later in the interview, shouting at the top of his
voice as though to intimidate the senator, Scaevinus' swollen face contorted in
derision and he reminded Rufus that he knew better than most people who the
insiders of the plot were.

Even Tigellinus' dark and suspicious mind had not expected to find a traitor
among Nero's elite officers. Perhaps the circle of conspirators included a few senators, some embittered patricians and an ambitious slave or two. He eyed Rufus
with a cock of his head. "Rufus, what's the fool talking about?"

Rufus might still have extracted himself from harm's way with a determined
denial, but his initial response was anemic. He stuttered as he spoke a few half-
hearted words of explanation. Tigellinus, who could read past a man's eyes with
the power of a sorcerer, drew his sword at once and ordered the guards to bind
him. Rufus fell apart more swiftly than even Natalis or Scaevinus, and from his
lips poured name after name. It was only then that Nero and his prefect
comprehended the magnitude of the disaster they had averted.

Once Flavus was incriminated, he was immediately sent for, and disarmed as
soon as he entered the chamber. Nero had long regarded his colonel with favor, and
this act of betrayal seemed incomprehensible. At first, Flavus denied the accusations made against him, and Nero was prepared to believe him, but then without
provocation from anything but his conscience, he threw up his hands and shouted,
"Caesar, I will bear this self-deceit no longer! I am guilty as you have charged me. I
am guilty of being part of a plan to set Rome free from your despotism!"

Nero walked up to him with the look of a grieved parent. "Then it is really
true. My most loyal subjects, my closest associates were plotting to kill me. Why
Tribune? Why? Why would you forsake your military oath? What possible harm
have I done to you?"

Flavus stood firm without flinching and glared at Caesar. "When I was a young soldier, I served you more faithfully than any other, as a son his own father. No more affection could a soldier have had for his commander than I had for you. But I realized in time that you did not deserve my affection. And I began to detest you. I detested your singing. I began to hate you after you murdered your mother, and then I hated you more when you murdered your wife. My hatred was sealed when you became an arsonist."

Nero's grief quickly was forgotten, replaced by a rage that manifested itself almost at once. "You will die," he said with his mouth quivering uncontrollably. "You all will die!" He stalked away, and the soldiers took Flavus to the dungeons where he was subjected to misery, and then killed.

Of those who were captured and tortured, only one individual refused to give any names away. Of all the officers, senators, nobility and slaves who were arrested, only one among them maintained a resolute silence—Epicharis, the whore from Misenum, who had been locked away in the dungeons and brought out only when the conspiracy came to light.

She was whipped, branded, and wracked until each of her limbs was dislocated. Through all of the indignities heaped upon her, she repulsed her tormentors' efforts to loosen her lips and protected those she was in league with, never realizing that those who exceeded her in status, rank and power were readily spilling names on the floor. On the second day of her interrogation, she managed to slip out of the bonds holding her to the inquisitor's chair, and before the guards could stop her, she wrapped the rope around her neck, and fell from the chair, snapping her neck and snuffing out what little life was left in her.

The name Nero was most eager to hear was the name he heard betrayed almost from the very start: Seneca. His brooding hatred of the philosopher seemed disproportionate and illogical, but then Seneca was the last vestige of Nero's conscience and for that reason, Nero despised him. The shadow of his logic and austerity hung over the emperor like the strand of a cobweb that refused to be shaken off. Now at last this irritant could be removed.

When the message came from Piso, Seneca was walking on the grounds of his villa with his wife Pompeia Paulina and another married couple, none of whom knew of the conspiracy. He read the message but stuck it quickly in his pockets and kept to himself its contents. All he said of it was, "Our plans for this

afternoon have changed. We will not need to go into the city today after all." He
surmised what the end of it would be.

So they spent the remainder of the day together, eating and talking by a pond
on his property, but as the afternoon waned, Seneca grew increasingly more quiet.
They moved inside for dinner, and as they ate, Pompeia reached out her hand to
his. "Lucius, you are melancholy."

"All silence is not melancholy, my love," he said in return, but the conversation remained muted, until servants suddenly rushed into the room.

"Master Seneca!" one cried out excitedly. "Soldiers are coming. They refused
to stop at the gate!"

They all rose from the table and walked outside. From across the wooded field
that encompassed the house, they could see at least ten soldiers advancing rapidly
on horses. They stood still until the party rode up and stopped.

Seneca looked up at the leading officer. "Centurion, why this intrusion? What
can we do for you?"

The centurion looked at him with a coldness that bordered on disrespect. "I
have a message from Nero. You may end you own life tonight with dignity, or
you may have your life taken from you in the morning."

Seneca's wife gasped. "Lucius, no! Why? What is this about?"

Seneca looked at the centurion with an understanding gaze. "I know why. My
name has been implicated in a plot to kill the emperor."

The centurion nodded his head. "The plot has been exposed. The conspiracy
has collapsed."

Pompeia began crying and embraced her husband, while their friends looked
at each other in confusion and distress. Seneca sighed. "I wish to read through
my will one final time before I release my hold on this life. If—,"

"That will not be allowed," the centurion said abruptly. "If the slightest hesitation or resistance is given, we are authorized to assist you. You are to proceed
at once."

"So there it is," Seneca replied. "Our impetuous Nero has spoken and will not
be disobeyed. Very well."

This was too much for his wife who fell to the ground and clung to his legs,
weeping hysterically. Seneca knelt down in the dirt beside her and rocked her tenderly in his arms, and then he began to whisper to her.

"My love, we are walled in on every side. You and I have discussed this moment many times. We always knew this possibility existed. I ask that you bear this with a grace and dignity that is becoming to our family name. I will go into the bath chambers, and let them do with me what must be done. You stay with our friends. My love, this will be our final kiss. These will be our final words spoken to each other." He kissed her then with sympathy, with passion, with love. "I have cherished our companionship these many years. You are my dearest friend."

She looked up at him with desperate eyes, and tried to speak but her voice failed her. At last she managed to speak and said simply, "Lucius, I love you!"

They embraced once more and then slowly stood to their feet. Seneca turned to his friends. "I'm sorry for putting you through this, but I don't think I could have gotten through this day without having you friends here with me. Please, would you stay and be with Pompeia, and see that she is looked after?" They too were weeping now, and they indicated with a short shaking of their heads that they would honor his request. "I leave you with one possession that cannot be taken from me by Nero and it is my best possession. I leave you with the pattern of my life. Make the pursuit of virtue your highest aim. There is nothing else to life. No other meaning to our existence."

"How could Nero do this to you?" the woman asked.

Seneca laughed. "How could he not? Certainly, his cruelty is no surprise to anyone, and he has made no secret of his habit of killing those who have been closest to him. Frankly, I am surprised it has taken this long."

He turned to Pompeia and placed her hand in the hands of his friends. "Go to the house now." Slowly, they left him, and more than once, Pompeia looked back, but then they disappeared inside. Seneca then turned to the soldier. "Around on the other side is my bath house. With your approval, can we take care of the emperor's business there?"

The centurion nodded as he dismounted from his horse, and bringing four other soldiers with him, they walked to the bath house. It was a small, glass enclosed atrium with three baths. As they walked in, they disturbed a small swirl of mist that hovered over the water. Seneca took a seat near a drain in the floor and pulled up the sleeves of his tunic on both arms.

"Centurion, if you would do this. It would be less painful than my own tentative strokes."

The centurion felt little compassion for the philosopher and so he quickly pulled out a knife from his vest and with the efficiency of a soldier, he made two deep and precise incisions across Seneca's thin wrists. Seneca had written many long, elegant essays on the subject of suffering, but now all of his eloquence failed to dull the tremendous pain that seized him. He bit his lips and closed his eyes.

After a few seconds, the centurion suddenly exclaimed, "Don't you have any blood?"

Seneca opened his eyes, and saw that the flow of blood which had initially spurted from his wrists had now slowed to a trickle. "I am an old man," he said, his head swimming in a fog of dizziness. "My circulation is very poor. Perhaps I should be lowered into this pool. That might quicken this affair."

The centurion helped him to his feet, and walked him to the steps of the bath. After he had settled into the water, the centurion again drew his knife across his skin to revive the wounds, then left Seneca to die.

With his eyes closed, and the water burning his wrists, Seneca's breaths became quicker and more stressed. "I am hemmed in on every side," he gasped, on the verge of nausea. "I see darkness all around. No light. There is no light."

Thirty minutes later, the centurion emerged from the bath house. The remaining soldiers were outside waiting impatiently, and one of them remarked, "Centurion, it's been over a half hour!"

He ignored the exasperation of his men, and with a sourness to his voice said, "Go in and help bring out his body. Let's get out of here."

Chapter 19

When it was all said and done, the Pisonian conspiracy was found to have included more than a hundred of Rome's brightest and most influential citizens. The movement drew recruits from virtually every arena of society, with the exception of the military. Though the Praetorian guard was heavily infected with the seed of sedition, it had not spread to the legions on the frontiers of the empire. Nero retired a few generals, but otherwise, he left his troops intact. However, he made sweeping changes in his Guard. Once every conspirator had been rooted out, he replaced his entire corps of officers, and consolidated all power into Tigellinus' hands. He then dramatically raised the salary for each of his guards to buy the favor of any who might still have reason not to serve him whole-heartedly.

As well, the conspiracy became the occasion to initiate wholesale purges of the Senate. Anyone whose name was even remotely linked with the conspirators was held under suspicion and either executed or driven from office. Though Nero desperately wanted to be rid of Thrasea Paetus, his name was never once raised in connection with the plot, and so Nero was compelled to leave him alone—for the time being.

Nero also found that eliminating Seneca was not enough. His distrust of others was growing exponentially, and he now moved against the very philosophy that motivated his mentor by initiating a violent assault on the popular philosophical schools in Rome, especially the Stoa. Teachers who propounded the gospel of peace and non-violence were assassinated or imprisoned.

Nero left no stone unturned in his search for opponents, and the reign of terror he launched turned Rome into a besieged city. Caesar ransacked the community of artists and writers when it was discovered that Seneca's nephew Lucan, a poet, had lent support to the plot. At the same time, it gave him opportunity to eliminate more than a few of his artistic competitors of whom he was jealous. The emperor's drift into paranoia was steady and irreversible. So in the end, though the Pisonian conspiracy ostensibly failed, it was the impetus for triggering Nero's emotional unraveling which would soon lead to his ruin.

The Christians in Rome were understandably disheartened when they became aware of the failed plot. It seemed to many of them inconceivable that God had somehow looked the other way when so many powerful forces had aligned themselves against Caesar.

"This has been the struggle of the ages for God's children," Judah explained to a group of leaders who had begun meeting with Judah weekly for times of prayer and training. "Habakkuk the prophet asked God, *Why do you remain silent when those who are evil devour those more righteous than they?* But we are commanded in the scriptures not to worry ourselves on account of the wicked. We are not to envy the prosperity they seem to enjoy. We are not to fear their threats. We are simply asked to wait upon God, and in the end, we have his promise that we will look on the destruction of the wicked."

"But how can Nero possibly be overthrown now?" asked an older woman named Ruth. "He's killed everyone who might oppose him."

"And he's my age," said Lucius, a man of about thirty. "He could rule the empire for forty more years."

"God's patience thankfully exceeds our own," replied Judah, "which certainly works to our advantage when we're the ones he's being patient with. It's when he shows forbearance to others that we accuse him of dawdling."

Clement shook his head in exasperation. "I have difficulty accepting God's patience when it means people must die."

Judah smiled empathetically. "Your heart is in the right place, Clement. There's so much about life we just can't understand. Things that we can only stomach by faith, and will only be made better by heaven."

"But I want to understand!" protested another young disciple called Mark. "Doesn't God see that this stretches a person's ability to believe sometimes? One answer, one explanation—is that too much to ask for?"

Judah, ever the teacher, looked at Mark with tenderness, and spoke again. "When a person is suffering, it's rare that an explanation is comforting. But there is an answer for why this kind of suffering exists." This perked their interest, and each looked at Judah, waiting for him to continue.

"God has given us creatures who bear his image a remarkable gift—the gift of freedom. But for freedom to be real, God must give us the space both to make choices and to live with the fruits of our choices. This of course has a disturbing implication. Of necessity, it means that evil men will also be given space to make choices. And the inevitable consequence of an evil person abusing his moral freedom is that innocent people will suffer, and God will not always intervene, for that would be to break his covenant of freedom with us. Until his kingdom comes in its fullness, and this age of sin is passed, it can be no other way than this."

"So the righteous must use their freedom to fight back," said Clement.

"But using only the weapons of righteousness," Judah answered. "We overcome evil with good, hatred with love, falsehood with truth. If the day comes when a disciple of Christ picks up a sword to advance his cause, it will be a day of such defeat for the Church that the Holy Spirit of God might very well evacuate his presence from it. The Church exists to show the world that another way is possible."

"In the meantime then, wicked kings are to be endured," Ruth said, though not convinced.

"We give to Caesar what is lawfully his. If he asks anything more, we'll tell him politely to stick it in his ear," Judah said, and the others smiled.

"Then he takes our freedom, our property and our lives," said Mark with a shrug.

"Even so. See then how powerless Caesar really is! He takes from us only those things we must all lay down in the end anyway. Our dignity, our conscience, our souls are left untouched. *Don't fear those who only can hurt the body and afterwards can do no more. Fear him who has the power to cast you into hell.* Isn't that what our Master said?"

There was a lull of silence around the table as Judah's words were digested by his students. Mark sighed. "Perhaps Nero is not in as much control as we think. There is still hope that a governor or general may yet revolt against him. Soon war is likely to break out in Judea. The whole empire might fall through his hands."

At the mention of Judea and the imminent conflict there, Judah's head lowered. His sadness was noticed by the others, and at once Mark was filled with regret. "I'm sorry Judah. That was thoughtless of me."

"You don't need to apologize Mark. Judea is a strange land to you. I wouldn't expect you to feel as I do about it."

"I may not be a Jew but I am married. I know how much you miss her, Judah. Forgive me for aggravating your wound."

At the thought of Esther, Judah was not able to suppress the dampening of his eyes, but he gathered himself together and resumed the conversation.

"Whether it is a general or a governor or a slave who brings Nero down is up to God. Frankly, we need to stop assuming that the kingdom of God is somehow limited by the politics of men. Don't forget, God chose little Bethlehem as the birthplace of his son's kingdom, not Rome or Jerusalem. And he chose a young peasant girl as the vessel of his incarnation, not an empress or a princess. God doesn't need important people or places to do his work. A shepherd or a carpenter or a fisherman from a tumbledown village will do just fine."

The others nodded in humble agreement. Judah then looked around the table at each one. "Let me say to you now what has long been on my heart. Nero will fall. Of that I am convinced. But it will not be of a man's plotting. Nero will destroy himself. The terror of God will consume him."

"When Judah?" asked Ruth. "You sound so sure."

"Not long, I sense. But we must be patient."

Ruth then asked the question that had long been on everyone's heart. "How long will you stay with us, Judah?"

He sighed. "Until this night is over. This long and bitter night."

*   *   *

Sometime during the summer, the voices returned. Nero had last heard them nearly a year before when the arsonists were being punished. Then they suddenly stopped and he was happy again. Now at some point in the past few weeks, his sleep had fled from him, and he could once more hear the whispers. Sometimes it was garbled, like a fly buzzing at the window. Other times, it was clear but distant, as though someone was speaking to him from outside his bedroom in the hallway. *Nero!* It was so obvious, so real, that more than once he had gone out into the corridor to see who was calling him. But each time he found the corridor dark and empty.

Sometimes it was a man's voice. Sometimes a woman's. The boy's voice he rarely heard, but it haunted him most. They came especially at night and always when he was alone, and most irritating of all was that the voices knew of only one word: *Nero!*

"I'm hearing them again," he confessed to Tigellinus one afternoon. He had confided in his prefect the year before about the strange occurrences.

"Shall I come and read you bedtime stories before you sleep?" asked Tigellinus dryly.

"Don't be an ass, Tigellinus. Try for once to suppress your natural personality. Are you telling me that you never hear voices in your head? You never talk to yourself?"

"Everyone talks to himself, Caesar. Not everyone hears an answer in reply though. My mind is usually quite at rest."

"Quite dormant, you mean to say," Nero snapped.

"So what are your voices telling you?"

"They just keep whispering my name."

"By all the gods, Nero!" Tigellinus exclaimed. "You're not satisfied with the adulation of the people. You've now gone to inventing imaginary worshippers."

"It's hardly worship. They torment me!"

Tigellinus appeared eager to leave the subject behind. "I don't know what to tell you, Caesar. Maybe if you started sleeping at nights, rather than whatever else it is you do, your voices would sort themselves out. Sleeping in the same bed with the same woman can do wonders for a person."

"Sleeping with only one woman is ludicrous," Nero said with a pathetic sneer. "How stilted a man becomes."

"I would rather be stilted and not hear voices calling my name out of thin air. And Lady Poppaea can, of course, take her own carnal holidays, as does her husband?"

The emperor scoffed. "Of course not. I will kill the man who dares to desecrate Caesar's temple."

"And you have no suspicions of her?"

A small dart of irritation landed on Nero's vanity, but he turned up his nose at the suggestion. "I need only keep her pregnant and there will be no need to worry, true?"

"Caesar, have I ever told you that you are an idiot?" Tigellinus' face remained void of emotion as he said this. Nero had lived with his sarcasm for years, but he still never knew how much Tigellinus meant of what he said.

"Why do I endure you Tigellinus?"

"Because you need me. Although I am sad to say, I cannot solve your current problem. I suspect you need a priest more than you need my advice."

With that, their conversation ended, and Nero never mentioned the voices to him again. But the voices would not stop. As each week slipped by, Nero's world changed by gradual degrees. The line between reality and illusion began to blur. He began to spend long, solitary hours peering out the windows of his suite which overlooked the city. Though he claimed to others that he was composing poetry, his mind was completely inert during these times, except for the flash of images from his past which burst into his thinking unannounced and unwelcome. He did not want the past. He hated it. It was a shadow-world that scorned him, and worse—it condemned him, and he did not know how to silence the tribunal of his conscience.

It was late in the summer when the shadow-world made its first violent foray into Nero's real world. The celebration of a third *Neronia* had been declared, and like the inaugural festival, Nero pranced, recited and sang on stage before his adoring public, only this time he did not give just one performance, but a string of them. Night after night, he entertained his people to the aggravation of even the few who sincerely did appreciate the emperor's artistic talent. For the rest, it was intolerable.

The distinguished general Vespasian, who had won glory for himself in Gaul and Britain, made the unfortunate decision of taking a furlough during this time, and was severely reprimanded for falling asleep at one of Caesar's performances. (He was forgiven the slight however, and when the war with the Jews began a year later, Nero chose his best commander—Vespasian—to lead the assault against the rebels.)

Nero's voice still bore traces of his confrontation with Paul, and he went to ridiculous measures to try and restore it for the sake of his singing. A physician suggested that eating only chives soaked in oil could soften the rasping in his throat, and the next day he ordered his meals to be stopped in favor of the new diet. Several days after this, Tigellinus found slaves stacking lead weights on

Nero's chest as he lay on the floor. Caesar explained that the exercise was an ancient Persian treatment that would strengthen his diaphragm.

On the day of his final performance, Nero returned to his apartment after having received the Persian remedy. His chest was sore, but his voice was little improved. As he undressed, he tried to sing a few measures from one of the songs he hoped to perform, but each high note seemed beyond his grasp and fell to the floor like a bird dying in flight. He cursed in disgust, and when his arms became caught in the sleeves of his tunic, he became angrier yet. He wrestled with the clothing for several seconds, his rage mounting furiously each second that he was unsuccessful. Finally, he extracted himself and threw the tunic against the wall as though it had deliberately thought to ensnare him. A paroxysm of foul language spewed from his mouth as he put on other garments and walked up to his windows, where he sat down and brooded.

How alone I am, he thought. *How alone and unappreciated. What can be done about my voice? Why can't someone be found who could lift the sorcerer's curse? How anemic our gods are. Precisely, because there are no gods!* Seneca's face suddenly appeared in his imagination, as he seemed to be in the days when Nero was still a pupil sitting at his tutor's feet.

"The gods impose an order on creation without which the universe would collapse," the philosopher said. "A tension exists between them which assures us that in the end, the good will prevail. In their own struggle for perfection, we see our own path marked out. We must strive for the good, though recognizing that virtue will not be acquired without first winning the monumental struggle of the soul."

Such gibberish. The philosopher could bore as no man could. And such a miserable man. Always speaking of denial and struggle and suffering. What a pathetic philosophy to live by. And where did it take him in the end? Fool. Think of all the pleasure I would have missed abiding by his counsel.

Octavia's face flashed into his mind next. She was eleven, he a couple years older. They used to play together as children.

"I will be married to you one day," he proudly announced, as they walked alone in a palace courtyard.

"Don't be foolish, Nero," she said. "We're so young."

"We're not young," he said, his voice taking on an aggressive tone. "Look how much we have changed already. Look at my face." She peered closer and he pulled on the skin of his cheek. "See, whiskers."

"You are a silly boy, Nero. I don't see any whiskers."

He was upset by her casual denial of his manhood. "Look you, I have whiskers! Feel them with my hand." She didn't like his yelling. She reached out and touched his face with her fingers.

"Okay, you have whiskers." She started to walk away.

"You didn't feel them closely enough." He grabbed her arm and pulled her closely to him.

"Feel them again."

This time he grabbed her face and pulled it to his and kissed her with an awkward roughness. She struggled, and the more she pulled back, the tighter he embraced her. "See. I am a man," he said firmly. "And you are a woman," and as he said this he squeezed her chest with his hand. When he did this, she pried herself away from him, slapped his face and ran away.

You never received me. You always pulled back. You always fought me. And where did it bring you in the end? Think of all that you threw away because you never appreciated the man I was. No one appreciates me.

"Nero."

His head pulled back with a jerk. *Not again. Not now. Why the voices again?*

"Nero."

He rubbed his forehead vigorously. It was the woman calling him.

"Nero!"

He looked up from his chair and glanced down into the room behind him. Standing in the middle of the floor, with her arms held out to him, was Agrippina. Her hair and the sleeves of her dress were flapping as though a wind was blowing right then through the apartment, but every door and window was shut. Her face was bloodless, pale and empty. Her eyes were red, as a dead person's eyes must be when they awake from the grave. Her fingers curled beneath her hands as she waved them at him. Her mouth looked contorted and twisted, but still she spoke.

"Nero."

He froze as though paralyzed, though each of his limbs convulsed and shook with abject terror. "Agrippina—it's not possible!" he stammered. Still the specter did its eerie dance before him. Overwhelmed with horror, he fell to his face on the ground and cried out, "Speak to me if you exist. Otherwise, leave me foul spirit and stop torturing me!"

"Nero!"

The voice was as a scourge on his back. He screamed as though to drown out the voice, but it spoke again and so he covered his ears with his hands, and would have ripped off his very lobes if it would have silenced her. "No, no, no!" he cried, rocking back and forth on his heels. Suddenly, he felt a hand touch his back.

"Nero!"

"Go away!" he cried, with sudden rage borne out of the sensation he felt of being cornered. When he looked up, it was Poppaea leaning over him with her long hair dangling in his eyes, but his mind could not adjust so quickly. He looked down into the room but the apparition was gone, then he looked back at Poppaea as her eyes searched his face for a way to comfort him.

"Nero, what's wrong? Darling, you look sick." He didn't respond nor was it likely that he could respond. His head jerked involuntarily as the shock coursed through him, and to Poppaea, his face looked more like an animal than human. She reached out to touch him. "Nero, tell me what's—," but before she could finish talking, he reared up with unexpected fury and pushed her back against the wall.

"Leave me alone!" he screamed, rising to his feet. She slumped to the floor, less stunned by the impact on the wall than startled by Nero's frightening outburst. She began to cry. Curled up on the floor as she was, the heaviness of her pregnancy was obvious. The sound of her weeping unnerved him further. He reached over to a table and snatched up a glass vase, then smashed it on the floor beside her.

"Shut up!" he screamed. "Why are you tormenting me?"

Her crying quickly strengthened into loud wailing which only intensified his anger. She pushed back along the wall to retreat from him, but recognizing her vulnerability triggered an instinct of abuse within him. "Leave me alone!" he howled. As he said this, he lunged at her and with all the power of his rage reinforcing his motion, he kicked her in the stomach with an iron blast of his leg. Poppaea gasped, then cried out as spasms of pain overwhelmed her.

At that moment, a clatter was heard from outside, and two guards burst into the room. Nero's head seemed to clear at once and he looked down in dismay at his wife, who was doubled over, moaning, and clutching at her stomach.

"Poppy! O no," Nero said with a whimper, as he knelt beside her. Then he beckoned the soldiers. "Guards, come quickly. My wife has fallen over a table. She's hurt herself, badly I think."

The guards rushed to his side and bent down over Poppaea. "Help me take her to my bed, then go at once and bring my physician," Nero commanded, and as they lifted her, Nero stared down upon her crumpled form with a scattered look of fright and confusion.

*   *   *

As soon as the physician emerged from the bedroom, Nero rose from his chair by the window and rushed over to him, but he could discern at once from the expression on his face what the outcome had been. The physician said nothing, but beckoned for Nero to come into the room with him.

Poppaea's motionless, nude form lay uncovered on the bed, and beside her was the body of a newborn infant boy, so silent and still, it looked like a wax figurine. Their bodies had been washed, but the bedding, the clothing, the floor were all stained with red, and two attendants were slowly picking up strips of bloodied rags and placing them in a basket. Nero stepped tentatively toward the bed. He bit his lips and began to mutter some words which the physician could not make out.

At last, the doctor spoke, with both a graveness and a trembling to his voice, prompted by condolence on the one hand, and a fear of reprisal on the other. "Emperor, I am so sorry. We lost both of them. Lady Poppaea died before the baby could be born. And once we were able to remove the child, it too was gone. I assure you we tried everything in our power to save them."

The physician reached down and tenderly drew up a sheet over the bodies. As the sheet passed Poppaea's waist, his hands couldn't help tracing over the obvious bruise that discolored her torso. He tucked the sheet under Poppaea's chin and backed away.

"Emperor, you have my deepest sympathy. The grief of this—accident—will be felt over the entire empire. We will leave you alone if you wish."

Nero didn't move and said nothing, so the physician motioned to his attendants and they quickly left the bedroom. There was a chair by the bed, and after five minutes of standing in stationary somberness, Nero pulled the chair over and sat down. His shoulders drooped, his head sagged, but his eyes remained dry.

"Poppy," he said feebly, looking down at the floor. "Poppy, why have you left me so? I am now utterly alone. I have no son. I have no wife. I didn't want to hurt you, my love. It was an accident. I was afraid. You know I would never hurt you."

More silence. Then he reached beneath the sheet and took her hand which felt as cold as clay.

"Poppy, wake up. I want you to wake up and get dressed. We must go to my final performance, you and I. We have survived so much together. And the people want to see us together. They want to see our son. We are just beginning to build our family. Soon, our home will be repaired. And Rome will be rebuilt. This is just the beginning of our golden age, Poppy. Now is not the time to be asleep. Wake up, my love, and I will sing to you."

He leaned over and cradled her hand against his face. "You enjoy my singing, you say. Octavia did not enjoy my singing. You should have been my princess before her. You appreciate me. It seems that no one appreciates me anymore. Come Poppy, and sit by my side tonight as I sing to our people. Then we will come home, and I will sing you to sleep. The future is still ours to claim, and I want you by my side, and all our children will play at our feet."

The room fell into a macabre silence as his waited for a reply, a movement, a sound. But the only movement was the shadows of the candles which fluttered on the walls. Nero sighed.

"Sleep then, sweet Poppy. I will leave you with a kiss and return for you when you are rested."

He stood slowly and stiffly, then leaned over her to kiss her, but suddenly jerked back with a gasp of fright and fell against the wall. The sallow skin of the face he saw staring at him from beneath the sheet was Octavia's. He fled from the room with a scream, to the dismay of the physician and his attendants waiting outside. Eventually, when it was clear that the emperor was not returning, they entered the room and took the bodies of Poppaea and her son away to prepare them for burial.

Chapter 20

April [A.D. 65]

My love Judah,

My thoughts have continually been of you since we were taken from each other, and there has not been an hour that passes where I do not feel a hollowness inside when I think of being apart from you. I know you can sympathize with me for how my heart has been wrenched with the ever-changing news of where you might be. When Seneca sent word of your deliverance, I cried in joy for weeks on end to know you were alive and coming home. And though you told me not to concern myself with any letter which told me otherwise, when Paul wrote to tell me that you had died in the fire, I cried all over again, this time in fear for what had happened to you.

Then months went by and winter came without you. I began to fear that you were gone. I'm sure I drove Tirzah and John mad with my anxiety. At last, several days ago Catus arrived. He said he was your servant and my spirit leaped to think that you were right then coming around some corner. But no, I was crushed again, this time almost beyond healing. In one stroke, I learned of the suffering of our beloved church, and then of your decision to go back to Rome.

Be assured, my husband, that I now am at peace, and I believe that the choice you made was right. But it was not without anguished prayer that I have come to accept this. I feel as though in the past year I have died a thousand deaths. Each time I think I will have you back, I soon discover that you are taken from me again.

Catus has now rested, and is eager to return to Rome. At first, I felt compelled to come with him, but I will wait for you to tell me what to do. Who knows, but maybe even now you have finished your task and are returning to me! (I know better, but so it goes in my dreams.) I will stay here and keep the space warm beside me in our bed, for you to come and fill it.

Tirzah and John, their children and grandchildren all send their greetings to you, and of course everyone is eager to see you again. The grandchildren never can hear enough of the stories I tell of our adventures together. "More, more!" they cry, when I tell them of their great-uncle Judah, the great charioteer. They love to hear of our travels with Paul, but oddly enough, they seem more interested by your involvement with Nero. Why do the young sometimes appear to be more fascinated by the wicked than the righteous? Were we this way when we were their ages, Judah? Or are there simply no more heroes left in our age for the young to imitate?

One thing is for certain. If the Romans continue their harassment of our people here, our children will learn soon enough that they are not worthy of admiration. Nero's new procurator in Judea, Gessius Florus, is an evil man. In just the few months he has been here, it seems that lawless men are multiplying in droves. John says he refuses to travel outside of Jerusalem any longer by himself. Robberies occur on the roads in broad daylight, and it seems that the soldiers look the other way and do nothing. The rumor in the streets is that Florus openly accepts bribes from any one who will proposition him. I am told that his wife and Nero's wife are good friends, which would seem to explain the similarities in their husbands.

The people are growing increasingly agitated, Judah. Skirmishes and riots seem to take place every day in some corner of the city. During the Passover, the priests led a massive delegation to Caesarea to appeal to Cestius Gallus, the governor, to do something about Florus, but it remains to be seen what, if anything, will be done about him. Jerusalem is not the same city we once knew, Judah. The church is large here, but opposition is strong, and many disciples find their lives made bitter here by both Roman and Jew. I fear there may not be any place on this earth where we may retire in peace. So far though, we have been safe and unmolested, so do not be needlessly alarmed. Finish the work God has called you to do, and send me word of what I should do next. I would give anything in exchange for one letter written in your hand.

And yes, my love. I will join you in prayer every sunset. Each day as the sun dips over the hills, you will find me atop our roof looking west, searching for your face. I will not lose hope that we will be together again soon. Whatever you may do in Rome, keep from the emperor's gaze. He would love nothing more than a second chance at destroying you, and what would I do without you?

Grace to you, my husband and friend.

Esther

September [A.D. 65]

Dearest Esther,

Peace and joy to you, my wife, lover and friend, from one who finds intolerable this unending separation between us.

The summer has been long and wearisome here. Nero has declared war on his own people, and Rome is a city under siege. As much as I wish for you to join me here, it is much too dangerous, and as much as I would like to leave, the situation in the church is still too uncertain. So for now we must continue to endure this gulf between us.

You would be very proud of your brothers and sisters here. As I came to Rome, my greatest fear was to find our work completely undone, but my fear was groundless and unrealized. Why did I ever believe otherwise? Didn't the Lord promise us that He would build His church?

The devastation though was indeed grievous. All of our dearest friends are gone, Esther. But hundreds of disciples yet remain, and those who were being trained for leadership when the storm fell have risen to the demands of the hour. Slowly, any who had fled or had gone into hiding are being gathered together again, and in time, the church will be even stronger than before. There is a spirit of grace on the community unlike anything I have ever sensed before. The Holy Spirit of God is here as fully as on the day of Pentecost. We have not been abandoned, and the greatest glory of the Lord's church yet awaits us.

By now you have heard of the conspiracy on Nero's life which failed. In the end, it was found to have involved a massive number of people, including our friend Seneca, all of whom have been swept away in Caesar's wrath. Presumably, the plot collapsed because of the betrayal of a senator's slave. The door of history often swings on the hinges of insignificant moments and people, and if we did not believe that in the end it is God who opens and closes the door, it would be enough to drive a person to despair. Instead, we choose to trust the guiding hand of our heavenly Father. He allowed his children to taste 400 years of captivity to Egypt before bringing them forth to freedom. If we must endure untold years of Roman tyranny that God's purposes might prevail in the end and the freedom of our faith be hailed across the world, then so be it. Caesar too will bow to the cross one day.

I will share with you what I have shared with the church. Nero will not live out his days. His wickedness is nearly full. God's judgment is often written in our very behavior, and the judgment which Nero is heaping up is soon to fall upon his head.

We reap what we sow, and already the signs of his unraveling are evident. Lady Poppaea died several weeks ago in childbirth, along with her son, and the story is circulating that Caesar himself killed her by kicking her. Certainly, his behavior after her death would not discredit this idea.

After her funeral—which was a disgusting and opulent affair as you might imagine—he engaged in a mock wedding ceremony with Sporus, the freeman from Greece you might remember. Nero had him dress in woman's garments, and what else went on is shameful to even write about. (How the Senate can endure this man is beyond my comprehension. How God can endure this man is even more of a wonder.) Nevertheless, I am convinced that his destruction is imminent, and he will bring it upon himself. The weight of his sins will crush him.

What you write me concerning Florus concerns me greatly. That he is depraved and barbaric is of no surprise, considering the man who appointed him. (It is easy to discern the character of a leader by looking at the men he appoints around him. You learn most about a person by observing the company he keeps.) I trust John's wisdom to know what is best in these situations.

If the voices clamoring for war win out in the end, it will not be safe to remain in Jerusalem. Nero is incompetent, but his legions are not. In the event that blood is shed, I will send for you, my love. If we cannot live together in peace, then let us face the danger side by side that at least we might die together. Can the Lord delay his coming much longer?

Grace and peace to you, my love, and greet everyone in the house for me, particularly my dear Tirzah, who will forever remain my little sister and the jewel of her brother's heart. With this letter I am sending little gifts for each of the children. I will think of you everyday Esther, pray with you everyday at sunset, and write you faithfully until we are together again. I love you.

I am yours in love and faith.

Judah

January [A.D. 66]

My love Judah,

*Do you feel the embrace I am giving you right now as you open and read this let-
ter? Do you feel the warmth of my kiss on your face right now? If ever you could feel
the passion of bodiless affection, feel it now, for I send this letter with all the love that
my heart and soul can create.*

*Your package arrived just the other day. The children were naturally thrilled by the
bronzed horses and chariots you sent along, and already several miniature arenas have
been dug out of the ground outside. Need I say that since then Judah Ben-Hur has
been declared champion of the circus numerous times?*

*Tensions continue to mount in Jerusalem as Procurator Florus presses on with his
policy of harassing Jews whenever he can. John believes—and I quite agree—that
Florus is deliberately trying to incite us to take up arms against him. That way, his
own brutality will be overlooked in the light of the Jewish rebellion, if it occurs.*

*Just a few days ago, an incident took place in Caesarea which has everyone still
simmering. The synagogue there is built on land owned by a Greek merchant, but he
has refused to sell the property to the local Jewish council even though they have offered
him many times its value. Recently, the merchant began to build upon the property, as
though to deliberately cheapen the synagogue's appearance, and then he allowed
friends of his to begin offering mock sacrifices in front of it to ridicule the Jews. There
was nearly a riot there the other day, and supposedly, a dozen or so council members
were given assurances by Florus that the construction would be stopped to keep the
peace. But his promise was meaningless and he did nothing. When the Jews appeared
before him a second time, he had each one beaten and arrested.*

*The high priests are doing their best to calm people down, but at every public
meeting, people begin shouting and often there is violence. A man named Manahem,
from Galilee, seems to have the loudest voice among those who want war with Rome,
and he is supported by several of the priests including Eleazar, the temple governor. It
feels as though we are being swept by some irresistible current which is carrying us
inevitably toward disaster.*

*Meanwhile, the church here continues to feel the strain of being caught somewhere
in the middle. There are a few who want to take up arms with their brothers to
defend their homeland, and the rest believe it to be forbidden by the Lord. I wish you
were here Judah to help bring some sanity to these debates. There seems to be madness
all around. Those among the church that seem poised for violence point to the*

persecution in Rome as a sign of what will happen if we do not fight, but I'm sure you could provide a much needed perspective if you were here.

It seems that the Cross has been lost somewhere in the heated clutter of this discussion. In the meantime, I have tried to occupy myself with teaching some of the younger ones. The church is as large as ever, and there is no end of work to be done strengthening the new believers. Should the Lord return, I do not want to be found sleeping with little oil left to trim my lamp of readiness.

It is all I can do to make the time pass. But even so, the months away from you grind on so slowly, Judah. Believe me, if you told me to come to Rome, I would leave at once, so eager I am to see you. I will continue to wait for you to tell me what to do. Stay strong my dear husband in the faith that links us together as one. Soon our patience will be rewarded.

Under His wings,
Your loving Esther

June [A.D. 66]

Dearest and sweetest Esther,

How I miss you my love! Yesterday I saw a woman in the street whose movement and form so reminded me of you, I nearly called out your name aloud. Her face was veiled from my sight, but my imagination was aroused by the thought of how desperately I long for you. (Fear not though, my wife—I am not going out of my way to look at other women! Your features are so rare and precious to me, that I seldom even notice another, for so few come close to the loveliness that you possess.)

Summer has come early to Italy, and with the change of seasons I am reminded that it has been two years since I have seen you. Am I mad to persist on this course I have set for myself? Be encouraged though in that the church here continues its recovery. I have appointed bishops for all the congregations, and their training is going well. Linus seems to have emerged as the first among equals in the group, and Clement is right behind him in gifts and vision. I feel I will soon be able to comfortably release everything into their capable hands. But will there be a Judea to return to?

I have heard that violence has finally broken out in Jerusalem, and that thousands have already died. Such news terrifies me, my love, and I need to know if you are all right. If such is the state of affairs in our homeland, then perhaps it is best that I send for you now, and we will brave Nero's impetuousness together. I struggle to know what to do myself, for Nero's violence rages on unabated. Among his latest victims is the noble senator Clodius Thrasea Paetus.

Of what I knew of Paetus, he was a man who was deserving of great honor and respect. (That being the case, it would stand to reason why Nero would hate him.) As I understand it, charges of sedition were concocted against him, not on the basis of anything he did, but on the grounds of what he did not do. The essence of the accusations against him was that he had neglected his senatorial duties with excessive absenteeism, and because of this was influencing other senators to be insubordinate.

No one spoke a single word in his defense, the sad irony being that over his career, he himself had stood up in defense of countless people who were brought to trial unjustly. I have even heard from some that he stood to plead on my behalf when I was tried for my so-called crimes against the state. The end of the matter was that the Senate ordered his death, and his veins were opened that night.

Caesar may have stretched himself too thin this time. Paetus is held in high esteem by the people and is a favorite of many governors beyond Italy. A wise man would begin to wonder if his turn would be next, and take measures to prevent it from happening.

Thankfully, there has been no movement against the church during all of this. It is as though Nero has forgotten about us, which is as we would wish it to be. And soon there may be even better news for us. We have heard the rumor that Nero is planning on a lengthy trip to Greece after the summer. If that should be so, the threat may lift from off of us altogether, and I will send for you at once, Esther. But it is still too early to tell, and so wait a little while longer. I feel confident that we will be together before the year is through.

In spite of the danger here, do not be anxious for me. Though Nero repossessed our property two years ago, the church has provided me with a small home well outside the city, and I never have to go into Rome, so the risk of being discovered is small. I have also tried to minimize my public ministry, knowing that there are many visitors who find their way into our meetings. Instead, I am content—and the church is willing—that I work behind the scenes, encouraging and teaching in smaller groups, and sharing from house to house rather than in larger assemblies. Very few, it seems, know me by my Roman name, and the newer ones think of me as the "Old Man", and so I think I am relatively safe.

But your safety on the other hand is what concerns me the most. I want you to write me as soon as possible. I have lost many hours of sleep wondering what is *happening in Jerusalem. Send me assurances of your safety, and whatever happens, do not get trapped in the city! Should war break out, get out before it's too late. If Rome should lay siege against Jerusalem, there will be very few survivors. What lawlessness and famine won't kill, the Romans will finish off once they break through the walls.*

Promise me, Esther—leave the city, and get out of Judea even before I send for you if the worst happens. I love you, my dear wife. And I long to hold you in my arms. It's sunset now, my love. I am going to have fellowship with our Father in heaven, and I'm thankful that you and I can share this time together.

Grace and peace to you.

Your "Old Man" Judah

September [A.D. 66]

My dear Judah,

I am writing this to you even though I have no assurance that it will be sent. Your last letter arrived with your servant a few weeks ago, but there will be little else coming in or out of the country, for Judea has exploded into violence, and war has begun. The nation has gone mad and everywhere there is death and destruction.

Even as I write, Governor Cestius is moving on Jerusalem with thousands of soldiers. John and Tirzah have made plans to leave the city, but right now, the rebels are in firm control of the walls and gates, and no one is allowed in or out without their authority. Judah, I have never been so afraid in my life. And I need you more than I have ever needed you in my life. But you are not here and I feel so desperate and alone.

This conflict has been building for so long, it seems hardly surprising that it has reached this point, but finally it overheated several months ago when Procurator Florus raided the temple treasury of seventeen talents of silver. The people managed to suppress their anger even then, but Florus wanted a fight, and so he sent his soldiers through the city to incite a riot, and once it broke out, the soldiers began killing people at random. He slaughtered over 3,000 men, women and even children. Judah, you couldn't have imagined a more heart-wrenching scene!

King Agrippa's sister Bernice was in Jerusalem at the time, and appealed to Florus to show restraint but he scorned her to her face. Then Agrippa himself came, and at first, he managed to calm the people. I was there when he talked to the crowds. He told them how ludicrous it was that they could even consider fighting the Roman army. He reasoned with them and encouraged them to appeal to Caesar through

Governor Cestius. But when he said that Florus should be obeyed until he was replaced, at once rebels began to shout him down, and it's a wonder he and his sister escaped the city with their lives.

The final bridge was burned a few weeks later when Masada was attacked, and the rebels killed all the Romans there. They murdered the high priest and then took control of the temple and the lower city. They kept fighting until they had captured the Antonian fortress, and gained control of the whole city. Every Roman soldier has been killed by now, and any one who speaks against the war risks his life as well.

All of this has set off fighting in one city after another. I've heard that more than 20,000 Jews have been massacred in Caesarea, and thousands have been butchered in Alexandria as well. And in our own towns, the Jews are killing every foreigner in sight. Judah, it must be the end of the world. I never could have imagined that such madness could rule our nation. Didn't Jesus say that everyone's love would grow cold at the end? There is no love anymore. Just hatred and violence.

And now we are trapped inside this city of hatred. Gallus has gathered his armies and right now is moving on Joppa, and afterwards he will come to Jerusalem, and what will the end be? Judah, I don't want to die, but it seems so inevitable. You command me to flee the city, and how readily I would obey you, but am prevented!

Pray for us Judah, pray. For that is all that is left. And should you never hear from me again, then I want these to be my last words written to you by my hand. Engrave them on your heart, my husband. I love you!

*   *   *

Catus was terrified by the prospect of suffering in the impending Roman siege, and with a measure of duplicity and good fortune, managed to slip out of Jerusalem by night. He weaved his way across Judea to the sea where he caught a west-bound boat and returned to Rome. He brought this letter to Judah and placed it in his hands late in the winter. It was the last letter Judah would receive from Esther.

Chapter 21

Gaius Julius Vindex was the praetorian governor of the Lugdunensis region in northwest Gaul, from whose coast ships set sail across the channel to Britain. As a military commander, he was deeply loved by the soldiers who served under his leadership. As the governor of an isolated province far from Rome, the stature of his authority was magnified all the more in comparison with Caesar, whose rule seemed distant and irrelevant. It was easy for a provincial governor to develop a brooding sense of autonomy when so far removed from the Palatine Hill and all the decisions made upon it.

Particularly disturbing for men such as Vindex was the constant stream of reports issuing from Rome concerning the unrest and confusion caused by Nero. The burning of Rome was grievous; the prosecution of the Pisonian conspirators was disturbing; but the continued assault on the Senate, now intensified by the execution of Thrasea Paetus, was unpardonable. Vindex had never liked Nero—he disdained him from the beginning for his acting and singing. But now he hated him, and the hatred was only strengthened by the great love he bore for his nation which was being systematically strangled by Nero's repression.

It was his patriotism which motivated him to send letters to numerous governors broaching the subject of rebellion. A handful of favorable replies returned, and a secretive meeting was arranged in the Tarraconensis province in Spain, between Vindex and two other governors from the region—Sulpicius Galba and Salvius Otho. They met inside Galba's palace in the summer following the outbreak of hostilities in Judea.

"It is unfortunate there are only three of us around this table right now," Otho said, as their meeting began.

"I have sent out letters to many of the governors I felt would be sympathetic to our cause," Vindex said, "but it is too soon to be discouraged."

"I know that two or three of your letters have been summarily passed on to Rome," Galba interjected. He was an old man in his early seventies, and ugly as well. A mound of wrinkles piled up on his bald head, and his mouth seemed to be permanently contorted into a frown. Indeed, those who knew him said he never smiled, and he bore the reputation of having administered his province with taciturn sternness. A convicted murderer once appealed to him for clemency, claiming to be a Roman citizen. Galba responded by ordering his cross to be whitewashed and elevated above the others who were to be crucified that day. But with his callousness came an authority that few could deny, and Vindex recruited his services by promising him the throne should Nero be overthrown.

Galba held up a small scroll in his hand. "In fact, I am certain that there is no secret in what we are doing. I have recently intercepted this order. Caesar has commanded my assassination."

Vindex shrugged. "So be it. Let Caesar rant and rave. Nero is now in Greece and his pathetic band of freemen is in charge. Even if the idiot Helius sends the letters to Nero, we will have plenty of time to move against him. We are not alone, gentlemen. I have received word from Clodius Macer in Africa that his legion belongs to us the moment we give the word. Others will rally to our side as soon as we act. I cannot recall a time such as this when one emperor has inflicted so much injury on his people, not even Caligula. Otho, it's a wonder you have suppressed your hatred all these years. You, of all of us, are deserving of vengeance."

Though in his thirties, Otho had aged considerably in the years since his wife Poppaea was taken from him and he was banished from Rome to administer the lonely province of Lusitania. His sufferings were not overlooked by the people. A popular rhyme circulated among the taverns.

'Otho in exile?' Well, yes and no
But we ought not call it so
'And could we ask why this must be?'
They charged him with adultery
'But did they prove it?' Well, no and yes
It was his wife he dared undress

Otho cleared his throat. "There was a time after he stole my Poppaea when I thought my hatred had left. But now that he has killed my Poppaea, I have discovered that it was merely sleeping."

"And now it is awake," said Galba, nodding approvingly. "Which is good because hatred can cause a man to do great things he would not have the power to do otherwise. And we must do a great thing for our people."

"One thing is certain, if we do not act, the empire will unravel beneath us," added Vindex. "Already look at what happens under the anemic leadership of our divine Caesar. The Jews think to throw off our yoke, and reverse decades of stability we have brought to the region! How many others will be emboldened by their example to attempt similar rebellions? Will we sit idly by while division and decay eats away at the prosperity we have worked so hard to obtain?"

So it was that in that meeting, and others which followed, plans were made to topple the seat of Roman power. And while the seeds of revolt took root, Nero spent all of that year cavorting in Greece, as he had long planned to do since the earliest days of his reign. He intentionally bypassed the Senate in selecting the man to rule Rome in his absence, and chose instead a coterie of his freemen, headed by a flatterer named Helius, in whom he vested full power to confiscate property, and to punish or execute anyone as he saw fit. With Tigellinus by his side, Nero left Nymphidius Sabinus in charge of his Praetorian Guard.

Nero did not neglect his duties entirely. His most significant decision while in Greece was to appoint a commander to oversee the campaign in Judea, and for that he could think of only one man—Vespasian. Several months earlier, Cestius Gallus had laid siege to Jerusalem, and just as the city was on the verge of collapse, he inexplicably broke off the assault.

The Jewish defenders retaliated at once, and sent the Roman army scattering in a bloody retreat, which seemed to arouse the entire countryside into taking up arms. Thousands of Romans perished while the Jews suffered minimal casualties, and when word reached Nero of the defeat, he was made sick for more than a week. Vespasian was summoned and commissioned at once, and along with his son Titus, they landed their first legion in Judea in early spring. The fifth and tenth legions were brought from Alexandria and dozens of additional cohorts were recruited from the surrounding nations. The Roman ranks flooded with mercenary enemies of the Jews who wanted nothing more than to see the Judean province laid waste.

Once his forces were mustered, Vespasian marched on the region of Galilee to the north, with the intent of bringing the populated areas around Jerusalem to heel first, after which he could focus all of his military might on the capital city. Perhaps by then, the Jews would see the futility of their resistance and come to their senses, averting the long and costly siege which was otherwise inevitable.

By the first of July, the major Galilean city of Jotapata fell, and 40,000 Jews were slaughtered. In October, Gamala was the next to fall and before the winter, the final stronghold of Gischala was conquered. Having sealed off all the territory to the north and west of Jerusalem, Vespasian returned to his quarters in Caesarea for the winter, not only to give his soldiers time to rest, but also to give time for the unrest within Jerusalem itself to fester.

While the Galilean campaign was being waged, civil war slowly brewed within the great city. Though the rebels and zealots had remained solidly ensconced in power and continued to stand guard at the gates, a number of the high priests began to organize opposition against them. The eruption occurred when the rebels attempted to convert the temple into their barracks. With the priests leading the charge, the people turned on the rebels and forced them to barricade themselves in the temple.

But the rebels were supported by the Idumeans in southern Judea, and when news of the rebels' defeat reached them, the Idumeans dispatched an army of 20,000 men which overran the city and repulsed the priests' own forces. The rebels were released and regained control of the city, and the bloody purge which followed guaranteed that there would be no more resistance to their power. The stage was set. The zealots would have their war, and Jerusalem would have its showdown with Rome.

Judah could only watch these developments from afar, and as each report filtered back to Italy, his spirit grew more and more disconsolate as the reality set in that Esther was either hopelessly trapped or dead already. He felt paralyzed with helplessness. Travel to Judea was forbidden except for military personnel, and even if he could somehow sail east, he would find the country sealed off. All he could do now was wait until it was over and then pick through whatever rubble the Romans would leave behind. The only true hope he could cling to was that

Esther might survive as a prisoner—that is, if Vespasian even bothered to take prisoners. The winter which fell on Italy that year was the longest and coldest that Judah had ever remembered in his life.

*   *   *

At first, Nero discarded the written warnings that Helius sent to him concerning the tremors felt in the West. The Greeks had showered him with such acclamation that it tended to mute any criticism he heard elsewhere. During this time, he had taken another wife, Statilia Messallina, and he simply wanted to be left alone to his games, his performances and his vices.

Every city he traveled to in Greece hosted contests in music and athletics, and Nero again amazed the masses with his prodigious abilities, winning glory at every stop. He assumed—quite mistakenly—that the citizens back in Rome were desperately awaiting news of his triumphs and so he sent every prize and award back home as an assurance to the people that he was yet the Supreme Conqueror, and that his time away from them was being profitably spent. Helius merely took the crates of ribbons and wreathes and stacked them unceremoniously in a storage room.

As for the disturbances which Helius reported to him, Nero believed they could be smoothed over by simply ordering each of the accused generals and governors either to kill themselves outright or to come to Greece where he could then examine their fidelity himself. It never occurred to him that his authority had been so enfeebled that his orders would simply be disregarded.

It was the discovery that Vindex was conscripting an army of 100,000 men that finally so alarmed Helius that he went to Nero himself in late winter to beg him to return to Rome at once. Only Tigellinus' reinforcement of Helius' urgency compelled Nero to acquiesce.

"I will go," he said begrudgingly, "though of course you realize it would be far better for you if you had encouraged me to remain in Greece until I proved myself worthy of bearing Caesar's name. I have yet to hit my full stride and you are asking me to quit the race. This is nothing but shameful."

They returned to Italy in early March, and Nero disembarked at Neapolis, where he again descended on the city as before, with all the pomp of a victorious general. Again, a breach was made in the wall. Again he climbed atop the ramparts as the people shouted his praises. Again he paraded through the streets with elephants, dancers and soldiers. Yet this time, the exhibition was hollow and stale for all who watched it.

Soon after their arrival in Neapolis came the message flying swiftly across the Alps: Vindex had revolted, and his army was moving south toward Italy. Nero was exercising at the gymnasium when the message came, and at first he did nothing. He thanked the messenger, asked for a towel, and resumed his exercising. At dinner that night came a second message, which repeated the first. Nero yawned and waved away the messenger with a disinterested promise to show the rebels his trophies from Greece and then they would back down.

So it went for eight more days, and still Nero did nothing, though his lack of concern was not entirely unjustified. Vindex would have to march his army through the heart of Gaul to come to Italy, and in his way he would find one of the empire's crack legions commanded by Verginius Rufus, whom Nero had appointed as governor only the year before and could be assumed to be a staunch loyalist. In Nero's thinking, Vindex stood alone.

In the meantime, Vindex sent messengers ahead of his army into Rome, seasoning the city with his own propaganda. When Vindex ridiculed Nero as *Ahenobarbus* and questioned his ability to run the empire, Caesar scoffed lightheartedly. Only when he questioned Nero's ability to play the lyre did he become aroused to anger, and he at last dispatched a hurried missive back to Rome asking that the Senate stand with him no matter what shape the crisis took.

Finally, Nero returned to the capital and he quickly summoned his high council together. But to the bewilderment of each of his advisers, after providing just a brief report on the Gallic situation, he used the remainder of the time to give them a demonstration of several varieties of water organs he found used in the musical theaters of Greece. The only resolution Nero asked for was the approval to install the water organs throughout the city, but beyond that, the council took no action, gave the Senate no directives, and offered the frightened populace no assurances. More inactivity followed. And then all in one day, Nero's world collapsed around him.

A week after his meeting with the council, Caesar was sitting at his favorite perch in his apartment gazing out over the city when Tigellinus suddenly burst into the room and walked purposefully up to him. Nero looked up at him with a vacant stare.

"Yes, you bearer of bad news, why have you disturbed me now?" Nero asked with a disinterested frown.

"Vindex is not alone, Caesar."

Nero waited for more, but hearing nothing, asked, "And who might be foolish enough to join him?"

"We have thought till now that Galba was dead. He is not. He is in fact very much alive, and is right now marching two legions along the coast toward us, supported with additional troops and weaponry by your old friend, Governor Otho."

Nero's face turned white in an instant. "Galba is alive!" he uttered, as he struggled to his feet.

Suddenly, his eyes rolled shut, his legs gave way, and he fell to the floor in a senseless heap. At this, Tigellinus cursed under his breath. He called for guards to come, and stooped over to pull Nero back onto his chair. The guards came, and a company of servants followed close behind. Seeing their lord and master sprawled out on the floor, the servants immediately began running about the room like baby chicks let loose from a box. Somehow in the chaos, wet towels and fans were fetched, and Nero was wiped down, cooled off and even slapped for good measure. Tigellinus meanwhile waited impatiently for Nero to regain sensibility.

In time, he stirred and opened his eyes. Tigellinus was swift to scold him. "Caesar, you've wasted enough time up till this point. Now is not the time for napping."

Nero rubbed his temples as his head pounded away like crashing cymbals. "What will we do, Tigellinus? Is this the end for us?"

"Why should it be the end, Caesar? Do you actually fear this ancient baldhead? He comes at us as a dragon with no fire. All I see is smoke."

"Two legions are hardly smoke, Prefect."

"What are they to us, when you can raise up ten legions of your own by nightfall!" It was the most passionate that Nero had ever heard Tigellinus speak. "Simply give the word, Caesar, and we will summon home the units you have sent to the East. They can join Petronius Turpilianus' legion in the north. Not even if Hannibal rose from the dead to lead them would any invader break through such a wall. The legion from Misenum is already at our disposal. Verginius Rufus will easily stop Vindex in his tracks and his men will be available by the time Galba approaches. Caesar, there is no need to panic at all. For once, show yourself as more than just a musician, and this will all be over with in less than a month."

"And what exactly is that supposed to mean?" asked Nero, miffed at the insinuation.

"Caesar, there are times for singing and dancing, and then there are times when we need to put away our instruments. A wise leader will know which season he is in."

Nero sneered and wagged his finger in Tigellinus' face. "By the gods, do you realize how very near you are to sounding like Seneca?"

Tigellinus ignored him. "So is the order given, Caesar? Do we recall the legions and position them to the north?"

Nero waved his hand flippantly about in the air. "Do whatever you wish. I'm surprised you ask my permission. Don't you think it might be better to consult Vindex first?"

"And Caesar, you must appear before your soldiers and stand with them on the field of battle. They are all ready to serve you, but you must show yourself determined and fearless first, and then they will follow."

"But what if I do not feel determined and fearless?" For some reason, Nero's voice was sounding more ridiculous and effeminate as the conversation progressed, which began to grate on Tigellinus. He glared at Nero.

"I thought you were an actor!" he said condescendingly, then spun around and left the room. Nero huffed in response, and then took his seat again at the chair by the window. He stared outside as shadows cast by the setting sun began to paint the streets and buildings with a darker hue of color.

"Poppy. Poppy," he began to say under his breath. "Why have you left me so? Where have you gone? I have no son. And soon I will have no empire. Poppy, Galba is coming. What should I do? Tigellinus says I must fight him. I—who abhor violence. Must I stoop to be a soldier?"

He buried his face in his hands, and then slowly allowed his fingers to furrow through his hair. Then he looked up toward the window, and a curious brightness suddenly beamed in his eyes. He stood up and began to pace.

"Yes, I will fight him. I will lead my armies into battle. I will walk before them playing upon my lyre, with a thousand trumpets blowing behind me, and then the dancers and artists shall come, and together we shall lead our legions before Galba. And I will fight him by showing him the surpassing excellence of my world in comparison to his. And we shall stand before all of Rome, and they shall decide which future they prefer. His—a future of blood, and demolition and dust. Or mine—a future, a renaissance of spirit, culture, and peace. Then I will be vindicated. Poppaea, my precious bride, from your death will come rebirth. And I will dedicate all this to you, when once Galba has repented and I return to Rome."

Nero was the lone member of the audience he addressed, but the stirring speech was convincing nonetheless, and he marched from the room striding like a soldier going to battle. Without any further delay, he called the Senate together and in a matter of hours, issued a public condemnation of Galba and declared all of his goods and property forfeit to the state. At the same time, he forced the retirement of one of the two consuls residing over the Senate and assumed the seat himself, that he might be seen giving more active leadership during the crisis. Finally, the order was given to bring home every available legion from the surrounding provinces. With such forceful measures, Nero prepared himself and the city for the storm that was steadily gathering strength around them.

*   *   *

By May, Vespasian was prepared to move the bulk of his army toward Jerusalem to join the 800 horsemen and 5,000 foot soldiers he had posted there already. He was well aware of the convulsions shaking Italy right then, and was therefore motivated to bring the Jewish war to a close as quickly as possible. With ruthless efficiency, he mowed through Idumea to the south and then took Jericho to the west, fifteen miles from Jerusalem. Some fled into the desert and others ran into the mountains toward Jerusalem. Those who remained were cornered, then mercilessly slaughtered, and after their homes were raked through for plunder, the soldiers burned them to the ground. Each mile of Judean sand trod upon by Roman sandals was claimed by Vespasian at the price of a thousand Jewish lives, and the trail he blazed toward Jerusalem was marked by a gauntlet of crucified rebels.

Even so, it was nearly impossible to distinguish the the violence outside Jerusalem from the atrocities committed inside the city. Some Jews counted themselves fortunate to have escaped the city only to fall into the hands of Vespasian's army. Inside the city, the rebels preyed upon their own countrymen. They roamed the streets like wolf packs, robbing, pillaging and raping for survival or entertainment. Stores of grain which were intended to carry the city through a protracted siege were pilfered and wasted, until the first pangs of famine were felt even before Vespasian surrounded the city.

Lawlessness prevailed in the absence of authority, and there were factions even among the rebels who made war on each other. Disease as well ravaged the populace, but those were the lucky ones who perished by the hand of nature. Without graves to bury them, their bodies were stacked on street corners, left to putrefy in the heat of the sun. And so the city of Zion, once called by King David the *perfection of beauty* and by the prophets the *throne of the Lord* became instead a citadel of death.

*   *   *

The facade of confidence which Nero carried before the people was impossible to sustain, and soon fell apart as easily as plaster before a hammer blow. The hammer which broke him struck three times.

First, while still advancing on Italy, Galba declared himself *legate of the Senate and the Roman people*, which was an idle threat in and of itself, unless the Senate and the people believed it to be a credible claim. The second blow came when Clodius Macer, the commander of Africa's single legion, defected to Galba. It was this more than any other development which turned the tide against Caesar, for Africa was the bread basket of Italy, and the threatened embargo of wheat created panic in the streets.

Once more the hammer fell, and this time Nero would not recover. In late May, the expected clash between Verginius Rufus and Vindex occurred, and as Tigellinus had foreseen, Rufus' superior forces won the day. Vindex lost 20,000 men on the day of battle but before he could be captured, he fell on his own sword and perished with his army.

But the apparent victory for Caesar was short-lived, for no sooner had Rufus conquered than his men immediately began to hail him as their emperor.

Though he refused to acknowledge their acclamation, the mood of the soldiers was telling. Soon the report drifted down to Nero that even many of his troops in northern Italy were secretly sympathetic to Vindex and Galba.

On the morning of the ninth of June, Tigellinus came to Nero attempting to fan into flame the one spark of hope that remained. He found Nero in his arena, having just finished a ride on one of his horses. Two of his freemen, Epaphroditus and Phaon, were with him, helping him remove the tack from the animal, and when he saw Tigellinus enter the arena, Nero scowled and muttered something to himself which the others could not hear.

Undeterred by Nero's obvious displeasure, Tigellinus approached him with bold urgency. "Nero, I must speak to you privately—now."

Again, Nero grumbled to himself. He had been coiling a bridle in his hands, but all at once, he threw the bridle down into the dirt and then walked lethargically outside the barn while Tigellinus followed. Caesar walked over to a fence, braced his hands on the top railing and snorted, sounding not unlike an irritated horse. The hot sun overhead drew out several lines of sweat from his face, and a circle of flies quickly began to orbit his head.

"Nero, Galba is coming." Nero said nothing in reply. "Do you hear me?"

Nero stabbed at the flies with an angry sweeping of his hands, then glared at Tigellinus. "You have interrupted my morning to remind me of old news. Is that the best you can do?"

"What is not old news, Caesar, is that the people are now clamoring for Galba. You should see the marketplace today. The booths and shelves are all empty. People are hoarding up food and provisions, fearing they may not be available tomorrow. Thousands are milling about the Forum, growing increasingly restless. You have one chance left, Nero. You must address the people now. Then you must gather your legions together and go and stop him. You must not give your soldiers any more reason to doubt you. Assert yourself now! Half of Galba's army will desert to us if we but show the simplest resolve. Nero, the window is closing and tomorrow will be too late!"

"Soldiers' games, Tigellinus," Nero mumbled. "I don't have time for soldiers' games. Galba is bluffing. It is smoke and mirrors. The people love me."

"The people were prepared to love you yesterday when two grain ships from Alexandria arrived. And what did they find the barges filled with? Grain?

No—sand! Sand for the arena. Sand for your playbox. The people do not love you, Nero! You have lost them. All you have left are your legions, and if you lose them, you lose it all. Caesar, at least appear before them. Give them one speech, one exhortation, one reason to die for you."

Nero extended his finger at Tigellinus as though to lecture him. "No, you go and speak to them. And give them this reason. Caesar has ordered their obedience. What more needs to be said?"

"Nero, that will not do!" but Caesar waved him silent.

"Tigellinus, go. Leave me. Now! You are irritating me with your drivel. Not another word. I am going back to my house to write poetry and I don't want to be interrupted." He stomped away, but then before he had re-entered the arena, turned again to face his prefect. "How many of your soldiers could rhyme even two words if asked?" Then he went inside, leaving Tigellinus alone. And in that moment, Tigellinus knew what the end of it all would be. He was left with no other choice. That afternoon, he went outside the city and presented himself to Galba's envoy who had arrived in Rome ahead of the army to offer the terms of his master.

*   *   *

Toward the end of the afternoon, the early summer heat began to unsettle the atmosphere above the countryside, and off to the west, mountainous thunderheads began to pile up in the heavens, preparing to descend on Rome as a natural foreshadowing of Galba and his army.

The Roman church had taken advantage of the splendid weather to meet together in the outskirts of the city for a day of fellowship, and while the rest of Rome was succumbing to fear and foreboding over what was coming on the earth, the Christians shared in a day of rest and recreation unlike any they had enjoyed for a long time. Though Judah's heart was mildly uplifted, he found himself unable to share in the pleasure that flowed so freely through his people. He had fallen again into the valley of depression, and with it, came a sickness which began to weaken his body. Though he needed rest, each night his sleep was stolen from him by nightmares of what must surely have been unfolding right then around Jerusalem. He tried to keep a face of faith turned toward his brothers and sisters, but those who were closest to him knew that his soul was being ripped apart with anguish.

He had long since released Julius, Catus and Urbanus from their servitude, but each of them chose to stay by the side of his master, and so the four of them remained companions throughout the long months of waiting and uncertainty. Toward the end of the afternoon, the servants decided among themselves to bring Judah home. He had spent the day laying on blankets beneath a tree, talking to people as he had the strength, but his sickness was slowly getting the better of him, and they did not want Judah to be caught out in the storm that was poised to break around them. And so they helped Judah climb atop his horse, they bid farewell to the church, and then began the lengthy journey back home which was on the other side of the city. It would be dark and most likely raining by the time their long day was over.

*   *   *

Throughout the afternoon, Nero sat at his window and watched the storm roll in, his eyelids twitching and his feet rocking on the floor. He spoke to himself off and on, and when he was silent, the voices started echoing again in the cavern of his thoughts. Servants entered the room quietly and looked up at his silhouette, then turned around and left the room distressed at their inability to know what to do. From his window, Nero could see the streets teeming with people, and at this distance, the movement below seemed like the churning of a flooded river. A muddy, angry river.

"You see what is happening, Nero."

The voice was Tigellinus', who had entered once again, as the evening shadows were lengthening over the city. The room was already drowning in darkness, as the sun was lost behind the threatening clouds which boiled in the sky.

"The streets have exploded. You've lost control. You have one last chance to restore order and sanity to your kingdom. What will it be?"

Nero continued staring straight ahead.

"Ahenobarbus!"

The word stung. Nero twisted his head with venom. "How dare you use my childhood name! You mock me!"

"You deserve to be mocked."

"I'll have your neck, Tigellinus."

The prefect laughed in derision. "Not before Galba will have yours. You come now to the soldiers' camp or it is over. The people will not tolerate another civil war. If you rally your Praetorian guard and legions together, the people may yet support you, and the army may yet fight for you. Come with me."

He reached out and grabbed Caesar's arm, but Nero jerked it back in offense, then resumed his reflective posture. After a moment, he said, "Tigellinus."

"Yes, Caesar." Tigellinus waited, but not with hope.

"I am sitting here thinking that our sewage system is much too inefficient. Did you notice the system of aqueducts when we were in Greece? So much better than our own. Those Greeks are magnificent engineers."

Tigellinus pulled back away from Nero and retreated toward the door. He thought for a second that the noble thing to do might be to kill Nero right then and there, but he had made another promise which now had to be kept, especially if he wanted to preserve his own life. He walked outside and turned to the four soldiers standing guard by the door.

"Men, I am ordering you to withdraw from your post and return to the barracks this instant. You are to see that every guard on duty in the palace goes with you."

One of the soldiers appeared confused. "Sir?"

"And I want you to see that this message is passed on to the entire Praetorian Guard. Every member of the guard is to report to the soldiers' camp immediately. We are going to prepare a suitable welcome for Governor Galba."

Another soldier misinterpreted his meaning. "So Nero is going to fight after all, Prefect?"

"Didn't you listen to me, man!" barked Tigellinus. "We're going to welcome the new emperor and assure him of our full support."

There was a pause as each soldier digested what was said. Then each of them in turn saluted and marched away as commanded. Tigellinus scowled, and followed after them.

*   *   *

As the servants had feared, the storm broke well before they were even halfway through with their ride home. The rain fell so hard it sounded like iron marbles bouncing off the cobbled pavement. Judah pointed out a shelter that was standing off in the woods fifty feet away from the road, and the men dismounted and quickly walked their horses over to it. Just then a horrendous blast of lightning cracked overhead, and a huge limb crashed down to the earth behind them, causing the heart of each man and beast to race with terror. They managed to hang on to the horses which tried desperately to bolt.

"This night is fit only for devils!" exclaimed Julius.

"In that case, we keep moving," shouted Judah above the wind and rain.

"Master Judah?" Julius asked, perplexed.

"We don't fear devils, do we?" Judah replied. The others laughed, though nervously. "But we should fear lightning, especially when we're surrounded by trees. Forget the shelter. Let's keep on the road and stay clear of the woods."

The others agreed, and they pulled back to the road, then pressed on, though with their faces dipped low to ward off the stinging bite of the rain.

*   *   *

An hour after Tigellinus left, night fell. Nero grew weary of staring out at darkness, so he stood and walked out into the hallway, intending to find something to eat.

"Guards, I want—," he began to say as he pulled open the door, but then he stopped as he saw that the hallway was empty. "Guards!" He looked right and left as far as he could see in the dim light provided by the candles on the wall. "Is anyone here?"

He took a candle out of its stand and walked with it down the corridor to the staircase that took him to the main entrance of the palace.

"Hello!" he called out.

He trembled as the eerie silence swallowed up his call. He walked down the steps and called out again, and this time, he was startled by the cascading echo of his voice as it bounced off the domed ceiling. When he reached the main floor, he stood in the center of the vestibule and peered down each of the corridors that spun off like spokes in all directions. He saw no one and heard nothing except for the rumble of thunder from outside.

Quickly, Nero ran outside to the ambulatory and gazed down the expanse of steps that led to the sea of tiles down below. Each place where he expected to see a soldier standing guard was vacant. The only sentries he could see were the stone statues lining the steps and the Colossus keeping watch from below, and even that seemed small and pathetic as it stood alone in an empty courtyard. Nero was petrified now. He turned and ran back inside, then frightened himself anew when he saw Sporus standing in the vestibule.

"Sporus! You scared me half to death, though I am glad to see you. Where has everyone gone?"

The freeman seemed also to be in dread. "The guards have gone to the soldiers' camp with Tigellinus."

"Yes, well he said he was going there," Nero replied, trying to snatch control of the situation. "Why did he take all my posted men?"

"He's declared for Galba."

"Who has?" Caesar asked, acting shocked.

"Tigellinus. He told us as he left that anyone still in the palace by nightfall would be arrested. Everyone has gone, Nero. The slaves, the gardeners, the cooks. Everyone, except for me, Phaon and Epaphroditus."

"The traitor!" Nero spat. He paused to control the trembling of his body. "So you had better be on your way as well, Sporus."

"I am your servant, Emperor. I have no place to go but Greece."

Nero smiled. "Brave Sporus. More noble than Tigellinus. You shall be my Prefect when this has passed. Then we'd best be on our way, I imagine. I am an emperor with an army of three. Sporus, go and summon our army. We must sound a retreat from this place and pull back our line of defense. I will wait for you here."

Sporus bowed low, and then disappeared down one of the hallways while Nero returned to the doorway and looked out at the horizon, which was right then illuminated by a massive claw of lightning. He waited for twenty minutes, and then the three freemen appeared, and in their hands were rain cloaks which each of them put on before turning outside. Because of the ferocity of the storm which had just then unleashed its fury on the city, the streets were empty, and the four men were able to thread their way without detection through back roads and alleys. After an hour of miserable, wet progress, they found their way out of the city.

But the storm refused to abate. The men talked very little as they trudged on, if only because it took all their effort to keep the cloaks from blowing off their bodies. At last, Phaon cried out above the gale, "Caesar, we have to get out of this storm! My villa is up the road another two miles. Let's move there until this passes."

"Isn't the soldiers' camp that way, though?" asked Sporus.

"It's not far from here, but you can't get there by this road. We'll be safe," Phaon answered.

Caesar only nodded and the men pushed on, fighting the wind with every step. Another half hour passed. Because of the darkness, and the slipperiness of the slate beneath their feet, they were constantly stumbling or sliding into pockets of ooze, and once the first word of profanity fell from Nero's lips, it seemed to unleash a torrent of foulness from him which dirtied them all worse than the mud.

Epaphroditus suddenly called out, "What's that?"

There was an unusual noise mingling with the wind and the rain, a rhythmic sound, haunting, a ghostly chant of some kind. They all stopped and listened.

"It's coming from the soldiers' camp," said Phaon after a few seconds.

Nero suddenly stepped off the road and began walking into the woods toward the sound. "I need to know what it is," he muttered.

The others looked at one another and then followed him. They plodded through the trees about a hundred yards as the sound grew increasingly louder and more distinct, and then they came to the top of a bluff that looked down into a steep ravine. At the bottom of the hill was the soldiers' camp—the barracks where the Praetorian guard trained, ate and slept. Hundreds of soldiers were standing in rank outside on the grounds, ignoring the rain, and shouting one word high above the howl of the storm.

"Galba! Galba!"

To Nero, it was a deafening roar, a pounding cataract sweeping over him. He fell to his knees in the mire and buried his head beneath his hands, unable to bear the weight of the cursed name his own guards were proclaiming. The three freemen looked at each other, unsure what to do next. Finally, Epaphroditus spoke.

"We're not going to have much more time before they start looking for us. Once they learn you've fled, Caesar, it's only a matter of time before they start combing the woods. Perhaps we should keep going."

"Let's at least make it back to the road," Phaon said. "We'll get nowhere standing here."

Nero didn't move, so the three converged on him and helped him to his feet. If it was possible, the storm actually seemed to be worsening at that moment. Lightning flashed relentlessly above them, and each man harbored the thought inside that even the gods were now standing in opposition to their flight. Nero was of little help to them. He shuffled his feet along but had the strength to do little else. Sporus supported him by one arm, Phaon the other, and slowly they tramped through the muck back to the road. All at once, Nero cried out with an utterly inhuman shriek and fell to the ground again.

"Nero! What is it?" Sporus cried out.

Nero began to frantically rock on his knees, possessed by a crippling panic. "It's her! It's her!" he screamed out, in such fear that all three men were now covered with gooseflesh.

"Who is it?" they asked together.

"Agrippina!" Nero screamed again, and he pointed off into the woods. With each flash of lightning, Nero could see her standing amidst the trees, like the angel of death, reaching out to him with her long, white fingers, beckoning him to come. Her red eyes glowed in between the lightning streaks. They scowled at him with contempt and condemnation.

"There's nothing there, Caesar," said Sporus, breaking the spell.

Phaon reached down again to pull him to his feet. "Nero, you have to pull yourself together or you'll have no chance. It's bad enough out here in this weather without you going crazy on us and seeing ghosts."

They continued walking, though not without struggle, and as they passed the grove where she stood, Nero looked back. His entire body was convulsing, but somehow, they at last managed to drag him to the edge of the road. And then as they stepped onto the road, it happened again. A tremendous burst of lightning exploded directly over their heads, and each of them fell to their faces on the pavement. But accompanying the blast of thunder which shook the ground was the sound of horses whinnying, and the clapping of hooves upon the cobblestones.

The men looked up and silhouetted against the black sky were four steeds rearing up above them, each of their nostrils flaring. The men screamed, frozen in place, as the animals danced above them, but finally the horses backed away. Only then did they see upon the beasts the cloaked riders, who looked like ghouls in the darkness. Suddenly, one of the riders brought his horse near and turned it sideways, as though to get a better look at this pathetic party lying on the ground. All they could see of the man was his mouth, as it twisted down in anger. The rider reached up and pulled back the hood from his cloak. Each of the men expected to see a skull appear beneath the cloth. But the image was worse.

Nero's eyes bulged from his head, and his convulsions started again in earnest, and then one by one, each of the freemen also began to tremble uncontrollably. The rider was indeed a ghoul, a dead man who had come back from the grave. It was a cavalry from hell, led by Quintus Arrius!

"It's him! It's him!" Nero screamed. "Do you see him or am I the only one!"

"It's real, Caesar! It's real!" they all howled in unison.

Phaon summoned the courage to address the ghost. "Phantom of Quintus Arrius, leave us poor and desperate men!"

When Nero and his freemen had unexpectedly stumbled out onto the road, Judah and his servants were as startled as they. But when he recognized Nero, something surged up within him—more than human wrath, it was a filling of divine outrage brought on by the Spirit of God which welled up within him at that moment. Judah drew closer that he might look Nero straight in the eyes, and when he spoke, it was not with words of his own inspiration.

"Nero Ahenobarbus!" he bellowed. "The living God has wearied of your abominations against him and your crimes against men! Tonight your crown is handed to another and your soul returns to him who made it. One door yet remains open for you, but it closes swiftly. Repent of your evil! Call upon the holy God and beg that you might still receive the mercy of his son Jesus Christ!"

Nero wailed at this pronouncement. He heard but he could not listen. "Leave me, specter!" he yelled. "I am undone! Leave me ghost of Quintus Arrius!"

Judah looked down upon Caesar who cowered pitifully on his knees, and with a voice full of conviction, he declared, "I am Judah Ben-Hur!"

Judah looked at his servants and nodded for them to continue on down the road. All four of them passed by the frightened huddle of men on the road, and as they disappeared into the gloom, Judah intoned, "The door closes, Nero Ahenobarbus!" And then they were gone.

It took five minutes for the men to recover enough from the vision that they could stand to their feet. Sporus was the first who was calm enough to dare to speak. "If even the Furies oppose us, then we can go no further."

Epaphroditus nodded his head in agreement. "Nero, you must surrender yourself. It's of no use trying to flee. You won't be allowed to escape."

Nero had just enough strength to attempt a stab at self-preservation. "Surrender myself?" he cried. "Do you know what they will do to me? Do you know how they will kill me? And what they will do to my body after it is done? I can't allow for that to happen."

"You have no choice, Nero," said Phaon, completing the verdict of the freemen. "It is that, or else end your own life now before the soldiers come. My villa is just up ahead. Let's hurry there. Caesar, I would be honored if you would find your rest on my property."

Nero's head dipped down in a posture of submission, and began walking with the others' help. They continued down the road another mile until arriving at Phaon's property, and to their relief, the storm slowly lost its vigor, and soon the wind was all that remained of it. Behind the house was a small one-room storehouse, and at Phaon's suggestion, the men went there to share their last moments with Caesar. As they opened the door to step inside, Nero stopped.

"Friends, I would ask you here and now, that if you love me, you will dig a grave here in my presence."

It seemed an unusual request, but then the entire setting was strange to begin with. Phaon found some shovels, and as Nero sat down in the doorway of the storehouse, the servants began digging out a burial hole. As he dug, Sporus tossed aside a large white stone which rolled to Nero's feet. He picked it up and examined it, then held it out to Sporus.

"Sporus, this must not be wasted. I need marble to line my tomb." Sporus nodded compliantly and set the stone down beside the hole. "Is there more of this stone around?"

"It's scattered throughout my property, Caesar," replied Phaon. "You'll find it everywhere."

Nero seemed pleased. "Lucky man. In that case, while you men dig, I shall gather some. It is fitting for Caesar."

They continued their work for another fifteen minutes, but suddenly the quietness of the woods was broken by the distant sound of voices. "What's that?" Nero called out timidly.

Everyone stopped their digging to listen. More voices echoed through the trees. Phaon set down his shovel. "It could be soldiers. They would think to look here after awhile, knowing I was still with you. Nero, we may not have time to finish our digging. You don't want them to capture you."

Nero's eyes flitted back and forth in nervous denial. "We can still run, my friends. The storm is over. The roads are dry. We can make our way to the sea. I have friends in Alexandria who will receive me. Judea will be in need of a governor soon. There is so much that can yet be done!"

Phaon reached out and grasped his shoulders, then spoke with insistence. "They will capture you, Caesar. And once they capture you, you will lose the power you have over your own life. Is that what you want?"

Nero shuddered and slowly shook his head. "You are right, of course. There is a noble way to end this." He looked about the ground as though searching for something. "Does one of you have a knife?" Epaphroditus stepped forward and withdrew a dagger from his cloak. He held it out, and when Nero reached out to take it, the shaking of his arm was obvious. He took the knife, then turned it in toward himself.

"Phaon, my obedient servant, would you...would you...," he stuttered.

"I cannot do that," Phaon replied. "I will not raise my arm against Caesar."

"Lord Nero, you must do this," said Epaphroditus. "It is the way of Roman dignity."

Nero's hands were caked with dirt and sweat, and the knife slipped from his hands. He fell to his knees, clutched the knife again and leaned over the upturned blade with his throat hovering just above the tip. He remained as still as stone in this position for at least a minute, and then sighed with disgust.

"I have died a thousand deaths on stage. Why now when rehearsal is over can I not act the part?" He looked up. "Maybe Galba will pardon me. Maybe I can devote the rest of my life to art, and leave behind this foolish pretense of running an empire. I am not suitable to this role."

Phaon grabbed Nero by the chin and forced him to stare into his eyes. "Galba will burn the skin off your body, and break each of your bones one by one, and maybe then he will decide to kill you. He will inflict the wrath of the empire upon you. Caesar, if you do not act now, each of us will leave you to face them alone. We cannot help you anymore."

Suddenly, there was a renewed burst of voices, only this time they were noticeably closer and coming nearer quickly. Nero blanched and hovered over the knife again. He closed his eyes.

"What an artist dies with me! What an artist dies with me!"

Still he hesitated. Suddenly, Sporus reached forward and in one fluid motion, he grasped the knife in his left hand and drove Nero's head down onto the blade with his right hand. The knife penetrated his throat to its hilt, and Nero lifted up his head making a hideous gasping sound before collapsing on the ground. He convulsed for maybe thirty seconds and then was still. No sooner had his death throes ceased, than a line of soldiers came running around the house, led by Tigellinus. Seeing Nero sprawled on the ground, Tigellinus ran up to him and knelt down beside him.

"Nero. Nero!"

He reached down and pulled the knife from his throat. A final gurgle of air squeezed from Nero's mouth, and nothing more. Tigellinus threw down the knife and walked away.

Part 4: A.D. 70

Chapter 22

The sea was a sailor's dream as the ship glided into the harbor at Caesarea. Not a wave or ripple seemed to disturb the smooth plane of water, until the keel came along and made music by slicing through it with a *hiss*. Every passenger was on top the deck to take in the pleasure of that moment. The white marble of Herod's palace shimmered in the bright September sunlight that beamed down upon it.

Judah was among those who looked on at this beautiful scene, and as he leaned out over the railing, his mind was taken back to the last time he was here nearly eleven years before. How his world has changed in that time. All the ones he knew and loved were gone. All the ones he had grown old with, built memories with, worked and laughed beside, all of them were no more. If an old man could feel like an orphan, Judah knew that emptiness well.

But the pain cut deeper yet, for now he was a man without a country. Caesarea had no beauty for him. Where once it was a doorway to Jerusalem and happiness, now it was a doorway to death. The sky for him was black. The path that had brought him to this point was paved with nothing but misery.

When Nero had died, a chapter in Rome's history that was both glorious and infamous was closed. Nero was the last of the Julio-Claudian line which had occupied Caesar's throne for more than a century. With no heir to replace him, when he died the vacuum of leadership was predictably filled by anarchy, and for the next year civil war raged in Rome. Galba and his army swept into the city, but his brutish demeanor and the arrogance of his soldiers quickly alienated the citizens. He then insulted Otho—whom the people loved and whose support he had relied upon—by selecting someone else as his successor. In January, Galba was assassinated on the Forum and his head was brought to Otho and laid at his feet, and the Senate hailed him as Caesar.

But the legions in Germany, who had grown weary of Galba, had already determined that their commander Vitellius was the true ruler of the empire and were then marching on Rome when Otho ascended. Otho's short and bitter life came to an end with a self-inflicted wound on a battlefield in north Italy, less than a hundred days into his reign. But Vitellius and his soldiers proved worse than Galba, and the outcry of the people for a worthier man was heard all the way to the eastern frontiers of the empire. In June 69, a full year after Nero's death, the eastern governors and legions proclaimed Vespasian as the rightful heir to Caesar's mantle.

During the year of unrest, Vespasian refrained from beginning the siege on Jerusalem, but instead had the city encircled, then returned to Caesarea to monitor the situation in Italy. When the eastern provinces rallied behind him, and the Senate offered favorable signs that he depose Vitellius, he at once dispatched a section of his army to Italy led by his commander Mucianus, while he went to Alexandria to secure additional forces. One province after another quickly fell in behind him, and Vitellius' army was defeated by the Mysian legions who attacked even before Mucianus' forces had arrived.

A Roman mob killed Vitellius in December, and the *Principate* was conferred on Vespasian by the Senate. He entered the city peacefully without ever having to lead his own soldiers in battle. But before he sailed to Rome, Vespasian's first order as emperor, given to his thirty year old son Titus, was that he resume the siege on Jerusalem at once and bring the Jews to heel.

As all of these events played themselves out, Judah was effectively stranded in Italy by both the political disturbances and his own health. With Nero's death, the sword of violence that hung over the church was removed, and he wanted nothing more than to return to Judea at once, but travel to the East was restricted, and danger abounded in the unsettled climate in Italy, so his way was blocked.

As soon as the disorder in Italy was resolved and the door appeared open, Judah's illness worsened, and for the next few months, he hovered between life and death. The image of Esther's face imprinted in his mind sustained him at the lowest moments. He fought the illness with all his mental powers, and in the end, his resiliency prevailed and his strength returned. Though Judea was still a forbidden province, he decided to leave and get as near to it as he could.

He sailed from Rome and came again to his old home in Antioch. He sailed alone, denying Julius, Catus and Urbanus' collective plea to go with him. He also refused the offer of the church to provide him with companions. His face was set on one consuming task—to find Esther—and for that task he wanted only God beside him.

From Antioch, Judah followed each of the reports that drifted out of Judea. As soon as his father had commissioned him, Titus wasted no time in assembling the bulk of his forces and marching to Jerusalem. The rebels refused to surrender and in April, the assault resumed. Jerusalem would not be easy to conquer. Positioned in the mountains of Judea, it was actually two separate cities, one elevated above the other. Impassable valleys and cliffs served as a natural defense on one side of the city, and fortifying these were three massive stone walls that encompassed the whole.

Warfare in this age required incredible patience and commitment. Holes first needed to be opened up in each wall and for that task, massive battering rams were employed. Measures then needed to be taken to protect the operators of the rams, for the defenders on the wall did everything possible to harass the workers. They rained down arrows, poured cauldrons of boiling oil upon them, and hurled over flaming logs to stop their progress.

The Jews were relentless in defending their city, and finally Titus stopped the work and had his men construct three towers, each 75-feet high and taller than the city's walls. From these towers, he was able to fire down upon the walls, and scatter the defenders, and at last, the outer wall was breached in early May. Titus took the second wall only five days later. From the prisoners that were captured, Titus learned that famine was overtaking the city, and so he decided to pull back his forces, and allow hunger to be his next weapon.

Between May and July, more than 100,000 Jewish bodies were piled up in one section of the city as the famine intensified. Scavengers roamed the streets, searching through dung heaps for food. Bands of robbers broke into homes demanding bread. One day, a rebel leader smelled meat cooking from a nearby house. He and the robbers with him immediately burst into the house and demanded to be fed. To their horror, the starving woman they found there brought forth the roasted body of her infant son.

Each day, the Romans lined up outside the city and ate their fill of meats and fruits which they had in abundance, to the torment of the starving Jews who watched. Hundreds attempted to escape the city, but each was captured and crucified, in full view of their relatives and friends on the wall. At one point 500 a day were being killed, and Titus ran out of wood to make crosses. Two at a time might be nailed to a cross. The carnage during the siege was simply beyond description, and as Judah heard each report, his despair became complete. He realized he would never see Esther again.

When Judah heard that Titus had resumed his offensive assault in August, he knew that the city would not last much longer. He decided at that point to sail to Caesarea and see if he might find a way to go to Jerusalem, if for no other purpose than to see with his eyes the result of the disaster and put to rest his impossible yearning to see his wife again.

As the ship finally drew near and he looked out over Herod's palace, he saw the pier filled with hundreds of soldiers, and stacked up as far as he could see in huge piles was an astonishing array of military equipment and materials. Judah felt numbed by the display of power he saw spread out before him.

"O my God," he whispered to himself as a prayer and a plea.

An elderly man standing next to him overheard his sigh. "The crimson stain of Rome goes with us everywhere, Judah. It cannot be escaped. Especially in Judea."

"I've never seen so many soldiers, not even in Rome," Judah said.

The old man reached out and placed a consoling hand on Judah's shoulder. "Judah, my brother. I fear you have come too late. These soldiers can mean only one of two things. The siege is over and the extra legions are returning home. Or else they are stepping up their attack and bringing in reinforcements. Either way, you will not find what you are looking for in Jerusalem. It is a doomed city."

Judah's eyes were red with sleeplessness but his skin was colorless. He rubbed the gray stubble spread over his unshaven face. "Oh Samuel," he said with a groan. "I cannot believe God would bring me so far, through so much, only to crush me in the end. I must know what happened. I must know where she is."

The ship was nearly docked, and after a few minutes, Samuel spoke again. "I have been blessed by your companionship on this voyage, Judah Ben-Hur. Should you find that hope has deserted you, and you have no place left to turn, seek me in Joppa. Though we have just met, you are to me as a brother."

Judah managed a small smile of gratitude. "Thank you, Samuel. I too have drawn strength from your friendship."

The men embraced, and as soon as the ship came to a stop, Judah left him to find his baggage. Once on shore, he had to join the line of passengers being interviewed by a battery of customs officials who were spread out on the pier, and after waiting nearly an hour, he was called forward.

"Your name?" the young agent asked gruffly, looking down at his scroll on which he wrote.

"Judah Ben-Hur. I am known in Rome by my adopted name of Quintus Arrius."

He had hoped this would make some impression, but the man merely kept looking down and writing. "Do you have a certificate of your citizenship?"

Judah reached into a pouch and withdrew the diptych which confirmed his identity and credentials. The man inspected it and then handed it back. "Why have you come to Judea?"

"I am here to complete some business, and afterwards retire."

This drew a response. "I hope you're not retiring here! I can't wait to leave this forsaken land. What is your destination?"

"Jerusalem."

The officer laughed and shook his head. "Everyone wants to see Jerusalem now, but I'm afraid that's one place you can't go. Titus wants to keep all the treasure hunters out of there. Supposedly, there are mountains of gold and silver lying around. I wouldn't mind walking through there myself. But all travel to and from there is prohibited."

"The siege is over?"

"I'll say," he said matter-of-factly, and resumed writing.

Though Judah didn't feel that his spirits could sink any lower, and though this news certainly wasn't a surprise, hearing the confirmation of his nation's final defeat nearly caused the strength to go out of his legs. He leaned forward on the custom's table to keep from falling over. *Now everything has been taken away from me,* he thought.

He sighed and looked up. With this news, he was more determined than ever to see the city of his birth, if only that he might die there. Judah couldn't remember the last time he had told a bold-faced lie, but at this moment, he didn't care.

"Well my young friend, I will see Jerusalem, especially now, because as a legate of the Senate, I am authorized to give them a report of its condition and of the prisoner transport."

This caught the agent by surprise. Before he could ask another question, Judah continued. "Here is my authorization." He took up a clay tablet from the table, and stamped his ring upon it. "Check this seal with your records. It belongs to Quintus Arrius. I was serving Caesar and the Senate long before you were born. The shorter my stay in this province the better, so if you don't mind, do what you must to get me clearance on a military caravan even this afternoon."

He spoke with such authority, the agent could say nothing in reply, except nod his head submissively and walk off to find a superior officer to assist him. As Judah anticipated, the clearance was given, and he was placed in a supply convoy that was heading for Jerusalem the next morning.

The caravan took four days to traverse the sixty mile road to Jerusalem, and they were far from alone on the way. Military traffic stretched in both directions as far as could be seen. Judah watched as an unending stream of armory wagons, soldiers, horses, and food carts passed by returning to the coast. The uniforms of many of the soldiers he saw were torn and bloodied, and the epic nature of the siege was written on most of their faces.

On the third day, Judah's grief was aroused to new depths when they passed a line of wagons carrying artifacts from the city, among them an extensive collection of articles used for worship in the temple—censers, candelabras, gold trumpets, lavers and basins of silver, a variety of musical instruments, and beautiful panels of carved cedar. Judah couldn't help but notice that much of what he saw was smoke-scarred or burned.

And then to his horror, the train of prisoners began to pass by. A procession of lost souls being ushered into Hades itself would not have looked more appalling. Hundreds of them streamed by one at a time, their wrists bound in chains. Some of the fortunate ones were clothed with rags around their waists and the others were naked. Each one was emaciated; some hardly seemed human. And what alarmed Judah was that each of them was young. Not one elderly person was a member of this pathetic cavalcade. Of course, Judah understood why, because he had seen this all before.

These were Titus' trophies which were to be put on display before the conquering race as part of his triumph. They would be hauled to Rome in slaves' galleons, and then on a day of the emperor's choosing, would be made to walk the streets of Rome while tens of thousands of her citizens would come out to cheer and jeer. A memorial arch would be built to glorify Titus, and each slave would pass under it to signify his subjugation. When the parade was finished, some of the slaves would be sold, some sent to the mines, others would perish in the arena. So naturally, the prisoners were young. They could survive the voyage. They could endure the triumph. They could fetch a price for their servitude. Judah knew what had happened to the old and the sick. He knew what had happened to Esther if she had survived until now.

As Judah's thoughts tossed these bitter realities in his head, he suddenly noticed one of the prisoners staring at him. In that moment their eyes met, Judah saw himself. So many years ago, it was he walking in chains, without hope, and destined for an early grave. God helped him then, but what could be done for this one? And the one behind him? And the hundreds more that were coming over the next hill? The enormity of the suffering sprawled out before him was beyond comprehension. Still the prisoner stared at him, and Judah could not look away.

Suddenly the man's face, which had been void of emotion till then, contorted into a defiant snarl, and then he spat in Judah's direction. He was too far away for it to matter, but to Judah—the Jew, the patriot, the Christian, the pastor—the gesture struck with an accurate and awful power. Judah turned away, unable to look any longer.

On the fourth day, nothing of the scenery changed. More dust, more soldiers, more prisoners—it all looked the same. But Judah knew the terrain of the land well, and his soul was pricked with anxious melancholy as Jerusalem drew near. Then by the middle of the afternoon, they crossed a line of hills and suddenly it appeared before them, less than a mile away. In his imagination and nightmares, Judah had seen pictures of the devastation, but it had not prepared him for what he saw.

The outer walls were demolished. Judah could trace with his eyes the trail of rubble where they once stood. It snaked across the valley, and Judah could see off in the distance teams of workers hauling the larger pieces of stone away in wagons. The buildings of the city were in ruins. He saw perhaps three or four complete structures still seemingly intact, but the rest were leveled.

As for the temple—Jerusalem's dazzling ediface which from afar looked like a snow-capped mountain—it had disappeared. There was nothing he could see of it left behind, except for a few barren walls. It was as though it had been lifted off from the earth and removed, and in a sense it was, for the Romans had burned it, then dismantled major sections of it stone by stone in their search for gold or silver.

Then Judah noticed the bodies. Outside the city, he counted five distinct piles of corpses—massive piles, at least thirty feet high. Even as he watched, he saw two workers tossing a body over the edge of one of the inner walls, and it landed atop a pile and rolled halfway down before stopping in a tangle of arms and legs. Scattered over the terrain around the city were what looked like hundreds of spears in the ground, and Judah realized that these were the beams of crosses that had not yet been torn down. Judah slipped from the wagon he had been riding on and stepped off the road, but the intensity of the sight was too great for him. He grew nauseous and fell to the ground, as the caravan continued on without him.

When his strength returned, he picked himself up and continued moving toward the city, but when he was several hundred yards from the walls, he found he was unable to come any closer. An officer walked by him, and looked at him strangely for a moment then continued on. Judah called out to him.

"Are there any Jews left there at all? Is anyone living in the city?"

The officer turned and a look of bemused disbelief crossed his face. "Old man, your eyes are failing you," he said with a chuckle. "This city is being erased from the map."

He walked on. All Judah could do for the remainder of the afternoon was limp around the city and survey it from a distance. Somewhere inside the smashed city was the wreckage of his own home, but he could not bring himself to search for it. Lost in the rubble somewhere were streets he had once played in and ran through as a child, but he could not look for them. His journey was over. He would look no further. His ambition to live was now gone. His wanderings would cease at the very spot where Esther's own pilgrimage had come to its close.

Judah chose a spot on one of the hills and dropped to the dirt, and there he sat for three hours, completely motionless, staring out as though in a trance. Once the sun dipped below the hills, the small breeze that had been blowing became cold and unwelcoming, but Judah didn't notice. His throat was parched but he had no desire at all to seek for a drink. Across the valley, campfires began to appear but Judah was left alone.

Finally, he moved. He reached out his hand and brushed at a small wildflower that was growing from the sand beneath him. He touched its leaves, then cradled its frail flower between his thumb and forefinger. Then his hand slid down the plant, and he suddenly grasped it by its stem and yanked it from the dirt. It gave way without resistance, and he lifted it in front of his eyes and studied it for a moment.

"This is all we are to you, God," he spoke aloud. "We're like the desert grass. And you uproot us, and you destroy us so easily. Do our lives mean nothing to you? Does our suffering matter to you at all? Does our obedience move you one way or another? Do you even know we are here?"

He crumpled the flower in his hand and threw it from him, then lowered his head into his knees and began to weep. As he cried, he fell to his side in a fetal position, doubled up with grief.

"Take me home, God," he said with little more than a whimper. "Let me die now. I cannot live another day. I have lived too long."

The shadows around Judah suddenly deepened, and a voice called out to him.

"What's the matter, my father?"

It was a boy's voice, that sounded young and tender, and echoed with compassion.

Judah looked up and saw a young teenage boy standing over him. His face was smooth and there was no dirt on it. His clothing was ordinary but clean. And hiding beneath his innocent look of concern was a smile. Judah was too tired to wonder why a young shepherd boy would be loitering on this hillside at this particular moment.

"I am too weary to even begin to explain," was all Judah could say.

The boy sat down beside him.

"Why have you come to this valley of death?" he asked.

"I thought I would find someone still alive here."

"They must not be here then," the boy said with childlike simplicity.

Judah laughed scornfully. "I'm sure she is dead."

There was a moment of silence between them, and then the boy spoke again. "A long time ago, a young rabbi named Jesus prophesied that this would happen."

Judah was not especially interested in discussing theology right then. He wanted to be alone. "I know about Jesus. I am one of his disciples," he said tersely.

The boy's face brightened. "Then the one you are searching for is one of his also?"

"She was my wife. We served him together. We became separated by circumstances beyond our control, and she came here to wait for me. I thought I would find her. And now I will die alone, if only death would find me."

"My father, no Christians perished in this disaster."

Judah slowly raised his head as he apprehended what the boy had said, and he looked at him with confusion. "What do you mean, no Christians died here? The people of God suffer like everyone else does, more so even."

"But none suffered *here*," the boy said, and now he was smiling. "An opportunity was given for people to escape the city before it was destroyed."

"What?"

"Some time ago when Cestius Gallus was in command, the Roman soldiers withdrew from their assault. All of the Christians left. Most of them went to Pella, and to villages beyond the Jordan. They weren't here when the Romans came back."

They weren't here when the Romans came back. At once, a resurrection of hope exploded within Judah, but the emotional upheaval was too much for him to bear, and he began to cry again. He lowered his head onto his arm as a shower of tears fell, washing lines into his dusty, dirty face. As he wept, the young boy reached over and laid his hands tenderly upon his head. He spoke again with a soft, assuring voice.

"May you have strength to finish your journey. The race is almost won. Home is in sight."

He withdrew his hand, and Judah's head remained lowered for awhile longer. His sobbing stopped, and quietly, he said, "Thank you. Thank you for telling me this."

He looked up to say more to the boy but to his astonishment, discovered that the boy was gone, and he was alone on the hillside.

*   *   *

Judah slept until dawn, and then sprang to his feet. His legs felt fresh and his heart beat with renewed vigor. The leader of the convoy allowed him to fill a bag with provisions.

"Where are you going so early this morning?" he asked.

"I have business now in the Decapolis," Judah said excitedly.

"We have a caravan which leaves for the Dead Sea at noon," the officer said.

"That's too late for me," Judah exclaimed. "I'll walk." He took a long drink, saluted the officer who marveled at his determination, and began walking east.

Pella was a Greek city fifty miles north and east of Jerusalem. It was a member of the *Decapolis*, a confederation of other Greek cities in the region which enjoyed municipal freedom within the Roman province of Syria. To reach it, Judah would first walk twenty miles to the Dead Sea and then follow the Jordon River straight to the north. He covered half of the distance by the end of the first day. It had been months since he had walked with such purpose. He never realized how crushing the weight had been which had oppressed him for the past four years until now that it was gone.

He rose even earlier the second day and as he walked, he tried to reason with himself concerning this line of hope he had been thrown. Was the enemy of his soul toying with his mind one final time before obliterating his faith altogether? Was he chasing down a reckless dream that had no chance of fulfillment? Even if Esther had escaped, would she have survived these last few years? One mile he walked with ecstasy, the next with dejection. One hour he strode in sunlight, the next he limped in shadow. *Insanity is not an improbable outcome of this*, he thought to himself.

He marveled at his own resiliency that he was able to press on, but he simply could not stop, except for a brief nap after his lunch. And when it was through, the fifty miles seemed as if it were five, and he found himself within sight of the city by the early evening as the sun was starting to set.

He came first to a spring outside the city on its western side, out of which a number of wells had been dug. When Judah arrived at the wells, he found five young women filling buckets for their households. The women watched him hobble up to them, and when he touched the masonry of one of the wells, he nearly collapsed in exhaustion.

"Peace to you, daughters," he said politely, though it must have seemed strange to the women, who weren't used to seeing old men walk alone out of the desert at nightfall.

"And peace to you, my father," said one of the women. "Have you just come through the desert alone? You look as though you've been walking for days. Here, take a drink."

She offered him a ladle of water which he accepted with a nod of thanks, and drank lustily. She offered him another and he poured it over his feet.

"I've been walking for years, my daughter. I have come from Rome. The journey has been very long." His words came out in sporadic bursts as he paused to catch his breath. "This is Pella?"

The women each nodded. An old man walking out of the desert alone *from Rome* was stranger yet. This was quite unique and they were thoroughly intrigued with Judah.

"Why have you come here?" one of them asked.

"I am hoping to find someone here," he replied. "Someone I have been looking for, for a long time."

"Who are you looking for?" each one of them asked, nearly in unison.

"Her name is Esther."

"That's a common name," said one. "My mother's name is Esther."

"And a pretty name too!" said another with bubbly enthusiasm. "I'm going to name my first daughter Esther."

Judah smiled at their girlish charm. "The Esther I am looking for is my wife. If she were here, she would be found in a community of those who are called Christians. Are there any of these people here?"

Each of the women smiled broadly. "We're Christians! There are many of us here."

Suddenly, one of the women dropped the jug of water she had been cradling in her arms. "You're Judah!" she screamed. "Judah Ben-Hur—from Rome!"

Judah's heart leaped within him. "Yes child, I am."

"This is a miracle!" the lady screamed out deliriously. She reached out and took both of Judah's hands in hers, and the other women at once surrounded him and began to dance in joy. "Esther is living in the house of John and Tirzah. They live on the other end of the village. The last street. We'll take you there!"

Leaving their water jugs strewn on the ground, the women at once began to usher Judah through the town, each of them chattering away like a nestful of baby birds. "Esther never stops talking about you!" "Did you really drive a chariot?" "What are the men in Rome like?"

Judah hardly noticed the blisters on his feet. He seemed to be floating. And he scarcely could hear the women talk to him, for he seemed to be in his own private world. In that world, he knew of only one other person, and as they walked through the village, his eyes searched up and down each street for her. The sky behind them was a brilliant orange as the sun now exhausted its last stores of light, and ahead of them as they walked the first stars were peaking through the eastern twilight. Slowly, the shops thinned out, and the neighborhoods became quieter, and soon Judah could see the outer perimeter of the village up ahead. Even the women started speaking more softly now, for they sensed that something wonderful was about to happen.

As they came to the last row of houses, Judah noticed that a field stretched out beyond the village, and he saw the figure of someone walking slowly through the field. The silhouette was of a woman, and she was looking up at the sky. The women smiled, started giggling and pushed Judah away in her direction, so he stepped out into the field and walked toward her. He came to within fifty feet of her and stopped, for her back was still to him and her head was yet tilted up to the stars. But then it was as if she knew that she wasn't alone, and slowly she turned around.

It was her!

They both looked at each other and neither one moved, as though they each feared the other was a vision which might disappear. Then the starlight betrayed the glistening under each of their eyes. Esther cried out and ran toward him. Once she moved, his feet were loosened as well, and they fell against each other with a loud exhalation of sobbing and laughter.

"Remember," she said through her tears, "you told me to pray with you each sunset?" He nodded. "I was praying with you tonight, and here you are! I knew you'd come. I knew you'd come back, Judah!"

He pulled her close to him. "I never took my eyes off of you, my love."

Then he kissed her, and the feel of her lips against his was the surest sign that there was a heaven. The love that flowed through them in that embrace was a cleansing flow of water, washing away all of their frustrations and fears. In an instant of time, it filled all the barren and empty spaces in their souls.

They kissed and danced. They fell to the ground like two children and rolled on the sand. They cried and laughed, then cried some more. And as the sun set behind them, five silhouettes could be seen against the sky, and each one was dabbing at its eyes with the sleeves of its garment.

Epilogue

Judah and Esther never let another day go by where they failed to take a walk together. The wilderness east of Pella became a place of holy beauty for them, and in the quietness of the desert, the noise of their past was silenced and they rediscovered the still, small voice of God.

They shared their story with any who asked and were of great encouragement to the company of believers they found in the region, but they spent most of their time together, and alone. Since they had no home to return to, they remained in Pella, and for the first time in their lives they were able to rest, mulling over no great plans for the future, and giving no thought to going anywhere else, except one place.

Several months later, a beautiful day drew them outside, and they headed off into the wilderness toward a favorite spot they had come to love. It was a long, narrow ravine, at the bottom of which flowed a small stream which babbled over a bed of boulders. A grove of trees grew near the brook and there they would sit for hours at a time, serenaded by the water and watching small desert animals come near to drink.

They found the stream drier than normal, and Judah ventured out onto the rocks to walk across the stream.

"There's still a little boy in you," Esther called out to him, as she sat down on a ledge under the trees. He smiled in agreement. "Just be careful. The little boy may be in your mind, but the old man is in your legs."

No sooner had she said this, than he slipped and tumbled into the water, causing her to yell out in concern, but he waved her off, and climbed back onto the rocks and crept to shore.

"Ouch," he said in some pain as he sat down beside her. "I didn't need to do that." The wind whipped up right then and it chilled his wet skin.

"You'd be foolish to break a leg out here, because I am not carrying you back," she said with mock insistence.

They rested for awhile, and then he took her by the hand. "Esther, everything we've gone through has been worth it, because it has brought us to this moment."

"If only this moment would last," she lamented. "But couldn't we have done without all the other to enjoy this?"

"I could do without the pain right now," Judah answered, wincing as he rubbed his back. Then he laughed. "Somehow it all belongs together, I suppose. As long as joy wins out in the end. Either way, I am happy right now, and that's what matters."

Just then, Judah's eyes narrowed as he looked down the length of the ravine. "Look at that, Esther."

He pointed off to where the stream cut through two arching stone cliffs, maybe a hundred yards in the distance. A thick cloud of sand was blowing toward them.

"What is it?"

The wind was blowing harder now. "I think it's a sand storm. It's coming right at us, whatever it is. Let's sit behind this tree over here and cover up."

He stood and helped Esther to her feet. With some struggle, they managed to secure themselves behind the tree. By now, a virtual gale was blowing through the ravine and sand was starting to bite at their skin. Judah pulled a blanket up over their heads. "Hang on, love. We'll ride it out."

No sooner were they covered up than the wall of sand hit them with full force. The wind violently stabbed at them, driving sand, sticks and debris in all directions around them. When Judah attempted to look out from under the blanket, there was nothing to be seen. The sky and sunlight had been swallowed up in the storm. He pulled Esther closer to him, and in an instinct of fear, they gradually sank to the ground and curled up flat in each other's arms. They both screamed out as the sand stung them, and they found it difficult to breathe. An inescapable dizziness overwhelmed them, and then all suddenly went dark.

Judah came to his senses first. His immediate thought was that the storm had subsided, but when he opened his eyes and pulled the blanket back, the sand was still whipping about and he could see nothing. Esther stirred beside him, and moaned slightly.

"Are you all right, Esther?" Judah asked, still trying to catch his breath.

"I think so," she answered weakly. "That was so sudden. I feel dizzy."

"So do I. And I'm hearing a ringing in my ears. It sounds like ocean waves."

She rubbed her face. "I'm so light-headed. And warm."

Several minutes passed, and again Judah pulled the blanket back and sat up. The wind was now a whimper of what it had been, and the last of the sand was now clearing out. As visibility returned, Judah looked about him—and gasped.

"Esther, look! Something's happened."

She was still rubbing her eyes, so he helped her sit up, and her vision swiftly returned to her. Her mouth dropped open in dumbfounded amazement.

"What's happened to us, Judah?" she whispered.

No longer were they sitting up against a tree beside a stream. They found themselves instead sitting on a beach of white sand alongside an ocean, whose surf was gently nipping at their feet. The sand stretched on for as long as they could see in either direction, and behind them, the beach was framed with towering granite cliffs which stretched up for a hundred feet or more, and the beauty of it left them breathless. The sky was crystal blue, and the sun was right then cresting over the horizon, scattering a translucent shimmer over the water.

"I'm afraid to even guess where we might be," Judah said, in a voice hushed with awe. "I'm afraid to move, in fact. As though I might spoil it. Are we dreaming?"

"It's not a dream, Judah. It's really happening to us."

Slowly, but ever so gingerly, they stood and took in their new surroundings. Not a footprint indented the sand anywhere. Not one strand of moss or piece of litter detracted from its loveliness. And then as they looked on down the beach, the brightening morning light revealed a group of people walking toward them. From a distance, there seemed to be thirty or forty in the group, and all they could discern at first was that they each wore robes made with a sparkling array of colors. They drew nearer and voices began to echo off the cliffs. Judah and Esther looked at each other, completely mystified.

Suddenly, Esther's hands went to her mouth, as she covered up a squeal of delight. "Judah? Judah, look! Look who it is!"

One person broke out of the group and ran toward them, calling out with a rich and familiar voice.

"Welcome dear ones, welcome!"

The face was remarkably younger than the one Judah had remembered—a face no older than twenty-five—but there was no question about it. It was Paul.

He ran up to Judah and embraced him with a robust hug worthy of their deep friendship. Judah was speechless. Seeing his shock, Paul grabbed both of Judah's cheeks and pinched them with a jovial shake.

"It's me, brother Judah! Can you have any doubt about it? But what took you? Goodness, how you've been dawdling. And look what you did? You let me win the race! Here I had thought you'd crossed the finish line ahead of me, and come to find out, you'd tricked me. Ha!" He turned to Esther and engulfed her in his young, strong arms. "Dear sister, you've come together. I'm so pleased."

Paul had a beard, but there was not a streak of gray within it. Judah reached out and tugged on it, and Paul slapped his hand with a smile. "This is really happening?" Judah asked. "Is this…? Are we…?"

Paul nodded vigorously. "Welcome home, Judah. Your odyssey is over."

"But…I don't remember dying," Judah said slowly.

Paul laughed. "Nor I. But what we call death is just another birth. And whoever remembers being born?"

The others drew nearer and Judah and Esther began to recognize faces, though it was difficult with some for everyone was now young. They were both stunned, as though they were sleepwalking in the most beautiful dream they had ever had. Luke, Andronicus, Aquila and Priscilla were there, along with others who had been martyred for their testimony to Jesus. The crowd was much larger than they had first realized, but they slowly worked their way through it, adding joy upon joy with each reunion, till they felt their hearts would burst with the gladness they felt.

As Esther turned away from one friend, she saw a face she knew at once—a face which had not changed hardly at all, except that now her eyes sparkled with happiness. Esther reached out and held her close.

"Octavia, my dear child."

Octavia wept on Esther's shoulder. "Our sufferings are over, Esther. Thank you so very much for helping me."

Another face appeared beside her.

"And Julia, our princess in the Lord!" exclaimed Esther, marveling at how beautiful she looked. "I hardly recognize you."

Julia beamed. "I'm glad you've come home, my sister."

Each face brought a renewal of love and affection. Just when Judah did not think he could experience any deeper emotion, he came across another man and woman whom he knew at once, and his knees nearly buckled beneath him.

"Mother! Father! Is it really you?"

They held each other close, and Judah instantly remembered the last time the three of them embraced, when he was ten years old and his father was sailing out to sea. So long ago. Or was it just yesterday? Suddenly, the chasm of time which was so grievous on earth seemed inconsequential now. Judah's father reached out and placed his hand firmly on Judah's shoulder.

"I want to say something to you, son, that you didn't get a chance to hear from me before." Judah looked at him and waited. "My son, I've been watching you. And I am so proud of you."

Somewhere inside Judah, the little heart of a boy, which Esther had only just joked about, swelled with satisfaction and peace.

"You're so young," Judah exclaimed, as his tears poured down.

His mother leaned forward and whispered in his ear. "Don't worry, Judah. You start breathing in this air, and before very long, it'll start happening to you too."

Paul had been hovering close behind, but now he tapped Judah on the shoulder. "Judah, there's someone back here who insisted on being included in your welcoming party."

They moved through the group until it opened up, and there standing at the outside was an old friend, though now young.

"Burrus!"

Burrus stepped forward and gripped the arms of his friend. Judah noticed at once that his crippled hand was completely healed. "Not wasted, Judah, my friend. My life was not wasted. Thank you for sharing your hope with me. Thank you!"

Judah simply had no words left to say. All he could do was marvel. The fellowship was not broken after all. There were some whom Judah simply didn't know at first. He drew a blank with one man and woman in particular, though with them it seemed he should somehow know them best of all.

The young woman seemed shy, but she spoke first. "Father?"

Then Judah knew, and he sobbed afresh. "Rachel! My daughter! And Samuel my son! O my God. My good and wonderful God. What a gift I have been given to see you again!"

He called out at once for Esther, and when she came and realized that the children of her womb had not been lost, but would be known by her for eternity, she fell on them with the passion that only a mother's love could bring. The four of them fell to the sand and did not rise for a long time, while the rest of the group surrounded them and worshipped the One who had made this moment possible.

And then He came. He was walking toward them on the beach by himself. Judah looked up and saw him coming, and at once he reached out and touched Esther, and pointed with his finger. A look of reverent awe overshadowed her face when she saw him. They rose to their feet with their children, but Rachel and Samuel smiled and stood back from their parents so that they could go and meet him. Judah and Esther joined hands and as they started walking in his direction, every person in the group rejoiced with them.

The robe he wore was brilliant white, his hair was long and rich, as a lion's mane, his posture was gentle and welcoming, and his face—his beautiful face—radiated with the glory of heaven. When Judah and Esther reached him, they looked in his eyes but for a short time, for there was something far more fitting to be done in this moment. Weeping in gratitude, they fell to their knees before him and worshipped at his feet. As they clung to his legs, Jesus reached out his hands and gently caressed their heads.

With a smile, he said, "I bless you, my children. Well done my faithful ones. Welcome home!"